TRICK SHOOTER

Morgan heard Bender shouting, "I'm a law officer. Stay back, I'm warning you! This man killed his father and mother. Let me through!"

Morgan had to shove hard to get through the mob of shouting people. Then he saw Ryan with handcuffs in front of him. Bender was holding Ryan with one hand and fumbling in his pocket with the other when Ryan suddenly smashed the back of his head into the detective's face, and he went down bleeding from the nose and mouth. Ryan whirled and grabbed the shoulder-holstered revolver from under Bender's coat and pointed it at his face.

Ryan was edging the hammer back before Lee's pistol cleared leather. Morgan had to draw fast, or his friend was a dead man!

BUCKSKIN #34

TRICK SHOOTER

KIT DALTON

LEISURE BOOKS NEW YORK CITY

A LEISURE BOOK®

January 2006

Published by

Dorchester Publishing Co., Inc.
200 Madison Avenue
New York, NY 10016

ISBN 0-8439-3360-7

Visit us on the web at www.dorchesterpub.com.

Chapter One

The corn-fed whore with the yellow hair and blue eyes was as pretty as a prize cow—and just as dumb. Morgan knew the comparison was a bit farfetched, but there definitely was something cowlike about Birgitta. She was placid, liked her comfort, and took things pretty much as they came to her. The only thing that got her excited, apart from sex, was talking about money and the good life she was going to have when she got enough of it.

Sweet 16 and just weeks off a Minnesota farm, she made up in good nature what she lacked in brains. Right now she was stroking Morgan's cock, resting briefly after many hours of vigorous sex but already showing new signs of life. "Don't let me down, darlin'," she crooned to Morgan's shaft, using her tongue a little. "Show the pretty lady what you can do, big fella."

Birgitta hadn't been in the business long enough to be soured by it. That would come, as it came to them all,

Morgan knew, but for the moment she thought she had a good deal. The house was clean and well-run; Mrs. Lally, the madam, was a strict woman but not a tyrant. Instead of employing a tough pimp to keep order, she relied on her sturdy self and the town marshal and his two deputies, who got enough protection money to be dependable in a pinch.

"I like this work. There's money here," Birgitta had told Morgan more than once during the two days he'd been in her bed. "Anything is better than slopping hogs on a bitter cold morning. My mother died when I was young, and I got to do all the things she used to do. Dawn till dusk, nothing but work. Baking bread, feeding chickens, killing chickens, plucking chickens, fetching water, washing clothes, mending clothes, and how could I forget it— scrubbing floors. Us Lunds are a very clean family."

One of the things about her that amused Morgan was the way she said anything that came into her head; she had told him matter-of-factly that her five older brothers had been fucking her since she was 12. It didn't bother her. It was a fact of farm life, nothing more. Morgan could well understand why they'd want to fuck her. Any man would. And the peach smooth skin, the soft, pink, slightly plump body, the way she sucked her lower lip wasn't all of it. The instant you met her you knew you wanted to fuck her, and she was ready to fuck you to a fare-thee-well if she liked your looks. She liked Morgan a lot and in just two days was convinced that he was madly in love with her and wanted to marry her. Morgan had no such notion, but he said or did nothing to change her mind.

"I know you'd like me for your bride," she said. "We could be happy together if you were rich, but you're not and I have to look at the practical side of it. Don't be too sad."

Morgan said he'd try not to be.

Birgitta had it all figured out. Although she was a new-comer, she was one of the top moneymakers in the house, and she planned to save most of what she made, holding out just enough money to pay for subscriptions to two Eastern magazines that offered tips to young women who wanted to get ahead in the world. Why waste money when Mrs. Lally provided everything she needed in her work—soap, douches, petroleum jelly and a complete medical examination once a month. Her timetable called for her to have her own whorehouse at the mature age of 25; by 35, when a woman was nudging middle age, she'd be rich enough to retire, move to some faraway city and look for the right kind of husband, a man of substance.

Morgan hoped she'd get what she wanted; only a few whores ever did. But for all her planning, what she really wanted deep down, Morgan was sure, was to go back home and "show them." Naturally they'd still want to jump her, but there would be none of that. Morgan almost felt sorry in advance for the five horny brothers. Now, as she stroked his steadily hardening cock, he knew he'd be fucking her in a few minutes. Birgitta was what they called a honeyfuck, the kind of sweet woman who brought out affection as well as lust in a man. Sliding it into her was like sliding it into a jar of warm honey. No matter how many times you had her, you always wanted more. Everything about her was sweet—even her sweat—and the yellow hair that grew between her legs was as soft and smooth as the rest of her.

Watching her stroke his prick and loving the way she did it, Morgan decided the best thing about Birgitta was her good-natured willingness to do anything or have anything done to her by a man she liked. Dog style, taking it up the glory hole, any which way of doing it was fine with her.

In two days, Morgan had tried every position he could think of, had done everything to her that could possibly be done, and yet he wanted to do more. Once, in a sort of crazy impulse, he had pulled his cock out of her just before he came and squirted hot, steaming jism all over her belly. Birgitta, instead of wiping it off, wet her fingers with it and rubbed it on the backs of her hands, saying, "Good for the skin, a girl told me." Another time, late the night before, he told her he wanted to put it between her breasts, and she smiled and smeared her breasts with petroleum jelly, then held them together so he could mount her that way.

Ready now, Morgan spread her legs and thrust into her. She gasped and tightened her vaginal muscles and the surge of pleasure he felt was the same as the first time. He didn't try for anything fancy because, goddamn it, there wasn't enough time. But after two days of sex he'd never forget, what was he goddamning about? He drew his penis back until only the head was in her, then thrust in all the way and came with such intensity that he was shaking all over when it was finally done.

He sat up and used a corner of the sheet to wipe the sweat from his chest. "I have to leave now or I'll miss my train to Talcott." Birgitta pouted prettily and wanted to know why he couldn't stay another day.

"Please stay," she said. "You're so different from the other men. For me they're just business. With you it's fun, and you make me laugh."

"Can't do it," Morgan said. "I'm due for one last visit with my friend Bronc Larson before he goes back East. Bronc is old so I probably won't see him again. Wrote me a letter saying he's been selling off his land and horses and plans to pull out on the tenth. I'd be good and mad if I missed him."

"Is he that good a friend?" Birgitta said.

"I would say so," Morgan said. How could he explain to this good-natured but selfish child-woman that Bronc was the best friend he ever had. Five years before, stranded in Talcott after losing his last few dollars in a card game, Bronc had saved his life when he came down with typhoid after eating lamb stew in a dingy restaurant run by a dark-faced foreigner with a big mustache. The town doctor burned down the restaurant after tracing several fever cases there, and the foreigner ran away before they could burn him, too. Morgan dimly remembered how they dragged him out of his cheap hotel room after he began to show all the symptoms—fever, diarrhea, weakness, blinding head-aches—and dumped him 20 miles out on the prairie with a warning not to come back, even if he survived, or he'd be shot on sight. After that he blacked out and came to two days later in Bronc's extra bed.

"I thought you were a goner when I picked you up out there," Bronc said after looking at him. "I guess you'll live. Get some sleep."

The next morning, while Bronc fed him whisky-laced milk, Morgan asked, "You ever have typhoid?"

"Never have."

"Aren't you afraid you'll catch it from me?"

"What's there to be afraid of?" Bronc said. "I'm sixty-six, got a leather liver from too much booze and a bum heart that could quit anytime." The old man patted the Remington Army revolver hanging from his belt. "I got a cure here for anything that can ail a man. Long as I can get around, though, I'm not ready for the .45 caliber cure."

That was five years ago, and they had remained friends. Bronc Larson raised, sold and traded horses and seldom left the Talcott area now that he was old. But Morgan always paid him a visit when he was even remotely close by. Though Morgan wasn't much of a drinker, he got drunk with Bronc. Stumping around on bowed legs, Bronc always did what he called his Wild Indian War Dance whenever they were halfway through the second bottle. Morgan never got drunk enough to join him, but they had good times all right.

Bronc wanted him to come in as a partner, but he knew it wouldn't work. Two loners with quick tempers, it was bound to end in a falling out. So Morgan said no and got the feeling that Bronc, after thinking about it, was glad he did. Morgan came to Talcott as often as he could, and between visits they exchanged letters.

Thinking of how much he owed Bronc, Morgan said, "Bronc probably wonders what's keeping me."

Birgitta turned to face the wall. "A telegram came for you yesterday," she said nervously. "Somebody slipped it under the door when you were asleep. I put it in the top dresser drawer. I didn't want you to be called away so soon."

Morgan grabbed the Western Union envelope from the drawer and ripped it open, then looked at the bottom of the yellow sheet for the sender's name, which was RUSSELL BOWDRY, ATTORNEY AT LAW, TOPEKA. The message read:

BRONC LARSON SAID YOU MIGHT BE REACHED MRS. LALLY. BRONC IN TOPEKA JAIL. FEDERAL CHARGE COUNTERFEITING. COME SOON AS POSSIBLE.

Morgan dressed and pulled on his boots. He kissed Birgitta and put a $50 bill on top of the dresser. "I'll settle up downstairs. You're a nice girl and I had a good time, but I have to go."

"Don't be too sad," Birgitta called after him.

On the train, heading for Topeka, Morgan wondered what the hell was going on. Bronc was as likely to be mixed up in counterfeiting as Carrie Nation was to get drunk. It didn't wash, didn't make sense. It had to be one goddamned awful fucking mix-up for a man like Bronc to land in jail on such a charge. Morgan threw his half-smoked cigar on the floor and stared out the window.

Off the main line, the train was no cannonball and made frequent stops, but finally he managed to curb his impatience. Nothing could be done until he talked to Bronc, talked to the lawyer and heard all the facts. The federals—counterfeiting meant the U.S. Secret Service—had Bronc in custody, and they must think they had some kind of case or they wouldn't have locked up a sick old man past 70. He rubbed his eyes, gritty from lack of sleep, and found himself wondering if Secret Service agents wore false beards. He knew he must be very tired to be having such notions.

After a while he slept, worn out by his exertions with Birgitta, and didn't wake up until the train slowed, the locomotive bell clanged, and the conductor started calling the station. "Topeka! We're coming into Topeka, folks!"

The jail was near the station, and he got there in minutes, though he guessed there was no hurry. There wasn't. Chief jailer Macurdy wanted to show that his jail was no tank town jail where people just walked in and got to see prisoners with no regard for the formalities. A sour, swag-bellied man with a belt that would have gone round a horse, he waddled instead of walked. If Morgan wasn't a lawyer representing the prisoner or a blood relative, he would have to come back during the regulation visiting hours of two to four on Saturday afternoon.

"Today is Monday," he said, like a man who had just won some points in some dumb game. "Sorry, mister. Rules are rules and must be followed." He offered his hand to show he was a good fellow at heart. Morgan had been in other jails, as visitor and prisoner, and he knew how it worked. A five dollar bill was already folded under his thumb when he shook hands with the jailer who muttered, "Well, since you come so far," and unlocked the gate that led to the cellblock.

A guard with a club sat on a stool inside the gate. Jails gave Morgan the creeps, but Macurdy at least tried to keep his clean. The stone walls were whitewashed, and the strong disinfectant tried to tone down the stink of the slop buckets in the cells.

"You got a visitor, Larson," Macurdy shouted. He had to shout because a colored prisoner with a razor-scarred face started singing a militant hymn as they came in. "Pipe down, you black bastard!" Macurdy roared with no real anger. To Morgan he said, "Holler for the guard when you get through." He unlocked the cell door, then slammed and relocked it when Morgan went in.

Bronc sat on a stool with his boot heels hooked into the rungs. He wore the same old worn-out Levi's, white at the knees, and a shirt that could have used a boiling in lye soap. His hat and leather vest hung from a peg in the wall. Older and sicker-looking than Morgan had ever seen him, he raised his head and said, "Good to see you, Lee. They got me in the shithouse, and I ain't sure I'll ever get out."

"I'll get you out, old friend," Morgan said. "One way or another I'll get you out." Morgan meant what he said. If the only way to get Bronc out was to break him out, he'd do it. There was no place to sit. The iron-slatted bunk was hinged up by day, jail rules, and Bronc had the only stool. Morgan leaned against the wall.

"Tell it from the beginning," he said.

Bronc wandered a bit, but his account of what happened was simple enough. A man he'd never seen before came to the ranch and said he'd heard Bronc was selling off his horse stock. Since that was what he'd been doing, there was no reason to be suspicious. The man, who said his name was Coakley, picked out a likely horse, and they settled on a $100 sale price.

"Fella haggled a bit, prob'ly to make it look good," Bronc said, "but he caved in kind of quick when I stood my ground. That should have made me suspicious. It didn't. I was just glad to get the money. Rotten sneaking sheep-fucker paid me in ten new ten dollar bills, like he just got them outen the bank. Anyhow, that same day I went into town—that's Talcott, as you know—to buy a few things at the general store. Paid with one of the new tens, then went to get something to eat. I was leaving when the marshal—that's Marshal Finney—told me to hold up. He had the ten I just spent, and he says, 'This is counterfeit, Bronc.' 'Bullshit it is!' I says. 'Don't argue,' he says. 'It's a dud. Storekeeper's wife spotted it after you left. Smart woman.' Well, my eyes ain't too good, Lee, but I took the bill from the marshal and looked at it up and down and sideways. Looked all right to me, but the marshal says again, 'It's a fake.' Then he says, 'You got any more this queer money, Bronc? You got it, hand it over. Don't make me search you.' What could I do? I had nine more of the buggers in my pocket, and I gave them to him. He checked them real careful and says, 'They're all fakes. Sorry, Bronc, I'm going to have to lock you up till this is straightened out.' Well, sir, you know how mad I can get . . ."

"Never mind that," Morgan said. "The marshal sent for the Secret Service."

"Never heard a them before," Bronc said. "Marshal said I'd be in his jail a while. Shitass Secret Service agent had to come all the way from Kansas City, their closest office.

Marshal Finney asked me about this fella that bought the
horse. Was he a local man? Was he tall, was he short,
fat or thin, how did he talk? Not tall and not short, I
says. Maybe on the skinny side. Didn't sound foreign or
Eastern. Talked like everybody else. 'You ain't helping
your case much,' the marshal says. I says back . . ."

"Get to the Secret Service agent," Morgan said.

"This agent name of Washburn finally arrived in
Talcott," Bronc said. "Serious son of a bitch for such
a young man. Right off I started calling him 'Washboard'
and he didn't like it." Bronc eyed Morgan. "You think I
was too scared to call him 'Washboard?' You think I'm
making that up?"   "I don't give a damn what you called
him," Morgan said. Sometimes good old Bronc could be
a pain in the ass. "What happened next?"

"What do you think? Bastard asked the same questions
as the marshal, only there's a lot more a them. I got mad and
asked him, 'Do I look like a counterfeiter to you?' 'That's
neither here nor there,' he says. 'You had just passed one
spurious—there's a word for you—one spurious ten dollar
bill and you had nine more in your possession when you
were arrested. If you had just one bogus ten you might
be given the benefit of the doubt. But nine! Do you have
any more counterfeit money at your ranch?' That made
me madder, and I says sarcastic-like, 'Sure I do. I got a
whole trunkful out there.' "

"That was smart," Morgan said. "How did he take it?"

"How did he take it? His eyes lit up like somebody
just shoved a red-hot poker up his ass. Then he got hold
of himself and says, 'You're going to be transferred to
Topeka to appear before a federal judge.' So here I am in
Topeka. I appeared before the judge this morning. Bowdry,
my lawyer and a very fine man, asked for bail—after all,
I have money—but this Washburn opposed it. 'This is a

most serious charge, your honor,' he says. 'Several western states have been flooded with counterfeit money, which is a serious threat to the nation's currency, and the criminals responsible, big and small, must be punished to the fullest extent of the law. The accused has already made plans to return to the East. If he is granted bail, he may simply disappear.' The judge, an old turd with a quavery voice, agreed with him. No bail. Then he set a trial date in the Kansas City federal court two weeks from today. They're moving me tonight, the cocksuckers."

"I better go and talk to the lawyer," Morgan said. "Is the federal agent still around?"

Bronc made a sound like a man about to spit. "Federal dick-puller's gone back to Kansas City, so at least I don't have him coming in here every day saying, "Why don't you make a clean breast of it, Larson? Name your fellow criminals, Larson. Make it easy on yourself, Larson." The shit-faced child-fucker kept throwing names at me, men I never heard of. The bastard is trying to frame innocent people, if you ask me."

Morgan moved away from the wall and slapped white-wash from his sleeve. "I better get moving." He looked hard at Bronc, surprised at all the foul language he'd been using. Bronc had been a hellion in his youth but had given up obscenity as well as whisky when he married his long-dead wife 40 years before. After she died he went back to whisky but not to cursing and swearing. Now he was as dirty-mouthed as a mule skinner. It had to mean he was scared bad, trying to sound tough the way he did.

Bronc started to say something, then his voice broke and the tough front was gone. "You got to help me, Lee. I don't want to die in a cage."

"I'll get you out," Morgan said again, "but I'm doing you no good here. Anything I can get you?"

Bronc tried to smile. "They don't allow whisky in here," he said. "Will I see you at the trial?"

"I'll try to be there," Morgan said. "If I'm not I'll be working for you somewhere else. You can count on that." They shook hands and Morgan called for the guard.

Russell Bowdry's office was on the second floor of a new commercial block. One end of the red brick block was still unfinished with men working there. Morgan hoped Bowdry wasn't as new to the law as his building was to Topeka. Upstairs he found a burly man locking the door to the lawyer's office.

"You Mr. Bowdry?" Morgan said.

The man turned and put the key in the trouser pocket of his gray summer suit. He wore a gray derby with a curved brim. His thick mustache had grey in it, and he was in his late forties.

"I'm Bowdry. You'll have to come back. I have to go out."

"I'm Morgan. You sent me a telegram. I just came from the jail."

The lawyer unlocked the door and stood aside so Morgan could go in. It was hot in the office with the windows closed, but Bowdry shoved them open and sat down behind his desk. There was a film of brick dust on the glass of his framed law school diploma, State of Kansas license to practice law, and various other documents and photographs. Some of the bookshelves were filled with law books, while boxes of still unpacked books stood against the wall.

"Confounded brick dust," the lawyer said. "Just moved in. Should have waited another month. Sit down, sit down. I was on my way to the jail. Macurdy sent word there was a stranger there talking to Bronc. Macurdy and I have an agreement." Bowdry made a sour face. "Fat grafter! But he serves his purpose. I don't like my clients talking to strangers. Too often the police send in informers posing as clergymen or something. They get the prisoner to talking and later testify against him in court. I doubt if the Secret Service is any different. How did you find Bronc?"

"Scared," Morgan said. "What are his chances?"

"I can probably guarantee he won't go to prison," the lawyer said. "He's seventy-one, has a bad heart, an enlarged liver and high blood pressure. My doctor has examined him and will testify in court. As to winning an acquittal, I just don't know. He has no criminal record, so that's in his favor, but the government is out for blood. In the end, it's up to the jury. Washburn, the federal agent, searched his ranch for a trunkful of queer money he made a dumb joke about. I was surprised he didn't find at least a few more dud tens. These people are not above planting evidence."

Morgan said, "Maybe Washburn is an honest policeman."

"Could be. I just don't like policemen. My father was a policeman," Bowdry said but didn't elaborate.

"You talk to Washburn much?"

"Quite a bit. He wants me to plead Bronc guilty in return for leniency. Otherwise, sick or not, he could get a long sentence, depending on the judge he draws."

"He wouldn't last three months," Morgan said.

"Maybe less than that," the lawyer said. "I don't want to take the deal but . . ."

"Let it ride for now. The trial won't take place for two weeks. Maybe I can turn up something by then."

Bowdry made another sour face. "What can you hope to do? I've had a private detective from Kansas City working on the case, a real professional, but he hasn't turned up much, if anything. He hasn't been able to find the man who gave Bronc the queer money."

"Tell me what he did find out."

"Well, after he talked to Washburn he went to the cities and towns where the counterfeits were turning up. Washburn gave him a list. Finally he concluded there had to be some kind of link between Colonel Hardesty's Wild West show and the bogus bills."

"A wild west show. How did he tie that in?"

"Every town he went to had Hardesty show posters plastered up all over the place. The queer money and the show turned up at much the same time. Coincidence? I don't know."

"Is he still working on it?"

"No, unfortunately. Bain took sick, may be laid up for weeks. Runs a one-man operation so there's nobody to replace him. There's only one other agency in Kansas City, but I don't know them. Odd thing, the Hardesty show's next stop is Kansas City. They open there sometime next week."

Morgan stood up. He liked Bowdry and his blunt way of talking. Bronc would be well-represented in court, if that meant anything, but he couldn't let it get that far. "Skip the other agency for now. I'm going to take a look at this wild west show. It's worth the price of a train ticket."

Bowdry came out from behind his desk. "You can reach me here or at the Royal Kansas Hotel two days before the trial. One last thought—there must be some pretty bad people behind this counterfeiting. They'll kill you if they catch you snooping around."

They shook hands. "I'll wear a false beard like Secret Service agents do," Morgan said. They both laughed.

Chapter Two

Morgan studied the huge billboard poster advertising Colonel Judson Hardesty's "stupendous, colossal, breathtaking" Wild West Show, "the Ninth Wonder of the World." The billboard stood high above the city's busiest intersection, and at night it was illuminated by glaring naphtha lights. Smaller posters, garishly colored and illustrated with pictures of Colonel Jud and his show's main attractions, were pasted up on every bit of free space that could be pressed into service. Pretty young women in fanciful Wild West costumes distributed handbills on busy corners; the streets were littered with them. Famous preacher C. Vernon Detweiler would supervise a raffle advertised in the *Kansas City Star*, and the lucky winners would receive free ringside tickets.

Studying the billboard from the sidewalk, Morgan decided that the advance man for the show sure as hell knew his business. Maybe Buffalo Bill Cody had a bigger show, but you'd never know it from the way the drums were beating for Hardesty's. The show wouldn't arrive until the following day on its own special train, so he went to see Detective Lieutenant Nathan Bender, "the only honest policeman in Kansas City," according to Russell Bowdry, who had given Morgan his name. The lawyer said Bender would make an outstanding chief of police, but didn't have a chance unless Jesus Christ reappeared on earth to work some of his sleight-of-hand. "I'll send a telegram telling who you are," Bowdry said. "He's a suspicious man but with good reason. Chief Gallager would like to get something on him and pluck the one good apple out of the rotten barrel. Gallager's a drunk but a crafty drunk."

Looking at the crowded streets, Morgan hoped the Hardesty show would lead to something. If not, it would be like that goddamned needle in that haystack. Among so many people there had to be an awful lot of crooks, but he couldn't just walk around asking dumb questions. Maybe Bender could point him in some direction. His meeting with Bender wasn't until three in the afternoon in the Texas Saloon near the stockyards. He had telephoned Bender from a booth in the Telephone Exchange. All Bender did was grunt a few times and ask him if he knew where the Texas Saloon was. He didn't. Bender said, "Ask anybody. I'll be at the last table in the back."

He'd eaten a late breakfast and was now idling over a mug of beer in a saloon. Bronc's name was in that morning's *Star*, a couple of inches on page two, so he knew the old buzzard was in the city jail. Earlier he'd gone to the jail, insisting that he was Bronc's only son, but he had nothing to prove it and they wouldn't let him in. He was told to come back Saturday, the only day visits

were allowed. The five dollar bill folded under his thumb
had got him kicked out.

After another slow beer he started for the stockyard
district and could smell it long before he got there. He
didn't have to ask where the Texas Saloon was; it would
be hard to miss. It took up half a block, and from the name
it's main business would be with the cowhands who rode
in on the trains with the livestock. The trains rolled in day
and night so the place did land-office business.

Morgan went through the doors and pushed his way
through the mob of drinkers. Above the bar, on a raised
platform, three musicians, piano, fiddle and cornet, were
adding to the noise. As Morgan came in, the cornet player
put down his instrument and sang through a megaphone.
Bender was at the last table in the back, as he said he
would be. A short man with a drooping mustache and
wide shoulders that would have looked better on a taller
man, he was talking to a shifty-looking young man with
yellow hair, a lemon suit and yellow boots. Bender got rid
of him with a wave of his hand.

"I'll give you three guesses what they call that sneaking
rat," Bender said as Morgan sat down.

"The Yellow Kid," Morgan said.

"First guess wins," Bender said. "How is Bowdry keeping himself? Does he still hate the police?"

Morgan smiled. "He said he *disliked* them. That's not
as strong."

Bender laughed. "I dislike a lot of them, too." Bender's
smile faded, and he set down his beer mug. "What do you
want from me, Morgan? Yes, I know. Your friend is in
jail, and you want me to help get him out."

"I'd appreciate anything you'd be willing to do."

"Don't be too appreciative. There may be nothing I can
do. Counterfeiting is way out of my line. We have the

Secret Service for that. Bowdry couldn't say much in a telegram. Tell it, but don't make a book out of it."

Morgan finished his account of Bronc's troubles with the private detective's idea that the Hardesty show was somehow involved in the distribution of counterfeit money. "You think there's anything to it?"

"Sounds like there might be," Bender said, "but it doesn't have to be somebody working for the show. Could be one crook or a gang of crooks trailing along behind, using the crowds the show draws as a smoke screen. A wild west show or a circus brings the crooks out all right. They come from all over—con men, pickpockets, card cheats, drunk rollers, strong-arm boys. All out to fleece the honest citizens who come to gawk at the trick shooters and bareback riders. By the time the show opens they'll be all here. You'd have your work cut out for you, trying to find a few queer money shovers in a crowded city."

"That was my thought," Morgan said. "I'll stick with the wild west show to start with."

Bender wiped beer from his walrus mustache. "If your man or men aren't working for Colonel Jud, you won't find them at all. The minute the show leaves, the town will empty out. You don't have much time. Your friend's trial is in two weeks."

The band was back from taking a break, and the cornet player was splitting the smoky air with his high notes.

"I'm going to stick with it even if they send him to prison," Morgan said.

Bender's big shoulders slumped a little, as if they were carrying too much weight. He took a deep breath and blew it out, making the ends of his mustache flutter. His eyes were more blank than tired.

"From what you tell me, your friend won't last behind the walls, but they could send him there. Get used to the idea. And what can you do then? What can you do now, for that matter?"

"Get a job in the show and look around."

"Play detective, is that it? Listen at keyholes, peep over transoms, look for secret messages written in invisible ink?" Bender brayed out a loud laugh.

Morgan said, "The hell with you, Bender," and started to get up. Bender's thick fingers closed on his arm, and it felt as if a bear trap had snapped shut. He wasn't smiling now.

"Sit down and simmer down, cowboy," Bender said. "I just wanted to see how serious you are. Some people behave like stage actors when they get mixed up in something serious. They swear they'll do this and that, die for their friends if they have to, then do nothing but talk. You think you owe that old man?"

"I owe him my life."

"Can't owe more than that. No more smart-aleck talk, but listen to me. I have been searching for a child killer for six years. Little girl about my daughter's age was tortured and raped before she was killed. Looked a little like my daughter even though she'd been blinded by the killer. I swore to catch that animal if it was the last thing I ever did. Gallager took me off the case, said I was taking too long, but I didn't give up. I worked on the case every free moment I had. I still haven't caught him. Probably never will."

"I haven't even started yet," Morgan said.

"I wasn't trying to discourage you," Bender said. "Just letting you know not every case gets solved. All right, here's what you should do. You can probably get a job with Hardesty—tent show people are always quitting— but try to aim for something higher than roustabout or horseshit shoveler. In a job like that you'd never get close to the kind of people you want to talk to—performers, section managers, men and women on the business side. You agree it's unlikely that a stall cleaner or a roustabout is passing queer money. A lot of them are drunks. No clever operator would trust them."

"Makes sense," Morgan said.

When a drunken cowboy threw a beer bottle at the cornet player and missed, the band went on playing as if nothing happened. Two huge bouncers grabbed the cowboy and tossed him into the street.

Bender rotated the beer in his mug until it got a little head on it. "What can you do that might get you hired? Don't be modest now."

Morgan said, "I'm a top rider and a dead shot with a six-gun. If they want a fast draw artist, I can do that, too."

"Sounds all right," Bender said. "Try for riding or shooting. Maybe you'll get lucky, but I guess you'll have to take any job they give you. Better than nothing. At least you can walk around without some guard wanting to know who you are."

"What will you be doing?"

Bender smiled. "What I'll be doing is putting out the good word among my many friends in this city's under-world. That won't happen until the Hardesty show is in full swing. The people who pass the word like the Yellow Kid over there at the bar will say that Lieutenant Bender wants to know who's been passing queer ten dollar bills of the highest quality. Top quality tens, nothing else. As a reward for this information, Lieutenant Bender will take an interest in your case next time you are arrested. On the other hand, if you withhold this information and Lieutenant Bender finds out about it, he will put you in prison for a very long time. Is that good enough for you, Morgan?"

"Couldn't be better," Morgan said. He didn't know what to make of Bender, who was unlike any detective he'd ever met. Jokey one minute, dead serious the next. But whether he was smiling or deadpan, he was a man to be trusted, Morgan decided, if only because his relentless honesty had made him a loner.

Both men got up at the same time, knowing there was nothing more to be discussed. "I usually stop in here two or three times a week," Bender said. "Around three o'clock, same as today, If I'm not here, leave a message with the Yellow Kid. The sneaky bastard is always here, pimping for one of the houses. Don't worry. That lowlife is completely trustworthy where I'm concerned. Don't get yourself killed, Morgan. These queer money merchants aren't old, starving printers making one dollar bills in the cellar."

"Bowdry said the same thing," Morgan said.

"Russell Bowdry is a very smart man," Bender said.

The next day was Tuesday, and the Colonel Judson Hardesty Wild West Show arrived at noon, a time when thousands of people were on their lunch break. From locomotive to caboose, the long train glistened with red, white and blue paint; flags and bunting hung from the roofs of the cars, and on a flatcar, a brass band dressed in red, white and blue uniforms boomed out a lively marching tune. Colonel Hardesty, every inch a showman, was on another flatcar astride a magnificent white stallion that looked as if it had been doped just enough to keep it quiet. The train stopped in the depot so Colonel Jud could make a short speech about the glories of his show and the United States of America, which in his humble opinion stood for the same wonderful things. After urging one and all to come and see the show, Colonel Jud and his train were switched onto the side track that ran down to the city fairgrounds.

Morgan knew it would be better if he waited a day before he tried to see Colonel Jud, but every day lost brought poor old Bronc closer to a possible prison term that would kill him. The fairgrounds were a mile away, on a wide stretch of reclaimed bottom land by the river. Morgan took his time getting there.

He had seen wild west shows before, but never anything like this. It was more like a huge military encampment than anything else. Only the bugle calls were missing. Tents and light wood-and-canvas buildings had already been erected on the edges of the vast, square-shaped site, leaving a clear space at the center for the enormous main tent. Men were working everywhere, moving fast and efficiently, while foremen yelled orders through cupped hands. The train stood on a siding, and Morgan walked along the side of it without being challenged. He was looking at a car with flowers in cut-glass vases in the window and what looked like a chandelier hanging from the ceiling when a raspy voice said, "What the hell do you think you're up to?"

Morgan turned to face a big middle-aged man wearing buckskins, a white Stetson and a gold-plated badge. The badge had MARSHAL/ TOWN OF HARDESTY engraved on it. Around his thick waist he wore a gunbelt with imitation silver stitching; the pistol in the holster was nickel-plated and pearl-handled.

"I asked you what you're doing here," he said.

"Looking for Colonel Hardesty," Morgan said. "Is this his car?"

"What if it is?" The big man took a step closer. He had the look of a prison camp guard. "What business would the likes of you have with the colonel?"

"Personal business. The colonel will want to hear what I have to say. Why don't you ask him if he'll talk to me? It's important. I wouldn't bother him if it wasn't." Morgan thought that sounded polite enough, but this thug didn't want to listen. He took another step closer; in a minute he'd be using his massive fists like clubs.

"Get the fuck out of here before I kick your ass all the way back to town," he roared.

The door of the fancy car banged open and the colonel stood at the top of the steps, wearing only a shirt and trousers and rubbing his eyes. His beautiful long white hair and beard were mussed as if he'd been asleep.

"What in hell is going on here, Scully?" he said irritably. "Can't a man take a nap without all this commotion going on underneath his window. Who is this man, and what's all the fuss about?"

Morgan cut in before Scully could answer. "My name is Morgan, and I must talk to you, Colonel. It's important to both of us."

The colonel drew his bushy white eyebrows together in a frown. "Did you say *must*, young fella? I don't *must* do anything I don't want to. Just recently I said the same thing to President Hayes, God bless him. Rutherford was pushing hard to get me to campaign for him."

"I didn't mean it like that," Morgan said quickly. "I have the greatest respect for you, sir. I would have written you a letter, but there wasn't time. All I ask is a few minutes of your time."

Scully finally found his voice. "You want me to kick this bum out of here, Colonel? I guarantee he won't bother you again."

The colonel looked at his hired thug. "Stay right where you are, Scully. I'll call you if I need you. Meanwhile, I'll talk to this young fella and see what he wants. Young fella, you better give Mr. Scully your gun and let him conduct a quick search for other weapons. Can't be too careful these days."

Morgan knew he had to hold still for it. He handed Scully his gun and let the vicious bastard run his hands over his body. Scully looked in his hat and pushed his fingers into his boots, hoping to turn up a derringer or a knife.

"Nothing," Scully said. Morgan knew he was disappointed. Maybe he could get Scully alone before this was over. Then he told himself not to be such a goddamned fool. Bronc's life was at stake; there was no place in this for personal grudges. He climbed the steps and followed the colonel into his private car. If the colonel had set out to make himself comfortable, he had more than succeeded. The car was divided into three compartments with sliding doors between them. The doors were pushed back now, and Morgan could see all the way to the end of the car. If the car hadn't been shaped the way it was, the three compartments would have looked like a small but elegant suite of rooms in a luxury hotel.

Once Morgan was inside, the colonel seemed in no hurry to get down to business. Instead, he took Morgan on a little tour. "This first room is my office," he said proudly. "The next is my sitting room, and last but not least is my bedroom. What do you think, Mr. Morgan."

"It's truly magnificent, sir," Morgan said.

"Not bad for a poor Ohio River boy who ate muddy catfish three times a day. God, how I hate catfish!" They went back to the office, and the colonel waved Morgan into an overstuffed chair. He sat behind a desk, pulled a large gold watch closer to him, took note of the time, and said, "Time is money, Mr. Morgan. Say what you came to say."

Mindful of the watch, Morgan kept it short. He need not have. The colonel had a red face which grew redder as Morgan told of Bronc and his trouble. It took on a really dangerous color when Morgan got to the possible connection between the counterfeiters and the wild west show. The colonel had remained silent until then, but now he exploded with rage and consternation; for a moment he became incoherent.

"Christ on the cross, Morgan, what is this you're telling me? Are you mad, or am I? I can't believe what I'm hearing." The colonel's bellowing must have carried clear across the fairgrounds. Morgan tried to say something but was drowned out. "Who would dare?" the old man roared. "I am an American institution. I am the friend of presidents and captains of industry. Look at them."

On the wall were photographs of important men. Morgan recognized Rutherford B. Hayes, Ulysses S. Grant and Commodore Vanderbilt. It would take some time before the colonel stopped ranting. When he did he said stiffly, "Excuse me, Mr. Morgan. Wait here. I must get dressed." He went to the bedroom and pulled the sliding doors shut.

"Now I am more myself," he said when he came back and settled in behind his desk. He was in full Colonel Jud regalia, from white boots to enormous white Stetson hat. His beard and shoulder-length hair had been combed. "You took me completely by surprise, Mr. Morgan. I was expecting some wild tale of a lost gold mine or some fantastic invention that would change the world. I like crackpot stories. They give me a chuckle." He turned and closed the window behind him. "Did I say anything that might have revealed your information?"

"No, sir. You just sounded off. It could have been about anything."

"Good." The colonel leaned forward, his elbows on the desk. "Are you sure you're telling the truth? You seem like an honest man, yet."

Morgan said, "It's the truth as I know it. The rest is suspicion. They may be using your show, or they may not."

The colonel nodded. His hat was the biggest hat Morgan had ever seen. "We must proceed as if they are. I cannot take a chance of a scandal that could ruin me. My God, the newspapers—and wouldn't Cody laugh! What do you want me to do?"

"Give me a job so I'll be on the inside. I can ride and shoot better than most men. I can show you."

A little of the colonel's suspicion returned. "So you want to be a rider or a trick shooter?"

Morgan said, "You wouldn't have to pay me."

"Nonsense! You'd have to be paid and go down in the books as paid. Let me see. How would you feel about working under a woman? And don't tell me you'd rather work on top of one." Colonel Jud laughed at his own joke. "Our star's warm-up shooter just quit on her. Wanted her to show him some tricks in bed, and she wasn't interested. Well, what about it?"

"I'm game if she'll have me," Morgan said.

That got a frown. "Oh, she'll have you all right. Kitty may be temperamental, but it's my show. In this business there's only me and Cody and Crawford. Big-timers. Cody has Annie Oakley, and Crawford has Little Laura Chase. Our Kitty Carson is very young and not in their class yet. I admit it. I doubt if anybody will ever outclass Annie, but Kitty is sure to beat out Little Laura, given time." Colonel Jud opened the window and called down to Scully. "Go fetch Kitty Carson and be quick about it. If she gives you an argument, tell her I'll come down and fetch her myself."

While they waited, the colonel asked Morgan if he wanted a drink, but Morgan declined. Colonel Jud said, "I have the name of being a bigger drinker than Cody. Fact is, I don't touch the stuff. See that bottle over there marked private?" A row of bottles stood on a sideboard. "There's nothing in that but cold tea. Now and then I gargle with bourbon to keep my breath strong."

A few minutes later, Kitty Carson's boots sounded on the steps, the door banged open, and she stalked in, angry and very beautiful. She was tall, slightly on the wiry side, and had long legs. What a boss! Morgan thought. She stood there breathing hard until the colonel told her to sit down.

"Next time you want to see me, Jud," she raged, "send somebody else. That Scully makes me sick to my stomach. What do you want anyway?"

The colonel put an edge in his normally mellow voice. "I want to talk to you. Is that all right? Would you like to go back out and compose yourself? Good. Don't you feel better now?"

Kitty took a hard look at Morgan. "I feel all right. You still haven't said what you want. Does this bird have something to do with it?"

"Soft pedal it, Kitty." Staring her down, the colonel told her he had just hired Morgan to replace the warm-up shooter who had quit.

"Without talking to me first?" Kitty was ready to throw another tantrum.

Colonel Hardesty said, "I'm talking to you now. It's your job to find out if Lee is as good as he says he is. His father was one of my oldest friends, but I can't let that get in the way of business. See what he can do and fire him if he doesn't measure up. Naturally he'll never be as good as you, but at least give him a chance." The colonel turned to

Morgan. "Sorry for talking like that, Lee, but you'll have to take another job if you don't pan out as a shooter."

"Fair enough, sir," Morgan said.

Kitty Carson glared at him. "What are you waiting for, big man?"

Chapter Three

Kitty's living quarters were three cars down from the colonel's. As a star, she rated half a car all to herself, the other half being occupied by the show's top knife thrower. They came and went by their separate entrances. Morgan got the feeling that she didn't much like the knife thrower. Maybe she didn't much like anybody.

Kitty's place, one large compartment, wasn't a patch on the colonel's but it was fit for a star. It was more feminine than he expected it to be, even with the rack of chained rifles, mostly .22 calibers, on the wall. Flowered window curtains stirred in the hot summer breeze; on the wall was a colored copy of the famous painting "The Little Match Girl." Glowering down from another wall was a tinted photograph of a man and a woman, grim and elderly, in dark clothes. But it was the huge fourposter bed that got most of Morgan's attention. He knew Kitty was very proud of it. She sat on the edge of it and bounced her ass a few times.

Morgan stood because she hadn't told him to sit down. He didn't want to rile this fiery bitch—she even had the red hair to go with the temper—but when he thought she was looking at him too long, he said, "How soon are you going to try me out? I mean, the shooting."

"A wisenheimer," she said. "That's what you are, Morgan. Is Morgan your real name?"

"You heard the colonel. He knew my father in the old days."

"I heard him all right. What old days were those? When elephants flew and there was an honest Republican in the White House? I think there's something fishy going on around here."

"The name is still Morgan. What's your real name?"

"Kitty Mulligan, Irish and proud of it. But Kitty Carson, granddaughter of good old Kit, sounds better. Where are you from, Morgan?"

"Idaho. Where are you from?"

"Tenth Avenue, New York, is where I'm from. I'll ask the questions here."

Morgan shifted his weight to the other foot. "Ask away. I just want to know when you're going to try me out."

Kitty bounced her ass a few more times. "Don't be such a rube. I'm going to try you out right now. Peel off and let's see if you can fuck as well as you say you can shoot."

This wasn't the most romantic invitation Morgan had ever had thrown his way, but he grabbed at it like the drowning man and the straw. God, she was a beauty! A nasty beauty to be sure, but maybe she had a heart of gold underneath all that big city brashness. He didn't give a damn if she had a heart of stone. He didn't care if she had no heart at all, provided he could get between those lovely long legs. His cock stood to attention, and he had a little trouble shucking his pants. Kitty, out of her clothes in a flash, came over to help him.

"Ramrod straight," she said approvingly, handling his cock. "Maybe you'll do all right, big man."

"I'll try to, ma'am," Morgan said modestly.

She gave his prick a twist that hurt but did no damage. "Don't call me ma'am, you fucking rube. I'm twenty-two years old so quit trying to make me sound like a dried-up schoolteacher. You've heard of the three R's, hayseed. I'm going to teach you the three F's. Furious Fancy Fucking!" She gave a wild laugh and pulled Morgan onto the bed. Maybe she was crazy, he thought. Some of the crazy ones made the best bed partners, as long as they didn't try to kill you. Just watch yourself, he told himself. Think of Bronc. The hell with Bronc!

Kitty wasn't at all like Birgitta, who was content to let the man do the work. In bed or out of it, she was aggressive, impatient and wanting to be the boss. Some women were like that, Morgan thought, because the man had the driving rod and they didn't. But for a while Kitty acted as if she did. She spread her legs and guided him into her, pushing down hard on his ass so she'd get every last inch of his cock in her. "Ram it into me," she kept saying. "Get it in there, big man." Morgan didn't know what else he could get into her unless he got his balls in, too. As soon as he was in her, she pulled and grunted and rolled over until she was on top of him. Now she was—or thought she was—shafting him. It took only a few moments of impaling herself on his cock before she came like a wild woman, shuddering and biting her knuckles to keep from screaming. Sweat dripped from her long lean body, but instead of resting she went at him again, calling him "big dick" and "big hard man." Morgan rolled her back over. It

looked as if there hadn't been a cock in her for a long time.
Morgan felt like the water in the desert, the unexpected
food on the edge of starvation. He shafted her steadily,
wanting her to know that he was the boss from here on
in. She was warm and wet, and he felt her dripping. Her
warm juice ran down between her legs and puddled on the
silk sheets before soaking in. Kitty was a talker; she never
stopped talking. "Oh yes!" and "Jesus Christ—yes!" she
cried out, and even while his cock was sliding in and out
of her she tried to feel it with her hand. She came again,
and it felt as if the massive bed was being rocked by an
earth tremor. Morgan hadn't come yet, but he didn't want
to stop for even the short time it would take him to get
hard again. He wanted to wear her down, tire her out
so she'd finally know that here was a man big enough
for her.

But it looked like he was wrong, because there was no
let-up in her fierce energy. Still quivering from her last
orgasm, she clawed at him, demanding more and more of
the same. The bed was wet with her juices and the sweat
that rolled off both of them. Now she was saying, as if
he'd showed any sign of it, "Don't go soft on me, hard
man! You want me to stiffen it for you?" She was lean and
muscular, but Morgan was far stronger than she was, and
he drove in and out of her like a piston. At one point she
raised his face and held it, staring into his eyes and biting
on her lower lip. She mumbled because of the way she was
biting her lip, but he knew what she was saying. What he
was doing wasn't enough and wouldn't ever be enough.
Maybe she wanted him to fuck her to death. No wonder
she was lean and muscular. If she fucked like this, even
once every three months, she wouldn't need any exercise
for the rest of the year. Now she was urging him to come.
Maybe she was tiring, but he wasn't going to let her off the

hook just like that. If she beat him in bed, she'd try to beat him everywhere else. She'd try to do that anyway—it was her nature—but she'd always know she hadn't been able to beat him where it counted.

Morgan didn't mind any of it. All women were different and all women were the same. Except for those who had something wrong with them, all women wanted cock, big and strong and tireless. Any way they wanted it was all right with him. They were entitled to it. Without them a man was just a lonesome cock with nowhere to go. He was happy to be in this bed with this woman, and what was in her head didn't matter a whole lot. "Jesus, Mary and Joseph, all together in a bed!" she was saying.

That was one Morgan hadn't heard before. Maybe she was crazy. Maybe it was just something she'd learned underneath the elevated tracks in Hell's Kitchen. It had just been days since he'd worn himself out with Birgitta, and here he was pronging away like a mountain man down from the high valleys for his yearly rendezvous with the Indian whores. Ah, Kitty my love, he thought with his face pressed against the side of her head, I'm going to fuck you until you'll have to crawl out of bed.

Though her energy was waning there was life in the old gal yet. And as though she knew what he was thinking, she took a deep breath and raised her ass to meet the thrust of his cock, urging him on like a racehorse owner urging on a faltering nag. Now he was shafting her without mercy. There was no meanness in it, just the determination to beat her down until she couldn't come anymore and had to lay there weak and gasping. He knew he was winning when she said, "Come! I want you to come. I want to feel you coming. Don't you want to come?" And when he didn't come she asked, "You want me to help you to come? You can come, can't you?"

A little nastiness there, he thought, holding back a smile because she could see his face. "I don't want to stop," he lied. "I don't want to let go. It's so good I want to keep doing it."

The bed battle went on like that, neither side wanting to give up. Kitty's legs, tight around his back, grew tighter as if she meant to break it. She had him in so tight a hold that he had to raise up hard to shove it in and pull it back. Kitty came again but trembled with fatigue as well as pleasure long after it was over. She tried to roll him over to get back on top, but she no longer had the strength. He reached back and untangled her legs, then pushed them down on the bed until they were wide open and he was fucking her without so much of a struggle. She loosened her muscles down there, and he put less force into his thrusts. Kitty responded to that, eyes closed, and legs wide open, and he fucked her gently, not wanting to hurt her anymore. The hard part of it had been good, but this was better. Her talking stopped altogether, replaced by sighs of contentment, and he knew he had broken her hard, big city shell with his cock. That was all to the good, and he thought it wouldn't be such a fight-to-the-death next time they went at it. Not that he didn't like spirit in a woman, far from it, but it was just that he liked other qualities as well.

It was time, he thought, and after pulling back all the way he drove in hard and came like he'd never wanted to come before. Kitty screamed and came with him, and they lay pressed together until the shuddering stopped. Kitty looked happy—happy for her—and was talking again before he rolled off her. There was no stopping this gal, he thought.

Kitty sat up in bed. "I love this bed," she told him. "When I was a kid back in New York, we slept four to a bed. All that kicking and fighting for space. I swore if I ever got out of there, I was going to have a great big bed all to myself."

"But why a fourposter?" Morgan liked her better now.

"I saw a picture of Martha Washington's bed in Mount Vernon. It looked big enough to sleep the whole Mulligan family. I bought this bed in Chicago. I was new with the colonel, but he advanced me the money. A good way to keep me with the show."

Morgan said, "The colonel thinks highly of you. How did you get into trick shooting anyway? Doesn't sound like something you'd learn in a city."

"That's what you think," she said. "My father ran a shooting gallery on 14th Street. Didn't own it, but just ran it for his brother Johnny. Lucky for him. My father was half-drunk all the time. Every morning before he went to work on the El he stopped at Sweeney's hose joint for a few mouthfuls of rotgut. You know what a hose joint is?"

Morgan said no.

"I guess they don't have them in Idaho," Kitty said. "A hose joint is a place where instead of a regular saloon they have hoses with numbers sticking out a wall. A guy sits in front of a row of taps, and when a customer comes in and pays his nickel that number hose is turned on and he gets a big mouthful of whisky. My father's morning ration was always fifteen cents worth. So he was half potted when he arrived at work. Uncle Johnny had serious thoughts about firing him, but then I got to be thirteen, old enough to handle a gun. When things were slow, like in the morning, I practiced till I couldn't see straight. I paid for the ammunition—Uncle Johnny always did a count of cash and bullets—out of my tips and a little short-changing on the side. Then

Uncle Johnny died, and that was the end of the shooting gallery. I got my first shooting job when I was sixteen, a real mangy show in Jersey. Pay was peanuts but I got experience—and here I am. I've been with the colonel three years."

Morgan yawned and stretched; the fourposter was the most comfortable bed he'd ever been in. "I was thinking I might . . ."

Kitty was way ahead of him. "Not a chance. Nobody bunks in with me, pardner. Maybe later but not even then, probably. I like my privacy. It's nice to lay here early in the morning and listen to the sounds of wherever we are. Sometimes I read till all hours. Did you ever read *Under Two Flags* by Ouida. I read a lot. My mother taught grammar school till she had the misfortune to marry my father. I've read *Under Two Flags* five times."

"Can't say I've read it."

"You can read, can't you?"

"Sure I can read. I read the papers."

"I'm glad you're not illiterate," Kitty said thoughtfully. "It would distress me to know I'd been to bed with an illiterate. I may be from Hell's Kitchen but I have high standards. Time to get up, Morgan. We got to mosey over to that thar shootin' range. I'll introduce you to some of the people you ought to know."

The last part was what interested Morgan; any one of the people he was going to meet could be the counterfeit bill passer. Could be Kitty was doing it. She was well-paid, but maybe she was greedy. He didn't want it to be Kitty, but if it was, he'd send her up as quick as he would a son of a bitch like Scully. Easy boy, he told himself. You're not going to meet everybody in the show in one afternoon. You're not about to clear Bronc by nightfall.

*   *   *

The shooting place had seen set up south of an outer line of tents. Tent show shooting was done at close range, Kitty said, so the distance between the shooter and the targets was not great. The man who would release the targets was already there and would work behind the protection of a thick wooden shield. Behind him was another shield 12 feet high and 20 feet long. The back shield was to keep some trespasser from getting shot.

On the way there, Kitty introduced him to a bareback rider, an Indian maiden who threw a tomahawk at targets, a female rope and whip virtuoso, and a champion bronc buster. The rope and whip gal was the best-looking of the three young women; it would be no hardship to be roped, though not whipped, by her. None of the women was particularly friendly to Kitty, who was one of the colonel's favorites despite all their bickering. Kitty called the old man 'Jud' and he didn't object. Morgan thought the bronc buster gave him a funny look when Kitty said he was Lee Morgan from Idaho. The man's name was John Ryan. Morgan had been battering around long enough to know that west of the Mississippi 'John Ryan' was the 'John Smith' of the criminal fraternity. Maybe the funny look didn't mean anything.

Morgan also met the advance man for the show, an affable gent named Cargill who looked like he knew all the latest jokes. The chief purchasing agent, who spoke with a strong lisp, said he had no time to talk. He gave Morgan a quick handshake, welcomed him to the show and hurried off. His name was Schlegel, short in stature, short in manner, and clearly not one for jokes. The joke Cargill told—"These three Irishmen bought an elephant, see"—got Kitty's back up, and later she said, "Fuck him and his paddy jokes. You'd think he was the happiest man in the world, but he's a born loser. A gambler that couldn't pick a winning horse even if there was only one horse in the race. Loses at races, cards, dice, anything you could name. The man is a legend in the tent show business. Owes money from here to San Diego. It's a wonder they don't kill him. Even drew a losing number when he got married. His wife smokes hop—opium to you, Snodgrass."

A possibility there, Morgan thought. A hard luck gambler who got around. He smiled sourly to himself and thought of Bender's sneering remarks. Detective Morgan on the job!

They got to the shooting area, and Kitty handed Morgan the long barreled pistol she'd been carrying in an oil-damp wool-lined leather case, a nickel-plated double-action Colt .22. "You may be better with your own gun, but it's not showy enough. This is what you'll be using. Get used to it. You have till next week."

Morgan hefted the fancy .22. It had a nice balance. Most tent show shooting was done double-action, fast and showy. That didn't bother him, though he preferred to thumb back the hammer when he fired a gun. Kitty called to the man behind the shield, and he set clay pipes spinning. This was kid stuff, and Morgan broke six pipes with six fast shots.

"Give the man a kewpie doll!" Kitty called.

Next the man tossed up three eggs, and he broke them. Then he broke three more eggs with the three rounds left in the pistol. He reloaded and waited.

"That's enough," Kitty told him irritably. "You're good, Morgan, but take heed now. Try to take my job and I'll shoot your balls off."

Morgan handed her the loaded .22. "I'm not near good enough to do that."

"That's right, buddy." She took a walnut from her pocket, tossed it high in the air and broke it before it started to fall. Then she shoved the Colt .22 back at Morgan. "Keep it and clean it. It's yours."

Walking back, she asked if he wanted to take the warm-up shooter's place, in a car with four other men, or would he rather have a small tent to himself. Morgan opted for a tent, and she showed him where it was after talking to the man in charge of living quarters.

"I'll leave you to get settled in," she said. "You might stroll by about nine. I don't go out nights. After New York, what does a hick town like Kansas City have to offer?"

The tent was all right. It had a cot, a duckboard floor, a pressed wood pulp table, a gasoline lantern and a chair. Morgan was stretched out on the cot, cleaning the Colt double-action, when the colonel stuck his head in. "Let's us take a little walk, boy. I always have a walk and a talk with my new people."

Nobody took any notice of them except to wave or say hello to the colonel. "I've got the common touch," Colonel Jud said grandly. "The secret of my success. Kitty said you did fine. First time I ever heard her praise anybody."

"I love her, too," Morgan said.

"Just as long as you mean it lightly," the colonel said. "That gal will break your heart as quick as she'll break your balls."

They walked out into the wide space where the big top was yet to be erected. Morgan asked Colonel Jud about the advance man, Cargill, and his gambling losses. "Kitty says he's in over his ears. A man deep in debt will do a lot of things, specially if he owes leg-breakers and acid-tossers."

Colonel Jud took off his huge hat and fanned himself with it. "In this business you get a lot of funny people. I've got a man—I won't mention his name—a top money-maker who can't seem to keep his hands off other men. That's fine as long as he stays at home, which is here amongst his own kind of people. If he bothers a man or boy here, he gets kidded about it. It's when he tries it away from here the trouble starts. I don't know how many times I've had to buy him out of scrapes. Naturally I don't do it myself. You know who does? Cargill, that's who. I help Cargill out, too, which is not to say that I go around the country buying up his markers. His losses are constant but not all that great. A story gets started and along the way it gets embellished. Whatever he is, Cargill is the best advance man in the business. That, and the fact I like him, is why I protect him. If any of his creditors get too nasty, I let it be known that I can call fifty roustabouts together, give each man a five dollar bill and a bottle, and send them into the creditor's place of business."

Morgan was seeing another side of the old man. It figured though; you couldn't run his kind of operation without being tough. "You think I shouldn't waste time on Cargill?"

Colonel Jud put his hat on and squared it on his head. "Oh, I didn't say that. No man really knows what another man will do. See what you can find out about Cargill, poor bastard. That wife of his is as much a burden as his gambling. Lays there in bed with her opium dreams. Hardly knows her husband exists. But don't get me wrong. Maisie isn't all withered away like some dopers—far from it. She seems to thrive on the fiendish stuff. I doubt if you can find out much about Cargill through her. Starting tomorrow, Cargill will be gone for a week or so, spying on Cody's new acts. Try to be discreet, my boy."

* * *

He spent most of the night with Kitty. She didn't like drinking and kept no liquor in her place, but she had brought in two bottles of beer just for him. He drank one before he got into bed with her and now, six hours later, it was time to go, she said, and he was sitting on the edge of the bed, pulling on his socks and drinking the second beer. He had been trying to think of a way to get her to talk about money. Now she did so in a roundabout way. He was aware that she'd been staring at him.

"What made you start so late?" she said. "In this business, I mean. You're no kid. You're well into your thirties."

"I heard it paid well," Morgan said.

"You said you raised horses."

"I said I used to raise horses. Ran into a streak of bad luck and lost my ranch. I could have found work in my line for forty a month. Here I get fifty a week and the grub's better. A year or so I'll be able to go home and start over. That's my big plan. What's yours?"

Kitty lay back on the silk pillows. "I don't think I have any big plan, Morgan. Life is too good now to be thinking so far ahead. I've been after the colonel to give me a whole railroad car, not this sawed-off thing I have now. I think he'll do it. Jud is an old darling. I'd like to make more money, but I get a lot now, so I don't fret about it. As long as I can live in the lap of luxury, I have no serious complaints."

Morgan pulled on his boots and stood up after bending over to kiss her. "You wouldn't want to invest in a horse ranch, by any chance?"

Kitty threw a pillow at him. "No way, mister! Now get the hell out of here so I can get my beauty sleep.'

*   *   *

He spent part of the next morning shooting at eggs
and balloons. Even Annie Oakley had to practice, though
Colonel Cody's publicity agents put out the story that
she didn't. After an hour, he gave it up and went back
to his tent. On the way, he saw Cargill walking along
the side of the train with a grip in his hand. He had no
idea how he was going to get into Mrs. Cargill's bed or
even get close to her. He couldn't just walk in and say,
"Let's smoke a pipe together" like a redskin chief at a
powwow.

Morgan was a little surprised when John Ryan stopped
by for a chat, if that's what it was. A few minutes later,
he decided it wasn't so casual. The man was digging
for information. Trying for good ol' boy affability, Ryan
was as nervous as a cat with a new dog in the house.
Morgan sat on the cot, and Ryan took the chair. After
lamenting how hot Kansas City was in summer, Ryan
switched abruptly to Idaho. Morgan felt like smiling. The
son of a bitch sure as hell didn't have much polish to
him.

"What part the state you from anyhow?" Ryan asked.

"Thirty miles west of Boise," Morgan said. "My people
were country people. Tried raising horses but went bust.
Been doing this and that ever since. Yourself?"

Morgan's answer seemed to have settled Ryan down
a little. "I'm from Colorado," he said without the strain
he'd been showing before. "Always was good at breaking
horses so took a chance and asked for a job when the show
was in Denver. Been with Colonel Jud nine months. Nice
old fella. You been with other shows?"

"This is my first." Morgan knew it wouldn't be hard for
Ryan to find out if he was lying. Wild west shows were
a small world where everybody knew everybody else, or

close to it. He meant to check if Ryan had been hired in
Denver; the colonel would know. What he didn't get was
what Ryan was up to. He got an idea a few minutes later
when he took the .22 from his belt and started cleaning it.
After that was done, he would take it over to the payroll
office and have it locked in the safe. Kitty didn't allow
him a key to her gun rack.

Ryan stared at the gleaming revolver as if he'd never
seen any kind of gun before. It was a fine weapon, Morgan
thought, but not at all unusual; it was used in all kinds of
shows, and once in a while you saw one in a pawnshop
window.

Ryan said, "You must have a lot of experience to shoot
the way you do. I guess you've done more than raise
horses." He laughed nervously.

"I told you I did this and that after I went bust, but
I was always good with a gun. That's why I got this
job."

Ryan leaned forward, his hands on his knees. "A man
as good as you could be a top lawman. There's money in it
if you're the best, like Earp or Wild Bill. Course a bounty
hunter can make a lot more than that. A lot of uncollected
rewards still being offered. Never been tempted in that
line, have you?"

"Never have. It's a dirty dollar." Morgan put the .22 in
its case and got up. He understood now. Ryan was on the
dodge, which was no business of his unless Ryan got the
idea that he was on his trail and wanted to be sure he had
the right man before he dropped the hammer. Ryan had
done something pretty bad in Idaho, or he wouldn't be
sweating. There had to be a sizable reward out on Ryan
or he wouldn't be talking about bounty hunters. Only the
scurviest bounty hunters, generally old men, worked for
small money.

Outside, Ryan said, trying again for affability, "We ought to go into town one of these nights before the show opens. A few drinks."

"Maybe we'll do that," Morgan said.

Chapter Four

Morgan went into the Texas Saloon and sat at the last table in the back. All the other tables were occupied, but not this one. It looked like Bender had staked his claim at this table, and though nobody dared jump it, he wasn't there. A waiter shooed Morgan away from the table when he tried to sit down, but the Yellow Kid, who was standing at the bar, whispered something in the waiter's ear, and he smiled and waved Morgan to a chair. The Yellow Kid gave Morgan the thumb and forefinger okay sign and turned back to his drink.

Bender came in about 3:30, and the waiter brought a mug of beer without being asked. "Thought I wasn't going to get here. A state senator's son got himself shot and wounded in a nigger whorehouse. Why a nigger whorehouse? They got black women in the white places. Likes the danger, I guess. What have you been doing, Detective Morgan?"

Morgan told him about getting the warm-up shooter's

job, then he went on to Cargill and John Ryan. "I'm pretty sure Ryan is wanted bad in Idaho. Can you check back on him?"

Bender said, "I can't telegraph every city and town in Idaho, but if what he did was bad enough, it might have made the newspapers besides where it happened. I'll get Fletcher on the *Star* to telegraph a few inquiries. Fletcher is the managing editor and ought to get some results. Now Cargill. What's he done besides lose his shirt and marry a woman that likes her pipe? You know, your Colonel Jud could be right. Just because a man is a fool doesn't mean he's a crook. But I'll look into it. Cargill will be harder to check, so I'll start with Ryan. John Ryan, eh?" Bender laughed. "I've put the cuffs on a lot of John Ryans in my time. Anything else?"

Morgan had to lean forward to be heard. A drummer had been added to the band. He had a bandage around his head, and maybe some bottle thrower had put him in the infirmary. He liked the cymbals a lot.

"Can you check a guard named Patrick Scully?" Morgan asked, describing the man and what he thought he'd been before he joined the show as chief guard.

"I don't have to check him," Bender told him. "I know who he is. Pat is a reformed badman who turned state's evidence against the Bannister Gang, of which he was a leading member. It was in all the Missouri papers. Judge gave him five years, a mere twist of the ear, and he got religion inside the walls. Nothing like the rockpile to turn a man's thoughts to the Almighty. I hear he's some kind of lay preacher on the side."

Morgan said, "You'd never know it the way he walks around behind that badge."

"Probably thought you were planning to stick-up the colonel. Pat hates badmen now. You can cross him off

your list, I'm pretty sure. A word of advice, Detective.
Don't be suspecting too many people or you'll end up
suspecting your grandmother. And I have other work to
do. Now I better get moving. Gallager has just promoted
his halfwit nephew from patrolman to detective behind my
back. I'm just Chief of Detectives so naturally I'm the last
to know. Kid is a greenhorn from Ireland, a flatfoot less
than six months, and suddenly he's a detective. Why can't
he get shot in a nigger whorehouse?"

Morgan smiled at this strange man. "Why don't you
quit and take Scully's job?"

"Probably pays better, but I like the dirty job I have.
I'll let you know about Ryan. Like I said, Cargill will
take more time. Watch out for this Ryan. If he thinks
you're planning to cut off his head and take it back to
Idaho in a bag of salt.well, watch out. You know, I could
pull the bugger in on suspicion and hold him till this is
over one way or another."

"I don't know," Morgan said. "Could be he's been
asking around about me. Probably has. The man is not
too bright. If they tied me in to his arrest I'd be out in
the cold. Nobody would talk to me."

"Then don't walk down any dark alleys with Ryan."

Bender went out first, while Morgan drank another beer
before he left. There was no sign of John Ryan. He'd kept
a lookout for Ryan on the way to the saloon. Now he did
the same on the way back.

Colonel Jud laughed. "You're asking about Ryan, and
he's been asking about you. Fell into step with me on my
afternoon walk, my tour of inspection, so to speak. Well,
sir, I don't mind that. I'm a plain man. Anybody can talk
to me. Ryan is a bit of a sneak, but I don't mind that either.
Sneaks have their uses. I thought he was about to relate

some juicy morsel of gossip, but no—he started asking questions about you. He started off by saying he thought he'd seen your picture on a wanted poster for bank robbery in some town we played in. Then, begging my pardon and all, he asked what I really knew about you. Had you just walked in off the street, so to speak, or had somebody sent you? No, you hadn't been sent, I told him, but you looked all right. Your story was the story of many men who fell on hard times, and you could shoot extremely well, so I hired you."

"You did fine, Colonel," Morgan said.

"Of course I did," the colonel said. "Then he started up with didn't I think it strange that a horse rancher could shoot like that. I said no. A lot of men like guns and like to shoot them. Next he suggested maybe you were a fast-shooting lawman gone bad. I asked him if the reward poster had said anything about that, as it would be sure to. That threw him, and he said he couldn't remember. I think he may be short, as the country people say. It took a while to get rid of him. What's all this about, my boy?"

Morgan told him.

"I did hire him in Denver," the colonel said. "At least that part is true. What difference does it make? I've got to get rid of him."

Morgan said, "Please don't do that, sir. If you fire him, either he'll just take off or start lying in wait for me. Who can say what a man like that will do. I'd rather you kept him where I can see him. Besides I have a police lieutenant checking his background this very day. If he is what I think he is, he'll be arrested inside of a few days."

Somebody knocked on the door and a man's voice called out, "Bruno, Colonel!" It was the colonel's barber come to trim and wash his beautiful white hair and beard.

"A few days, Morgan," the colonel said. "I won't have him under my canvas longer than that."

Morgan had just left the colonel's car, walking along the side of the train, when he saw a woman getting out of a hansom cab with a lot of packages in her arms. He stopped and watched while she stopped in front of Cargill's car, fumbling in her bag and trying to hold the packages at the same time. The packages fell, and Morgan was right there offering assistance.

"My shining knight," she drawled in a deep southern accent. She was slender but not skinny. She had yellow hair and very sleepy green eyes. There was something catlike about her, the lazy way her body moved and the look of contentment on her heart-shaped face. "I am a damsel in distress. Please help me, kind sir."

"My pleasure," he said. "If you'll just unlock the door I'll carry in your packages."

"You are most gracious, sir," she said, holding the door open so Morgan could go in ahead of her. Cargill, as a married man and a top member of the colonel's staff, had an entire car. Like Kitty's, it wasn't as luxurious as the colonel's, but it was all right. Instead of being divided like the colonel's, it was one long room with the sitting room set off from the bedroom space. Mrs. Cargill—Morgan knew her name was Maisie—came in, locking the door behind her. "Won't you stay a while?" Morgan had muttered something about leaving. "I'm practically a hermit so seldom do I see anyone. Mr. Cargill is away so much. Do sit down, sir. May I fix you a drink? I do not drink myself but I do not object to others doing so. But I'm afraid all I can offer you is rye whisky."

Morgan said rye would be fine. She opened a sideboard, poured a drink and held up a water pitcher. "Straight it shall be, sir. And I shall have coffee."

Morgan sipped his drink while she lit an alcohol burner with a coffeepot on top of it. Then she filled a large mug with black coffee, the blackest looking coffee Morgan had ever seen. It looked like India ink coming out of the pot. An old story told to him by a mush dog driver who was trying out teams in Idaho came back to him. Mushers in the far north of Canada used to boil a chunk of plug tobacco in a pot of coffee, then add a pinch of gunpowder for good measure to keep them from falling asleep and freezing to death. No matter how tired they were, this awful brew revived them. Sometimes it drove them a little crazy. He'd seen one ancient musher dancing naked in the snow.

"Call me Maisie," Mrs. Cargill told him. "Would you like me to freshen your drink?" Morgan said he was okay, and Maisie went back to the sideboard for another mug of Canadian Special, if that's what it was. Her drowsy eyes got brighter a few minutes after she got it down, and then she had another. "You must think it odd of me to drink so much coffee, sir, but you see, I am the lethargic type. Coffee picks me up."

"Nothing like a good cup of coffee," Morgan said. "I'm a bit of a coffee fiend myself."

Maisie gave a trilling laugh. "Did you say 'fiend?' Oh, I'm nothing like that. What is your name, if I may ask?"

Morgan told her, thinking that every time she went to the sideboard there was a quick, hidden movement as if she'd poured something into the coffee. He got it. She was a laudanum drinker, not a pipe smoker. That figured. Any place where opium was smoked regularly had a thick, sweet, not unpleasant smell about it. He knew because he'd once had to drag one of his hands out of an opium den in Seattle. The drunken clown had thought he was in a Chinese whorehouse.

She was smiling now, flying high on tincture of opium and coffee. Tens of thousands of people, mostly women, drank laudanum. People who wouldn't be caught dead with an opium pipe drank it. There was nothing illegal about it, since you could buy laudanum in any drugstore. What he didn't get was why she wanted to stay awake instead of drifting off into those sweet dreams they said it brought you.

"I haven't seen you around, have I, Lee?" she said, slurring her words a little.

Morgan told her he was the new warm-up shooter.

"So you'll be working with the lovely Kitty," Maisie drawled, sounding even more southern than she had earlier. She added in a sharper voice, "That little guttersnipe! Don't be taken in by her city tricks, Lee. She's trash!"

"We get along all right." Morgan felt a little disloyal for not standing up for his redheaded boss. "We both come from poor people."

"Yes, but with you it doesn't show. After a mere few minutes acquaintance I can see you are a natural born gentleman. My own family lost everything in that dreadful war, but we managed to live graciously nonetheless."

Oh Christ! Morgan thought. She's going to tell me one of those apple pan dowdy stories. The house with the white columns. Happy darkies singing at dusk in the slave quarters. De Ole Massa sitting on the veranda, a tall julep in his hand.

But she didn't tell it the way he'd usually heard it. Her father had been an Alabama country doctor with a small plantation. The Yankee blockade ruined the English cotton trade, and even her father's once rich patients had little money to pay his fees. After her parents died she had worked for a dressmaker in Dothan.

"That's where I met and married Mr. Cargill—Fred."

She primped her hair a bit. "Of course I was a mere child at the time. But you would never take me for thirty, would you? Be a gentleman and say no."

Morgan said no. "I'd say you looked younger if I didn't know when the war ended." He took her to be about 35, but the years hadn't left much of a mark on her. He wondered if she'd started drinking laudanum pilfered from her father's medical supplies.

"You must be lonely with your husband away so much," Morgan said. That brought some annoyance to her voice, and he knew all was not well in the Cargill household. That figured—a beautiful woman left alone all the time, even if she had laudanum to console her. "Must be just as lonely for your husband."

The annoyance turned to a sort of distracted anger. "Fred has his cards and horses and dice to keep him company. I wouldn't mind if he didn't keep losing all the time. Lordy me! Poor Fred was not born under a lucky star when it comes to gaming. His addiction sometimes leaves us in severe financial difficulties, but we manage."

Her voice trailed off, and Morgan said, "It must be hard being strapped for money all the time. I know. You think maybe a bank loan would put you back on your feet."

"A bank loan, if he found a banker stupid enough, would send him straight to a poker game or a bookmaker. He's already had two bank loans, both largely unpaid. They keep dunning us. Luckily we move around a lot. I really don't know why I'm telling all this. It can't be of any interest. Suffice it to say that while we're not exactly poor we're a long way from being well-off. We manage. You know, all this talking has made me rather tired. Would you mind if I lay down for a while?"

"Not a bit," Morgan said. "You want me to leave?" He knew she didn't.

"Oh no, it's been so nice talking to you. Come and sit by me, and we'll talk some more."

Morgan followed her into the sleeping area, and she stretched out on a double bed. "Pull a chair up close. It's so nice having nice company." She closed her eyes, and he hoped she wasn't going to fall asleep. Apart from the other questions he wanted to ask, there was a bone in his pants he knew she'd noticed. It looked like Cargill was broke all right. If he had big money coming in from counterfeiters he'd be lavishing at least some of it on this strange, lovely woman. The colonel said he was mad for her.

After a minute or so, with her eyes still closed, Maisie drawled, "Wouldn't you like to stretch out for a while, Lee? If that sounds unconventional you must remember I'm an unconventional girl. Come on now. The door's locked, and there's just the two of us. I feel as if I've known you for ages."

Morgan didn't know why she had to go through all this genteel shit, but some women were like that, especially those from the South. He shucked his duds and got in beside her, and she giggled when she reached over and fondled his rigid shaft. "So big, so hard," she told him. She giggled some more as he got her out of her clothes and put his hand between her legs. "So wet," he said, knowing it would make her laugh. He was getting a handle on her now. She was a funny woman, and the spiked laudanum made her funnier. The stilted way she spoke was a mockery of the old life she had left to go on the road with Cargill.

"You are a terrible man, Lee Morgan!" Morgan had her legs wide open and was diddling her with his middle finger. She came quickly, and she held his hand where it was, getting all the pleasure out of it she could. He wondered if Fred Cargill was any good in bed. Maybe not; men who gambled like he did often neglected the things they should be looking after. Yet from the way she talked, she appeared to have affection for her husband—maybe even loved him a little at times—and Morgan liked her for that. Two lost souls supporting each other in a hard world.

"Put it into me, Lee," she murmured. "Let me feel you putting it in. Ah, wonderful! I hope you don't think I'm one of those randy ladies who go wild every time their husband leaves town on business. Poor old Fred knows many jokes about such ladies."

She yawned and her voice trailed off, but she revived considerably when he got between her legs and drove into her. Laudanum and coffee were fighting for possession of her; with his help, the inky black brew was winning. Her voice grew stronger and so did her movements. He quickened his thrusts to keep her from drifting off. That must be how she spent her days—longing for the drug, but wanting to feel its effects with her eyes open. What surprised him was that she loved a big hard cock as much as she did; drunks and dopers usually didn't have that much interest, but this was no pretense with her. He doubted that in her strange state of mind she would be able to pretend to love sex if she didn't. The Godawful brew she drank put her in the land of dreams, and maybe she thought what he was doing to her was a dream, but she was feeling every moment of it.

After she came again he knew the laudanum was getting a good grip on her, and he didn't try to stop her when she padded out to the sideboard in her bare feet. He heard a splashing sound as she filled her mug too quickly; when she came back, her eyes were brighter, and she laughed and crawled in beside him and reached for his cock. "Goodness gracious, boys and girls, will you look at what I have found. Santa has been good to me this year. I have what every girl needs, a toy that will not break or wear out. I sincerely hope your wonderful apparatus will not break or wear out, sir. Answer me, Yankee. You *are* a Yankee, aren't you?"

It looked as if she wanted him to answer. "I don't know if I am or not. I come from Idaho." He was back between her legs while all this foolishness was going on. He didn't think he would get any more information, but she was a nice woman in her dreamy way, and since there was no pressing reason why he should dress and leave, he didn't mind if he stayed till she finally fell asleep. He might even get some sleep himself, which was not a bad idea when he thought about it. His tent was right in the middle of everything, and the noise never stopped. He could sleep through noise, but why do that when he was in bed with a lovely woman and the door was locked?

"I can feel you smiling," she drawled. Before he could answer, she indicated by gestures that she wanted him to roll her over and mount her from behind. "I like to feel it invading my little treasure that way. I have a nice cushion for you to press against. By that, sir, I mean my posterior. A man less endowed than you are might find it difficult to do what I ask. However, your magic wand is so long and strong. If you had a willing little sweetheart back in the tall woods, I hope she does not miss your magic wand, your lightning rod, too much as she lies awake in her bed in the wee hours of the morning and has no solace other than her finger. Would you be shocked, sir, if I told you that all too often my own finger is my only friend?"

Morgan was shafting her with a steady rhythm, something that seemed to please her, and she responded. "I wouldn't find it a bit shocking," he said, knowing she'd keep at him if he didn't give her an answer. None of it made any sense, and maybe that was the good thing about it. She had been dreamy-eyed when he helped pick up her packages; there was a chance that she might not even remember him. If that was so, it would be the first time he'd ever been a dream. He had fucked women who could well be described as a sailor's wet dream, but that wasn't the same thing. That's what he was thinking when she reached back and pushed up so that his cock came out of her. "Put it in love's other hole," she murmured. "But be gentle, kind sir, and do not hurt me."

Morgan had no intention of hurting her. He edged it in, taking his time, but it was easier than it was with other women who wanted to spice up their pleasure by doing something forbidden. One woman had called it that and became angry when he smiled and asked her what was so forbidden about it. She wanted it to be forbidden— sinful—so she could enjoy it more. Not all women came when they did it like that, but this one did. "It's such an exciting sensation," she drawled, "that I don't quite know how to describe it. Inside me I feel it in a different place. Do you feel something like that?"

"You bet," Morgan told her, but didn't say anything else because she had finally fallen asleep. He fucked her ass until he came, then he stretched out beside her and fell asleep.

Chapter Five

It was past midnight, and Morgan thought he'd better get back to his own bed. Maisie was in a deep sleep. Morgan was dressed and reaching for his boots when shouting broke out somewhere toward the end of the train. Lights were burning in some of the cars and tents; others were being lit as he ran down the side of the train. He overtook a running man and asked him what was going on, but the man didn't know. A crowd was gathered in front of the tent where Ryan lived, then he heard Bender's voice shouting, "I'm a law officer. Stay back, I'm warning you! This man is a double murderer. He killed his own father and mother, and I have a warrant for his arrest. Let me through!"

Morgan had to shove hard to get through the mob of shouting people. Then he saw Ryan with his hands cuffed in front of him. Bender had him by the back of the collar and was trying to move him away from the tent. A woman screamed, "How do we know you're a policeman? Where's your fucking uniform? Let's see a badge, you flatfoot son of a bitch! John Ryan never killed anybody. You're lying!"

Bender was holding Ryan with one hand and fumbling in his pocket with the other when Ryan suddenly smashed the back of his head into the detective's face, and he went down bleeding from the nose and mouth. Ryan whirled, bent down, grabbed the shoulder-holstered revolver from under Bender's coat and pointed it at his face. The hammer was edging back when Morgan shot Ryan twice in the back of the head. He dropped like a stone. The gun in Ryan's hand fired but hit nothing but grass. Bender staggered to his feet, groping for a handkerchief, but everybody looked away from him when the colonel bulled his way to the front. He wore nothing but a quilted dressing gown and his hat.

"What in blazes.?" he bellowed, but stopped when he saw the dead man.

Holding a handkerchief to his face, Bender took a folded piece of paper from his inside pocket and shook it in the colonel's face. "This is a warrant for the arrest of the man who called himself John Ryan. His real name is Otis Drury. He is wanted in Idaho for the murder of his parents. If your people hadn't interfered he would still be alive to stand trial." Bender pointed at Morgan. "This man saved my life. Drury would have killed me. What kind of people do you have working for you, Colonel?"

Colonel Jud's face swelled with anger, and he turned on the gawkers like a fierce old lion. "Get away from here, you goddamned fools! There's nothing more for you to see. Go to your beds, I say. By Christ, if you're not gone in five seconds, I'll fire the lot of you!"

Most of the crowd went back to their quarters, but a few just backed away and watched and listened from a distance. The colonel didn't seem to notice. He tried to take Bender's arm, but the detective pulled it away. "Officer," the colonel said in a shaky voice, "I don't know what got into my people, but you have my humblest apologies. You say he killed his own father and mother? Horrible."

"Killed them with a billhook," Bender said. "Chopped them to pieces. Stole their life savings, not very much, and ran away. There's a five thousand dollar reward out on him. A big local rancher put it up all by himself. Reward still stands." Bender turned to Morgan. "I guess it's yours. What's your name?"

"Lee Morgan."

"Come and see me tomorrow, Morgan. Any time in the morning."

"I don't want it, Lieutenant," Morgan said. "Blood money brings bad luck. I didn't kill him for money."

"Come and see me anyway," Bender said. "We'll talk about it. Maybe you'll change your mind."

Bender turned back to the colonel before Morgan could respond. "Colonel, I'll send a paddy wagon for the body as soon as I get back to headquarters. Meanwhile I guess you better cover him up. Good night."

Morgan decided Bender had played it just right. He hadn't even thanked him for saving his life, the tough detective right to the core. And the colonel wasn't bad either. As soon as he noticed the people who were still there, he said to Morgan in a voice that really carried, "Must be hell, son, killing a man you had nothing against and didn't even know."

"Spoke to him a few times, Colonel. That's all."

The colonel took Morgan's arm and led him away, ignoring the stragglers who were already drifting off. "Come on, son," Colonel Jud said. "What you need is a good stiff drink."

Morgan didn't feel like listening to the old man's blather, but he went along to make it look good. Most men who weren't killers needed a drink after killing somebody. Morgan didn't give a damn, one way or another. Ryan was dead and that was all to the good since he couldn't ask any more awkward questions. He wasn't sure how his fellow performers would take it—whether they'd give him the cold shoulder, freeze him out, or see him as a right brave good fella, the righteous killer of a despicable monster. He hoped they'd look at it that way. Probably they would. Performers were sentimental people for all their tough fronts, and the murder of poor old Ma and Pa wasn't likely to sit well with them.

"There you are, my boy," the colonel said, handing Morgan a big drink. And that, as you'll know after you taste it, is gen-u-ine Jack Daniels. God knows, you've earned it. A point of interest. Did you shoot him in the head to shut him up for good, or . . . ?"

"I shot him in the head to save Bender's life," Morgan said. "A bullet anyplace else might not have stopped him quick enough. With a head shot the body quits like a finger snap."

A little rattled by Morgan's coldness, the colonel changed the subject. "At least you're five thousand richer after tonight. I liked that sanctimonious little speech you made to the lieutenant. 'Blood money brings bad luck,' and so on." Colonel Jud laughed.

"I could use the money. The blood money bullshit was for show, like you say. It would give me a new start in the horse business. Don't rightly know I want to do that. I've been on the move so long."

The colonel toasted Morgan in root beer. "Success in all things! Put the money in the bank and feel good that it's there. Of course you may have to split it with that lieutenant. He could drag his feet on your claim if you don't."

"Not Bender, Colonel."

"Good. No word yet on Fred Cargill?"

"Too soon. If you believe his wife he's in the clear."

"Didn't I tell you that? I am nothing if not a sound judge of character. How did you find the delightful Maisie, by the way? Did you smoke a friendly pipe with her?"

"No pipe. She drinks laudanum."

"Why, that's almost respectable. A maiden lady of my acquaintance could not get through the day without it. Usually she's comatose by late afternoon. You had no trouble in that regard?"

"Maisie managed to stay lively in spite of it," Morgan said. He sure as shooting didn't want to give the old man a blow-by-blow account of what happened in Mrs. Cargill's bed. "They've had no windfall, I'm pretty sure. I got the feeling she likes Cargill in spite of all his dead loss gambling. Could be she loves him."

Colonel swigged the rest of his root beer. "Kitty's going to be mad when she hears about it, as she's bound to. Ours is a small world." There was a faint hint of malice in the colonel's voice.

"Why should she be mad? A lot of the time she talks to me like a hired hand."

"But not all the time, my boy. And what other hired hand do you know with such privileges? But you'll weather the storm, I feel certain." Colonel Jud tapped his slipper on the carpeted floor of the office. "You are no closer to your man than when you came here. Cargill is out unless that detective turns up something we don't know about. Ryan never was in. What does the lieutenant think?"

"He thinks I may not be able to clear my friend in so short a time."

The old man chewed on that for a while. "I've been thinking much the same thing myself. A scandal could ruin me. They might even suspect *me!* Ridiculous, of course, but once a man's name is dirtied there's no way to fully get rid of the dirt. I don't know that I shouldn't cancel this engagement, plead illness or something, and take this show to England. I haven't been there for five years. These bastards couldn't very well pass fake American money in England."

Morgan didn't like the sound of that. "But you couldn't stay in England. You'd wear out your welcome if you tried."

"What do you know of show business?" Colonel Jud was annoyed because he knew Morgan was speaking the truth. "You said yourself you've spent your whole life raising horses, whereas I . . ."

Morgan knew he had to settle down the old man. If he got mad enough he might close the Kansas City show and start sending cables to England. "What I meant, sir, is England is too small for a show as big as yours. You need a country like the United States. Go to England and stay there and Cody will have the whole shooting match all to himself."

That got a smile. "Don't try to fox me, boy. I know you're trying to play on my vanity. What you forget is that England isn't the only country in Europe. There's France, Germany, Austria, Denmark—we packed them in in Copenhagen last tour. I could make a tour last two years."

"But do you want to?"

"No. I don't like foreigners."

"Then why do it?"

"Didn't I just tell you? To get far away from this counterfeiting business."

There had to be some way to stop the colonel from moving the show to Europe. Could be he was just bullshitting, but you never knew with old men. Once they got their false teeth into something they kept chewing at it until they swallowed it or spat it out.

"All right," Morgan went on. "If the counterfeiters' man is part of the show he'll go to Europe with the show. When you come back eventually, all he has to do is start up again."

A moth flew in the window, and Colonel Jud slapped at it with his slipper. "Got you!" he growled. "The counterfeiters may be out of business or in jail by then."

"You don't know that, Colonel. If the phony money starts dogging the show all over again you'll be no better off than you are now."

"Then I'll sell the show and retire," the colonel said without any conviction at all. Morgan let him stew for a while, then the colonel let out a roar that made the chandeliers tinkle. "Like hell I will! Nobody's going to drive me out of this business. Goddamn you to hell, Morgan! You win. You stay and I stay and the show stays and the fucking, damn counterfeiter stays!" Colonel Jud picked up his empty glass and smashed it against the wall. President Hayes' picture fell to the floor in a shower of glass.

The colonel got up and walked away. Over his shoulder he said, "Do the best you can, Morgan. I'm tired. I'm going to bed."

Next morning Morgan discovered that his fellow show people now regarded him as a hero, especially the women. This didn't go down with some of the men, but most of them were friendly. So the killing of Ryan had paid off after all. The morning *Star* reported the shooting, gave it a fair amount of space, but didn't get worked up about it. A year-old murder in faraway Idaho, even a double murder, didn't attract much interest in Kansas City, which had more than enough murders of its own. Maybe he wouldn't get the keys to the city for what he had done, but here in Colonel Hardesty's small world he was a hero and a small celebrity. How big or small his celebrity was didn't matter to his admirers, the women most of all. To show people anybody that got his name in the paper, and wasn't being charged with a criminal offense, was a celebrity. In the grub tent young women crowded his table while other tables remained unoccupied. There wasn't enough they could do for him. Did he want more coffee? More ham and eggs? A few men gave him dirty looks, but that's as far as it went, and there was a good explanation for that. Not so many hours before some of them had seen him put two bullets in a man's head without taking aim, and he was still wearing the same gun he'd used to do it. It was enough to discourage the thorniest man in the bunch.

Morgan was ready to leave when "The Last of the Mountain Men" walked in and sat down, threatening to break the bench with his weight. Two men sitting at the table got up and left without looking at him. Morgan had seen him around, but they hadn't spoken. He looked like a good man to avoid, and most seemed to do just that. He was well over six feet, and his hair and beard were long and shaggy. His billowing buckskins were dyed bright green, such as no real mountain man ever wore, and a skinning knife, a tomahawk and a flintlock pistol were slung from his belt. Now and then he muttered to himself, showing strong brown teeth.

Morgan smelled trouble and tried to walk away from it, but somehow he knew it wasn't going to be that easy. It never was, not when the bully boys were determined to push it. He was nearly out the door when the so-called wild man called after him, "Hey, Morgan, what else can you do besides shoot men in the back of the head? What good are you when you're not killing men and pulling down the bloomers of women?"

Morgan kept going, but it wasn't going to work. Unless the colonel was there to stop it he would have to turn and face this bird-brained son of a bitch. Backing down would just land him deeper in the shithole, and he wasn't about to do that. Once he lost face these people would turn on him, and if they didn't freeze him out completely they would think less of him. That would be bad because of what he was trying to do. He needed to be able to talk freely to everyone.

He was still walking, and the wild man was coming up hard behind him, still throwing out insults. When Morgan stopped, the footsteps behind him stopped. He knew he could shoot the legs from under the huge bastard who had to be at least 250 pounds, but that wouldn't be the end of it. It would turn the show folks against him for sure. The wild man was smiling viciously when he turned to have it out once and for all.

"What do you want with me?" he said. "You want trouble, is that it?"

A crowd was gathering, and there was no sign of the colonel. It looked like Colonel Jud was away somewhere or the wild man wouldn't have been so bold.

The wild man got going with his harangue, talking more for the crowd than for Morgan. "This fancy shooter thinks everybody's afraid of him cause he's fast with a gun. This fancy shooter forgets I have a gun too, but not such a good gun as he has. I'll show you." The wild man pulled the flintlock pistol from his belt, put the muzzle to his head and pulled the trigger. Nothing happened, and a few of the men laughed. "I forgot to load it. All right, the pistol is no good right now. The knife and the tomahawk don't have to be loaded, but I'm so good with them it wouldn't be fair to the fancy shooter here." The wild man spoke good English with just the trace of a foreign accent. A fierce-looking woman shouted at him, "Why don't you go back to Russia, Chenko? You're a pain in the ass over here!"

Chenko showed his big brown teeth. "Go home and put your bloomers back on, Marie. When I get through with fancy man here he won't be able to walk for a month. Maybe longer. Maybe never."

"Fancy man," he started off again, "I'm going to give my weapons to Charlie over there. Come on, Charlie, lend a hand." Charlie stepped forward and took Chenko's gun, hatchet and knife. Chenko raised his arms and turned around. "See, no more weapons, but fancy shooter still has his gun. What'll you do if I try to waltz with you, fancy shooter? Shoot me in the head? We all know you can do it. Get rid of the gun, fancy shooter. Quit hiding behind it for once in your life. What do you say?"

Morgan knew he had to make up his mind fast. There would be no more smart talk from this man; in a minute he'd be coming at him like a runaway locomotive. Where in hell was the colonel? No help there. No help anywhere. An inner voice told him to shoot the bastard and then walk away for good. But that was shit advice. He had to go through with it. Charlie took his gun.

"Your move," he said, then jumped forward and kicked Chenko in the knee. The kick was aimed to tear the big man's kneecap off, but it didn't connect right. Chenko grunted with pain, but an instant later he was smiling again. "You don't fight fair, then I don't fight fair." Morgan knew Chenko had no intention of fighting fair. He had a wad of chewing tobacco in his mouth, so he was a spitter as well as a butter, eye-gouger and nose and ear-biter. Nobody had to tell him that the wild old mountain men did all those things.

Chenko didn't try any kicking. Underneath his oversized trousers his legs were thick and muscular, too much so. Morgan expected a rush powered by all that weight, and it came right away. If his knee hurt he didn't show it. He lowered his head like a bull and came at Morgan full tilt. If he could butt Morgan in the stomach and knock him down he could throw his weight on top of him, get him by the neck and start tearing with his teeth. The rush was fast, but Morgan dodged it and tripped him. Chenko went down on his face and was down for about ten seconds, his thick legs kicking out hard to keep Morgan away. Then he was up again and coming at Morgan like a wrestler, body bent, arms out wide and clawing the air. Morgan jumped high and aimed a kick at his face. The kick landed without doing much damage, and an instant later Chenko grabbed his foot with two hands and Morgan felt himself being swung around. Chenko swung harder and harder, moving toward a pile of lumber at the same time. Morgan's eyes were blurred and he was dizzy, but he knew the Russian was trying to get close enough to smash his head against the stack of boards. Suddenly the boot Chenko had hold of came loose, and Morgan arced out wide and landed in a tangle of arms and legs on a folded tent with plywood underneath. A fierce pain stabbed through his left shoulder which he thought was dislocated, but when he tried to move it it moved all right in spite of the pain that was now running down to his fingertips. Chenko was getting set for another rush when Kitty appeared. Everybody looked at her. Even Chenko held back to look at her. Chenko looked too long, and Morgan kicked him in the same knee. This time Chenko's grunt was louder, but even though the leg didn't buckle under him, the knee was damaged. Morgan could see that. Chenko was moving toward Morgan, dragging the injured leg. Before he was close enough to try for a hold, Kitty drew a pistol and fired a shot in the air. Now she had everybody's attention. Chenko backed away from Morgan so he couldn't land any more surprise kicks.

Still with the gun pointed at the sky, Kitty was something to see. Instead of her show costume she wore a straw boater with a colored band, a white silk shirtwaist, white duck trousers tight at the top and very loose at the bottom, and a pair of white ankle boots. She was the picture of summer elegance except for the worn .38 caliber Colt in her hand. A plain brown holster was clipped to the waistband of her immaculate white trousers. When she spoke it was with the tough slum kid's accent of her early life. Some of them might not have liked her, but they listened attentively because she was the colonel's favorite, had a loaded gun and knew how to use it better than anyone in the whole state of Missouri.

"Listen youse bums," she began. "That's you, Idaho, and you, Ivanovitch, or would you rather be called Ivan the Terrible? You sure look terrible. Maybe youse oughta take a stomach powder an' go lay down." That got a laugh, but Kitty stilled it by firing another shot. "Now, as I was sayin', youse bums think youse is havin' a fight when all youse is doin' is mixin' it up like two bears in the zoo. Ain't you never heard of rules?"

"You talkin' about the Queensberry Rules, Kitty?" some wiseguy called out.

"No, the Mulligan Rules," she shot back. "Pipe down, Shorty. You ain't on the rules committee. Like I was sayin', dis fight has got to be conducted in a gentlemanly manner. Which means no eye gougin', bitin' off ears and noses and private parts. It also means you let Idaho put his boot on,

Ivan. How can a man fight with one boot on, one boot off? After Idaho gets his boot on, youse two stiffs got to fight like the great John L. an' udder notables of the ring. You got to try it, boys, or I'll get mad."

Chenko had been listening to all this like a perplexed gorilla. Now he shouted, "What if I don't like all this shit? What'll you do if I tell you to go fuck yourself? Go fuck yourself, Kitty!"

"You're fined ten bowls of borscht for that," Kitty shouted, dropping the Hell's Kitchen accent. "You'll fight fair, Chenko, or not at all. That goes for you too, Morgan, so quit your kicking."

Morgan had his boot on by now. His shoulder still hurt, but it would see him through the fight. Now he had some kind of chance. If he could move around and tire the big bastard, then maybe he could bring him down.

Chenko wasn't ready to let it go just yet. He'd been counting on his bag of dirty tricks to kill Morgan or cripple him for life, and now he couldn't use them if Kitty had her way. Chenko didn't like it and told her so. "I'll fight any fucking way I like."

Kitty pointed the .38 at him. "I'll put bullets in your arms and legs if I see you trying to break this man's back. Anything like that you get shot." To make her point she pushed out the three spent shells and reloaded. "Hey, Chenko," she added, "you look so sore maybe you want to quit? How about you, Morgan?"

Morgan knew Chenko would back down if he did. The fight wasn't going the way the big ape had planned it. Tough luck for him. "Chenko started it. It's up to him."

Kitty said to Chenko. "You heard him. Make up your mind."

"I can beat your dick any way I fight him," Chenko roared back, then moved toward Morgan with his arms stretched out and his fists turned up, trying to look like a prizefighter. Women in the crowd laughed. So did a few men. Chenko tried for a haymaker and it went wild. Morgan danced in before Chenko could regain his balance and landed two hard blows on the big man's heart. They circled, Morgan light on his feet, Chenko lumbering after him. Morgan got in punishing rights and lefts before Chenko landed a powerful right on his bad shoulder. Pain flared white hot, and suddenly he wanted to kill this dimwitted troublemaker. Chenko saw the rage in his eyes and showed uncertainty for the first time. When he tried to grab Morgan's throat, Kitty fired a shot that kicked up dirt at his feet. Morgan landed a ferocious right to the jaw when Chenko jerked his head halfway around to curse at Kitty. Chenko had a massive jaw, but Morgan felt teeth breaking under his fist. Bewildered and howling with rage, Chenko rushed at Morgan with his head down. Kitty's pistol barked again, and when Chenko stumbled Morgan's right fist came up in a terrific uppercut that cut off an inch of the huge man's tongue. Morgan moved around him almost at will, always going for the head or the heart. Every blow Chenko took to the head made him more confused than before. Chenko moved his left hand back to protect his heart, and Morgan went after his belly. It was wide and banded with muscle, but there was fat there, too. All Chenko did was grunt when Morgan landed a blow to his gut, but his movements were getting slower and slower until finally he was just standing there trying to keep from being hit. Morgan moved behind him and punched him in the kidneys until his knees started to buckle. In spite of everything, he managed to turn and face Morgan, trying for one last punch. His right arm went back but stayed there, and he slowly sank to his knees. Morgan swung and hit the side of his head, knocking him sideways in spite of his weight. It was over. Chenko lay on his back with his eyes open. Blood dribbled from his mouth, and his chest heaved as if his lungs couldn't get enough air. Kitty was walking away by then. Morgan called after her, but she didn't slow down.

Morgan shrugged and went to look for the doctor.

Chapter Six

"What happened to you?" Bender asked, looking up from his newspaper. "Did Mr. Cargill and his five brothers catch you in bed with Mrs. Cargill?"

Morgan told the detective about the fight. His left arm was in a sling, and the right side of his face was bruised from the fall he took after Chenko swung him and the boot came off. The shoulder wasn't dislocated but badly wrenched, the doctor said. He should keep the sling on for two weeks, taking it off only when he had to appear in the show. He ached all over.

Morgan drank whisky for the pain and repeated what he'd told the colonel about Fred and Maisie Cargill. "There's nothing there, I'm fairly sure. How about you?"

"I sent out four inquiries about Cargill and so far got one reply. Cargill just doesn't fit into this counterfeiting thing, but I'll wait for the other replies. Now about this reward for Otis Drury . . ."

"Don't you want it?" Morgan asked. "You got the goods on the bastard."

"And you killed him. I'd be in a coffin now if you hadn't acted as fast as you did. About the reward, I can't touch any part of it. Police officers aren't permitted to take rewards."

"I can claim the reward, get the cash and give you half."

"Can't do it. If Gallager got wind of it I'd be out, facing a reduction in rank and a transfer to the yards. Not that I'd accept that. Gallager and his sneaks have searched my house twice. Gallager's sneaks know their business, but I can always tell. Gallager would frame me into jail if he didn't know I'd kill him when I got out."

Morgan sipped the second whisky instead of belting it back. He didn't want to look like Maisie Cargill after she'd been at the coffeepot. Bender's newspaper was folded in half and spread out on the table. The detective had been reading about John Ryan. Bender said abruptly, "I guess you've been wondering why I didn't put the cuffs on behind. First rule with a dangerous criminal, put the cuffs on behind."

"Why didn't you?" Morgan hadn't been thinking about handcuffs.

Bender looked embarrassed. "Bastard had something wrong with his left arm. Deformed or something, like he'd broke it in a fall and wasn't set right. I made him turn over and lay face down on his cot, then tried to get his two wrists together behind him. Bastard yelled when I pulled on the twisted arm. Thinking I better cuff him any way I could, I cuffed him in front, hoping the freaks hadn't heard his yell. They'd heard all right and started gathering round. Then you came along. I didn't handle that too smooth, Morgan. Gallager's been grumbling about it.

Why didn't I take men with me? Did I want to claim the reward all by myself? You can see why I couldn't touch a nickel of the claim money even if I wanted to."

"There will be twenty-five hundred waiting for you in the bank. Yours anytime you want it. That's my last word on it."

The waiter came and went to get black coffee for Morgan. Bender was using a pocketknife to cut the John Ryan story out of the paper. "I hope it's your last word." Bender folded the clipping and stowed it away in his worn wallet. "Now here's *my* last word. Go to police headquarters to put in your claim. Sergeant Praed handles rewards. After you fill out the form, he'll forward it to me for my approval. They'll send a man or write a letter when the bank draft gets here from Idaho."

For some reason, the band wasn't playing today; the player piano pressed into service wasn't half as bad. It was battered and tired after so many years, but Morgan didn't need the piano to remind him he too was tired. Bender looked even more beaten down than he was himself.

"You look tired," Morgan said.

The detective yawned. "Tired is right. I went home after I got Ryan squared away. Couldn't get to sleep I was so mad at myself at the way I handled Ryan's arrest. Nearly got myself killed. I was still mad when I got up this morning. Couldn't eat my goddamned breakfast. I still feel stupid. At least Gallager has an excuse—he drinks."

"For Christ's sake, Bender, nobody's perfect. Go home early and take a few big belts of whisky. That'll get you to sleep."

Bender managed to smile. "You look worse than I do, but I'll take your advice. I'll get something to eat here. My wife's at her sister's today, and I can't cook. I'll down a few boilermakers and go to bed. You want something to eat?"

"I ate too much this morning. The ladies kept piling my plate with food. I'm a hero for killing Ryan."

"Lucky man. But you'll get tired of all that as you get older. I've been with the same wife twenty-one years. You ever thought of getting married and settling down?"

"Only when I have bad dreams," Morgan said.

The waiter didn't have to ask Bender what he wanted. What he wanted was a porterhouse steak minus the onions. No potatoes, no side dishes, just the big steak. "Kansas City has everywhere else beat when it comes to steak," the detective said.

Nothing much was said until Bender was halfway through his meal. "I should know better," he said. "You can't think right on an empty stomach. Look. We agree the man making these plates is one of the best. I shouldn't say 'plates.' The plates are made and turning out bad money. In a minute I'm going to tell you something that may surprise you. The man who made the plates is probably old. How old remains to be seen."

"Why not somebody new?" Morgan said. "Somebody new is always coming along."

Bender swallowed and took a sip of beer. "That's true, but let me go on. Why I say somebody old is like this. I asked Fletcher, the *Star* editor, about counterfeiting because like a lot of editors he writes mystery stories in his spare time and knows a lot about crime. Fletcher said there were no great engravers around today. Crooked engravers, he meant. Most of the great ones were presently in prison, serving long sentences. Naturally, not all the crooked engravers were in prison, but more than when the Secret Service started. 'What crookdom needs is a new star to light up the murky half-world of make-believe money.' That's what he said. You'd think he was talking about baseball batters or opera singers. Of course, I'm not taking what he told me as one hundred percent accurate. It's possible some new crook has just started up, some bird he never heard of. He can't know everything, but he does correspond with top detectives and crime experts all over the world. I wouldn't have known that if my wife hadn't showed me an article on him in some ladies' magazine."

"Sounds good, the way you lay it out," Morgan said. "If the man is old he must have been in prison for a long time and just got out—or decided to come out of retirement."

"Not too likely. A few old crooks do that, but it's not common. No old man wants to spend his last years eating slop and sleeping on a dirty mattress. A judge might go easy on an ordinary crook, but not a counterfeiter, even if he's old."

Morgan said, "If he got jailed as a fairly young man, why does he have to be so old?"

"Because unless he was a boy wonder, he couldn't have been all that young when he finally learned his craft to perfection. Engraving is like diamond cutting, I guess. Years of study and hard work with an older man looking over your shoulder. Few people hit their stride till they're thirty or thirty-five. It's all guesswork, I know, but what else have we got?"

"So if he got thirty years he could be sixty or sixty-five by now."

"Older than that, maybe. It could have been years before he got nabbed. Give him five working years, say, before they caught him. He could be seventy or over."

"A granddaddy crook."

"Don't fool yourself. Old men can be the worst of all. One thing is sure. He can't be turning out these bills from his old place before he was sent up, and he can't be where he told the prison authorities he was going to live when they released him."

"Why is that?"

"The Secret Service keeps a watch on ex-con counterfeiters. Anyway, they try to. They're shorthanded but they try, Fletcher told me. I'm thinking this old bird has long flown the coop."

"Can you check all that? I know it's asking a lot. When he was sentenced, who his cellmates were, when he was released."

The detective gave Morgan a tired smile. "You must have been first on line when they gave out the brass balls. All you're asking is for me to stick my nose into federal business. The feds don't like that. Gallager would like it less if they told him. If something is of no profit to him, he gives it the stiff-arm. I'd be riding the train with you when you leave for Denver. Washburn is the man to start with if you can get him to help. Want to try it?"

The piano slowed down and rattled and stopped playing. A cowhand kicked it, but it remained silent. The Yellow Kid, at the bar as usual, slouched over to the piano, saying, "You got to kick it the right place." The Kid aimed and kicked and the tinny music started again.

"You know Washburn?" Morgan asked Bender.

"I've seen him and know who he is, that's all," Bender said. "Has his office in the city hall, two rooms commandeered by the government. The mayor doesn't like having him there. Mayor Yost is a retired meat packer, a dollar-a-year man, but his son does business with the federal government. Army beef contracts and such. Having a government agent under his roof makes Yost nervous. Who knows what this Washburn might be investigating? One of Gallager's sneaks keeps an eye on Washburn all the time."

"But Washburn wouldn't tell Gallager I went to see him?"

"Of course not. Washburn wants nothing to do with the local police, but Gallager knows what he's doing. Washburn has a secretary in his office, a local lass probably related to Gallager or a poor relation of Yost's. She reports everything Washburn says and does. That's what I hear, and there's no reason to doubt it."

"I'll try it," Morgan said.

Bender said, "Gallager will hear about it as a matter of course. What difference does it make? Your friend is in jail, and you're trying to get him out. You see my reason for wanting you to do it. If Gallager fired me for cause— and messing about in federal business is cause enough— I'd be no more use to you. Once a detective is off the force he loses whatever influence he has. In my case no copper would talk to me for fear of Gallager. The two good friends I once had are gone, one forced out, the other dead. As for the crooks it would be like I had leprosy. See the Yellow Kid over there? Even that shitfaced rat wouldn't talk to me."

"I think I get your point, Bender." Morgan laughed in spite of his bruised face. "You make it like a man driving a six-inch nail into an oak knot."

Bender laughed, too. "The Kid seems to bring out the mean streak in me. Maybe it's because he's here all the time. I'm sick of looking at the shifty bugger. If he'd just take a few days off I might like him better. You want some advice? Get yourself some decent clothes before you go to see Washburn. From what I hear, he's a prissy sort of fellow. High collars, dark suits, hat just so. You look like a tramp cowboy."

"These are my working duds," Morgan protested.

"Play the game, Morgan. Try to look respectable. I'm told these federal agents set a great store by that. Respectability, yes sir! Look, Morgan, I can't talk anymore. I've got to get some sleep. I'll be here tomorrow if I can. That state senator's son has taken a turn for the worse and may die. We'll be turning niggertown upside down, a thing Gallager likes to do."

On the way to city hall, Morgan bought new whipcord pants, a dark gray shirt and a hat of the same color. He looked at his boots and decided the hell with it. He wasn't going to break in a new pair of boots just for Washburn, who might not even talk to him. He told the storekeeper to throw his old clothes and the sling in the trash.

City hall stood high on its own grounds, surrounded by well-tended grass, shrubs and statues. He went up the white stone steps and into the lobby where a uniformed police sergeant, smelling of whisky, made a dumb joke when he asked him how to find the Secret Service office. "It's a secret so I can't tell you," the clown said. "But you're a nice fella so I'll break the rules this once. Anyway, the name is on the door."

"I'd appreciate it if Mr. Washburn could see me for a few minutes," Morgan said after he went in. "Sorry, I haven't got an appointment, but he may want to see me anyway." Morgan told the secretary his name and why he wanted to see her boss. The girl sat behind her machine checking a typewritten sheet with a pencil. She wore a long brown skirt and a severe shirtwaist, and her black hair was tied back in a bun. She was as cool as her deep blue eyes.

"Please take a seat," she said. "I'll see what I can do. You may have to wait."

Morgan remained standing. He wasn't going to sit around for an hour so Washburn could look important. If Washburn kept him dangling he'd walk out.

The walls of the office were painted green. A chromo of President Hayes hung between two windows. On another wall was a picture of a stern looking man in a U.S. Army uniform with the single star of a brigadier general. He was nobody Morgan recognized but most likely the boss of this outfit. Standing on a small table in back of the girl's desk was a telephone box with two brass bells and a hand crank.

The door of Washburn's office opened, and he came out in front of the girl. He was tall and thin and wore the stiff, high collar Bender thought so prissy. His long neck could be the reason for the collar, Morgan thought. Instead of being high like his collar, Washburn's voice was deep and solemn. It matched the solemnity of his face. "Mr. Morgan, unless what you want to say has some bearing on the Larson case, I see no point in discussing it. Larson's attorney can't have sent you here."

"I'm here on my own," Morgan said. "It may be to your advantage to listen."

Washburn darted a look at the girl and told Morgan to come into his office which had a desk, two chairs and two oak filing cabinets fitted with padlocks. Two furled flags stood at either side of an empty fireplace. A mass produced copy of "Washington Crossing the Delaware" hung over the mantelpiece. Washington was standing up. Did it mean don't rock the boat? Washburn's chair was the same as the one Morgan sat in, a plain wooden chair with arms but no cushion. Nobody could say the Secret Service was going hog-wild with the taxpayer's money.

Washburn leaned forward. "Keep your voice down, Mr. Morgan. Miss Quillan has big ears. Now what do you want?"

So he knows, Morgan thought. Bender has him pegged as a prissy fool, but he knows what Gallager and the mayor are up to. He wasn't all that surprised. Long ago he had learned not to judge men too quickly by their appearance.

Morgan said, "Did Bowdry's detective ever get back to you? He thinks there's a link between the wild west show and the phony money."

"I had already decided that before he came to see me. No, I didn't send him on a wild goose chase. I didn't send him anywhere. It's not my job to teach private detectives how to detect. I see you have joined Colonel Hardesty's show. It was mentioned in today's *Star* in the story about the Idaho fugitive you killed. You're wasting your time. You'll never catch the counterfeiter by yourself."

"It's my time."

"You're still wasting it. This scheme was well-financed and well-planned. By now it must be paying for itself. All it needed was a man to make the engravings and to print the bills, a man to finance his operations, a man to act as wholesaler. Everything is supposition at this point. The engraver and the printer may be the same man. Same for the financier and wholesaler. Two men. But whatever the number of men at the top, they need a big crew of pushers to get their dud bills into circulation. Forget them. How many head men are there? It makes a difference. Conspiracies are threatened as the number of conspirators increases. Two men are harder to catch than four and so on. Mr. Morgan, you still haven't said what you came to say."

How can I when you do all the talking? Morgan thought, but he wasn't about to object to that. At least Washburn was talking to him. He told the agent the idea that the engraver was probably an old man recently released from prison after serving a very long sentence, but he didn't use Bender's name.

"I think it must be an old man because there aren't any master engravers around these days. I mean master engravers who are crooks."

The agent eyed him suspiciously. "Where did you get this information? Surely not in a wild west show."

"In a saloon," Morgan said. "I've been talking to every crook that'll drink with me. Some will, some won't. I could be a plainclothes policeman. Most of what I've heard is horseshit, as you might expect, but one very drunk guy told me he used to pass queer money in Chicago and had to turn to something else because the counterfeiting racket was too dangerous to be in. All the old crooked engravers were in prison, and the bum amateurs that had taken their place were producing bills so poor a blindman could spot them."

"He told you that, did he? And you believed him? What's his name?"

"Come on, Mr. Washburn," Morgan said. "I didn't ask him his name. If he gave me a name it wouldn't be his real one. You think he was telling the truth?"

Washburn fingered his high collar before he answered. "It so happens he was. I'm not convinced that you really spoke to such a person. I'll reserve judgment on that. But it's true that most of the crooked master engravers are in prison and will remain there for a great many years. Not every single one of them is behind bars, but the two that are not are too closely watched to do anything criminal."

"Somebody's out there making top quality fakes."

"And you think it's an old engraver just out of prison. It's possible, but let me tell you something. From my own experience and checking the files, I haven't come across a case where an aged counterfeiter risked what criminals call a goodbye sentence—meaning a sentence that can only end with his death."

"But suppose this old man is different," Morgan said.

Washburn went to the door and listened at it, then went back behind his desk. "What you want me to do is to check if an elderly master engraver has been released within the last . . . Let me figure it. The quality counterfeits began to appear about two months ago, so if he exists he was released before then. I'll give him a year to find a backer. Perhaps that isn't enough time, so I'll give him two years. I'll check back three years."

Morgan nodded. "Anything you say, Mr. Washburn."

"You look pleased, Mr. Morgan," the agent said. "Don't be. Just because some old criminal has been released from prison doesn't mean he's our man. Of course, he becomes a suspect if I find he's disappeared. The federal system doesn't parole counterfeiters, but they are asked where they can be found. It's not legally binding on them to give this information, but they usually do. Thirty years will break the spirit of the most recalcitrant criminal. I've seen some of them on the day of their release."

The agent made it sound as if everyone should see this spectacle, the dithering old ex-cons lurching through the gate of the penitentiary. Law-abiding citizens might take comfort from it; would-be criminals might take fright and forsake their wicked intentions. Morgan was beginning to understand this gloomy man, who had been so hard on Bronc. Bender was a very hard man, but you sensed an underlying compassion. If he didn't think the world would gain much by locking up some guy, he might let him go. Not so with Washburn. His view of the law and life was as rigid as his starched collar.

"I'm still thinking about your old man," Washburn said. "He emerges from the penitentiary at an advanced age. What he has earned, a few cents a day for thirty years, comes to very little. He is dressed in a cheap new suit and shoes. His original belongings have long rotted away. Now where is he to go, and what is he to do? Is there a son or daughter or even an elderly wife there to greet him? If there isn't a family, is there an old friend from the past?"

"You mean an old cellmate?"

"That's what I mean. But how many cellmates can a man have in, say, thirty years?"

"You mean there isn't a record?"

"There's a record all right. Everything is recorded in a federal penitentiary. There is one problem, however. There were no federal penitentiaries until . . ." Washburn was annoyed because he didn't know the year or had forgotten it. "I'm sure they existed when your old man was sentenced. If they did exist then, every visitor your old man received would have had his name and address recorded, which is not to say that some of these names and addresses may have been false. But for the moment we must proceed as if they were genuine."

Morgan said, "A lot of those visitors, if there were any, are gone by now."

"I was about to come to that," Washburn said irritably. "It's interesting in a way. We may be looking for a man who visited your old man frequently, sporadically, or not at all."

"Or who sent somebody else."

"Or who never laid eyes on your old man until he was approached for money. I am inclined to the view that someone who came to visit your old man only infrequently is now an important part of this counterfeiting ring. I don't know why, but I do."

Morgan said, "There may be only two people—the old man and the cellmate. The old man engraves the plates, makes the money and gets it to the cellmate. I think the cellmate picks it up instead of having it sent. Too risky, having it shipped. Anything could go wrong. It could be given to the wrong person or opened by mistake. There could be a go-between who delivers the dud money, but I doubt it. Like you say, the fewer people taking part, the fewer chances of getting caught."

Washburn liked that. "That's what I said. Now let's move on. If the cellmate is with the show, he must be able to move around and be absent at times without attracting attention. Is there anybody who fits that description?"

Morgan hated to drag the Cargills into it. He was pretty sure, and so was Bender, that they had nothing to do with it. Just the same, he had to go through with it. "There's the advance man for the show, Fred Cargill. He works ahead of the show for days, maybe weeks. The colonel may check his movements, but I doubt it. He likes and trusts Cargill in spite of all his gambling losses. The colonel has paid off some of his creditors and has kept others from pressing too hard, but the Cargills have no money. There's nothing that smells of fresh new money coming in."

The agent gave Morgan a cold look. "Who told you they have no money? Mrs. Cargill?"

"Yes. Mrs. Cargill."

"What did you expect her to say? Why, yes, Mr. Morgan, we recently came into a sizable amount of money. Good lord, man!"

"They have no money."

"I'll decide that after I do some checking. Who else?"

"There's the colonel's financial manager and the chief purchasing agent. I met the purchasing agent for a minute. Schlegel is about sixty, with a lisp. I haven't even seen the financial manager. He handles the show's finances and the colonel's investments in various parts of the country. Both men travel around as part of their jobs."

Washburn did some more pacing, then he stopped and said, "What's the financial man's name?"

"Tillotson. Charles P. Tillotson. His name is on the door of his car, where he has his quarters and office."

Washburn looked at his watch and frowned. "I have business I must attend to. Go back to the show and keep your eyes and ears open. I'll start working on what we have discussed. I must ask you not to get in my way at any point, so don't tell me Cargill is a losing but honest gambler. Don't vouch for his good name because you can't know anything about it. And you don't know the financial man at all. Don't come here tomorrow. Come the day after. Come at nine o'clock in the evening."

Morgan got up. "Why not tomorrow evening?"

"Because I'll be busy. That's why."

Chapter Seven

Morgan was going out through the lobby when he heard a woman's voice calling his name. It was the Quillan girl, and she was slightly breathless from walking so fast. She had looked good in the office; now she looked even better, with her cheeks a little flushed and her hair not so tightly bunned.

"Miss Quillan," he said.

"Oh, you remembered my name. Did Mr. Washburn mention it?"

"Yes. You're on your way home, I guess."

Offices were closing for the day, and city hall was emptying out. You could tell the working people from the politicians, who looked the same everywhere. Women made up only a small part of the homebound office workers. Even these days, with all the talk about women's rights, most secretaries were men.

"Home is where I usually go at the end of the day."

She tried to make it sound dreary, but Morgan didn't buy that. A woman as good looking as this could have her pick of men. "I was thinking perhaps you'd like a cup of tea or something stronger if you prefer. I share a flat with another girl, but she's out of town at the moment. You must think me bold, Mr. Morgan."

"Call me Lee. Washburn mistered me to death up there."

She laughed, pretending to be torn between loyalty to her boss while admitting the truth of Morgan's remark. "Then you must call me Nancy. Mr. Washburn is on the formal side, but he's a very nice man and a most considerate employer."

Well, she got that off her chest, Morgan thought, and a very nice chest it was. She was foxy without having a foxy look. Gallager or Yost, whichever one it was, had picked a very smart girl to do their snooping.

"He seems all right," Morgan said. "Are you from Kansas City, Nancy?"

"Born and bred here." She took his arm without making it look forward and steered him in the direction she wanted to go. "I can tell you're not."

"Does Idaho show so much?" he asked. This was the kind of small talk he wasn't so good at. They crossed the street and turned into another street lined with slate-fronted houses. It looked like a street where city hall office workers might live, not grand but solid and respectable. The lace curtained windows had potted plants in them.

"My flat is two blocks down," she said. "No, I don't think Idaho shows so much, but what's wrong with Idaho? I'm sure it's very nice." First Washburn got his pat on the head; now it was Idaho's turn. "Here we are, Lee."

The flat was four rooms on the third floor. It smelled of women and wasn't too tidy, but what did you expect from working girls? She took his hat and hung it on a coatrack in the hall. "Elly has her two rooms and I have mine," Nancy said. "We try to keep out of each other's way. We share the kitchen. All in all not a bad arrangement. Elly has to travel in her job, and she won't be back until next week. Sit down, Lee. The sofa is the most comfortable place. The flat is furnished so we can't be too choosy. Now, would you like tea, coffee or something stronger?"

Morgan sat on the slightly sprung sofa. A brass lamp with a decorated chimney stood on a table at one end of it, but the lamp was just a leftover from some earlier year. There were gaslights in frosted globes which Morgan had helped to light when they came in.

"Something stronger if you don't mind," he said, wondering why she was moving so fast. He would have expected her to get orders from Gallager or Yost after making her report on this new visitor to Washburn's office. It was kind of funny. She was spying on Washburn, and he was spying on her. Right now maybe he was out there on the fire escape with bucket and rags, disguised as a window cleaner.

"I can offer you rye, bourbon, Scotch or Irish," she called from the kitchen, which was separated from her sitting room by an arch. "I'll bet you've never had Irish. Why don't you try it?"

"Sure," Morgan said. There were magazines and several old newspapers on the table in front of the sofa, but not that day's *Star*. Maybe she'd read it in the office.

She brought in a tray with a bottle of Irish whisky, two glasses, a bowl of ice and tongs for the ice. "I always let a gentleman fix his own drinks," she said without being coy about it. "You have to become accustomed to Irish whisky. It has its own special taste. Would you like water? No. My dear old father used to say, 'Why drown something so dear to your heart?' "

Morgan drank his Irish with ice. It tasted as if it had iodine in it. "Tastes good," he said, looking around. "You have a nice place here. I live in a tent. Just a joke, Nancy. I work for the wild west show."

Nancy was on her second drink. She hadn't knocked back the first one, but she hadn't sipped it either. "Yes, I know, Lee. I read about you in the *Star*. How you saved that detective's life. I didn't bring it up because I thought you might not want to talk about it."

"It's over and done."

"The paper said you were a newcomer to the show. What did you do before that?"

"Raised horses in Idaho."

"A big jump. Raising horses to trick shooting."

"I did a lot of things in between."

"Were you with the show before Kansas City?"

"No. I came here to see an old friend who's in jail on a counterfeiting charge. Somebody passed some phony money off on him. He couldn't prove where the fake bills came from, so the marshal held him for the Secret Service. Your Mr. Washburn took charge of the case. My friend comes up for trial in about ten days. He's as innocent as you are, and I have to see him through this. I needed money, so I tried for a job with the show."

Morgan's glass stood empty on the table. Nancy reached over and filled it halfway to the top.

"Whoa there," Morgan said. "I need a steady hand in my work."

"It's early," she said, pouring herself a third drink. "And so you went to see Washburn about your friend's case. Did it do you any good?"

"Not a bit of good." Morgan drank a little of the strange tasting whisky. "Washburn says the case is out of his hands now."

The third drink was getting to her. "I know all about your friend's case, Lee. I should have stopped you before, but I wanted to hear your side of it. I don't know if Washburn really believes your friend is guilty. He does believe a bird in the hand is better than no stone left unturned." She giggled. "I didn't get that quite right, did I?"

"It's close enough," Morgan said.

"The trouble is," Nancy said, "I'm not close enough to you." She swayed a little as she got up and came over to sit beside him on the sofa. A moment later she unbuttoned his pants and started playing with his rod. Still playing with it, she put her mouth close to his ear and whispered, "Tell the truth now. How do you like being a Secret Service agent?"

Morgan smiled at her. "You're joking."

She smiled back. "Perhaps I am, perhaps I'm not. But really—are you one? It's all right to tell me. I'm practically one myself."

Sure you are, Morgan thought, except you work for Gallager and Yost. "I'm no kind of agent," he said, still smiling, "Secret Service or soap powder. Besides, what would a Secret Service agent be doing in a wild west show?"

Her hand went down his shaft and fondled his balls. "Looking for counterfeiters, that's what. I used to type Washburn's reports to Washington. He believes there is a link between the wild west show and the recent flood of counterfeit money."

"What do you mean you *used* to type them."

"That's right. Now he writes them himself and doesn't show them to me. You know, it's terrible not to be trusted. He even padlocks his files. I admit it. I'm nosy. What woman isn't? It helps to pass the time."

"Doesn't have to mean he doesn't trust you," Morgan

said. "Most likely he got new orders from Washington. This looks like it's turning into a big case. All information is restricted to this office and yourself. Something like that."

"That makes me feel better," she said. "I hope what I'm doing makes you feel better. I'm sorry I asked you those silly questions. There was nothing about you in the reports I read."

Morgan's hand was under her bloomers and was moving up her thigh. "How could there be? My only connection with Washburn is my poor old friend. Now can we drop it?"

"It's dropped." She took him by the hand and led him into the bedroom. It seemed natural, the way she did it, as if they might have known each other for a long time. The odd thing was, for a snoop there was something innocent about her. Lack of experience with men was more like it. But how could that be when she'd fondled his cock and liked it when he stroked her clit? Her bloomers were wet when he got his hand in there. When he first touched her clit, she made a sort of hissing sound and trapped his hand with her thighs, but then she put her free hand on top of his and opened her thighs so he could go on stroking her. She made oohing and aahing sounds as she helped him stroke her clit; that seemed to give her greater pleasure than if he'd been doing it by himself.

Whatever she was, she pulled him right down on top of her when they got to the bed. Enough light came from the window in spite of the heavy brocaded curtain so he could see her face clearly; it was twisted with more lust than he'd seen in a woman for a long time. There was none of that playing around that some women liked so much—she wanted it *now*. Her legs were wide open, and her knees were slightly raised; most women crooked their knees to one side. Her bush was as shiny black as her hair; it was so thick that he had to part it with his fingers before he slid his cock in. She was tight and groaned when he pushed hard; she was clumsy or pretending to be clumsy. She might be putting on an act for him, but he didn't care. Her body was soft and curved.

Nancy's eyes were closed tight and her mouth kept working, but no sounds came out after he got his cock all the way into her. He got his hands under her ass and raised her so he could really drive it in and out. Her hands wandered all over his back as if she didn't know where to put them. Finally she moved her hands to his ass and gripped him as he was gripping her. Whatever that did for her, she began to moan, then her mouth came up to meet his. Her tongue pushed into his mouth, and he sucked on it. That made her groan all the more, and she raised her ass high without any help from his hands. Then she wrapped her legs around him and came so violently that he thought she was going to pass out. He pushed in hard and shot his load into her, and when he felt it spewing into her hot and thick, she came again and again. One shuddering orgasm followed another; she clawed at him now, her nails tearing into his flesh. There was pain as well as pleasure, the two sensations, so different, making his cock hard again. Her spasms finally subsided, and she lay back, her black hair a tangled mass on the white pillow, and looked up at him as he drove in and out of her. She seemed to be studying him like someone wanting to learn about something they had wondered about but had never experienced. She gripped him again when he sent another load of jism into her, but she didn't come herself. That was all right; she had come enough for ten women and in a very short time. Only a short time before he had been talking to her, prim and proper, in Washburn's office.

They lay with their faces close together; she touched his face with her finger. "You are my first man," she said quietly. "Does that surprise you?"

"Nothing surprises me very much," Morgan said. "We all have our reasons for doing things." He thought that sounded pretty deep, coming from a shitkicker like him. She was a great poke, but he couldn't decide how much about her was real. Her awkwardness in bed could be real, or it could be a well-staged act. Her tightness down there didn't have to mean she'd never had a cock in her before, just as it didn't mean a woman wasn't a virgin because it was easy to drive it all the way on the first thrust. He didn't try too hard to decide what she was; as long as she was ready and willing to be shafted, he didn't care.

"I have had men friends, but it never went this far," she said. "Not that some of them didn't try. I would not have felt myself desirable if they didn't try. More than once I wanted to let them have their way, but I always held back, not from prudishness or what the consequences might be, but from the feeling that the moment wasn't right. I saw you today and hoped you would come home with me if I followed you. Is that terrible?"

"No," Morgan said. "I think it's great."

"You are not making fun of me?" she said, combing his hair with her fingers.

"Lord, no. Why would I do that?"

"Because you've had me—and it was so easy. Perhaps you're not like that at all. I sense that you are a good and kind man. But tell me honestly—and I shouldn't really press you—will this be the only time I'll see you? Will you be coming back to Mr. Washburn's office? I'd like that, and you mustn't think I'm going back to that silliness about working for the Secret Service. I'm sorry. I was making fun of you."

Morgan touched one nipple then the other with a fore-finger. "I can take a joke," he said. "I don't know if I'll be coming back to Washburn's office, least on business. I wouldn't mind coming back to see you."

She gave a little laugh. "I don't know if Mr. Washburn would like that. I'll give you a key and we can meet here. When you first walked in, I thought you might be connected with the Secret Service. A job like that wouldn't interest you at all?"

"Not a bit," Morgan said. "For one thing, I'd be no good at it." He felt like smiling. She was trying to steer him back to the Secret Service bullshit to find out if he was an agent, but she could find no way to do it. He sensed her irritability; he wasn't sure she didn't want to slap his face. Why she had chosen the virgin act he had no way of knowing; maybe she thought it was a change from the woman of experience approach. All he knew was he was going to fuck her again in a minute. "Oh, Lee," she cried out when he shoved it into her again. "I want you to come back. I want to know you. I want to know all about you."

I'll bet you do, Morgan thought, fucking her like a pile driver.

The colonel laughed heartily at the idea that Charles P. Tillotson might be mixed up in counterfeiting. "Why Tilly's nearly as rich as I am, maybe richer. He invests for me and for himself at the same time. Therefore, his investments are sound. If I lose, he loses, and there have been a few investments that made little or no money. That's the nature of the business, and I certainly have no cause to complain. Write him off, my boy, just as you've written off Fred Cargill."

It was an hour after he'd left Nancy Quillan's apartment; she'd gone to work at the same time, a little hungover but smiling tightly, not quite as friendly as the night before.

"That leaves Schlegel," Morgan said.

"It leaves him as the only one who gets around a lot," Colonel Jud said. "You won't find it easy, getting James to talk about anything. And for heaven's sake don't forget yourself so far as to call him 'Jim.' Matter of fact, a young whippersnapper like you better not call him anything but Mr. Schlegel. He's all business—eats, lives and sleeps business. You'd think he owned the show, the way he works. Years ago, when I first hired him, I used to josh him about why didn't he loosen up a bit, enjoy life, smile once in a while. No good. He remains what he is—a sour old bachelor with ink in his veins."

"How old is he?"

Colonel Jud thought about it. "I don't rightly know. Between fifty and sixty, I would say, the sort of man that looks much the same for years."

"What excuse can I give for wanting to talk to him?"

"Beats me. I can't send you. Why would I send you and for what? Why do you have to see him at all? James has no wife you can sweet-talk. If I didn't know him better I'd say he was queer, but I doubt he's human enough even for that. Make up any excuse you like. Just remember James thinks everybody is out to get the better of him. That may be an uncharitable attitude, but it has saved me a great deal of money. He may just show you the door. He'll show it to you quicker if you try to use your rustic charm. Even the Jersey Lily couldn't charm James."

Morgan put on his hat. "I'll keep you posted, Colonel."

"Do that, my boy. I feel as if I'm playing the part of a wise old uncle in a melodrama. By the way, Miss Kitty has been looking for you. No, she wasn't wearing a gun, but you know what I mean. Mad. Mad as a wet hen."

Morgan knew he'd have to talk to Kitty, but now wasn't the time. He walked down the train to Schlegel's car. The windows were open, the door closed. He had to knock hard before the door banged back and Schlegel glared down at him. "You're the new man with Kitty," he said as if Morgan had denied it. "What do you want?"

"A few words with you, Mr. Schlegel. I just came from the colonel."

"Oh, you did, did you? Come on in then, but don't waste my time." Morgan again noticed his lisp.

Oak filing cabinets took up an entire wall of Schlegel's office. Gray filing boxes were stacked against another wall. There were wall calendars going back five years. No pictures of any kind. If Schlegel smoked or drank, there was nothing to show it. He took a file box off a chair so Morgan could sit down. Instead of sitting behind his desk, he propped himself up against the front of it, as if he didn't intend to talk to Morgan for very long.

"Well, get on with it," he said, twitching with impatience. It was summer in Kansas City, but he was wearing a black serge suit and a vest. He was short and wide, with not much hair left on his head. He'd been reasonably civil when Morgan was with Kitty; now his curtness was close to downright hostility.

Morgan said he'd raised horses before he went broke and hoped to make enough money with the show to go back to Idaho and make a new start. "I had to sell all my stock, all but two fine stallions I couldn't bear to part with. A neighbor is looking after them."

"What has all this to do with me?"

"I've decided I like this life here. I want to sell my horses."

"Then why don't you do it?" Schlegel looked at him

as a cranky schoolteacher might look at a particularly stupid child.

"I'd like to sell them to you. My neighbor—everybody, in fact—knows I'm hard up and wouldn't give me a good price."

Now Schlegel was more puzzled than annoyed. "How can you be hard up with five thousand dollars reward money coming to you? I hear you don't want to accept it. Forget I asked you. I don't want to hear your reasons. What about these horses? They're in Idaho. Idaho is not next door."

Morgan said, "I'd take some time off without pay and get them down here after the show closes. They're fine horses, sir, the best. I know you'd want to buy them if you saw them."

"Then you know more than I do. What makes you think I'd give you a good price if I did buy them? Buying cheap is what I'm paid to do."

"Whatever you paid me would be better than I'd get in Idaho. There's a slump in the horse business—won't last, but it's there now."

Schlegel heaved himself away from his desk, making it clear that the conversation was over. "I'll have to think about it," he said. "I'll let you know. Wait a minute. My curiosity's got the better of me. Why did you tell that detective you wouldn't claim the reward money? You said it was blood money. Is that all of it? For the life of me I can't see any sane man turning down five thousand good American dollars. Are you some kind of religious fanatic? You don't look like one or behave like one, from what I hear."

Morgan knew Schlegel meant Kitty and Maisie Cargill.

"I refuse to profit by a man's death," Morgan said.

Schlegel went to the door with him. "As you get older

you'll learn to profit any way you can. Don't bother me again. I said I'd let you know." The door banged, and the key turned in the lock.

He was hungry since Nancy Quillan hadn't cooked breakfast. The head cook complained about people coming late, but there was coffee and leftover eggs and he was welcome to that. Kitty was outside, pacing like a tiger, when he left.

"I knew you'd finally drag your ass back here." Her voice was cold, but he knew it wouldn't stay cold for long. "You were with that southern bitch the other night and last night you were with some town bitch. Don't lie, Morgan. You were seen sneaking back this morning."

"I didn't sneak. What are you so mad about?"

"I'm mad because you're a birdbrain that shouldn't be let out alone. The minute I'm not with you, you take a belly flopper into the shithole. First you stick your nose in where it shouldn't be and end up shooting a killer. The next morning a killer tries to kill you. If I hadn't saved your worthless hide, Chenko would have killed or crippled you for life. I don't get you, birdbrain. Why didn't you just shoot him the first move he made toward you? With a gorilla like that, it would have been self-defense. But you live by the Code of the West, am I right? Code of the Assholes is more like it. Keep back from me, birdbrain. You smell like you've been in a cheap whorehouse."

Though people were gawking, he'd taken a step toward her. "I don't want you near me till you take a bath. You stink of whores! Stay back, I said." Her eyes snapped like firecrackers.

Morgan stayed where he was. "I wasn't with any whores."

"But you were with somebody. Is that why you bought the new clothes? To impress some town girl? If she'd known what you were really like, she'd have called for the police. What're you trying to do, Morgan? Wear out your cock?"

Nothing he said would have been believed. "If you must know," he said, "I was sitting up with a sick friend."

It was the wrong thing to say. Everything was the wrong thing to say. She got madder. "You'll be the 'sick friend' if you hang around with any more whores. Forget about the bath, Morgan. Forget about coming to see me. I don't want to get a dose from one of your bitches. Knock on my door and I'll put a bullet in you."

A few people smiled but nobody laughed as she stalked away. Kitty had too fierce a temper to be laughed at to her face. Morgan liked her but didn't understand her. Well, yes, he did in a way. She was vain and bad-tempered and lonely, to name a few things. Apart from that, she was a wonderful gal. He knew this was not the time to go after her. It would only make things worse. But he might take a chance and knock on her door when it got dark.

He stretched out on his cot, listening to the sounds outside the tent. A man was cursing another man for dropping a mallet on his foot. Morgan's shoulder hurt, but he wasn't sorry he'd gotten rid of the sling. Snooping around, it was too easily remembered.

It was Saturday when visiting hours at the jail started at noon. Bronc was depressed after too long in three jails and didn't feel much like talking. "Tell me all about it when you get me out of here—if you ever do. Me, I ain't so hopeful. It's not that I don't 'preciate what you're trying to do, boy. I'll always remember that no matter how it turns out."

Morgan stood around for a while, then left. When it was time, he went to see Bender.

Chapter Eight

"If I ever decide to break my marriage vows," Bender said, "I'll try to break them with her. I've seen her just once, at a political rally, but she can have my vote anytime."

"Down boy!" Morgan said.

They were talking about Nancy Quillan; Morgan had just told Bender the things he ought to know about the night before. They had two mugs of beer in front of them; the ache in Morgan's shoulder didn't call for whisky.

"I still can't figure why she came after me so fast," Morgan said. "She'd never risk telephoning Gallager or Yost with Washburn there."

"She works for Gallager," Bender said. "Gallager's her uncle. Maybe she just liked your looks."

"She hits the bottle pretty hard."

"Maybe she likes to drink. Maybe she doesn't like what she does. Gallager is a son of a bitch to work for. I tell you

that from bitter experience. You told her no more than you
had to, I hope."

"I stuck to the same old Idaho story. I don't know if
she believed me when I denied being an agent."

"Don't fret it," Bender said. "Gallager has no interest
in counterfeiting. He wants to know everything Washburn
does—so does Yost—but that's more to do with federal
contracts than anything else. The Quillan girl will report
every last detail—well, not every last detail. Gallager's a
very pious man, a bigshot in the Knights of Columbus,
and wouldn't want to hear dirty talk like that. He might
like to know if you're a federal agent, but I doubt he'll
go out of his way to find out. The show is outside his
grafter's world. It'll be moving on in a few weeks, and
so will you."

Morgan told Bender about his talk with Washburn. "The
man surprised me. He started off by giving me the high hat,
then agreed to do everything we talked about—checking
the prison release dates of old engravers who got out in
the last few years, the cellmates they had, the visitors,
where they went or said they were going to go after they
left prison. He doesn't know how long it'll take."

"Better than we hoped for," Bender said.

"He read me the riot act for giving Cargill a clean
slate without knowing more about him. Then we got onto
Tillotson, the colonel's financial whiz, and Schlegel, the
chief purchasing agent. The colonel told me Tillotson is
too rich to get mixed up in a scheme that could put him
away for life."

"That figures. Most moneymen are a trifle crooked, but
they like to shave their risks close. You steered clear of
Tillotson?"

"I talked to Schlegel," Morgan said. "It wasn't easy.
Schlegel does not like his fellow man. You never saw

a man so grim and wary. Comes with the job, I guess, but he overdoes it. My story about the horses didn't go down too good. It wasn't so much he thought I was lying. He looked like he thought I was a little short on brains."

"Don't be so quick to decide what people are thinking," Bender said, "but we'll agree he thought you were harebrained rather than somebody to be wary of."

"He's wary of everybody."

"Not wary like that. If we cross off Cargill and Tillotson, that leaves him. Anything else about him you're forgetting to tell me?"

"A couple of times he asked me why I wouldn't take the reward money. He said it was none of his business, yet it was like it was nagging at him. I told him I didn't want to profit by another man's death. He thought that was crazy and said I'd learn to profit by everything, given time."

Bender smiled. "That kind of thinking describes most of the men in the world. Only monks and saintly priests who care for lepers may not think like that. You're ready to pin the tail on Schlegel because he's a mean, grasping son of a miser. But like you say, he's the only one left."

"Unless we have this whole thing figured wrong."

Bender made a sour face. "Thank you, Detective Morgan. You want to blow down our house of cards?"

"No. I think we have it figured right. I have a gut feeling."

"That may be too much beer," Bender said. "I don't know where my feeling is, but it agrees with yours. We'll have to wait till you hear from Washburn. Just remember, he may not be completely straight with you. These federal men play it close to the vest. If any glory comes out of this, he won't want to share it. Don't be looking daggers at me friend. You think let Washburn stick his glory up his ass. All you want to do is clear your friend. Washburn may *know* that, but he doesn't *feel* it."

Morgan smiled at the detective. "Don't be so quick to decide what other people are thinking."

"A wise man once said that, and it wasn't the Yellow Kid over there." The Yellow Kid was at his usual spot at the bar, whispering now to a drunk cowhand who could barely stand up. Morgan couldn't decide if Bender really hated the Kid, as he claimed to, or had a soft spot for the scurvy little bastard.

"I guess we should keep an eye on Schlegel," Morgan said.

"Not me and not you," Bender said. "Schlegel knows you and everybody knows me. Too many people would stop me, trying to talk about this and that. I could get one of my men to follow him, but it might get back to Gallager and he'd want to know what I was doing. What could I tell him? That I'm working on a counterfeiting case that's none of my goddamned business?"

"Then who?"

Bender looked over at the bar and crooked his finger at the Yellow Kid. "Pull up a chair, Kid," the detective said when the pimp detached himself from the cowboy he was trying to steer. "This is Mr. Lomax from Wichita."

"How do, Mr. Lomax?" the Kid said.

"Mr. Lomax wants some information on a bird named James Schlegel, a bigshot in the Hardesty wild west show. Guy is about sixty, wears a black serge suit, sour face, no mustache or beard, talks with a lisp. Trouble is this Schlegel knows what Mr. Lomax looks like, so he can't do it."

"You want me to do it, Mr. Bender? Just say the word!" The Kid quivered with excitement. "I'll stick to him closer'n a corn plaster."

Bender patted the Kid on the arm. "I knew I could count on you, Kid. I told you what he looks like. Follow him anytime he leaves the show. If he takes a cab, you take one. If he goes into a hotel bar or a good restaurant, you do the same. Here's some money." Bender took ten dollars from his wallet and gave it to the Kid. "Don't lose him if you can help it. You'll have to get rid of the yellow get-up. Too easily spotted."

The Kid was upset. "Gee, Mr. Bender, I don't wear nothin' but yella."

Bender gave him two fives. "Buy a normal suit of clothes. Same goes for the shoes. Buy a hat to hide the yellow hair. Get going, Kid."

"I won't let you down, Mr. Bender." The pimp's voice was sincere. "What did this bastard do anyhow?"

"Swindled widows and orphans," Bender said.

"The rotten fuck," The Kid said.

"You must know what you're doing," Morgan said after the Kid went out. He pushed twenty dollars across the table, and Bender put it away.

"The Kid would cut off his right arm for me, because he knows I'd cut off both arms if he didn't. He'll do a good job—he's a born sneak. Of course, if Schlegel stays close to home he can't do any kind of job. We'll have to wait and see."

"Waiting is a pain in the ass, Bender."

Bender shrugged. "That's the detective business for you. You think Washburn will have any information by tomorrow night?"

"If he uses the telegraph—maybe. What's his rank anyway? I didn't think to ask Nancy."

"He's head of the Kansas City office. One night when Gallager was three sheets to the wind I heard him saying Washburn had two agents on paper, but they hadn't showed up because they were needed somewhere else. If you're thinking Washburn has agents we don't know about, forget it. Gallager usually gets his dope straight."

Morgan had been thinking about something. "You ever had the feeling you were being followed?"

"Sure I have, but I've been wrong. You could be wrong. If you're not, it must be one of the paper agents Gallager says aren't here yet."

"All I know is today after I left the show I felt somebody was in back of me. It started right after I got through the crowd that came to see them putting up the big tent. I checked a few times, but there was nothing to see. If there was, I didn't see it. With the gawkers and all, streets were pretty crowded. Guess it doesn't have to mean anything."

The detective looked around the saloon, jammed with drinkers at that time of day. "No, it doesn't," he said. "Gallager's sneaks used to follow me. Not any more. One day I doubled back on one of them, did a little choking and asked him how he'd like to swim the Missouri River with an anvil on his back."

"Maybe I was wrong," Morgan said.

"Don't change your mind so fast," Bender said. "There could be something to it. What I don't know." Bender took another look at the mob of drinkers. "If it's somebody new on your tail they could just walk in here, and you wouldn't know and neither would I. Better take a closer look behind you when you leave. If you spot anyone, all you do is fix in your head what they look like. You may not spot them at all, specially if they switch their hat for a cap or take off their coat and carry it. Gives them a different look for a while."

"Maybe I was wrong," Morgan repeated.

"Don't keep saying that. Stands to reason an old frontiersman like you would know when some varmint is dogging his trail."

The detective was joking, but Morgan knew he was serious. "You ought to join the show, Bender. You sound more like a fake cowboy than the fake cowboys they got. I'll do what you say."

Bender stood up. "I'll go out first. Try to see if anybody follows you when you leave. Give it a minute or so."

Morgan didn't see Bender when he walked out of the saloon. And he didn't spot anybody following him on his way back to the show. The bigtop was up and some of the gawkers were still there, marveling at its bright colors and size. Kansas City people were still small-town enough to be dazzled by a spectacle. Scully and his buckskinned guards were on the job, keeping a lookout for trespassers and thieves. Scully gave Morgan a mean cold look before he turned his head the other way.

Walking over to look at the big tent he ran into Marie, the woman who had been calling down Chenko before the fight started. "I been looking for you, Morg," she said, looking around her and lowering her voice at the same time. She got a grip on his arm and pulled him toward her so she could whisper. "The colonel fired Chenko this afternoon. Hadn't heard about the fight at first—nobody wanted to tell him—but he heard anyway, and boy, was he good and mad. To make it worse, Chenko'd been drinking so it took Scully and three men to throw him out. Would have taken more men than that if Scully hadn't beat him bad with a blackjack. You should have heard the way he carried on. Cursed you and Kitty, the lousy foreigner, and kept saying this wasn't the end of it. Come hell or high water, he was going to get the both of you. You better watch out, Morg, and

tell Kitty to do the same. He means business, Morg. He's
probably off somewhere getting drunker than he was."

Morgan thanked Marie and went looking for Kitty. It
was all over the place by now, and several people stopped
him to tell him about Chenko and his threats. He thanked
them but cut them short. Kitty was in her car, still mad at
him, and wouldn't open the door. "Save your breath," she
told him through the window. "I know all about Chenko
and his bullshit. I don't need you to look after me, yokel.
I'll shoot the bastard dead if he tries to lay a hand on me."
She closed the window, but before she did she added, "You
do the same, hayseed. Right between the fucking eyes."

Morgan walked back to talk to Scully about Chenko.
The miserable son of a bitch scowled when Morgan asked
if he'd seen him. "No, I ain't seen him and I ain't going
to see him. I laid enough jack on his head to keep him
in headaches the rest of his life. What're you so scared
of, Morgan? You always got Kitty to protect you."

Morgan kept his temper and walked away before it went
too far. There was no point in looking for Chenko—and
what would he do if he found him? Beat him with a rock?
Kill him? By now Chenko could be anywhere in the city.
Best let Chenko be unless he came looking for trouble.
Morgan knew he could handle Chenko, but he wasn't so
sure about Kitty. She was city tough, but dealing with men
who just pestered her wasn't the same as dealing with a
savage like Chenko. Chenko was a brute, but even brutes
had some kind of cunning. He might be on top of Kitty
before she had time to grab her gun. She said she hardly
ever went anywhere, but it would be just like her to start
going out now to show everyone she wasn't afraid of any
man in the world, especially not a dimwit like Chenko.

He found the colonel inside the bigtop and asked him to
get Scully to post a guard outside Kitty's door. "You think

it's that serious?" the colonel asked, raising his eyebrows. "I warned him I'd get him a long jail sentence if he showed up here again. That usually scares the meanest of them. But I'll do as you ask, though Kitty may holler like hell."

"She'd holler louder if I hung around there," Morgan said.

"Sounds like true love, the way you two fight all the time. Goddamn, boy, I wish I was young enough to get into fights like that."

Morgan walked clear around the edge of the fairgrounds as the sun was setting. Scully had stationed a few guards, but after it was fully dark, Chenko could crawl in anywhere. The colonel didn't take Chenko's threats seriously, and Scully might be more than willing to let Chenko have a crack at Kitty as well as himself. He had tangled with Scully, and Kitty despised Scully and made no secret of it. Most likely that would be enough to make a mean man like Scully look the other way.

When it got dark he edged his way down to Kitty's car and took up a position behind a stack of scenery flats that hadn't been used yet. The guard was there, sitting on the bottom step of the car, dozing the night away. Chenko could kill the guard with one hand if he crept up without being heard. But there was no sign of Chenko, then or later.

Morgan went back to his tent before it got light. He lay on his cot and listened to the sounds of the fairgrounds coming to life. He would look after Kitty as best he could, but he couldn't do it day and night. Anyway he knew she'd scoff at the idea.

It was three o'clock the next day, and Bender was talking to Morgan in the saloon. The Yellow Kid came pushing through the crowd like a man with news that couldn't wait.

He threw himself into a chair, saying in a querulous voice, "Gee, Mr. Bender, I wish you'd let me come to your office. I could have told you what I'm gonna tell you first thing this morning."

"Tell me now, Kid." Bender told the waiter to bring a beer for the Kid.

The Kid stuck his face in the foaming mug and drank deeply. Bender took the mug and moved it away from him. "Okay! Okay!" the Kid said. "Here's what happened. Yesterday I hangs around all day, and it's dark when Schlegel comes out of the fairgrounds an' heads for town. No cabs down that way, so he walks. Hardly anybody around so I hangs back so I don't tip him. Suddenly this bird steps out from behind a wagon and starts walking after him. First I thinks this is just a guy going in the same direction, but the guy hangs back like I was hanging back on him. No mistake, Mr. Bender. Schlegel has picked up a tail."

The detective allowed the Kid one swallow of beer. "Get on with it, Kid."

The Kid wiped his mouth with his sleeve. "Here's where it gets spicy. Schlegel makes for the Twin Rivers Hotel on Mottram—you know it, Mr. Bender, not class but not too bad—goes in and don't come out. I figure he's checked in, but the tail stays outside and picks a spot where he can see the door. I walks past the tail like I'm a regular guest. I tell the night clerk I'm a private detective, and for a buck he tells me Schlegel's room number. Room thirty-eight, third floor. I sit there and read the paper, thinking what I'm gonna do next. Then in walks this not bad looking pross—she had the look—and tells the clerk she ain't sure the party she wants to see, Mr. Simmons, is in room thirty-eight or some other room, like room twenty-eight. Clerk gives her the right number an' she goes up. Ain't no time before she comes down looking fucking mad. I figure

Schlegel is quick on the trigger or something happened up there. Then a few minutes later Schlegel comes down an' asks the clerk for change of a twenty. I figure he's going to take a hack, and no hack driver will have that kind of change. Schlegel reaches for his wallet, then gets mad an' sick-looking at the same time. 'My wallet!' he says like he's going to cry."

The Kid licked his lips, and Bender let him finish the beer.

"So anyhow," the Kid went on. "Before the clerk can say anything, Schlegel rushes out of the hotel, and the tail starts tailing an' I tail him. Never got a real good look at him. Hat brim down over his eyes."

"Wait a minute," Bender cut in. "You didn't find out who the woman was? Jesus Christ, Kid!"

"I ain't that dumb, Mr. Bender." The Yellow Kid looked hurt. "After the pross goes upstairs I asks the clerk who she is. I have to give him another buck before he tells me she goes by the name Daphne, just Daphne, an' that's all he can tell me. That's his story, Mr. Bender. He don't know her last name or where she lives. I ask him how she does business, and he says he don't know. What do you want from me, Mr. Bender? I could have followed the woman, but for what? Stick to Schlegel, you said."

"You're right, Kid," the detective said. "So you followed Schlegel back to the fairgrounds?"

"Guy goes in and don't come out," the Kid said. "The tail calls it quits about twelve. I give it another hour before I figure Schlegel is tucked in for the night."

Bender gave the Kid two dollars to replace the money he had to lay out at the hotel. "Can you find out who this woman is, Kid? You find her, and I'll owe you big."

That was the kind of talk the Kid liked to hear. "I'll find her, Mr. Bender, but you got to remember the Mottram

Street district ain't my reg'lar stomping ground. I'll find the cunt, yes sir."

"Quick as you can, Kid. The quicker you find her, the bigger bonus Mr. Lomax will pay you. Soon as you find her, take a cab right to my office. I'll be working, or sleeping on the couch, depending how late it gets. Move out, soldier!"

They both watched the Kid until he was gone, then Bender said, "If she still has the wallet maybe it'll do us some good, but I don't expect to find phony tens. Schlegel wouldn't be that kind of a fool if he's our man. Goddamn! I hope she still has it. It could turn up names and addresses, something that could nail this case shut. If the Kid comes up with a winner, I'll be banging on her door before you can blink."

Morgan was thinking about Schlegel's closed-in face, the dead eyes and the grim mouth. "Funny, a cold fish like Schlegel wanting a woman. Any woman. colonel thinks he's as dead in the crotch as he is in the head."

Bender looked as if he's smelled something bad. "The colonel is thinking like a normal man. Who's to say what Schlegel wanted her for? Maybe he wanted to piss on her and she wouldn't go for it. Whores aren't all the same. So she walked out and managed to lift his wallet."

"I wonder how Schlegel got onto her," Morgan said.

"That's what I intend to find out," Bender said. "She may not want to talk, but she will after I explain things to her. Maybe she'll sing like a canary after I tell her what Judge Beddoes thinks of wallet lifters. I better shove off in case the Kid hits the jackpot on the first pull. What'll you be doing till nine o'clock?"

"Laying down in my tent," Morgan said. "Nothing much else to do. Then I'll go see what Washburn has to say."

*   *   *

It was eight o'clock, and Morgan was about to leave for city hall when the kid from Western Union cleared his throat and called out, "You in there, Mr. Morgan? I have a telegram for Mr. Lee Morgan."

What in hell! Morgan thought. He gave the kid a quarter, turned up the lantern and ripped open the envelope. Two telegrams inside of a week! He hoped Bronc wasn't dead or dying. The telegram was from Bender:

NO WALLET SEARCH TONIGHT.G LEADING
CHARGE ON DARKTOWN. NAME YOU WANT
DAPHNE LATROBE HOTEL CENTRAL DEN-
TON STREET. GOOD LUCK.

J.T. SNOW

It was 8:30 by the time Morgan walked to the center of town. He asked a patrolman where Denton Street was. "It's a good mile," the flatfoot told him. "Go to the next corner and turn right . . ." Morgan listened to the instructions he wasn't going to follow. If Daphne Latrobe had gone home, he'd go talk to her after he got through with Washburn. If she had the wallet now, she'd probably still have it an hour or two later. He had to make a decision, and Washburn came first.

When he got to city hall, he stood at the bottom of the steps and looked back across the wide intersection he had just crossed. On Sunday night that part of town was dead—no politicians or office workers, no newspapermen or visiting farmers. A streetcar rumbled past without stopping. Before he started up the steps, he looked at the city jail, squat and grim under the night sky. Bronc was in there somewhere, the poor old son of a bitch. Suddenly he was tired of all this detective shit—talking out of two sides of his mouth, watching his back instead of walking down the street like an ordinary man, trying to put a jigsaw together with most of the pieces missing. But he was in this stinking game and he had to play it to the end—win, lose or draw.

He went up the steps and rang the bell for the night guard. He wondered how long it would take Bender to shake loose from Gallager's invasion of the black district. A state senator's son was dead, so it could be a long or short haul, depending how drunk or vengeful Gallager was. Working without Bender would not be easy.

He heard the guard's boots sounding on the marble floor.

Chapter Nine

Washburn jerked the door open, then slammed and locked it after Morgan came in. Morgan didn't need the door slamming to tell him Washburn was mad. Anger showed itself in the grim line of his mouth and the thrust of his bony jaw. The lights in the outer office were turned off. Washburn walked ahead of Morgan and sat ramrod straight behind his desk. "Close the door," he ordered. A moment later he was out from behind the desk and pacing the floor. Morgan waited.

Washburn stopped pacing and pointed a finger like a prosecuting attorney. "Do you deny that you've been meeting with a Detective Lieutenant Bender of the Kansas City Police Department? Why didn't you tell me? I regard it as a breach of good faith."

Morgan knew he had to settle the agent down before he got too abusive. Start eating shit and that's all you'll get.

"Good faith, my ass!" Morgan said. "Why did you have me followed, Washburn?"

Washburn forced himself to sit in his chair and stay there. "How do you know you were followed?"

"Somebody spotted your sneak and told me."

Washburn allowed himself a bleak smile. "But he didn't give you a good description, isn't that so? Otherwise you would have seen him drinking at the bar while you and the detective were talking. My man followed you today and yesterday, and you never spotted him once. You just thought you might be followed, so you were ready to believe it. Why shouldn't I have you followed? For two days I've been burning up the telegraph lines, checking the possibilities we discussed the other day. I had to know if you were as straight a man as you pretended to be. Now I have grave doubts about you. Why didn't you tell me about Bender?"

Maybe it was too late to be believed, Morgan thought. "I thought you might tell Gallager, the chief of police. Gallager is a grafter and out to do Bender dirt any way he can."

Washburn was more outraged than he had been before. "Do you think I'd tell *anything* to Gallager? I know all about Gallager, and I wouldn't tell him the time of day. Gallager is a drunken disgrace to the uniform. He isn't fit to be dogcatcher." Washburn got back to finger pointing. "Bender sent you to me, didn't he? All your ideas about old convicts, cellmates and visitors were his ideas, right?"

"We talked it over together."

"Why didn't he come himself? If he knows anything about the Secret Service, then he must know that we do not share information of any kind with men like Gallager."

"Bender was afraid you'd see him as just another grafting policeman and show him the door. He's an honest man,

Washburn. Nothing would make him happier than to see Gallager gone."

"You keep insisting he's honest," the agent said, "and perhaps he is. He'd like to be chief of police, no doubt."

"What's wrong with that?" Morgan said. "Makes no difference if there is. He wouldn't stand a chance if Gallager dropped dead tomorrow. Yost, the mayor, would appoint somebody just like him, maybe worse. The reformers would like to see Bender made chief, but they have no power in this town."

"The reformers need help and so does Bender if he's as honest as you say he is. I may get into that later, or I may not. but to get back to the reason you came here tonight, is there any reason I should trust you after your underhanded behavior?"

Morgan had to fight to keep his temper; the pompous son of a bitch kept twanging away on his one-string harp. "Trust me or don't trust me, Washburn. I can't make you do anything."

The agent rubbed his long, thin hands together like a man trying to keep warm on a cold night. "Of course you can't make me do anything. I'm glad you know that. There is a certain arrogance about you that annoys me. Just the same, I have decided to tell you the results of my inquiries. After all, what harm can you do?"

An easy answer could be made to that, but Morgan held his peace.

"I telegraphed the warden at Leavenworth, the principal federal penitentiary, and he was able to provide a fairly detailed history of one Henry Glidden, master engraver and criminal, released from his custody just eighteen months ago. Don't interrupt, please."

Morgan had no intention of interrupting.

Washburn went on. "Glidden was born in Philadelphia seventy years ago. He was apprenticed to the master engraver Felix Bok at the age of fourteen. It was a ten year apprenticeship. After his graduation, so to speak, he worked for the U.S. Mint in Philadelphia for seven years. Then he worked for Bedloe and Company, Philadelphia engravers, until his arrest on a charge of counterfeiting. He was sentenced to thirty years and served every year of his sentence."

Washburn did more hand rubbing. "Aren't you going to say something, Morgan?"

"Congratulations," Morgan said, adding, "I mean it."

"Thank you," the agent said. "Let me proceed. Glidden's only cellmate for four years and ten months was a Baltimore swindler named Franklin Swain who was sentenced to five years for having United States Treasury bonds in his possession. Sometime after Swain's release, drawings of the new currency were found in Glidden's cell. He was immediately transferred to a one-man cell in the solitary wing. No, it wasn't the hole, as convicts call it. Prisoners in the solitary wing are housed in ordinary cells but are not allowed to mingle. There Glidden served his thirty year sentence, and his only visitor in all those years was his former cellmate, Franklin Swain. I suppose Swain gave his real name because he knew he might be remembered. Swain visited Glidden several times a year and his address in Omaha, Nebraska, recorded in the visitor's book, remained the same year after year. Five years ago, Swain's visits ceased."

The agent poured himself a glass of water from a jug on his desk. "After I received the communication from the warden at Leavenworth, I telegraphed the chief of police in Omaha, inquiring about Swain and the correctness of the address. His reply stated that nobody knew of anyone named Franklin Swain and the house on Railroad Avenue that Swain claimed as his home burned down many years ago. That house—a boarding house—was never rebuilt. An undertaker's has stood there for about fifteen years. Through the years, Swain continued to give the boarding house as his home address, unaware of what had happened to it."

Washburn drank more water, giving Morgan time to ask, "Do any of the guards remember what Swain looked like?"

"Many of the guards from the early years have retired or quit. The ones still there told the warden all they remember about Swain was his heavy beard. To the younger guards he was just a short older man who did nothing to attract attention."

"Goddamn!" Morgan said.

"However, there is one man who should remember Swain better than any of the others—the guard in charge of the visitor's book for all the years Glidden was in prison. None of the other guards had any reason to speak to Swain. This one had to. Vickers—that's his name—retired a few years ago. He lives in the town of Leavenworth, but the warden was unable to get hold of him. He's off on a fishing trip. His wife is dead and his sons and daughters have all moved away, so nobody knows where he is. He'll be questioned as soon as he can be found."

It didn't look too good for Bronc, Morgan thought. "What happened to Glidden?"

"He gave prison authorities an old folks' home in Philadelphia as his future address. The Secret Service in Philadelphia kept a lookout for him, but he never turned up. Since then they have not been able to trace him. He could be anywhere. We may never find him unless somebody breaks down and talks. It can't be Tillotson because Colonel Hardesty says he's tall and slim. The guards all agree that Swain was short and heavy-set. If we can get a better description from Vickers and match it to Schlegel, we may be able to break him down."

Morgan didn't share the agent's enthusiasm. "I doubt it. I've talked to him; you haven't."

"I can accuse him and see what he does."

"Maybe nothing. He knows you'd arrest him if you had evidence. It'll take more than one elderly guard to nail him. Swain had a heavy beard, and Schlegel has been clean-shaven as long as the colonel knows him, which is five years."

Washburn looked smug. "That's around the time Swain stopped visiting Glidden. I think Swain deliberately set out to establish a new identity for himself. Changed his name to Schlegel, shaved off his beard, and joined Colonel Hardesty's wild west show. He must be competent since the colonel has the reputation of being a hard man when it comes to business. Schlegel has been with the colonel only five years. The question is, what was he doing before that? Given time, that can be checked."

"Checking small shows that have gone out of business may not be so easy. Small traveling shows did better years ago than they do now. I saw a few of them as a kid in Idaho. People today don't want to pay to see a bunch of threadbare performers riding around on cavalry rejects."

The agent gave Morgan a wary look. "You seem to know a lot about wild west shows for a horse rancher."

The son of a bitch never gave up, Morgan thought. One minute he talked like he was ready to trust you, the next he saw you as part of some plot.

"I've been up and down and all over," Morgan said. "You learn a little about a lot of things."

Washburn rubbed his hands when he was pleased and fiddled with his collar when he was uncertain. Now he pinged the water jug with his middle finger. Morgan couldn't stand men who couldn't keep their hands still. There was a hard knock on the outer door, and Washburn got up to see who it was. "Must be the guard," he said.

But it was Bender, as wary of Washburn as Washburn was of him. He hardly looked at Morgan. "I heard you were looking for me, Washburn," he said in a rougher voice than Morgan had heard him use before. "No reason for me to talk to you, but you'd find me anyway. What do you want?"

"To talk." Washburn got a chair for Bender from the outer office. "You say there's no reason why we should talk. I think there is. You can look at your friend Morgan. I know all about your meetings. Don't try to deny it. My agent followed Morgan and was right there in the saloon when you talked."

Bender shrugged. "All right, you know. What are you going to do about it?"

"I won't tell Gallager if that's what you're thinking. Gallager is a crook and a drunkard. I want to talk to you because I think you might be useful."

"Why me?" Bender said. "I could be as crooked as Gallager for all you know. What makes you think I'm any better?"

The agent permitted himself a thin smile. "Because Morgan says so, and I've done some checking. You are far from being a model policeman, but they say you can't be bribed."

"I thought you federals despised all flatfeet, even the honest ones."

"That's not quite so," the agent said. "The Secret Service has always respected honest, competent police officers, but I do admit there is a certain lack of trust. How to tell the bad from the good, and so on. However, that is changing as the

Service itself is changing. Let me explain . . . why do you keep looking at your watch?" Washburn was annoyed. "Do you have some pressing engagement?"

Bender smiled. "My pressing engagement is with Chief Gallager. We caught the black pimp that killed State Senator Decker's son, but Gallager isn't satisfied with that. He wants me in his office"—Bender looked at his watch—"sixty minutes from now. I can be late but not too late."

Washburn put his own watch on his desk. "Then I'll be as brief as I can. As I've said, the Service is changing. Our old chief is retiring, and a new man has already taken over and issued a directive regarding our new duties. Tracking down counterfeiters will remain our principal activity, but we will also investigate threats against the President and other public figures. Discreetly, of course. Investigating government contracts for fraud comes under the same heading. And last but certainly not least, our new chief wants to establish better working relations with the police."

"How can you do that with crooks like Gallager holding top jobs?" The detective took a quick look at his watch. Morgan could tell that Washburn's windy way of talking was getting on his nerves.

"Our new chief is as much aware of the widespread police corruption as you are." Washburn leaned forward as if to say something highly confidential. "His directive stresses that we will work with no more than a handful of carefully selected officers. What I'm going to say next should make you feel better. Police officers working with us will have the protection of the federal government. The corrupt or recalcitrant chief who dismisses a man for cooperating with us will find himself in hot water. We will make sure his name gets into the newspapers, and we can look for secret bank accounts with false names.

Time consuming but possible. We can get some respectable young lady to accuse him of something. Do I make myself clear?"

Bender pretended to wipe his forehead. "Clear as a bell. I'm glad I don't have the Secret Service after me."

"No law-abiding man need fear the Secret Service," Washburn said piously. "But if a policeman proves himself disloyal, he must look to the Lord for mercy. He will get none from us."

After pausing to think about it—or pretending to—Bender said, "What if I say I don't want to work with you?"

"Chief Gallager will be informed that you have been conducting an illegal investigation of a federal case."

"I'd be out on my ear."

"So you would. But I'm sure you see the advantages."

"How could I not see? Now I've got two bosses I don't like instead of one. You're not strictly my boss, but you can put the boot to me anytime you like. I thought you were a federal officer and a gentleman."

Washburn rubbed his hands. "I try to be both. What you regard as threats are simply alternate means of persuasion."

"In a pig's eye," the detective said, putting his watch away. "I'll work with you the best way I can. But right now I still work for the KCPD. I've got to see what Gallager wants." Bender stood up and looked at Morgan. "I guess we better tell him about Daphne."

"I guess so," Morgan said.

Impatience made the agent's face twitch. "Who is this Daphne? What have you been holding back, Morgan? What about it, Bender?"

Bender told him about the Yellow Kid and Schlegel, the Secret Service agent the Kid spotted, the hotel on Mottram

Street, the prostitute called Daphne Latrobe and the stolen wallet.

The agent jumped up from his chair. "I must interrogate her immediately. Daphne Latrobe. Hotel Central. Denton Street." Washburn grabbed his hat and jammed it on his head.

Bender held up his hand. "Wait a minute. I don't have time to do it, but Morgan would do it better, Washburn. Messing around with prostitutes can get ugly. You don't know whores like I do or like Morgan does. They can go crazy if they're taking drugs. You want to tangle with maybe a crazy woman and maybe a killer pimp. It's not your line. Let Morgan do it."

It took some time before the agent made up his mind. Tangling with whores and pimps was not his line of work, and he knew it. "All right," he said at last, slumping back in his chair. "You'll keep me informed. Goodnight, gentlemen."

Out on the street, keeping pace with Morgan, the detective said, "I just can't figure that son of a bitch, can you? He's a pompous fool, an old woman and a blackmailer all rolled into one."

"He can sound foolish, but I wouldn't peg him as a fool." They crossed the street at a fast pace. There were no cabs around and Bender cursed. "I hope he doesn't change his mind and come banging on that woman's door."

There was still no cab when the detective looked behind him. "I think I scared him off with that crazy whore talk." When they got to police headquarters Bender said, "Here's where I leave you. I don't know how long I'll be with Gallager, maybe half the night. Can't say what he'll do when he has the booze in him. Before I left he was mumbling about making another raid in the morning. So it's best we meet at the Texas. Good luck with Daphne."

A lone cab came along just after Bender went into the police station. Traffic was light on Sunday night, and Morgan got to the Hotel Central ten minutes later. It looked like the way the Yellow Kid described the hotel on Mottram Street—not class but not too bad. He asked the night clerk where he could find Miss Daphne Latrobe. The clerk smirked and told him she was in room 26. On the way up he checked his gun, not expecting any killer pimps but just checking to make sure.

"Who is it?" a woman's voice asked after he'd knocked twice.

"Miss Latrobe?" Morgan said. "I'm Detective McGurk, Kansas City police. There's a man on the fire escape so don't go throwing the wallet out the window. Open up now. You don't want me to break the door down. Mr. Simmons is willing to forgive and forget."

There was a long pause while she thought about it. Then the retaining chain rattled loose and she unlocked the door. Daphne Latrobe was about 30 with pale skin and dark brown hair, eyes of much the same color. She was wearing a yellow dressing gown with dragons on it. Powder made a mask of her face, and she wore too much rouge. If she washed her face and you met her on the street you wouldn't give her a second glance. Her voice, trying for her idea of elegance, had a Missouri twang to it.

"I'm sure I don't know what you're talking about," she said, leaving the door half open. "What was that about throwing something out the window? And I'm afraid I don't know any Mr. Simmons." Her eyes swept down from his hat to his boots. "Are you sure you're a detective?" The moment she said it, her eyes grew frightened.

Morgan closed the door with his heel and reached back to lock it. That frightened her some more. Let it, Morgan thought. "I'm not the police," he said. "I'm what they call an expediter. Mr. Simmons wants his wallet back and sent me to get it. No police, no arrest, no jail cell. You still have it?"

"I'm sure I don't—"

"You're wasting both our time, Daphne." Morgan tried to sound as weary as Bender. "Give it up or I'll search you and then the room. You want that?"

Her eyes narrowed, and she stamped her foot. "For Christ's sake, all this fuss for a lousy forty dollars." No more phony elegance now. "I'll get the goddamned wallet for you."

She took the wallet from a shoebox in the closet and gave it to him. Morgan checked the money first and found two twenties, like she'd said. No tens. Schlegel would have asked the hotel clerk for change of a ten if he had tens in his wallet. He looked through the other compartments in the wallet and found nothing, not even a business card. It looked like Schlegel took no chance of being identified when he went whoring—or whatever it was he did with women.

Daphne looked at him in astonishment when he gave her back the wallet with the two twenties still in it. "What is going on here, whoever you are?"

"Never mind that," Morgan said. "I'm not the police and Simmons didn't send me. Let's sit down, and you tell me everything you know about Simmons." He didn't tell her Schlegel's name because she looked capable of blackmail. "How did you get his name, and who sent you to him?"

She was on the edge of the bed; Morgan was in a chair. "Nobody sent me," she said. "I met him in the park, where girls like me do a little bit of business. It's a quiet corner of the park, and the patrolmen don't bother us as long as we make it worth their while."

"Men go there to try their luck?"

"You could say that. They wander through to see if there's anything they like. I met Simmons there yesterday. He sat down beside me, we came to terms, and we arranged to meet at the Mottram Street hotel that evening. I haven't been there that often, but the night clerk knows what I do and knows my first name is Daphne. I don't know how he knows. I must have been tight or something when I told him. That's how you traced me?"

"That's right," Morgan said. "What made you run out so soon after you got there?"

"The bastard wanted to put handcuffs and leg-irons on me soon as I got in the room. Said there was no harm in it, just a little game he liked to play. It wasn't till then that I remembered when I'd seen him before. The same toys, the same voice. Only back then he had a real heavy beard."

"When was that?"

"Let me think a minute. Eight or nine years ago, I think. It was eight. I remember. The President passed through town or something. Simmons wasn't calling himself Simmons then. I think the name he gave was Shelby or Shipley, but it was the same man all right—with the same lisp as Simmons has. The only thing different is he has no beard these days."

"You have any idea what his business was?"

"Some kind of a traveling man, I guess, but not a salesman. It takes a little charm or something to sell things. Shelby or Shipley—whatever his name was—had about as much charm as a snake. Sort of sour-faced and rattled inside. He tried a few smiles, but it was more like he was constipated."

It was starting to fit together, Morgan thought. It wasn't enough to put Schlegel in jail, but he knew more than he knew when he walked in here. Too bad he wouldn't be able to talk to Bender till tomorrow. He thought of telephoning Washburn but decided against it. He'd listened to enough of Washburn's bullshit for one night. Bender was more his kind of person, for all his city ways.

At the door he turned back to her. "Better stay off the streets till Simmons leaves town. If he's still a traveling man, he should be gone soon. Simmons is a mean bastard and could do you harm. Should you see him, walk the other way. Don't think you can squeeze him for money or you'll be sorry."

Daphne lay back on the bed. "You sure you wouldn't like to stay a while? Maybe I'll remember something else about Simmons."

"Have to go," Morgan told her. Daphne Latrobe wasn't bad, but she really wasn't his kind of woman. Compared to Kitty she was about as exciting as cold turnip greens.

He walked back to the fairgrounds because he couldn't find a cab. Normally he'd never think of taking a cab, but he wanted to see how Kitty was. The night guard was still posted in front of her car, so everything was all right. It was late and there wasn't much else to do but turn in for the night. Sleep didn't come right away, and he lay on the cot thinking of all the things that had happened since he'd set out to visit Bronc for a few days of drinking, tall tales and good humor. The more he thought about Schlegel, the more he was convinced that Schlegel was the man he meant to put behind bars—or kill if he had to.

That made him feel better, and he slept.

Chapter Ten

Morgan spotted the Yellow Kid when he left the fairgrounds later that morning. The Kid wore a black suit and a black hat, giving him the look of a slightly crazy boy preacher. If he hadn't been looking around for sneaks, he would never have spotted the Kid smoking behind a broken, abandoned wagon not far from the entrance. The Kid was still on Schlegel's tail, he figured, and took no further heed of him.

Earlier, after a big breakfast, he strolled through the big tent and out the other side, on his way to do some practice shooting. Kitty was shooting when he got there, blazing away without looking at him once. Damn that woman! What in hell was she so worked up about? Show people were as randy as goats; crawling in and out of other beds was as common as fleas on a dog. It wasn't like she owned him; more than once she'd made it plain that she was on her own and liked it that way. Before she walked away, she made a snap shot at a target he'd missed through carelessness and hit it without effort. Nothing was said; she just walked away.

He didn't go after her. If she thought she could break his balls then she'd have to think again. If she wanted to be the goddamned queen bee of the show, so be it. He wasn't one of those men who sniffed around after women and always got his nose caught in the door when it was slammed in his face. All things aside though, he would try to see no harm came to her. If Chenko showed and made one wrong move, he would get a bullet in the brain.

There wasn't any sign of Schlegel but there was nothing so strange about that. The man who liked to put handcuffs and leg-irons on women took no part in the easygoing life of the show. Schlegel's guilt had to be proved before a judge sent him away for the rest of his life. It didn't matter how they took Schlegel away, on a train or in a coffin, just as long as they put him where the dogs don't bite.

On his way to beg more coffee from the complaining cooks, Morgan finally spotted Schlegel making for the street that went all the way to town. Schlegel saw him but kept on walking. He didn't know if Washburn still had a tail on Schlegel. You never could be sure about the shifty, stringbean agent; he always held something back.

Waiting for something to happen ate at Morgan like a small beaver gnawing down a big tree. It was like being trapped by a heavy snowfall in a shack in the middle of winter. He could eat and sleep but not much else. Waiting was part of the detective business, Bender said, but he wasn't sure he'd ever get used to it. He could be patient when he had to be, like when he was hunting some animal that had no mind to be shot. That was different, but this was enough to wear a man down and make him hold conversations with himself. Morgan smiled. It was natural enough for a man alone to ask and answer his own questions, just as long as he didn't start doing it where people could hear him. Shit! Why couldn't he get Schlegel to some deserted place and beat the truth out of him? Patience, boy! Fuck patience!

One of the guards was outside Kitty's car, but he didn't look as if he could fight off a blind man with one leg. Morgan took care not to be seen by Kitty. Why provoke the fiery bitch?

Morgan hoped Bender would be there when he went to the saloon at three o'clock, but if not, it would be useless to try to find the detective. He could be anywhere, catching a few hours sleep on the couch in his office or following along behind Gallager's unsteady banner. Washburn might be expecting him to show up, but he would dodge the agent as long as he could.

The Yellow Kid wasn't there when he left the fairgrounds, and neither was the wagon he'd been hiding behind. Most likely, somebody in the show had complained about the broken wagon being an eyesore and city workers had hauled it away. Trying to kill time, Morgan stopped to look at a man replacing the glass in a broken window. The man glared at him, muttered something about "sidewalk superintendents," and went on with his work. You'll be arrested for loitering if you keep this up, Morgan told himself. Yes sir, trying to kill time was hell. It was as bad as a bad dream where you're in bed with a beautiful woman and your cock won't do what she wants it to do. Frustration all the way, yes sir!

Time crept around the face of his watch until he was finally pushing his way through the mob of drinkers that threatened to spill out into the street. The Texas Saloon never closed, and they never changed the air. Bender was at the back table, and Washburn was with him. They had mugs of beer in front of them; Washburn's beer looked as if it hadn't been tasted and it had gone flat. Bender snapped his fingers and the waiter fetched Morgan a beer. Washburn said peevishly, "You took your time getting here." The wall clock said it was five minutes to three. "Come on, Morgan, what have you got to report?"

"Hello Washburn," Morgan said, then he told them about Simmons and Shelby or Shipley. "The woman isn't sure of the name, but she swears it's the same man." Washburn grimaced when Morgan told about the handcuffs and the leg-irons.

"Filthy pervert!" he said.

"We want him for counterfeiting not perversion," Bender said. To Morgan he added, "I hope you really tore that wallet apart."

"There was nothing in the wallet but the money," Morgan said. "Two well-used twenties. They weren't counterfeits, Washburn. They had different serial numbers. Sorry to disappoint you. At least we can be fairly sure Shelby-Shipley and Schlegel are the same man."

The agent wanted to take it further than that. "I'm not fairly sure—I'm positive. Based on what this Latrobe woman told you, I'm going to arrest Schlegel on suspicion."

Bender cut in. "You can arrest him, but you can't hold him. A big money lawyer will hit you with a writ before Schlegel takes his first jailhouse piss."

The agent had an answer for that. "The Secret Service has extraordinary powers in counterfeiting cases. We can hold him as long as we like. No writs need apply."

The detective looked tired after whatever it was Gallager had inflicted on him the night before or earlier in the day. Washburn was looking at a fly drowning in his beer. "What good is holding him if you can't convict him?" Bender said. "You could cook up evidence, proof of counterfeiting. How do you go about doing that? Get the mint to make ten dollar plates with the same serial numbers as the duds? I guess you could do that."

The agent was never slow to take offense. "I have no such intention. It could be done, but it won't be. For one thing, too many people would know about it."

The man was a weasel, Morgan thought. His only concern was to put counterfeiters in jail, but he was still a weasel. The son of a bitch would frame his kindly old grandmother into jail if he thought he wouldn't get caught at it.

"I feel I must do something," the agent said. "What if Schlegel smells a rat and disappears? How would that look to Washington?"

Morgan looked at the agent. Either the man would rise to the very top or fall flat on his face. "Why would he skip town? Nothing has happened to make him skip town unless he's spotted your sneaks and knows he's being followed."

"My agents are trained men, Morgan."

"Don't be pointing the finger at the Yellow Kid," Bender said. "The Kid is so sneaky-looking nobody takes him for a sneak. He's a better sneak than a pimp. Why don't you take him on, Washburn?"

Washburn ignored the idea. Nothing about the saloon was to his liking, especially the band. They were going at it hammer and tongs, and every time the cornet player got inspired the agent pinched the bridge of his nose as if he had a headache. Too bad bar floozies weren't allowed in the Texas, Morgan thought. Washburn would wet his pants if some dolly plonked herself down on his lap and asked him to buy her a drink.

"He'd have to curb his activities if he knew he was under suspicion." The agent had taken his attention away from the band. "Under the circumstances, only a foolish, desperate or reckless man would continue to distribute counterfeit money, and Schlegel is none of the three. We are short-handed, but three agents can be assigned to him to watch every move he makes. Wherever he goes, he'll know he's being watched. If that doesn't stop him, nothing will. It's a start, Bender."

"It will slow him down, but it won't stop him unless he decides to call it a day, which is unlikely if he's the kind of a man we think he is—cunning, calculating and above all greedy. We figure Schlegel is the wholesaler, the man who sells the bad money to some top retailer who in turn sells it to the pushers or let's them have it on consignment. We don't know how the printer gets the money to Schlegel, whether it's carried or shipped. If he knows you have a watch on him, what's to prevent him from finding another wholesaler besides himself? How can he arrange anything with anybody with agents on his tail?" The detective took a sip of beer. "He can duck you, that's how. I've been a policeman for twenty-three years, a detective for sixteen, and I've never known a tail that couldn't be lost."

"Not if the men are smart and dedicated." The agent didn't like having his balloon shot down before it was clear of the treetops. "If my men lost him, as you say, they would have to answer to me."

"A lot of good that'd do," Bender said sourly. "While you'd be giving your agents hell, Schlegel would have a new operation set up. He couldn't use his job as a cover anymore, but paying a new wholesaler would be better than a cell in Leavenworth. Even if he had to take the new wholesaler in as a full partner, it would be worth it. The operation would continue much as it is now, except Schlegel wouldn't handle any of the hot money."

Washburn snapped his fingers at a waiter and told him to remove the beer mug with the dead fly in it. The slightly drunk waiter, a cheerful fat man with some kind of foreign accent, started to tell Washburn the joke about what the waiter said to the man who complained about the fly in his soup. Bender told him to get lost.

"Then we really haven't made any progress," Washburn said. "What's the use of keeping Schlegel under surveillance if he can duck out any time he wants to?"

A fresh mug of beer was placed in front of the agent, but it remained untasted. Bender drank some of it before it got flat. "I didn't say that, Washburn. Schlegel would have to plan to duck out. It might take some time, but he's crafty enough to do it."

"Same difference," the agent said. "He'd still be in business. It infuriates me to think—"

Morgan interrupted. "Can't the warden at Leavenworth light a fire under his men? Speed up the search for Vickers? He's an old man and can't be gone fishing that far from home."

"They haven't found him," the agent said. "The warden has thrown every man he can spare into the search. The county sheriff is helping out. They still haven't found him. I'd know if they had. Christ, I hope the old codger hasn't fallen into a lake and drowned."

The detective looked at Morgan, his expression wearier than ever. "I doubt it," he said.

"Why do you say that, Bender? What do you know about the man's state of health? He's old and could suffer a heart seizure, a stroke, momentary dizziness. I better get back to the office and send a telegram to the warden. If I weren't needed here, I'd go out there myself. I'll let you know what happens."

Washburn fought his way out of the saloon, while Bender looked after him and shook his head. "That is a very nervous man. One minute he's rubbing his hands, pleased as punch with himself; the next he isn't sure the country will last to the end of the week. Nothing happens that isn't some kind of a personal dig at him. It's like Schlegel is a personal vendetta with him."

"It's personal with me," Morgan said.

"I know—your friend," Bender said.

Morgan asked the detective if there had been any reports of Chenko making a nuisance of himself in town. "The bastard drinks and likes to beat people."

"Something like wrecking a saloon wouldn't get as far as me. Even beating somebody to death, if they had him locked up for it, wouldn't get as far as me. I look for the killers they don't have locked up. Take some sound advice from somebody Washburn says isn't a model policeman. Kill the bastard. Some men should be killed for the general good. This Chenko sounds like one of them. Even if a judge sends him away he'll get out sooner or later if the other jailbirds don't kill him.

"The hell with him! I'm more afraid for Kitty."

"With good reason, I would think. That's why I say kill him. He'll go after the woman first, if I know my man and I think I do. Kitty humiliated the fucker, and he won't forget it. Lamebrains like that get an idea in their head and it stays there because it's the only idea they have. There will come a time when you won't be around to protect your woman. Okay, call her what you like, but she's something to you now."

"I guess so," Morgan said.

The detective drained the rest of his beer and got up. "While you're deciding whether it's true love or just a fleeting romance, I've got to get back and see what Gallager's doing. More arrests are expected to follow, the paper says. I don't know who Gallager's going to arrest since the black pimp did it by himself. I'm going

to telephone Washburn when I get through. Grit your teeth
and do the same."

Kitty wasn't in her car when he got back. The guard
said, "She's been gone about an hour. Looked like she was
dressed to go to town. She don't confide in me, mister. She
don't even talk to me."

Scully said he didn't know any more than the guard did.
"That lady don't need nobody's permission for nothing
and wouldn't ask for it if she had to get it. Why didn't
I send a man with her? Why didn't I go myself? How
could I do that when I didn't know she was gone till my
man told me? Here one minute, gone the next. It's already
been reported in case you're thinking of running to the
old man. I'm in the clear on this, Morgan. Report me all
you goddamned like." Now I got work to do even if you
don't."

Morgan waited near Kitty's car long after it got dark.
Maybe he was making too much out of this; she could
have gone to one of the big new stores or the theater. She
had the right to go anywhere she pleased; still he cursed
her for her recklessness. Of all the times to go traipsing
around a strange city after dark!

She'd told him she didn't know a soul in Kansas City
so he had no idea where to look for her. But goddamn it
to hell, he'd have to do something soon.

He gave it another hour before he started for town. There
was light in Schlegel's car when he passed it. Schlegel
could wait; the son of a bitch wasn't going to run away.
Thinking maybe Kitty had come back and was somewhere
in the fairgrounds, he asked the guard at the gate if he'd
seen her. "Not a chance she'd come in here without me
seeing her. I been right here all evening. Sure I'm sure.
I ain't laid eyes on the lady."

Nothing but stray cats moved on the street to town. The show's working day was over; no more wagons or buggies or cabs came from town. The street was dark except for a streetlamp here and there. Walking fast, Morgan saw what looked like a covered buggy about 100 yards ahead. It was hard to tell what it was because of the bad light. He got closer and could feel the eyes of the driver turning to watch him.

He was walking past when Schlegel's voice said, "Over here, Morgan. Climb in. We're going for a ride. Get in, I said."

He walked toward the buggy, his hand close to his gun. It was hard to see Schlegel in the deep shadows. It was a warm night, but he wore a light topcoat with the collar turned up; his hat was pulled down over his eyes. There was no one else in the buggy.

"What's going on?" Morgan said. "You've been waiting for me to show up. Why?"

"I told you to get in," Schlegel repeated. "Never mind the gun. It won't do you any good. If you value Kitty's life, take your gun out of the holster and put it on the seat."

Schlegel picked up Morgan's gun and put it in his pocket. His dull voice was the same, but there was something new in it. The menace in it was controlled; Schlegel's twitchy hostility had been replaced by a complete lack of feeling. Morgan had never heard a voice with such emptiness in it.

The horse and buggy started off on the crushed rock surface of the street. Morgan started to say something, but Schlegel cut him short. "Ask no questions. I'll tell you what I want to tell you, nothing more. If there are questions to be asked, I'll ask them. I have Kitty, and there's no way you can find her except through me. She will remain unharmed as long as you do what you're told. I want some information from you, and holding Kitty prisoner is the only way to get it."

Schlegel urged the horse to a faster pace; there was no impatience in the way he touched the animal lightly with the buggy whip. They passed a uniformed policeman smoking a cigar in a dark doorway. Up ahead, some lights showed in the center of town; except for the saloon drinkers, Kansas City was still a town that went to bed early. Far away there was the rumble of a trolley.

Looking at Schlegel, who kept his eyes straight ahead, Morgan knew he had been marked as a Secret Service agent. It couldn't be anything else. But who had given Schlegel the information? He thought of Nancy Quillan, but what connection could there be between her and Schlegel? The thought that she had broken into Washburn's files, seen his name and sold it for money was all wrong. For all his peculiarities, Washburn was a clever man; more than likely, his filing cabinets contained nothing that could be used to ruin or sidetrack the investigation.

"How do I know you've got Kitty?" Morgan asked.

Schlegel didn't take his eyes from the road. "You know I have her or you wouldn't have come this far." There was no gloating in Schlegel's voice; he was simply stating the facts. "But if you want proof, reach into my side pocket and you'll find Kitty's revolver. It's not loaded, but you wouldn't use it if it was, for the obvious reason that you know I'm telling the truth."

Morgan looked at the worn .38 in its scuffed holster. There was no mistaking the gun or the holster; the gun in his hand had saved his life. From the moment Schlegel spoke Kitty's name, he knew he had her; this man was not the kind to try a bluff. Everything Schlegel did was thought out in advance; he calculated the odds, and bluffing had no part in his final decision.

"What information do you want?" Morgan asked. Schlegel was certain he was an agent or he wouldn't be doing something as desperate as this. But there was nothing desperate about him; not once had he raised his voice. Even his threat to harm Kitty sounded matter-of-fact, like one practical man talking to another.

"I want all the information you have to give," Schlegel said, "but I don't want to talk to you here. I want to question you with Kitty there, so you'll know I mean to get at the truth. You owe your life to Kitty. I know you are the kind of man who feels honor bound. You'll tell me what I want to know. I have invested many years of my life, and not you or the Secret Service will keep me from reaping the reward. Be quiet now."

"How far?" Morgan asked, not expecting to get an answer.

"Not far," Schlegel said. "You know you won't be coming back. Now is your chance to overpower me or call for the police, but you won't do it because of Kitty. I am not sneering at you, Morgan. I don't care about you one way or another. All I care about is what I have worked for all these years."

Morgan tried other questions but got no response. He wasn't even sure Schlegel heard him. Now they were in the center of town and heading for the new bridge over the Missouri; he could see the lights of Kansas City, Kansas, on the other side of the river. When they reached the approach to the bridge, Schlegel flicked the reins and drove down under the bridge. Houses and warehouses, old and rundown, lined the left side of the cobblestoned street, facing the side of the bridge. No lights showed anywhere; the sound of the iron-hooped buggy wheels echoed in the dark cavern of the bridge.

Morgan could smell the river, lapping at the pilings of the old steamboat docks that ran north and south from the bridge. The street went under the bridge, and Schlegel followed it. Schlegel turned the horse again and drove along the side of a high brick wall with broken bottles embedded in cement at the top. Schlegel halted the buggy in front of a high, sagging wooden gate, then he got down and pushed one side of the gate back until there was enough room to drive the buggy through. He told Morgan to drive the buggy into the yard, then bolted the gate. "Over there," he said, pointing at a squat brick building that might have had offices in it at one time. When Morgan got closer, there was enough light to make out the weathered sign over the door: MISSOURI STEAMBOAT & WAREHOUSE COMPANY.

The door was open, sagging on rusted hinges. Schlegel told Morgan to go in ahead of him. The room they were in smelled of rotting wood and old paper; a glimmer of light came from under a door on the far side of it. Schlegel opened the door and told Morgan to go in. The light, dull and yellow, came from a kerosene lamp standing on a packing case. Morgan smelled Chenko before he saw him. Before he could turn, an arm snaked around his neck, cutting off his wind, and he felt himself being lifted. His breath rattled in his chest. The smell of Chenko's huge body was strong. His feet were off the floor and he heard Schlegel saying, "Put him down. Don't kill him. Later you can kill him." He felt Schlegel struggling feebly with the big man. Chenko used his free hand to push Schlegel away, and there was a thump as Schlegel hit the floor. Chenko turned Morgan without effort and took hold of his throat. He lifted him off the floor and held him out at arm's length. Everything went black. . . .

"Wake up. Drink this," Schlegel was saying. Raw whisky trickled into Morgan's mouth, He was on the floor, with Schlegel kneeling beside him. The ;light had been turned up. "Stay still." Schlegel took the bottle away from his mouth, and Morgan lay on the floor until he was able to sit up. Schlegel helped him, solicitous as a male nurse. Morgan's throat hurt, and he wasn't sure he could stand. He turned his head and saw Kitty lying on a cot and Chenko sprawled on the floor with his own knife buried in his back. Morgan knew the knife, had seen it on the day of the fight. A smell of shit came from the dead man.

Chenko was dead and Schlegel had Kitty's revolver in his hand. There might be a chance now, Morgan thought. Schlegel reached into his pocket and tossed a pair of handcuffs toward Morgan. "Put them on," he ordered. "I want to hear them click shut." The handcuffs were the new kind with a chain joining the loops, and they didn't need a a key to lock them shut. Morgan picked them up and put them on. There was still a chance, he thought. He looked at Chenko. The back of Chenko's shirt was soaked with blood; it looked as if Schlegel had stabbed him many times before the blade finally pierced the heart. He wondered why Chenko hadn't been able to stop the short, elderly man from killing him. The shock of the first stab wounds must have weakened him, and of course he'd been drinking.

"I had to kill him," Schlegel said. "His job was to guard Kitty, to stop you from overpowering me when we got in here—and to kill both of you when there was no more to be learned."

Schlegel moved to the other side of the cot and put the muzzle of the gun against Kitty's head. "As you can see, she's alive and hasn't been abused."

Kitty was dressed in her town clothes as the guard had described. There were fingermarks on the white shirtwaist, but it hadn't been torn. Chenko must have grabbed her before he got too drunk. Kitty's wrists were handcuffed together, and her ankles were locked in leg-irons. She was in a deep sleep; a bottle labeled CHLORAL HYDRATE was on the packing case beside the lamp.

"You sit there and I'll sit here," Schlegel said, pointing to a chair set against the wall. There was another chair on the far side of the cot and Schlegel pulled it close enough so he could keep the gun pressed against Kitty's head.

Morgan didn't know how much chance there was, but as long as he was alive, there was some chance. Schlegel had done some quick thinking after he had been forced to kill Chenko. The set-up he had devised was pretty good. All he had to do was squeeze the trigger and Kitty was dead.

Kitty stirred on the dirty cot, but Schlegel didn't look at her. The gun was pressed against her ear and he kept it there. Morgan looked at Schlegel and hoped he could kill him. During the fight with Chenko there had been fierce anger, but he felt none of that now; he wouldn't need a killing rage to put an end to this man's life—if he got the chance.

"It's time to talk," Schlegel said.

Chapter Eleven

Right from the beginning, Morgan knew Schlegel wanted to do more than ask questions, though that's how it started out. But as he went on, some of the things he said were at odds with the cold, businesslike tone he wanted to establish. Whether he knew it or not—and Morgan didn't think he did—he felt the need to talk, not to explain himself—he was too coldly arrogant for that—but to tell someone what he had done and why he couldn't be stopped. It was as if he wanted to reassure himself that his plans would remain unchanged. Sometimes he seemed to be talking to himself, Morgan decided.

"You are a Secret Service agent or working with them," he stated. "Don't deny it. I have information that you are, and I believe that information to be correct."

"Where did you get it?"

Schlegel allowed the question. "I got it from the Chief of

Police. I suspected you were up to something—your sudden appearance at the fairgrounds, your lack of experience in show business, your farfetched story about the horses. But there was more to it than that. What made me suspicious more than anything else was your mealy-mouthed reason for not wanting to claim the reward money. No man turns down five thousand dollars if he's normal. I told you that when you came to me with your cock and bull story about the horses. From what I could see of you and what I had been told, you were a normal man, so I became suspicious. I am a suspicious man by nature. There was something wrong about you, I felt sure."

"That's hardly enough to send you to Gallager."

Kitty cried out in her sleep, and the handcuffs rattled as she tried to free her hands. The air was thick and foul in the shuttered room.

Schlegel said, "For you it might not be enough, but I am a respected figure in my business. Why not talk to the Chief of Police? Though not quite sober, he said he would do anything he could to help someone so close to Colonel Hardesty."

Just like that, Morgan thought.

"I asked the chief what he thought of your reason for not wanting the reward money. That was news to him, he said. Peculiar for a man not to want five thousand dollars. Then he winked at me and said maybe it wasn't so peculiar. I pressed him on the point and he talked to a Sergeant Praed. He said some lieutenant—Bender—had told Praed that you were coming in to claim the reward after all. If you lied about the money, you lied about other things. I asked the chief what he thought. He was getting restless by then. To get rid of me, he lowered his voice and told me there was no need to worry. You were not a criminal but a Secret Service agent. He couldn't give me any details, but it was absolutely true. And I mustn't tell anyone what he'd told me."

Just like that, Morgan thought. Gallager had put an X on him when all he wanted was another drink.

"I tried to get more information out of him," Schlegel went on, "but the telephone started ringing and suddenly his office was full of people babbling about a state senator's son who had been shot dead by a Negro. There was nothing to do but leave. My suspicions had been confirmed. You were a Secret Service agent or someone they were using. Which are you?"

"I am working for myself," Morgan said. "I can tell you how I got into this, and some of it can be checked."

Kitty cried out, "Don't touch me, you goddamned ape!" She raised her head, and though her eyes were open, she wasn't awake. Slowly her head sank back onto the dirty mattress.

"Tell me," Schlegel said. "I'll know if you're lying. Remember this, Morgan. I can revive Kitty and torture her." This was said with as much emotion as if he meant to wake her so she could look at a sample of new wallpaper.

Morgan fought back the urge to throw himself at Schlegel. The man was elderly but far from infirm, and the way he was holding the gun gave him the edge. Morgan told him about Bronc and how he came to be in the Kansas City jail. "I came here to try to clear him. I tried for the job in the show because the chief Secret Service agent here said he had linked the counterfeiting to the show. A private detective came to the same conclusion. The entire show was under suspicion before it even got here."

Schlegel stared at him. "Why did you suspect me? What had I done?"

"Nothing. Whoever was distributing the counterfeits had

to be someone who traveled, could go all over, stay away for days and weeks. That meant you, Cargill or Tillotson. They didn't fit, so that left you."

Schlegel kept on staring. Morgan thought it was strange to be having what sounded like a reasonable conversation with a man who intended to kill him and was ready to torture Kitty if he thought he was being lied to, but there was no other way to handle things. Threats wouldn't work; nothing he could think of would work. Getting old and with no bravado about him, Schlegel wasn't afraid because he believed he couldn't be touched. That in itself suggested that he was crazy behind the dull, quiet front he presented to the world. Maybe the deadness in the man was a sign of craziness.

"Then you know nothing about the Secret Service investigation itself?" Using his free hand, Schlegel bunched up a soiled pillow and used it to rest his hand holding the gun. Morgan had tensed, getting ready to spring forward if the gun moved away from Kitty's head. The gun stayed where it was.

"I know you are on Washburn's list of suspects," Morgan said. "If he has evidence against you, he hasn't told me." Morgan knew he had to tread warily now. If Schlegel caught him in a single lie, Kitty would suffer for it. With nothing better to offer, Morgan threw out what would surely be thrown back at him. "Why don't you get out? You must have enough money to go anywhere. Money buys anything if you have enough of it."

Schlegel's eyes bored into him; there was life in there after all. "Would it buy you, Morgan?"

"Sure it would."

"You're lying. You got into this because of a half-dead old man. You're facing death because of a woman. Money has nothing to do with it."

"If you think I'm a man of honor, let us go and I'll give my word I won't talk. Kitty will do what I tell her. What the hell do I care about counterfeiting? Chenko's just a pile of dead meat to me. Anybody could have killed him in a place like this. Could be weeks—months—before the body is found. Police won't bother much. What's to tie you in to Chenko?"

"Nothing. We had the show in common, that's all. Chenko approached me in the street, begging for a handout. He was drunk and had lost his money. I knew he had been fired. He started cursing you and Kitty, blaming you for the loss of his job. I had been thinking about you, what Gallager had told me. I told Chenko I would help him if he would help me. Chenko had been a tramp at one time and knew of this place. He abducted Kitty and brought her here. I waited for you."

"But why kill us?" You'll hang if they catch you."

"Thirty years in prison is worse than hanging, so why not kill you? The police will see it this way. Chenko abducted Kitty and got you here by threatening to kill her if you didn't come. Kitty had already been killed, stabbed to death with Chenko's knife. You stabbed Chenko to death with the same knife, but he managed to shoot you before he died. The police will close the case."

Morgan made one last appeal; it probably would do no good, but it might keep Schlegel talking. "You're killing us for nothing."

"You are nothing," Schlegel said.

"You should be talking to Washburn," Morgan said.

"There would be no easy way to get Washburn here. He wouldn't come alone. I wanted to find out what you knew."

"Then you mean to go on?"

"Yes. But I will quit the show and disappear as I have

in the past. I will lay low for as long as I have to, then the counterfeit money will reappear. I was a swindler when I was a young man. Forgery always fascinated me. I was sent to prison for having forged U.S. bonds in my possession, but I didn't forge them. I have no skill in that direction. My guilt was in doubt, the police perjured themselves, and the judge knew it. I got five years instead of ten or fifteen. In prison I met a man who convinced me that counterfeiting is the quickest way to a fortune. He was a master engraver, maybe the best in the country, but I had to wait for him to get out. I waited. I waited so long. I grew old waiting. Now it's all possible—everything. The ten dollar bill is just the beginning. Other plates have been made. I will flood this country and other countries with counterfeit money. I may never retire. Why should I?"

Somehow Morgan knew it was close to the end; Schlegel had talked himself out. He tried to think of something to say that would drag it out a few more minutes. "Listen to me, Schlegel—"

"No," Schlegel said. "I am going to kill you now." He moved the gun a few inches from Kitty's head. It was a double-action, but he thumbed back the hammer, a steadier way of shooting. Morgan braced himself for the bullet, but it didn't come. The door slammed open and Bender leveled his revolver at Schlegel. "Drop it or I'll drop you!" he shouted. Schlegel set down the hammer and dropped the gun on the floor. Then he raised his hands above his head. Bender moved into the room with Washburn behind him. Two men were behind Washburn. "You're under arrest, Schlegel," the agent said. "The charge is conspiracy to manufacture and distribute counterfeit U.S. currency."

This was federal business and Bender kept out of it. Washburn ran his hands over Schlegel's body, looking for weapons, and found none. The keys to the handcuffs and leg-irons were on the packing case. Bender unlocked Morgan's handcuffs before he freed Kitty from the handcuffs and leg-irons. Kitty groaned but didn't wake up. "Better cuff him," Bender said.

Schlegel's hands remained above his head. "Please, not yet. I want to talk." Washburn was staring at Chenko's body. "I want to make a deal with you," Schlegel said. "I killed that man there to save Morgan's life. Morgan will tell you that. Tell him, Morgan."

"No," Morgan said. "I was in handcuffs. Chenko wasn't doing anything. You stabbed him from behind and kept on stabbing him till he died."

Morgan glanced at Bender; the detective was rubbing his face to hide a smile.

"He's lying," Schlegel said. "He wants to hang me. Everybody knows Chenko is a drunken, dangerous lunatic. No jury will convict me of murder."

"At the moment, the charge is counterfeiting," Washburn said.

"You have got to make a deal," Schlegel said, as if there could be no question about it. "If I get thirty years, you will never find the plates. The money will continue to be made and distributed. There are other ten dollar plates and also plates in other denominations. I will take you to where the plates are, but you must guarantee a reduced sentence if I am convicted."

"You'll be convicted," the agent said. "No deal."

"Talk to your superiors," Schlegel said. "They will make a deal to get the plates."

"No deal." Washburn told the two men outside to come in.

Washburn turned to Schlegel. "I don't have to make a deal with you. Your confederate, Henry Glidden, is dead and you killed him." Schlegel's expression remained the same. "Our Philadelphia agents finally traced him through a doctor who had been treating him for a lifelong lung disease after his release from prison. Glidden was close to death and would make no more plates, so you killed him to tidy things up. Our agents discovered his strangled body in a closet in the little house he bought, and only you and the doctor knew about it. You and Glidden had keys to the bank strongbox where the plates and counterfeits were kept, except that you didn't know Glidden had removed the plates and money and destroyed them. Glidden suspected you were going to kill him, but what could he do? Go to the police? He was a dead man anyway, but he didn't want to die in prison. He destroyed everything to spite you."

"I should have checked the strongbox," Schlegel, talking to no one but himself. "I had his key. I thought everything was safe. A mistake."

Washburn was startled but recovered quickly. "I am going to hang you for Glidden's murder or send you to prison for thirty years." He turned to the two agents. "Put the handcuffs on him."

One of the men was moving toward him when Schlegel started to cough. He coughed until spit dribbled from his mouth. "My handkerchief," he gasped. "May I use my handkerchief?" Washburn nodded. Schlegel's handkerchief was stuffed in his sleeve, and he lowered his right hand to get it. Out came the handkerchief and the small one-shot derringer concealed in it. It was pointing at Washburn's chest when Morgan's gun snaked out and killed Schlegel with a head shot.

"That's two dumb policemen you've saved in less than a week. "You've got a lot to learn," Bender said to Washburn, who looked at Schlegel's body but didn't say anything.

One of the agents got a window open to get rid of some of the stink. Washburn still looked faint.

"Gallager will have to be notified," Bender said. "I don't want to be here when he gets here. Maybe I can come with him. A double killing will bring him out. Tell Gallager we have a woman here needs a doctor."

"I don't need any damn doctor," Kitty said from the bed. She was sitting up, yawning and rubbing her wrists. She saw the two dead men. "Jesus Christ, this looks like a slaughterhouse. What the hell's been going on?"

Morgan told her. "You mean I slept through all that?" she said.

"I better get going," Bender said.

"Stay," the agent told him. "Gallager is through, if I have anything to do with him. It's time you came out in the open, Bender. Gallager won't do a thing to you, nothing that will stick. Let him say what he likes."

Washburn told one of the agents to notify the chief of police, then went to the window to breathe fresh air. Kitty was sitting on the edge of the cot, still rubbing her wrists. Bender sat down. It wouldn't be long before the police got there.

"How'd you find this place?" Morgan asked Bender. With all that had been going on, nobody had thought to explain.

Bender said, "Washburn took the tail off you and I put one on. It looked like we were getting somewhere, and I didn't want you dead at the finish. I put the Yellow Kid to work. He followed you before you got into the buggy with Schlegel, and he followed the two of you here. The Kid got nervous when you didn't come out for a long time, so he came looking for me. I met Washburn rushing in as I was rushing out."

Bender let Washburn finish it. "News had just come in over the wire from the Leavenworth warden. He'd finally talked to Vickers, the retired guard. Apart from the heavy beard, the one thing he remembered about Swain was his lisp. Vickers himself has a lisp, and he remembered Swain because of it. His testimony won't be needed now. I feel rather let down." The agent looked at Schlegel's body. "I wonder why he gave up his gun in the first place."

Bender shrugged. "Schlegel was no desperado. With guns pointing at him, he dropped his. Then you told him he was going to hang or go up for thirty years. I guess he decided a quick death was better than thirty years in jail or waiting around to be hung."

Kitty stood up and would have fallen if Morgan hadn't caught her. Her face was a pasty white. "I'm going to be sick. Help me get outside." They got outside, and Morgan stood behind her and held her up while she vomited. It took a while before the spasms passed and she was able to talk. Morgan told her to take it easy.

Sick or not, she flared up at him, but there wasn't much fire in it. "Don't be telling me to take it easy. I've been manhandled, dragged through back alleys, put in irons—and you tell me to take it easy." Morgan said nothing. "I don't like a man to see me sick like that."

"Everybody throws up now and then," Morgan said. "He fed you dope. Better not go back in there. I'll find you something to sit on. The police ought to be here soon."

Morgan found an empty barrel, and she sat on the edge of it. "Jesus, I'm tired," Kitty said. "I started thinking about the river when they put those leg-irons on." A shudder ran through her body. "I could be at the bottom of the river. We both could."

"I guess."

There was a long silence. "I wasn't sure you'd come," Kitty said. "I don't know if I would. You knew they meant to kill you, but you came anyway. Was it because I helped you with Chenko?"

"That's right. One good turn . . . and so on."

"Would you have come if you hadn't owed me?"

Morgan was getting tired of this nagging at something that was over and done. "How do I know what I'd do? Some days I'm braver than other days. Let it go."

"All right, we'll let it go."

It wasn't like Kitty to stay quiet for long, but she did. What she'd been through had rattled her good. Who wouldn't be rattled? Morgan thought. Maybe the shock would do her some good; she could be such a bitch when she got going.

She gave a jaw-breaking yawn and rubbed her eyes. "I've been thinking of my lovely big bed. I won't feel safe till I'm in it with the door locked."

"Don't count on getting there soon." Lights were showing down by the docks; there was the rumble of iron wheels. "We'll all have to go down to headquarters and sign statements. Here comes Gallager now."

The gate was dragged open, and Gallager's black and gold paddy wagon led the way; the two other paddy wagons were painted in regular police black. According to Bender, Gallager had a single bed and a rack for bottles and glasses in the back of his wagon. Gallager's driver pulled up the horses, and Kansas City's top lawman climbed down. He was a squarely built man of middle height; only his face gave evidence of years of dissipation. Its pinkness was due more to hot barbers' towels than good health. His blue uniform glittered with gold buttons, and the peak of his cap was a tangle of gold braid. Two cabs full of newspaper reporters drove into the yard while Gallager was staring at Kitty. The yard was bright with the gasoline lights carried by uniformed policemen.

Washburn and Bender came out. Gallager's face lost some of its pink geniality when he saw the chief of detectives. "Well, now," he said with a slight Irish accent. "Nothing was said about you being here, Lieutenant. Was that an oversight, Mr. Washburn? It seems to me that something irregular is going on here."

The reporters were crowding round, and Gallager was getting set to make the most of it. Son of a bitch thinks he's finally found a way to give Bender the push, Morgan thought. If Washburn doesn't stand up for him, he'll be swimming in a cesspool.

"One moment, Chief," Washburn said as he took Gallager by the arm and led him aside. The agent talked quietly; at first, Gallager argued back, but a minute or so later he simply nodded his head and listened. His smile, not as genial as it had been, was in place when he came back.

"What was that all about, Chief?" one of the reporters wanted to know.

"No questions till we get through here, Alex," Gallager said. "Then you can fire away till you're blue in the face. Let's go in, lads."

Gallager and Washburn went in, followed by Bender, Morgan and Kitty; last came two reporters and two photographers, carrying bulky box cameras and magnesium flash holders. The uniformed policemen were told to stay outside.

"Well, will you look at what we have here," Gallager said when he saw the bodies. A strong smell of whisky came from Kansas City's top lawman. "Mr. Washburn, your agent was very close-mouthed. Wouldn't tell a thing except you had two dead men on your hands."

Washburn stated the bare facts, and the reporters scribbled in their notebooks. They didn't like the agent's way of telling it, and notebooks snapped shut when he refused to elaborate.

"I'm sure Chief Gallager will fill you in later," the agent told them. He raised his arm when the magnesium lights flared in his face. Gallager, a great favorite of the press, showed all his false teeth, like the old actor he was. Done with primping for the moment, he called in a uniformed lieutenant and told him to cart away the bodies, then he said he'd see them all at headquarters.

With Gallager gone, the reporters turned to Kitty, but she refused to answer any questions. "Talk to the show's publicity agent, Fred Cargill," she told them, getting mad when they kept on pushing it. "No, I don't want to ride in your cab. In fact, go fuck yourselves!" That was more like the Kitty we all know and love, Morgan thought. Better that than rehashing what she'd been through.

A paddy wagon took them to police headquarters. Kitty liked the policemen better than the reporters. She told them that her Uncle Cornelius was a patrolman back in New York. It was turning out all right, Morgan thought, except that Bronc was still in jail. He had tried to talk to Washburn about it but had been told, "Later. I'll talk to you later. I think something can be done." For now he had to be satisfied with that, but surely the stiff-necked agent wouldn't keep an old, sick man in jail when the two main counterfeiters were dead and the case cracked wide open. He didn't know what he'd do if Washburn didn't talk to the U.S. Attorney and get Bronc out from behind bars. The trouble with Washburn was you never knew what he was thinking; if ever a man was hard to figure, it was the agent with the high collar.

The taking of their statements was supervised by Bender who wanted to be sure nothing got in there that shouldn't be in there. After they signed the statements Bender said they could leave. There would be no inquest; it was a straightforward case. Just then Colonel Jud came bustling in, followed by Fred Cargill. The old man was in full wild west regalia and was hopping mad.

"Reporters got me out of bed. I thought I must be dreaming. What have they done to you, my child?" he said to Kitty.

"Nothing, Jud." Kitty yawned. "You mind if I don't go into it now?"

"Of course not," the colonel said, then started berating the dead Chenko. He called him a monster, a maniac, a crawling dog and a sack of cockroaches. When he ran out of words to describe Chenko, he started on Schlegel. Among other things, he called him a viper in the bosom of his family. Kitty yawned all through his tirade and finally said, "Sorry, Jud, we have to leave."

Knowing Kitty, Fred Cargill didn't try to detain her; all he did was sketch a newspaper page with his hands. "Hardesty show star rescued by handsome assistant," he said. "What do you think, Kitty? We can play this big or play it small."

"Go fuck yourself, Fred," Kitty said. "Talk to you tomorrow."

Chapter Twelve

Dawn was streaking the sky when Morgan and Kitty finally got to bed. Kitty was strangely subdued. She asked him if she could fix him breakfast, get him a beer—or was there something else he wanted?

"I want you," Morgan said. "As much of you as I can get. Let's get to it, lady."

A little spark showed in her eyes. "Let's not be giving me orders, big man. I'll spread them when I'm good and ready." She smiled at him. "I'm ready now."

This time she didn't fight him. At first he didn't know why she just stood there beside the bed, then he got it— she wanted him to take her clothes off. She kissed him as he did it, her hands unbuttoning his pants and reaching in for his cock. She brought it out, long and hard. We should be dead, but we're not, Morgan thought. He got the feeling that Kitty was thinking the same thing. Then they were on the bed and her legs were wide open, and she held his cock and guided it into her. It went in smoothly, and she sighed with contentment as her legs closed around his back. But it wasn't like the way it was that first day, when it had been a fierce tussle from beginning to end. They had been strangers then; now they were friends. Morgan hadn't minded her old way of fucking; any way was all right with him. He wondered if she was trying to make up for all the times she'd been bitchy. If that's what it was, that was all right, too. He shafted her steadily and she kneaded his ass, murmuring as she did it and nibbling at his earlobe with small white teeth. He was tired, as she was, after the goddamned awful night, but neither of them had any thought of sleep. The close call with death had changed Kitty, he felt sure. Her aggressiveness, her sometimes bitter humor had been sluffed off like a snakeskin, and he found himself thinking it might not be a bad thing to stay with her for a while, if she wanted him to stay, that is.

But even as he thought about it, he knew it wouldn't work. He had said no to Bronc's offer of a partnership for the same reason. Two quick-tempered people, even the best of friends, couldn't be together all the time. Sooner or later, a quarrel would flare, and because they were the best of friends, there could well be cause for lasting bitterness. He liked the new Kitty, but it was possible that all she felt for him was gratitude, which might be fine in the beginning but might not be enough to keep her from slipping back into her old ways. Matter of fact, there was no way to prevent that; people were what they were. He didn't want to leave her with curses ringing in his ears and things thrown at his head.

He had told her to take it easy the night before. Now he told himself to do the same; better to concentrate on the here and now than to waste time thinking of how it was going to end. The thing to do was to get out before tiredness set in, then they could remain friends. He knew a few independent women who couldn't stand the thought of being stuck with one man for their entire lives. Most of these women had remained good friends, and he always went to see them if his drifting took him close to where they lived. They took him into their beds, but he knew when he had to move on before it got stale. It wasn't a bad way to live, to keep women as lovers and friends, without ever crossing the line on the other side of which lay uneasiness and strain. There was no strain here and now; it couldn't have been more relaxed.

"Penny for your thoughts," Kitty said.

"I was thinking how good it is to be here in Martha Washington's bed where nobody can get at us and we can make love all day if we like."

Kitty laughed. "I'll bet George and Martha never had as good a time as this."

"Who knows? They didn't call him the father of his country for nothing."

"You'll be leaving any day now?" Kitty ended the question with a groan. "Oh Jesus, Morgan, what did you just do to me? Do it again."

Morgan kept on doing it till she came, then lay weak and happy under him. She pulled his face close to hers and kissed him. "I'm not sure I want to say goodbye to you. I guess this life, my kind of a life, wouldn't suit you."

"Fraid not," Morgan said, "but I might stay on for a while. Right now I have to stay because of Bronc. After he's released or locked up—I don't want to think about that part—I'll decide what I want to do."

"Take your time. There's no hurry. Those horses of yours can wait. Tell them a pretty lady needs you more than they do. I guess you'll be going back in the horse business after you get the reward money. Is five thousand enough to get started again?"

"It would do, depending on how big or small a place you had in mind. I'll have to think about it." He let Kitty get out from under him, and she sat clutching her knees. In a few moments she began to play with his cock which started to rise up again.

"Have you noticed I never suck your cock?"

Morgan smiled, amused by the directness of the question. "Well, no, I can't say that I have. I've been busy doing other things. But now that you've brought it up, why haven't you sucked my cock?"

"Because I didn't want to. Don't get mad. I think a girl has to like a man an awful lot before she gives him a blow job—unless she's being paid to do it, of course."

"Of course," Morgan agreed.

"Even J.P. Morgan doesn't have enough money to get me to suck his cock. Think about it. I'm going to give you a suck that all J.P. Morgan's millions can't buy. I'm going to give you the best blow job you ever had in your whole life."

"Sounds good."

"That's no way to describe it. I'll have you begging for mercy—"

A loud knock sounded on the door. Whoever it was knocked again when there was no answer. Then Morgan recognized Bender's voice and said, "I have to open it."

"Jesus Christ!" Kitty said. "Open the fucking thing."

"Sorry to break in, folks," Bender said as he came in, "but there's something I have to tell you." He tapped the gold badge pinned to his lapel. "Where do you think I got this?"

Morgan took a closer look at the badge. "You murdered

Gallager and stole his badge. You're really the new chief of police?"

"That I am. And I didn't have to kill good old Pete Gallager to get the job. Good old Brewster Washburn got it for me. Last night after you left and things quieted down, Mayor Yost came to headquarters, and the three of them—Washburn, Gallager, Yost—were in Gallager's office for an awful long time. I was not invited. My office is on the same floor as Gallager's, and at first I heard a lot of yelling, mostly done by Gallager. After a while, the yelling stopped, and I knew they were deep in conversation of a practical nature."

"You mean you had your ear to the door," Kitty said.

"No, it was the air shaft. I didn't have my ear to anything, but there are no secrets at police headquarters. The three of them were talking about me. Anyway, I was a good part of it. Washburn didn't pull any punches. Went right after Gallager and told him it was time he retired. If he didn't, there was a strong possibility that he'd be charged with obstructing the investigation of a federal case. Namely, Gallager had told Schlegel you were a Secret Service agent, putting your life in danger and jeopardizing the entire investigation. Gallager denied it—what else?—and wanted to know where Washburn got this false information. Washburn said, 'Schlegel told Morgan and he told me. We are both willing to testify to that.' "

"He lies pretty good," Morgan said.

"In the interest of justice, you bet," Bender said. "Yost was worried by the way it was going, but he tried to stick up for his man. He didn't deny the charge was serious; on the other hand, why should a fine chief of police like Gallager be made to resign? Not a bit daunted, Washburn said Gallager had been a rotten chief of police, and information about his longtime grafting would be made public at his trial. He would see to that personally. Yost was scared shitless but still hummed and hawed. It was then that Washburn came right out and said the government contracts held by Yost's son would be investigated by the Secret Service. 'Your son holds the contracts, but you are the real owner of the plant,' Washburn said. 'If we find any irregularities, the contracts will be nullified and you may find yourself charged with defrauding the federal government.' That did it."

Kitty wasn't as interested as Morgan was; she just wanted to get back to bed. So did he, but Bender had been a good friend and he wanted to hear him out. After years of walking a tightrope, Bender finally had his feet on solid ground.

"So Gallager got the shove," Kitty said. "Yost stays on as mayor?"

"That was the deal Washburn worked out. Gallager goes, Yost stays. I doubt if he could make the charge against Gallager stick. Yost was more scared of the publicity than the charge. In return for his cooperation, Yost's meat packing plan would not be investigated, but I wouldn't be surprised if Washburn double-crosses the Yosts the first chance he gets. That sure as hell would upset Mrs. Yost's plan to go to Washington as a senator's wife."

That struck Kitty as funny. "So Yost goes to Washington, maybe, and Gallager goes out in the street. Poor Gallager."

"Don't cry for Gallager," Bender said. "That man has grafted enough to retire to the finest castle in Ireland, but the rumor is he's going to go to work for Yost's son at a handsome salary. Gallager knows too much to be left out in the street."

"Funny man, Washburn," Morgan said. "I guess he gets things done in his own peculiar way."

"He's more than peculiar," Bender said. "He's as cold-hearted a man as I ever met. You know what he said to me after I was called in and Yost appointed me chief? He said, 'Congratulations Bender, but I'll be watching you, too.' I'll do my best, but there's no way I can guarantee a Sunday School police department. I won't last. I know that. Yost may get to Washington—stranger things have happened—but I won't last. No honest flatfoot ever does. But I'll damn well make things hum for a while."

"Try to last till suppertime," Kitty said impatiently. "Get out of here, Bender. Go and arrest somebody. You're spoiling the fun here."

Kitty found a DO NOT DISTURB sign in a dresser drawer, hung it outside and locked the door. "I should have thought of that in the first place," she said, getting back into bed with Morgan. "Now where were we?"

"You were about to give me the best blow job I ever had in my life. I'm still looking forward to it." Morgan smiled at her and stroked her breasts.

"As well you might, my good man. Jesus, it's so big. I don't know if it'll fit in my mouth." But she was just kidding; it fit fine. "Just lay back, Morgan. I'm going to drive you crazy."

And so she did. Morgan had been sucked by professionals, women who really knew what they were doing, but he couldn't remember anything as good as this. Every time he was ready to come—wanted desperately to come—she did something to his balls that allowed the almost unbearable excitement to go on and on. His hands cupped her face, feeling the movement of her mouth as she sucked him. Her eyes were closed, and he got the crazy picture of a woman praying. At certain moments, she took so much of his cock into her mouth that he wondered it didn't choke her, but she knew exactly what she was doing. Other times just the throbbing bulb of his cock was in her mouth and she tongued it until sweat broke out all over him. As long as he lived, no matter how many times he got sucked, this would be the blow job he'd always remember.

Kitty opened her eyes; they smiled at him, telling him to get ready. And then she began to suck him with all her might, and when he shot his load into her mouth it was pulled back into her throat by the terrific suction. He felt as if everything inside him was being sucked into her mouth and swallowed. His orgasm was so overwhelming that he could scarcely move after it was over.

She didn't wipe her mouth when she lay down beside him, one hand stroking his cock, the other brushing back her tangled red hair. Morgan's middle finger, wet with her hot juices, played with her clit until she came, and while she was coming his finger pressed against her clit, prolonging her pleasure and making her gasp.

"You'd think we were never going to get another chance to do it," Kitty said. "We've been going at it since cock crow—there's a funny word—and we haven't let up since. Why is that, would you say?"

"We're greedy. We can't get enough. That's why."

"You think there's something wrong with that?"

"Lord, no. I'd think there was something wrong with us if we didn't want so much. That's how I feel, and I hope you feel the same."

"You bet I do. What good is it if you're young and strong and have the right equipment and don't make use of your gifts. I like your equipment, Morgan. It fits my equipment like it was made for it. You probably think I've had a lot of cocks in me."

"Never gave it thought," Morgan said.

"I haven't had as many cocks in me as you think. I can go quite a spell without a big cock, then the moment comes when I just have to get fucked—like the day the colonel hired you. I wasn't so mad at you as I was horny. Didn't like you much and being horny made me worse. You were the answer to a maiden's prayer."

Morgan grinned at her. "It didn't look like it at the time."

Kitty grinned back. "I'll bet you really thought you were bucking the tiger when you got in bed with me. I was mad at myself, mad at you and mad at the world, so I tried to break your balls."

"They're still a little sore," Morgan said, "But I know you'll kiss them and make them well."

That got a loud laugh. "You conceited son of a bitch. Just a while ago I gave you a blow job like few men have ever had, and now you want me to kiss your balls. Why not, if it'll make you happy."

Kitty put her head between his legs and didn't just kiss his balls, she licked them. His hands were buried in her hair and he couldn't see her face, but he could feel her hot tongue licking the salt and her own come from his balls. Morgan lay back, feeling the need to sleep pressing down on him, but if Kitty didn't sleep, he wouldn't either. Of course, sooner or later they'd have to sleep, but for the moment they were like drinkers at a weeklong party, knowing they should quit if only for a little while, but not wanting to because something drove them on.

Morgan raised Kitty's head, and she stretched out beside him. "You've done enough for me. What would you like me to do for you that I haven't done? I won't mind what you ask me to do."

Kitty thought for a while. "I've never had a man put his tongue in me down there," she said almost shyly. "Somehow it never happened. I think about it sometimes."

She was still shy when Morgan started to position himself between her legs, but the shyness didn't last long. "Jesus Christ, I'm going to shoot somebody," she cried out in sudden rage when there was another knock at the door. "Can't they see the sign, the dumb bastards? Don't answer it. Let them go to hell!"

Somebody was calling out in an old man's complaining voice. Kitty told Morgan he was crazy when he said it sounded like Bronc. "I've got to take a look," he said. "If it's Bronc I have to let him in. If it isn't I'll get rid of whoever it is."

But it *was* Bronc, and he climbed the steel steps like the stiff old man he was. Kitty had her robe on by then and Morgan his pants. Morgan put out his hand and pulled Bronc up from the last step. Bronc, always a bit cranky, was building up a full head of steam.

"That fucking Washburn finally got them to let me out," Bronc said, groaning as he settled into a chair. "You know what that shit-brained bastard son of a bitch says to me on the steps of the city jail? 'Get yourself a pair of glasses,' he says. "As if glasses would've made any difference. That dud money that got passed on me looked like the real thing."

"Glasses might have helped you to spot the fakes," Morgan said. "You might have seen the serial numbers were all the same. Washburn is right—get some glasses. That way you won't take any wooden nutmegs."

"Nutmegs I wouldn't mind. That fucking Washburn, the nerve of the man." Bronc peered at Kitty. "You're a real good looker, ain't you? That red hair and all. You wouldn't have a bottle of whisky on the premises?"

Kitty pretended to peer back at him. "You ain't so bad looking yourself. But no whisky. And watch your fucking language. There's a lady present. That's your cue to say, 'Where? Where?' "

Bronc looked at Morgan. "I can't figure out what she's saying. Have you taken up with a crazy woman? No offense, missy. My first and only wife was a mite tetched in a holy sort of a way. Made me give up whisky and bad language."

Kitty winked at Morgan. "I'd say she failed in her efforts. About the whisky, you'll have to wait till you get back to town."

Bronc made himself more comfortable in his chair. "Had a few snorts on the way down here. I'm here to say goodbye, Lee. To tell you thanks for everything."

"You mean you're not going back to Talcott?"

"Nope. Can't stand the thought of going back to a town I was shamed in. Russell Bowdry will go over there to wrap things up. Sell whatever's left to sell, put the money in the bank, transfer my funds East. Guess you wouldn't want to come East for a visit, boy." Bronc gave Kitty another farsighted look. "Guess not. Damned if I would. You got yourself a real armful this time. Well, I'd best be going. Treat this boy nice, missy. He's the best."

Back in bed, Kitty said, laughing about it, "I wonder who else can come in here today. Jud and the show people know better. What do you say to Washburn? I don't know him, but you do. You want to bet he won't come knocking at my door?"

"I don't want to bet on a thing like that. Might bring bad luck, like a black cat or putting your hat on the bed. I wouldn't mind if I never saw Washburn again. I have a sneaking respect for the man. He gets things done. He got Bronc out of the hoosegow. If he had any sense, he wouldn't have arrested Bronc in the first place. Washburn, the goddamned stuffed-shirt, was what got me here."

"Washburn's not so bad," Kitty said, grinning.

"I just don't want to talk to him," Morgan said.

Kitty snuggled up close. "If he comes, we won't answer the door. Let him get a warrant if he wants to get in here."

Morgan yawned. "We'd do a lot better if we went to a hotel. I mean that. It's been like Saturday night at the crossroads around here."

"Or like Broadway and Forty-Second Street any time of the day or night." She coughed discreetly, giving him a hint. You were about to."

No amount of knocking could disturb what Morgan did next. Let them fire off a cannon; it would make no difference. Kitty wanted this and she was going to get it, come hell or high water. He opened her legs, stretched out so his legs were off the end of the bed, and began to tongue her. He did it slowly at first so she would get used to it. Her ass began to move and her crotch bumped up gently in his face. He tongued her faster, and soon she was crying out in sheer pleasure, begging him not to stop. Tears of happiness rolled down her face, and she cried out to him. Some of the things she said he understood, some he didn't, but the meaning was unmistakable. She screamed when he pushed his tongue up into her for an instant. "It feels like a cock! It feels like a cock!" And she came; God how she came! His mouth and face were wet with her hot juices; it smelled of her and he breathed it in. "Oh, I can't stop coming! Don't make me stop coming!"

But she had to stop because she was exhausted; her body was dripping with sweat and all her muscles were trembling. Morgan tried to lift his head, and for an instant she trapped it with her thighs, not wanting to let him go. Once again they lay together, and they both knew they couldn't go on. Soon they would drift off into a deep sleep, but they weren't ready to do that yet. A breeze blew through the open window, drying the sweat on their bodies. Outside the sounds of the show went on as before; he heard the colonel's voice booming at somebody who had done something wrong. There was the usual hammering as boards were nailed into place. A week or so ago he would never have believed that he would come to be in a place like this, but now it was over. Bronc was free and heading back East. The things that happen to a man, Morgan thought.

"I don't know that I'll ever get to Idaho," Kitty said, all the energy drained out of her. But the tension was gone too; after today it would be a long time before it returned. Morgan hoped that there was a man around—a man she liked—when it did.

"I may not even be there," Morgan said, "but I'll always know where to find you."

"You could be wrong about that. They say Little Laura Chase is losing her touch. I may go and talk to Captain Jack Crawford. He's got much the same show as Jud, but he isn't as old, not as set in his ways. Maybe I'd like a change. I started out in a shooting gallery and here I am. Too bad you can't see the show life. We could be a team."

Morgan kissed her. "No deal, as Washburn likes to say. Let's not even talk about it."

Kitty snuggled up to him. "You're right. I'm like a kid wanting things to stay the same. I hope you won't forget me. I'll never forget you. Like the man said, it's been a pleasure meeting you. Now you're supposed to say, but the pleasure is all mine."

Morgan said it, and it was true. "Don't be getting weepy about it. We're in a wild west show, not a melodrama. We'll get back together, you'll see."

"Damn right I will. I might even get up to Idaho. Can't guarantee it though. Well, we've finally worn ourselves out, my dear friend. I'm ready to drop dead of fatigue, but it was worth every minute of it. What say we get some sleep? Holy Mother of God, that can't be another knock at the door. Maybe it's time we went to that hotel."

"Don't answer it," Morgan said.

Kitty got out of bed and put her gown on. "No, I'm going to see who it is. I won't sleep easy if I don't find out who it is. So far we've had Bender and Bronc. It has got to be Washburn out there."

Morgan stretched out to his full length. It could be Rutherford B. Hayes out there for all he cared. He wanted to sleep, and maybe when he got enough of it he'd be ready to go again.

"It's Washburn, all right," Kitty said, coming back to the bed. But Morgan wasn't listening. He was already asleep.

FALCON'S MISTRESS

Donna Birdsell

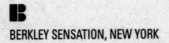

BERKLEY SENSATION, NEW YORK

THE BERKLEY PUBLISHING GROUP
Published by the Penguin Group
Penguin Group (USA) Inc.
375 Hudson Street, New York, New York 10014, USA
Penguin Group (Canada), 90 Eglinton Avenue East, Suite 700, Toronto, Ontario M4P 2Y3, Canada
(a division of Pearson Penguin Canada Inc.)
Penguin Books Ltd., 80 Strand, London WC2R 0RL, England
Penguin Group Ireland, 25 St. Stephen's Green, Dublin 2, Ireland (a division of Penguin Books Ltd.)
Penguin Group (Australia), 250 Camberwell Road, Camberwell, Victoria 3124, Australia
(a division of Pearson Australia Group Pty. Ltd.)
Penguin Books India Pvt. Ltd., 11 Community Centre, Panchsheel Park, New Delhi—110 017, India
Penguin Group (NZ), Cnr. Airborne and Rosedale Roads, Albany, Auckland 1310, New Zealand
(a division of Pearson New Zealand Ltd.)
Penguin Books (South Africa) (Pty.) Ltd., 24 Sturdee Avenue, Rosebank, Johannesburg 2196, South
Africa

Penguin Books Ltd., Registered Offices: 80 Strand, London WC2R 0RL, England

This is a work of fiction. Names, characters, places, and incidents either are the product of the author's imagination or are used fictitiously, and any resemblance to actual persons, living or dead, business establishments, events, or locales is entirely coincidental. The publisher does not have any control over and does not assume any responsibility for author or third-party websites or their content.

FALCON'S MISTRESS

A Berkley Sensation Book / published by arrangement with the author

PRINTING HISTORY
Berkley Sensation edition / October 2005

ISBN: 0-425-20634-3

BERKLEY® SENSATION
Berkley Sensation Books are published by The Berkley Publishing Group,
a division of Penguin Group (USA) Inc.,
375 Hudson Street, New York, New York 10014.
BERKLEY SENSATION and the "B" design are trademarks belonging to Penguin Group (USA) Inc.

PRINTED IN THE UNITED STATES OF AMERICA

10 9 8 7 6 5 4 3 2 1

To Mom and Dad,
with much love and gratitude.

Acknowledgments

I would like to acknowledge the men and women of the Carolina Raptor Center in Huntersville, North Carolina, for their dedication to the rehabilitation of injured and orphaned birds of prey. I would especially like to thank Elaine Cordivae and Larry Dickerson for answering my endless questions about the care of raptors and the art of falconry. Any mistakes are completely my own.

PROLOGUE

Lockwell Hall
England
October 1761

Forgetting the two hundred guests gathered in the ballroom for his birthday, the Duke of Canby ran through the woods, his gait uneven, his heart unusually light.

Overhead, a web of branches split the late afternoon sky into fragments. The falcon he'd been training for more than a year soared above the trees, its silhouette crisscrossing the crimson sky.

For a boy of twelve, there could be no better birthday gift.

Canby's neck ached from watching the bird, and more than once he found himself flat on the ground after tripping over a branch or rock. But he followed. He'd never seen anything so beautiful.

Behind him he heard Selena calling. He couldn't make out what she said, but he couldn't stop to listen, either. The falcon caught a current just as Canby burst out of the woods into a meadow surrounded by low-growing brush.

The raptor folded into a dive, chasing a smaller bird toward the ground. Canby's breath caught. He wished now he'd brought a dog to retrieve the prey.

As quickly as it dove, the falcon rose and flew across the clouds again. Canby's heart raced—in time with the falcon's, he imagined. He chased the bird's shadow across the meadow and charged through the brush.

Selena shouted, but before he could turn to answer her, the earth fell away. For a moment he thought he'd taken flight, soaring with the falcon against the darkening sky. Too late he realized his mistake.

The falcon had flown over the edge of a steep embankment and he had gone with it.

The force of landing knocked the breath from his lungs, and the heavy leather gauntlet he carried flew from his hand. A thousand limestone teeth bit into him as he slid downward, tearing his fine silk hose and satin breeches, scoring his flesh. Instinctively he reached out.

He grabbed at a tiny sapling growing sideways out of the rock. Miraculously, its roots held.

He hung there flat against the embankment, the toe of his finely cobbled shoe balanced precariously on the smallest of rock ledges. Below him, where the sun no longer reached, all was blackness. Above him the peregrine falcon perched on the rocks, gripping and releasing its talons in a nervous dance.

And then she was there. Selena, her face illuminated by the waning rays of sunlight reflecting off the rocks. She peered over the edge, no doubt searching for his body at the base of the ravine. He called out, but his shout emerged as a whisper.

Eventually she noticed him dangling from the sapling. "Canby, you're alive! Be still. I'm coming down."

She swung a leg out over the drop. Her feet, now bare, sought purchase on the stone. Her skirts snapped in the wind as she lowered herself down to where he clung. In an instant she was beside him.

Selena grasped his shoulder. Her touch gave him courage.

"When I go up," she said, "you move into my place. Take note where I place my hands and feet on the rocks."

She climbed up above Canby's head. He sidled into the place where the rocks had been warmed by her body's brief stay. He worked a toe into the space where hers had been but it slipped, sending gravel skittering down into the blackness.

"Kick your shoes off," she commanded.

He obeyed, trying not to listen for the thumps as they hit the ground below. Once he had discarded the impractical footwear, the climb became much easier.

They inched their way up the embankment, Selena stopping frequently to inquire after his safety. By the time they arrived at the top, the sun had moved below the branches of the trees.

Selena grabbed his jacket and dragged him away from the edge. He breathed huge, gulping breaths.

"Didn't you hear me calling after you?" she said, her voice tinged with the frustration she normally held for a hawk flying at check. "You don't know this meadow. The ravine is all but invisible behind the brush."

"The falcon . . . I wanted to see her."

Selena's voice softened. "She's beautiful, isn't she? But my father would take the leather to me if anything happened to you. Is your leg . . . does it hurt?"

"I'm not a cripple," he said, unable to control the quick anger behind his words. "My leg is just weak."

"Of course you're not a cripple," Selena said quietly. "It's your knee."

He looked down. A patch of bloody skin peeked out of a hole in his breeches. He should have known Selena would never mention his lameness.

Not for the first time, it struck Canby as odd how this

slender girl of fifteen could seem so powerful. He was a duke, a peer of the realm, yet she seemed so much wiser than he. Stronger in so many ways.

Of course, she *was* three years older than he, and he'd idolized her forever.

Beside him on the ledge, Selena's breathing finally slowed. "You've lost another glove."

"I know." He dared to move closer. Her unbound hair brushed against his arm, and he caught the scent of morning rain. "You saved my life. I shall never forget it."

"Too bad I wasn't able to save your fine party clothes," she said, fingering the hole in the knee of his breeches, a hint of amusement in her voice.

But Canby was serious. He took her face in his hands. "Someday, somehow I will repay the favor, Selena Downing. I vow to you I will."

Her cheeks warmed against his palms. Could she be blushing?

She pulled away. "Let's get you home. You have guests to attend to."

"They're not *my* guests. I'm just a falconer." He pointed to his bird, flying high overhead.

She laughed. "No, my father is the falconer. You are John Markley, Seventeenth Duke of Canby."

"Aristotle says we are what we repeatedly do."

"Then you are the loser of many gloves, the destroyer of many clothes." She pulled him to his feet. "Come. I must help my father prepare for the falconry demonstration tomorrow. We'll want to put on a good show for your friends."

"They're not my friends," Canby said bitterly. But she was already halfway across the meadow. He limped after her, eyes to the sky.

Overhead, his falcon and Selena's circled them, their wings spread out across the setting sun.

CHAPTER 1

Montainville, France
September 1776

Jack Pearce hid his loathing for the spoiled French aristo-
crats behind a carefully constructed expression of indifference and several layers of grime. They paid him not a
moment's notice, which was exactly his aim. He was
merely a cadger, carrying hawks to the field for the aristo-
crats' enjoyment.

He trudged behind them, mouth shut and ears open,
hoping he would soon be rewarded for his efforts. The
Marquis de Ligiers was deeply involved in France's foreign affairs, in particular the relations with the rebelling
American colonies. As of late, those relations had grown
even more intimate.

"Have you heard anything?" De Ligiers spoke in low
tones to the Compte de Vergennes as he removed the soft
leather hood from the head of the falcon resting on his
glove. "When will our friends arrive?"

The compte glanced in Jack's direction and gave De Ligiers a look of warning. De Ligiers waved him off.

"I received word a few days ago," said the compte. "The delegation is scheduled to depart New York this week, so all will depend on the weather and the seas."

De Ligiers's bird launched into the air, its wingbeat breaking through the morning mist that shrouded Montainville, a small village on the outskirts of Versailles where the Royal Falconer and his staff made their homes.

"I'm weary of Versailles," De Ligiers said. "Court has become a miserable place, everyone scratching and clawing for crumbs from the king. I plan to leave as soon as discussions are complete. That is, if there are to be discussions."

Jack suppressed a smile. Some men talked when they were drunk, others while in the throes of passion. The Marquis de Ligiers could be counted on, almost without fail, to discuss court affairs while hawking.

The Compte de Vergennes watched with disdain as Jack released several partridges from a small wooden cage. One flew toward a line of trees beside the meadow, but it was far too slow. When De Ligiers's falcon spied its quarry, it seemed to stop in midflight. In a blink it folded and stooped toward the unsuspecting partridge, attacking it from beneath and knocking it out of the sky.

Jack admired the falcon's swift efficiency and single-minded purpose, so similar to espionage. It was the falcon's way, and his own. Perhaps that was why he was so successful in his work. And why his codename was the Falcon.

The Marquis de Ligiers snapped his fingers. "Cadger! The dog."

Jack nodded, and ordered a spaniel at his heels to retrieve the wounded partridge as the marquis called the falcon back to his fist.

De Vergennes made a noise of disgust. "Why do you enjoy this barbaric sport? The partridge hasn't a chance."

The marquis laughed. "Much like the women you seduce, eh? And how was Madame Pelisseur?"

Now De Vergennes laughed as well. "A bit meaty for my taste, but good for a bit of sport."

"My falcon might say the same of this partridge," De Ligiers said as the dog dropped the unfortunate bird at his feet. It flapped weakly in the grass.

The Compte de Vergennes shook his head. *"Touché!"*

Both men averted their eyes as Jack picked up the partridge and, in a swift movement, snapped its neck. He held it out to the marquis, who looked at it with horror. "Keep it for your supper." He handed his falcon to Jack and removed his glove.

The two men strode across the field, mounted their horses, and rode off toward Versailles. Jack watched until they were out of sight. He rewarded the falcon with a taste of the partridge and secured the hood over its head before placing it back in the cage.

Choosing carefully from the remaining birds, he set a pair of hawks on his glove. He removed the leads attached to their jesses—the leather bracelets around their talons. "Do your duty, my friends," he said, "and you, too, shall have your reward."

The cast of birds took wing, kee-keeing to each other as they rose toward the clouds. They circled overhead in slow spirals, as if the heat of the early autumn sun made them lazy.

Sending this pair up indicated that Jack would drop a coded message in a tree just outside Montainville. The missive would then be retrieved by his partner, Ned, and sent on to England by way of carrier pigeon.

Jack withdrew a spyglass from his vest and scanned the hill to the south of the field. Within moments, a small bird with blue wings and a streaked belly—a merlin—flew out from the trees.

Jack's communiqué had been acknowledged. Ned had been notified of the drop.

Before Jack could call the hawks back to his glove, another bird, larger and of lighter coloring, joined Ned's merlin in the sky above the hill. Jack frowned. The appearance of this peregrine falcon meant Ned needed to meet with him as soon as possible.

One of Jack's hawks dove from the sky, snatching a rabbit that zigzagged across the field just before it could disappear into a hole.

The other hawk shrieked its appreciation, and followed close behind as the first dropped its quarry in the grass and circled above it. Jack sent the dog out to collect the rabbit as the birds flew back to his outstretched arm.

He gutted the dead rabbit retrieved by the dog and held it in his fist, allowing the birds to feed.

As they devoured the prey, Jack wondered what news could be so important that Ned would endanger their mission to relay it.

There wasn't a man of noble blood to be found in the dank common room of the inn.

That fact gave Jack little comfort as he wended his way through benches and tables crowded with drunken commoners toward the rear of the room, the darkest corner in the place.

Though his face was shadowed by the hat pulled down over his brow, he couldn't mistake Ned McQuirns's broad shoulders. The two had often been told they resembled each other. Jack wondered if it was because they'd worked together so often.

Jack slid onto a bench several tables away from his partner. Though it was unlikely anyone here would notice them together, they could afford to take no chances.

He grabbed the skirt of a passing serving maid and ordered a mug of ale. Before he'd finished it, Ned made his move. But it wasn't the one Jack expected.

"You insult me, sir," Ned said loudly in French to a

burly man at the table beside him. The man looked at him, confused.

Ned grabbed the man's shirt. "Apologize."

"Apologize for what?"

"You dare mock me?" Ned said. "Apologize at once, or I will thrash you for the insult."

The man rose from his seat, the vast expanse of his chest now level with Ned's nose. "*You*, thrash *me*?" He smiled, his lips catching on the space where his two front teeth had gone missing. He drew back a meaty fist and let it fly, straight toward Ned's face.

Ned ducked, and the behemoth's blow landed squarely on the back of another's head, knocking his tricorn through the smoke-filled air.

Within seconds the room was a battleground, fists and mugs and benches hurtling in every conceivable direction. Jack landed a few blows, and took a few as well, before Ned reached him. They fought back to back, Jack reveling in the physical release of the brawl even as he feared drawing attention to himself. But he behaved no differently than any other man in the place.

Suddenly, Ned spun him around.

Jack's old friend gave him a feral grin. Then he bashed him in the jaw.

Jack rubbed his chin. Bugger all, Ned hadn't even pulled the punch! He fought his way through the row, ducking flying mugs and splintering boards until he reached the door. He stumbled out into the alley behind the inn, taking a moment to catch his breath. What had Ned been thinking? He could have exposed the both of them to discovery.

He fingered the sealed missive Ned had slipped into his pocket during the brawl.

Jack knew he'd have to find a private place to read it. The cramped stone quarters he shared with a half-dozen other low-ranking falconer's assistants wouldn't do. The fact that a cadger could read might raise suspicion.

He set off toward the falconry, unconsciously adjusting

his stride against the old pain in his leg that had been aggravated by the damp night.

In the room he shared with three other men, he fetched a tallow candle and proceeded to the latrine. Securing the stub in a holder beside the door, he hunched over the note, breaking the plain red seal. He recognized Ethan Gray's sharp, slanting hand immediately. It took Jack only minutes to decipher the code he and his cousin had been using with each other since childhood.

Jack's pulse leaped as he read the message. This news simply could not be possible.

Selena had been arrested for murder.

His.

CHAPTER 2

As the other falconer's assistants slept, Jack crept off into the dark with nothing but an unlit lantern and a flask of wine.

He walked for nearly a mile, a sliver of moon his only light. He crossed the field where the Marquis de Ligiers had hunted that morning, walking along the edge of a wheat field until he reached the flanking wood.

The woods were more than dark. Jack had entered a seeming void. If it weren't for the rustlings of night creatures, he might have thought the world outside had disappeared. But he dared not light the lantern. Not yet.

An innate sense of direction his only tool, he walked until the rough path sloped gently upward, indicating he'd reached the base of a chain of small hills. He lit the lantern, now far enough away for the thin light to go unnoticed.

When he reached a broken ash sapling, he left the path, fighting through thick brush, searching for the subtle markers Ned had left so Jack could find him in the case of an emergency. He stopped twice to take some wine. It warmed him some, but the night air nearly froze his fingers around the lantern's ring.

He hardly noticed. His thoughts were consumed with Selena. Where was she now? Had she been mistreated? Was he too late to help her?

Jack arrived at the designated spot and covered the lantern with his sleeve, then uncovered it. He repeated this action three times as a warning to Ned not to shoot, should he happen to be awake and on lookout.

Jack continued on to the mouth of a fissure in the hill, where Ned had been living since the spring. He gave a low whistle as he entered.

The crack in the rocky hill was the width of three men side by side, but as high as a church ceiling. Jack made his way deeper into the crevice, where the wind did not reach.

There were a few subtle signs of inhabitance.

Moss rubbed off the stone at shoulder's height. The ghost of a footprint in the silt on the floor of the cleft. A whiff of fire smoke.

The fissure split off into three narrower veins. Jack took the one to the right, arriving soon at a small room that opened into the rock. There, Ned slept beside the embers of a small campfire, his face a mask of red light and black shadows.

Jack knelt beside his partner and shone the lantern in his face.

"Ned," he said in a low voice. The sound echoed off the walls.

Ned scrambled to his feet, a long hunting knife appearing suddenly in his hand.

"Careful, Ned. Put the knife down."

Ned's eyes glittered in the firelight. "Pearce?"

"Aye."

Ned exhaled loudly. He sheathed the knife in a scabbard strapped to his thigh. "Sit down." He motioned to a flat stone beside the fire. Jack sat.

"I must get back to the falconry as soon as possible," he said. "You're coming with me, as well."

Ned yawned. "Me? Why?"

"You're going to take my place as cadger until I return."

"Where are you going?"

"England."

Ned was suddenly alert. "Why?"

"I cannot explain. I'm sorry."

"The Wolf needs you?"

"No. This is a personal matter."

Ned stirred the embers of the fire with a blackened stick. "I'll need the names of our other operatives in Versailles."

"You know that information is closely guarded, and for good reason." As England's intelligence coordinator in France, Jack was the only one besides the Wolf who knew the identities of every operative in the country.

"But what if I must get a message to England? Whom should I contact?"

"If you hear anything of import from De Ligiers, just leave a message at the drop outside the palace's south entrance. Before I leave France, I will assign someone to check the spot regularly."

Ned threw the stick into the fire. "What story will we use with Vangorps?"

Jack picked up the weathered valise that had served as Ned's pillow. "We'll figure that out on the way back to the falconry."

Amant Vangorps, one of a dozen groomers under the Falconer of Versailles, turned his one good eye on Jack as he and Ned stepped into the weatherings. Hooded birds warming in the sun on blocks and perches grew restless when they sensed the presence of strangers.

A small man with coarse white hair covering his arms and hands, Vangorps squinted against the sunlight like a displaced creature of the night.

"This is my cousin," Jack said, jerking a thumb at Ned. "He comes with news that my mother is near death."

The groomer shrugged. "What should I care?"

"I must return to Arles."

"No. I cannot spare you. Not when the Marquis de Ligiers is about. You know he hawks every day. You are the only cadger he hasn't complained about."

"My cousin can take my place until I return."

The groomer spat, and wiped his mouth on the back of his sleeve. "Do he know hawks?"

"Yes. We trained under the same master. He brought two birds, as well. They're in the mews."

The groomer raked droppings from the sand beneath a goshawk's perch. The bird shifted and stretched, extending a long, pointed wing. Vangorps eyed it lovingly.

Ned shuffled in his place. "Well, what say you?"

Jack frowned at him.

Vangorps was a deliberate man, maddeningly slow but usually reasonable. Jack had painstakingly gained his trust over the last several months. If they showed him respect, Jack knew he would relent.

The groomer blinked his good eye at them. "When will you return?" he asked Jack.

"As soon as possible. My mother is not expected to last a fortnight."

Vangorps turned his attention to Ned. "You never speak directly to any of the lords or ladies. You carry the cages and clean them well after every use. You help me scour the mews and rake beneath the perches in the weatherings. And you take your meals last. Understand?"

"Of course."

"Very well," Vangorps said to Jack. "You may go. But you'll receive not a single franc from me, and neither will your cousin, until you return."

"Thank you, m'sieur."

The groomer grunted and turned back to his task, moving

through the perches and blocks as gracefully and deliberately as a debutante on a dance floor.

Jack and Ned walked toward the mews.

"Queer old bird," Ned said, laughing.

"You'll do best to respect the man," Jack said, "lest you jeopardize my position here."

"As if you aren't jeopardizing it enough yourself. And for what? I still do not understand all of this. Where are you going?"

Jack stopped dead. "Why do you press me? You know I would not leave unless I believed it was absolutely necessary. Do you not trust my judgment?"

Ned's lips curved into an odd smile. "I'm sorry, I don't know what came over me."

Jack stared at his friend and partner for a moment. The man had undergone some sort of subtle change. Jack couldn't put his finger on it. Perhaps he'd been living alone in the mountains for too long.

Jack took Ned by the arm. "Come. We'll take care of your birds, then I'll show you where you'll sleep."

CHAPTER 3

"Move away, move away. Accused comin' through."

The jail keeper's deputy led Selena, bound in shackles, from a tunnel that ran from Newgate prison to the courtroom at Old Bailey. The crowd parted as if Selena had leprosy, but hands snatched at her sleeves and hair once she'd passed. It seemed everyone wanted a souvenir.

It was a sensational case, a woman being tried for a six-year-old murder with nary a body to prove it.

The deputy took her to the dock, which was separated from the bar where the witnesses would testify by nothing but a railing. Who would stand there and speak against her? Selena couldn't imagine.

Her head ached. Having no family or friends, she'd had no one to bring food, clean linens, and other necessities to Newgate while she'd been imprisoned there. She'd existed solely on the scraps and water provided by the warden. Her simple brown gown hung on her like a sack, but what did it matter? It was filthy anyway, and the fit of her gown was the least of her worries.

What had become of her birds? She only hoped someone had been found to care for them, or at the very least, that they'd been set free.

The court bailiff called for order, but the manic chatter of the crowd persisted until he announced her case. "The court calls Selena Hewitt to stand before us."

The deputy gave her a shove. She stepped up to the bar to face a row of six judges lined up behind podiums on a riser, like falcons perched on blocks.

One of the judges—a thin, severe-looking man—stood. The courtroom grew suddenly quiet.

The judge skewered her with his gaze. "Selena Hewitt, you are charged with the murder of John Markley, Seventeenth Duke of Canby. How plead you, woman?"

"Not guilty."

The courtroom erupted.

It took several minutes for the bailiff to settle the crowd.

"Have you a barrister?" the judge asked.

"No," she said.

"Very well." The judge nodded to the bailiff. "Are we ready for the first witness?"

"We are."

The deputy dragged Selena from the bar and pushed her back into the dock. She tried to stand tall and steady, though her knees shook from weakness as well as fear.

Her gaze swept the faces of the jurors. Those who did not eye her with curiosity did so with unmasked hostility.

She looked away.

God help her, for surely no one else would.

Jack pressed a few coins into the court officer's palm and pushed his way through the solid wall of unwashed bodies. Commoners and well-heeled gentlemen stood shoulder to shoulder in the courtroom, riveted to the proceedings.

He made his way up a set of narrow wooden stairs to a bench overlooking the jury. Below him, the twelve men shifted and fidgeted in their seats, surreptitiously dipping snuff, scratching, checking pocket watches, and staring up at the brass chandeliers hanging from the ceiling.

He surveyed the courtroom. A half-dozen or so members of the *ton* had gathered in a tight circle near large oak doors, whispering to one another. The ladies fanned themselves furiously in the stifling heat.

Jack was momentarily taken aback. He had never considered the likelihood they'd attend. A stupid mistake.

English society loved intrigue, and this most definitely qualified. They would never miss the trial of a woman accused of killing a peer of the realm.

Jack hunkered down in his seat and pulled his hat low over his eyes, though he knew his chances of being recognized were extremely slim. Aristocracy did not make a habit of studying the faces of their lessers.

And after all, he had to be there. He had no choice.

In the dock he could see the top of a woman's head, the part in her hair a ghostly white line through straight black tresses. When she raised her head, a sharp pain shot through his chest.

Selena.

The last time he'd seen her, he hadn't been Jack Pearce. He'd been John Markley, the Duke of Canby. And she hadn't been Selena Hewitt; she'd been Selena Downing.

It was his twentieth birthday and he'd gone to ask her for a gift.

It seemed as if every event of the day had conspired to keep him from her—a long meeting with Lord Popper, the estate's administrator. An appointment with the tailor. An unexpected encounter with his mother. Requests for his time, his money, his attention. By the time he rode his horse up the lane toward the falconer's cottage, his mouth was as dry as dandelion tuft and his stomach full of butterflies.

When she opened the door, his heart squeezed painfully in his chest. She was so beautiful. So strong. He wanted her more than anything he could imagine.

"Canby, happy birthday! Would you like to come in?" She stepped aside, holding the door open for him. As he passed her, the crisp scent of autumn washed over him. She always smelled of wind and sunshine.

"Is your father here?" he asked.

"No, he's at the mews if you want to see him."

"It's not him I want to see." The warmth of the cottage overcame him. He took off his hat and unbuttoned his coat.

Selena watched him, her gaze warm and affectionate. They'd always been friends. Close friends. They'd even shared a few kisses growing up. And lately he'd begun to feel as if perhaps there could be more.

He hoped it, with all his heart.

"What is it, Canby?"

He twisted his hat in his hands. "Selena, you know I care for you deeply."

Her cheeks turned a delicate shade of pink. "And I you."

He shook his head. "Not merely as a friend. I . . . I want to ask you for a birthday gift. Something I probably have no right to ask. But . . ."

She smiled. "What is it?"

He took a deep breath, and looked into her eyes. They shone back at him, so bright and clear, filled with an emotion he couldn't readily identify.

He removed his ring and slipped it onto her finger. "I want you to be my mistress."

Selena's smile faltered. "Your mistress?"

"Yes." The words rushed out of him. "Selena, you will have the best of everything. I'll build a house for you. Big and beautiful, and nearby, of course. Or you could live in London if you wish. We'll have a grand time, I promise."

"I . . . I don't know what to say. Your mistress?" She looked down at his ring on her finger. "I suppose that's a wonderful offer for a falconer's daughter. The best I can expect, considering my lack of refinement."

"Selena, it isn't like that."

She shook her head. "I know, Canby. It's a fine offer. But I am afraid I shall have to decline."

He hooked her chin with his finger and tipped her face up to meet her gaze. The light had disappeared from her eyes.

The light he now realized had been hope. Surely she hadn't expected . . .

"Selena, I would ask you to marry me, but I don't want—"

She interrupted him. "I know what you want—" She looked away. "That is, I'm already getting married."

Her words hit him like a blow to the gut. He sucked a thin stream of air into his mouth. "You're getting married?"

She nodded. "In three weeks' time. I should have thought your mother would have told you."

"My mother? What does she have to do with it?"

"She introduced the man to my father and suggested we'd make a good match. I met him a month ago."

"Do you love him?"

"No."

"Then you cannot marry him."

"You'd rather I be *your* mistress than *his* wife?" She shook her head. "I want a respectable life, Canby. I want children. I don't want to be anyone's mistress."

So, she would marry a man she didn't love rather than be with him? Canby staggered backward to the door. "Well, I suppose there is nothing more to say, then."

"I suppose not." Her voice was brittle. She held his ring out to him, but he didn't bother to take it. He ducked through the door, not daring to look back.

As he rode his horse back to the stables, he decided he'd had enough. Enough of that life. Enough of that place. Without Selena, there was absolutely no point in staying at Lockwell Hall.

Her wedding took place the day he left. By the time she'd climbed into her marriage bed, he'd been aboard a ship to France.

What had happened between then and now, Jack couldn't guess. He stared down at her as she stood in the dock.

She was taller than he remembered, as tall as most of the men around her. Though thin and pale, she bore determination, even pride, in her posture, despite what must have been a terrible ordeal at Newgate. From the look of her, she could not have had much to eat. Was there no one to bring her meals to the jail? What of her father?

What of her husband?

That last thought caused the sharp stab of pity he felt for her to dull a bit.

A hush drew over the courtroom as one of the judges spoke. "Fetch the first witness."

The bailiff ran from the courtroom into the hall and soon reappeared, a stocky fellow in tight breeches in tow.

The witness stepped up to the bar, his buttons nearly popping from his waistcoat. He gripped the rail so tightly his knuckles turned white.

"Name?" said the judge.

"Albert Collins," he squeaked.

"Give us your story, man."

The circle of lords and ladies elbowed one another for a better view. The people in the gallery, Jack included, leaned forward in their seats.

Collins swallowed several times. "I was hunting off the marsh, and must've wandered onto Lockwell Hall propity by mistake." He swallowed again. Sweat gathered on his brow and he wiped it away with his sleeve.

"I come upon a grouse, a nice plump one. I took my aim an' nicked the wing, I s'pose, 'cause it fluttered somefin' awful. I gave chase, an' it come to rest on the roots of a tree."

Sweat now pooled in the folds of skin gathered above Collins's dirty collar. He swiped at it with his hand.

"Go on," the judge prompted.

"It was in that tree I found 'em."

"Found what?"

"The duke's clothes."

"The Duke of Canby's clothes?"

"Yes, sir. The one what died six years ago."

The courtroom erupted. A lady of the *ton* fainted dead away. Her escort dragged her from the courtroom, the spooled heels of her shoes jumping over the floorboards in rhythmic thumps.

Jack's attention fixed on Selena. She sat stone-faced. Did the thought of his death not move her at all?

Collins climbed down, no doubt leaving a puddle on the box, and hurried from the courtroom.

"The next witness is called," said the judge. "Her Grace, Charity Markley, Duchess of Canby."

A low buzz swept through the room as a statuesque woman dressed in jade green silk took the stand.

His mother.

She looked well, Jack thought. Her grief had hardly aged her. Too bad her looks were all there were to recommend her, as she was colder than the Channel in winter.

"What say you, Your Grace?" the judge asked, respect plain in his voice.

The duchess snapped open a simple green-and-gold fan and fluttered it beneath her nose. "As you might guess, we were all quite shocked when Mr. Collins brought the clothing to us. Seeing them conjured so many painful images."

Jack cursed under his breath. He'd been too careless with the clothing. He should have burned it, or sunk it into the marsh. But he'd been in a hurry, and never dreamed it would be found in a tree trunk in the middle of the forest.

His mother withdrew a delicate lace handkerchief from her sleeve and touched it beneath her eyes. "Of course, I immediately ordered a search of the grounds, in the hopes of finding something, anything else, to aid in the discovery of who killed my son."

"And was anything found?" the judge asked.

"Yes. A . . . a sort of knife, a tool for cutting leather, was found in the same tree. The kind of tool used by a falconer."

Jack rubbed his forehead. He'd used the tool to cut his arm, to put blood on the saddle of his horse. He strained to hear his mother's testimony.

The duchess looked down at her hands. "And finally, in Mrs. Hewitt's own house, we found . . ." She dabbed at her eyes.

"Take your time," said the judge.

"We found Canby's ring."

This last was nearly whispered but, owing to the utter silence in the courtroom, was heard by all.

Jack drew a sharp breath. Selena still had his ring? He couldn't believe she'd kept it.

His mind raced as his mother finished her testimony and the judge called the next witness.

A young maid in gray servant's attire stepped up. She gave a quick, nervous glance in Selena's direction before facing the judges.

"Tell what you know, girl."

She waggled her head in the affirmative. "There was a terrible row, sir."

"A row?"

"Yes sir. The night afore the duke went missin'. Him an' the falconer's daughter, out by the mews."

Canby frowned. He hadn't even seen Selena for weeks before he left Lockwell Hall.

"What was the row about?"

She shrugged. "Dunno. But I ain't the only one who heard it. Pete did, too."

"Who is Pete?"

The maid turned pink. "A stable boy, sir. We were out for a walk in the moonlight . . ."

"Is this Pete present?"

Indeed he was, as were a host of other servants and former servants of Lockwell Hall, all swearing to the animosity between Selena and the duke, and some confirming reports of an argument the night before he disappeared.

A few of them testified as well to Selena's skill with weapons.

Throughout the proceedings Selena stood silently in the dock, showing little emotion save exhaustion.

Jack could hardly believe the absurdity of it all. It seemed as if every servant who worked at Lockwell Hall had been down near the mews that night, listening to an argument that had never taken place.

In his mind, Jack willed Selena to speak up and challenge the testimony of these so-called witnesses. But instead she remained silent and pale in the dock, almost as if she didn't care one way or another for her fate.

Selena wanted to scream. Liars. Liars!

Most of these servants she'd never even seen before. What could they possibly have to gain, speaking against her this way?

She suspected it wasn't as much against her as it was *for* the duchess. Not a servant at Lockwell Hall would dare go against the woman, no matter the circumstance. Aside from putting their jobs in jeopardy, most of them sincerely admired her.

"Have you anything to say for yourself?" the judge asked.

Selena shook her head.

"Have you any witnesses to testify on your behalf?"

"No. There is no one."

What did it matter? Even if she should win the case against her, she would not be permitted back onto the grounds of the estate. She would never see her birds again. Never hold them on her arm, nor watch them take wing.

She had no husband. No children, no friends. Nowhere to go. If she had to spend the rest of her life in Newgate jail, who would care? Perhaps there was no point in fighting.

Dear God, she missed her father. And Canby.

This business served only to open wounds that had
never fully healed. Canby had been her best friend, her
confidante, and nearly her lover. That anyone would accuse
her of his murder . . .

She'd lost a piece of her soul the day he died. She'd arrived at her new husband's home, only to be greeted with
the news that Canby's horse had returned to the stables
without him. There was blood on the saddle, and after a
lengthy search, the duke could not be found, and was pre-
sumed harmed or dead.

Selena had locked herself in the pantry and cried for
hours. Her husband assumed she was afraid to consum-
mate their marriage. But that night she felt no fear. Only a
numbness that would last for a very long time.

The last witness left the courtroom, spurring the cease-
less chatter of speculation.

The deputy leaned over and whispered to her, his breath
rank with the smell of onions. "I think that went well, don't
you?" His laugh rattled in his chest.

Selena ignored him.

The members of the jury stared openly at her as they
murmured to each other behind their hands. The judges
milled about on the riser, talking, laughing, awaiting the
jury's recommendation.

Selena stole a quick glance around the courtroom. The
Duchess of Canby, Lord Randolph, and his betrothed,
Lady Letitia, were nowhere to be found among the lords
and ladies huddled by the door, craning their necks to get a
better look at her.

Selena returned their stares, her defiant streak taking
possession of her senses momentarily. A few of the men
she recognized from falconry demonstrations and outings
with the hawks at Lockwell Hall.

One of them she'd known since girlhood.

Ethan Gray, Canby's cousin, stood on the outskirts
of the knot. He caught her attention and gave her an en-
couraging smile. She returned it, standing a bit straighter.

Mr. Gray had been a close friend of Canby's since boyhood. One of his few friends, really.

If *he* didn't believe she'd murdered his cousin, perhaps she could summon the strength to face her fate with dignity.

Though it seemed like days to Selena, scarcely half an hour passed before one of the jurors approached the judges' riser. The thin judge leaned down, and the juror whispered in his ear.

The courtroom grew deathly quiet.

"Foreman, has the jury reached a verdict?" the judge asked loudly.

"Yes, sir," the jury foreman replied.

"What say you?"

"We find Selena Hewitt guilty of the murder of His Grace, John Markley, Seventeenth Duke of Canby."

Selena squeezed her eyes shut and sucked a deep breath of stale air to steady her.

Guilty!

She'd never had any real hope for a better outcome, but the word was a blow, nonetheless. She opened her eyes, fighting to keep her expression impassive. All that remained was the sentence that would seal her fate. She mustn't look scared. Mustn't look guilty.

The noise around her rose to a fevered pitch.

The judges huddled together behind the row of podiums, their bewigged heads nodding and wagging. Occasionally one would break from the group to consult a large black book propped open on a ledge beside the riser.

Eventually they resumed their proper places, staring down at her with a collectively stern countenance.

The thin judge rose. "For lack of a body, we will not sentence you to death. Rather, you shall spend the remainder of your days in Newgate Gaol."

Selena reached out to grasp the rail, hoping to steady herself. But she was too late.

Like the lady of the *ton,* she fainted dead away.

CHAPTER 4

"Take her back to the women's ward," said the judge, a note of pity in his voice.

The deputy picked Selena up off the floor and tossed her over his shoulder. Her skirts bunched up, exposing bare feet for all to see, adding further to her indignity.

Jack looked on with helpless fury as the deputy carried her like a flank of venison amongst the spectators. As he passed the crowd of lords and ladies, they regarded her with undisguised malice.

All save one, who stared directly at Jack.

Jack's nerves drew taught until he recognized the man as Ethan Gray. He hadn't seen his cousin and contact since leaving England for France six years before.

His cousin was impeccably turned out in light blue breeches and buff jacket. A beautiful woman in red Chinese silk clung to his arm. Jack smiled. The man was never without a distraction.

Ethan touched two fingers to his neck stock. Jack nodded,

almost imperceptibly. They would meet on the outskirts of Hampstead Heath at dusk.

The deputy carrying Selena finally managed to exit the courtroom and the bailiff called the next case. But most of the onlookers had seen what they'd hoped to see. They swarmed for the doors, Jack included.

Before he met Ethan, he had much to do.

At long last, her eldest son was dead. Truly, officially dead.

Charity couldn't help but smile. With one small word—*guilty!*—the jury had freed the title of Duke of Canby at last. Now all that was left was for Parliament to issue the writ that would install her younger son, Randolph, to his rightful position. How could he possibly be denied now?

It had been an endless six years. Randolph's fate hung in limbo as Lord Popper, administrator of the duchy, persistently ignored Charity's wishes. Lord Popper had been difficult to bear while Canby was alive, and positively intolerable after his disappearance.

As Dowager Duchess, Charity herself had no rights, of course. As second son, neither had Randolph. Until now.

She reached over her future daughter-in-law Letitia's lap and patted Randolph's leg as the coach jerked and jutted toward home. Things were going to be different now. Very different.

"Are you pleased, my son?"

Randolph turned from the coach's window. "What?"

"The duchy is within your grasp. Are you pleased?"

"Of course. Do you think I can build the mine now?"

Letitia caught Charity's attention and rolled her eyes.

Charity gave her son an indulgent smile. "The moment Parliament installs you as duke, you can build anything like."

Randolph was silent for a while. Then he said, "What will happen to Selena?"

"For pity's sake, what does it matter?" Letitia chided. "The woman murdered your brother. The jury said so. She's a criminal."

Randolph shook his head. "I just can't believe it."

"Well, it's true. We'll never have to worry about her again, will we? And we can finally get rid of those filthy birds of hers."

Randolph frowned. "But our family has kept falconry birds for more than three hundred years."

"Perhaps it is time for a change," Letitia suggested. Randolph turned back toward the window.

Charity gave her a meaningful nod.

Jack waited beneath a towering oak as Ethan dismounted a spirited gray mare. The two men hugged briefly.

"How are you, cousin? And how are my aunt and uncle?"

"We are all well. Mother and Father are spending a bit of time up north. They'll return to London in time for the opening session of Parliament in a few weeks."

"And the lovely Lady Frederica?"

Ethan shook his head. "A rare beauty, but quite difficult, I'm afraid. Mother and Father are at a loss what to do with her."

Jack laughed. "Some things never change."

"Quite right. But some things do." Ethan's voice turned serious. "How are things in Montainville?"

"Going well. I trust you received my latest missive?"

"Yes. Interesting development. Who do you suppose will be included in the delegation from the colonies?"

"If I were to guess, I would say Mr. Franklin," said Jack. "He and the Compte de Vergennes have corresponded in the past."

"We've been watching Mr. Franklin closely, of course," Ethan said. "One of our operatives serves as his secretary. You are to make contact with him should he happen to make it to Versailles."

Jack nodded. He kicked at an exposed root in the dirt. "What did you make of that trial?"

"A travesty. I can't understand why Selena would allow such lies to be spoken of her without objection."

"Would it have made a difference?" Jack asked. "You know how strong my mother's influence is."

"I suppose." Ethan leaned against the tree. "I don't think things have gone well for Selena. Her father died, you know."

"No, I didn't." Jack thought of his old friend and mentor, Daniel Downing, who'd helped him through the lingering effects of childhood fever and guided him to manhood, making him stronger than his mother's nettling ever could. "When did it happen?"

"In the spring. Selena was heartbroken, naturally."

"Of course. But what of her husband?" Jack practically spit the word from his lips.

"Gone. When Selena took her father's place as falconer of the duchy, her husband ran off with a milkmaid. He died shortly afterward from a kick in the head."

"From the milkmaid?"

Ethan grinned. "No, from a horse. He was a blacksmith."

So, Selena wasn't married anymore. A curious relief seeped into Jack's limbs.

He shook it off. This information held no significance. There was a job at hand, and when it was through, he would go back to France, to the work that was truly important.

"I gather you have a plan?" said Ethan.

"Of course."

"Would you care to explain it, or shall I guess?"

Jack grinned. "I plan to get her out of Newgate. I've arranged passage for her on a ship to Amsterdam. It leaves in a week's time."

"A week?" Ethan frowned. "What will you do with her until then? And what of Montainville?"

"Ned can handle the work at the falconry for a week. My instinct is that the delegation's visit is at least a month away. Perhaps more. As for Selena, she'll have to spend a bit of time with me in the country."

"When she finds out you're alive, she'll—"

"No. I don't intend for her to know who I am. I'll use a disguise."

"Are you insane, man?" Ethan's look was incredulous. "Your skill in that area is unsurpassed, but this is a woman who knows you. She'll recognize you in an instant."

"I don't think so. Look at me. I'm hardly the same man I was when I left. It's been a long time, and I've learned many tricks to alter my appearance."

"Still, she knew you well. How can you be so sure she won't recognize you?"

"Because I'm the last person in the world she'd expect to see."

Ethan was silent for a moment. "Things could become complicated if she knew you were still alive. And if she found out you were a spy . . . well, she'd have information not even Lord North possesses."

"Exactly. One slip of the tongue on her part could put us both in danger, and could put an end to my endeavors as the Falcon."

Ethan shook his head. "I think you should forget this. Let it be. I cannot afford to lose someone with your skills and experience."

"Then we shall have to proceed with caution. Make sure her rescue is planned to the last detail."

"I don't want you to risk it."

"She saved my life once," Jack said quietly. "I owe her."

Ethan nodded. "Very well. Tell me how I can help."

"Do you have any contacts in Newgate?"

The rest of her life.

She had the rest of her life to wonder why she'd been accused of such a horrible crime. To worry about her falcons. To think about her father and Canby.

The rest of her life.

Selena sat in the corner of the common area in the women's ward of Newgate, watching the activity about her with numb disinterest.

A young mother convicted of stealing food from the larder of a pub slept on the floor against the wall like a rolled-up carpet. Two prostitutes who'd robbed a vicar played dice with the guards. Visitors came and went, delivering food, clean clothing, darning needles, and brandy through the bars separating them from their kith and kin.

There would be no one to visit Selena. She would die the way she'd lived for months. Alone.

She closed her eyes and conjured good memories. She and her father hawking on warm afternoons. The thrill of training her first merlin. Canby teaching her how to read.

Canby. Golden hair and strong chin. Sparkling eyes. Soft hands that touched her so gently . . .

If only she could have swallowed her pride and become his mistress, she would have much better memories to sustain her now, for the memories of her husband's touch kindled nothing but nightmares.

"You there. In the corner." The guard's sharp voice startled her.

She stood. "Yes?"

"You've a visitor."

She sank back to the floor. "You must be mistaken."

"Stand up. 'Ere's a visitor, I says."

The guard stepped aside. Behind him stood a specter robed in black, his face almost completely concealed by a cowl. In her half-starved state, Selena thought the Grim Reaper had come to claim her.

The guard must have read her expression, for he laughed aloud. "He ain't here to take your soul. 'E's here to save it."

The man moved toward her. "I am Father Gregory," he said in a rasping voice thick with a German accent. "I've come to take your confession and administer the Holy Sacrament."

"Confession?"

" 'Tis the only way to save your soul."

Selena rubbed her forehead. "I don't understand. I'm not Cath—"

"Trust in God, dear child," the priest interrupted. "He will free you."

Selena laughed hollowly. "Where was God two days ago?"

"The day of your trial? He was there," the priest assured.

"Go away, please. I didn't request a visit. I do not wish to take the sacrament."

"A friend would like to help you save your soul."

She took a step back. "I have no friends."

"But you do." The priest reached through the bars and encircled her wrist with his fingers. His hands were warm against her skin. "Will you make your confession?"

Something about his touch stilled her. Urged her to relent.

"Very well."

The guard opened a gate and allowed the priest to enter the ward. "I'll be watching," he warned.

The priest said, "Let us walk."

He followed Selena through the women's ward and into a large common area crowded with male and female prisoners.

Selena withdrew her elbow from the priest's grasp, walking beside him until he stopped at a bench beneath a high, barred window. Sunbeams fought their way through the thick air and lay, as if exhausted by the effort, on the scummy brick floor.

They sat on the bench. Selena faced the priest, for the first time noticing that a dark, unkempt beard covered much of his face. His eyes were shaded by the cowl, but his cheekbones were high, his cheeks hollowed.

"Who sent you?" she asked.

He scrutinized her for a moment, as if unsure how to answer.

"Do you believe in God?" he asked.

She thought about the question. When she was a girl, she attended chapel regularly. She prayed fervently every day, for everything—for her mother to come back, for the falcons to be strong and healthy. For rain. For sun. For her father to be safe.

Some of her prayers were answered, but the truly important ones never seemed to be.

"If there is a God," she said, "He isn't with me."

"Is that why you're here? Because God wasn't with you?"

She shrugged. "I'm not so foolish to believe that God had anything to do with it."

"What if I told you that today, God *is* with you?"

The priest nodded to a man close by. In moments a scuffle at the other end of the common room drew away the guard who'd been watching them. In an instant, the bench they sat on was surrounded by a flock of dirty prisoners. The priest pulled Selena down to the floor and kneeled beside her. He pulled at the tie on his robes.

She panicked. Froze. But her inaction was soon replaced by a screaming voice in her head.

Fight, it urged. *Fight*.

Selena balled her fingers into a fist and punched the priest in the face.

"Damn me!" He sounded distinctly English. And distinctly unpriestlike.

She let out a scream. The priest quickly clamped his hand over her mouth. Her chest heaved with her efforts to breathe.

"Stop!" he ordered in a harsh whisper. "I'm not here to attack you. I'm here to get you out."

She had no reason to believe him.

Then again, she had no reason not to. Perhaps he'd mistaken her for someone else. Perhaps God really *had* answered her prayers this time.

She stopped struggling.

The priest untied his robes and slipped them over his

head. Beneath, he wore the same uniform of filthy breeches and a grease-stained shirt as the other prisoners. But the way the garments clung to his frame, he looked as if he hadn't missed any meals.

"Here." He shoved the ball of black cloth into her arms. "Put this on. Hurry."

"What—"

"No time to explain. Hurry!"

She slid the robe over her head and tied the belt.

"No." He pulled the belt from her waist. "Priests have no . . . curves." He pulled the cowl up to hide her face.

He used the rope belt to tie his wrist to hers. Then he pulled a packet of papers from the front of his breeches. They were warm, and she tried not to think about where they'd been.

"As we leave, give these to the guards. Try not to speak. If you must speak, keep your voice low and say as little as possible."

As if on cue, the prisoners around them disbursed as quickly as they'd gathered, leaving Selena and the stranger alone in the patch of sunlight.

Before she could get a good look at his face, her rescuer took her by the shoulders and spun her toward the main hall. "Walk in front of me. Do not look back. Go directly to the gate."

She nodded and set off, head down, hands in sleeves as he'd ordered. She knew he was behind her only by the occasional tug on the rope that bound their wrists to each other's.

For as odd as she felt in the priest's garb, she seemed to draw little notice. It was a typical day at Newgate. Noisy. Crowded. Chaotic.

They passed through several large day rooms and the warmer, cleaner wards of the prison where people who had money enough to afford decent bedding, food, and clean clothes resided. Soon she stood just an arm's length from freedom.

The guard at the gate was situated behind a small table, quill and parchment before him. Selena handed the papers to him, holding her breath as he examined them.

"Prisoner William Mather, leaving on Benefit of Clergy?"

Selena nodded.

The tip of the guard's quill ticked along the parchment once, twice, yet again. "I don't see . . . Ah. Here it is. Must've been added to the list this morning." He dipped the quill in an inkwell and scratched it on the paper. "Thank ye, Father Gregory."

She stood her place, her mind refusing to believe escape could be that simple.

The guard barely looked at her. "Go on, then."

The "prisoner" attached to her wrist gave her a gentle shove, keeping his hand on her back until they made a proper exit. Then he whispered, "Round the corner at Saint Sepulchre's. Wait in the carriage with the blue doors."

The rope connecting them went suddenly slack.

Selena turned to see him, but he was gone.

CHAPTER 5

The shades, drawn tight over the windows, made the interior of the coach dark and warm. Overly warm.

Selena debated removing the priest's robe, but decided against it. In a strange way, she felt protected by the garment. She tucked her hands inside the sleeves, thinking about the man who'd helped her escape Newgate.

Who was he? Had he mistaken her for someone else? She couldn't imagine a living soul who would take such a risk for her. Not when the penalty for helping a convicted criminal escape from prison was death.

As was the penalty for a criminal who'd escaped.

A wave of nausea rolled over her.

The latch on the coach door jiggled and she moved as far into the corner as she could.

The door opened.

The man was but a black form, silhouetted against the square of azure sky that filled the doorway. He ducked into the coach, pulled the door closed behind him, and pounded on the roof with his fist.

The vehicle rumbled into motion as he dropped on the seat across from her.

She moved to the window and reached for the shade.

"Don't."

She put her hands back in her sleeves. Perhaps it was for the best. If she let enough light in for her to see who *he* was, he'd be able to see her as well. Then he might realize he'd made a mistake.

"I assume you are the one who took me out of Newgate?"

"Aye."

They rode in silence for a while, studying each other as best they could in the shadows.

He was a large man, both tall and broad. His legs nearly spanned the space between the seats. She could not make out his features very well. His beard and hair curled around him, obscuring most of his face. And what his beard did not accomplish, the lack of light did.

"Are you comfortable?" The German accent had disappeared. His voice was low and smooth, barely above a whisper.

Her arms broke out in gooseflesh. "Yes."

"Were you harmed in the jail?"

"No."

In fact, she'd been by turns humiliated, terrified, dispirited, and desolate. The guards took no care when handling the prisoners, so she was covered with bruises. She was hungry, and dirty, and scared. And tired—so tired. She'd hardly slept since she'd been taken to Newgate. She'd feared to close her eyes.

But why would she tell this man these things? There was no point.

They bumped along in silence, the coach making an occasional wide, swinging turn. She noticed the man took great pains to keep his knees from brushing hers.

"Where are we going?" she asked.

"Somewhere safe."

Safe?

She almost laughed. How could she feel safe when she hadn't the faintest notion who this man might be?

Jack wished Selena would remove the priest's robe. He wanted to see her as best he could in the muddy light of the coach. He suspected she'd been mistreated at Newgate, despite her statement to the contrary.

He knew firsthand what prisons were like.

He'd once spent thirteen days in a stinking cell in Paris. The rats had been the size of small dogs, the food laced with maggots.

He hoped Selena hadn't had to face anything so grim. But of all the women he'd known in his life, she was the one who could handle such adversity.

He knew she was frightened, and a small, spiteful part of him took satisfaction in it. He straightened, and drew himself up to his most menacing posture.

Not surprisingly, she did a damned fine job of hiding her fear. "Where are we going?" she asked again.

"You will know soon enough." He kept his voice low, partly to disguise it, partly out of necessity. The strips of wax he wore between his gums and cheeks to change the shape of his face made it difficult to speak.

She gave no response, but stared at the windows as if she could see through the shades. What was she thinking about? He felt certain he could guess.

"What of your birds?" he asked.

She started, and sat up a bit straighter. "So, you do know who I am."

"Of course. I'm not in the habit of risking my skin for just anyone."

"But why? Why me?"

He hadn't thought of an answer to that yet. "In time you will understand. So, what of your birds?"

She sighed. "I don't know. I hope they are safe. If Lord Popper couldn't find someone to care for them, I pray they were released."

"How many were there?"

"Four. A peregrine, two hawks, and an eagle."

Jack pictured the mews filled with birds. The fine days he had spent there in the company of Selena and her father, cutting leather for hoods and jesses, making lures to train new birds, were too numerous to count. The fact that his mother hated him spending time there had made it all the more satisfying.

"I'd been treating a sore on the eagle's talon when all this . . ." Her voice trailed off, as if she'd caught herself telling a secret. "I suppose it doesn't matter. I shall never see them again."

What could he say? It was true. In a week she'd be aboard a ship and he would be on his way back to France. He felt a fleeting moment of pity for her. "Surely someone will take care of their needs."

She bowed her head and said nothing.

Even Jack wondered if this was true. Lord Popper cared little for falconry. His mother, even less. He had no idea what kind of man his brother had become. Was he a cruel person? An uncaring person?

Unlikely.

As a young man Randolph had been a bit self-absorbed, lost in his own world, but a decent fellow underneath it all. If he hadn't been, Jack never would have left the duchy knowing that someday there was a chance it would fall on Randolph's shoulders. It wouldn't have been fair to the people who relied on the estate for their survival.

In any case, Jack felt certain his brother would do right by the birds. But he'd speak to Ethan, just in case.

"What sort of man is Lord Randolph?" he asked.

But she remained silent, head bowed, face obscured in the hood of the robes. He leaned forward hesitantly, drawing back the hood of the priest's cassock with his fingertips.

Selena's breath came deep and even against his palm.

She'd fallen asleep.

When would this nightmare end?

Ethan despised the fancy livestock shows disguised as parties, with young women trotted out like horseflesh for inspection.

He had to admit, though, that in the case of Lord Shelbourne's daughter, that wasn't such a stretch. With her long face and large brown eyes, she might be described as equine. Her looks notwithstanding, she could prove to be an important source of information about her father.

Lord Shelbourne was a devoted Whig, supportive enough of the American colonies' causes to have drawn the attention of the Anti-British Activity Committee. He imported lumber from the colonies, and was staunchly opposed to the Townshend Duties that had spurred the tea rebellion in Boston three years earlier.

Ethan suspected that he was somehow involved in shipping goods, including weapons, to the colonies without record. Getting close to Lady Mildred might yield some information.

Across the room, Lady Mildred pulled awkwardly at the bows on her bodice. Ethan clenched his teeth and gave her a smile imbued with feigned interest. She giggled into her rather large hand.

Ethan groaned beneath his breath. He hoped Lord North appreciated the sacrifice he was about to make for his country. He threaded through the holes in the crowd until he reached her side.

"Lady Mildred, would you care to dance?"

The coach jolted to a stop, knocking Selena out of the most wonderful dream.

She and Canby were children, flying their hawks in a

field of wildflowers. Her father was there, as well, whistling the tune that was ever-present on his lips.

She tried to close her eyes again, but her mysterious stranger insisted upon pulling her to her feet.

"Come," he said in the same whispery voice he'd used since Newgate. "We've arrived."

She stumbled from the coach into the dark of night.

A large structure loomed before her, the edges of its roof shining in the moonlight like the blades of knives. She could sense its presence more than she could see it. The faint odors of hay and horse manure hung in the air.

A barn?

"Wait," said the man. He moved away from her. She could hear him murmuring to the driver behind the coach. Within moments he was back by her side. "Take hold of my cloak and watch your step."

Behind them, the coach rolled away.

Selena grabbed a handful of the rough wool fabric and followed close behind as he moved forward in the dark.

He led her into the structure and across a hard-packed dirt floor. The dank smell of animals grew stronger, but it wasn't fresh. It was clear no animals had lived there for quite some time.

The man stopped and she let go of his cloak. He moved behind her.

Her back warmed with his body heat. He leaned against her and the fresh smell of night air enveloped her. She felt light-headed with freedom and fear.

He reached around her, taking her hands in his and stretching them out before her, placing them on the rung of a ladder. The skin of his hands was rough against hers.

"Step up. Be careful of the robe."

She climbed slowly, acutely aware of his presence below her. The rungs of the ladder creaked beneath her feet. When her hand met the last rung, she reached out. A wooden floor lay beneath her palm.

"Crawl," he said.

She hiked the robe and her skirts up and inched out onto the floor, just far enough to allow the man to clear the ladder, too.

"Stand slowly," he said. "There are beams above you."

She reached overhead as she stood, her hand coming in contact with a thick rafter. The man moved in front of her and took her by the wrist, leading her straight to a wall.

A key scraped in a lock; hinges grated. The sound reminded her of the cell doors swinging closed at Newgate.

"Come in."

Crouching, she shuffled through a low doorway. A subtle change in the air pressure suggested she was in a small room. The man closed the door behind them and the key scraped again.

The potential danger of the situation struck her like a bolt of lightning.

She had no idea where she was, or whom she was with. As far as she knew, not a soul but the driver of the coach knew they were there, and it would seem he'd left them without a second thought.

Why hadn't she tried to escape? Surely she could have fought this stranger long enough to jump from the coach. She was quick on her feet. Of course, she was weak from her stay in prison, but if she could have made it to a patch of wood . . .

She took a calming breath. Giving in to fear wouldn't help her. If this man had wanted to hurt her, he'd had ample opportunity. She wouldn't let her guard down, but she wouldn't panic, either.

He passed her, his boots scuffing on the planks of the floor. He rustled about and in a few moments a shower of sparks split the dark. A small red spot flared, the devil's eye in the dark, and soon the burgeoning light of a tinder fire illuminated the confines of a primitive fireplace.

As the flames grew, so did Selena's view of the room. First a scallop of floor was illuminated, then the border of a rug, then the plane of a wall. When the logs caught, the room was whole, if not bright.

Shadows danced in corners and beneath a small oak table against the wall. Two wooden chairs were pushed beneath the table. A bench rested beside the door, and a small cabinet stood in the corner next to the fireplace. Two mattresses on the floor rounded out the sum of the room's furnishings.

Was she meant to stay here? If so, for how long? With him? Questions ricocheted through her mind like lightning trapped in a box.

"We will not be here for long," he said, as if reading her thoughts for a second time that day.

"Where are we?"

"You needn't concern yourself with that detail."

A spark of anger flared. "I see. I don't need to know who you are, or why you've taken me from Newgate, or where I am now, or what you intend to do with me. Why don't you tell me which details, exactly, I *should* concern myself with?"

Unruffled by the tone of her voice, her "rescuer" retrieved a basket from beneath the bench beside the door and set it on the oak table. "Perhaps you would care for something to eat."

He removed a cloth from atop the basket. The tantalizing aroma of food—not the putrid fare served occasionally at Newgate, but real food—seduced her. Her stomach rumbled loudly.

Selena made it to the table in three strides. She didn't bother to sit before grabbing what was closest to her hands: a giant leg of mutton.

She gnawed at the meat like a half-starved mongrel, unmindful of the picture she presented. She'd never been the dainty sort, and this was hardly the time to change.

As she ate, she eyed the contents of the basket he unloaded onto the table. Bread. Cheese. Apples. Nuts. She hardly knew what to reach for next.

She stopped eating only once, to remove the cumbersome priest's cassock. The sleeves kept dragging through the food.

"Thank you," she murmured between bites. "Thank you. Thank you."

Jack backed away from the table, partly to put some space between him and Selena, partly because he was afraid she'd mistake his hand for something edible. He'd never seen a woman eat that way.

Come to think of it, he'd never seen a man eat that way, either.

While she was distracted by the food, he had a chance to truly study her.

She'd changed in many ways.

Gone were the boyish angles of youth, replaced by the softer curves of maturity. The black braid that once hung to her waist now brushed the spot between her shoulder blades. He imagined she cut it out of practicality. Less time spent braiding her hair meant more time spent at the mews.

She'd always been the practical sort. While his head had been in the clouds, her feet had been firmly on the ground. He'd admired her for it. He used to think that, together, they touched both heaven and earth.

But that same practicality had driven them apart. Rather than become his mistress, she'd chosen to marry a man she didn't love because it was the sensible thing to do. It didn't matter to her that she had nearly destroyed him.

Jack clenched his teeth. Such memories, these fruitless old emotions, would do little more than interfere with the job at hand.

He caught the look of bliss on Selena's face as she savored the food.

"Have you finished?" he asked roughly.

She'd been licking her fingers and stopped abruptly, as if suddenly realizing where she was. She nodded.

He packed the remaining food away and removed one of several flasks from the basket. "Ale?"

She took the mug he offered, and drank as she'd eaten, with much enthusiasm and little decorum. When she had finished, she looked at him as if she wanted to say something.

"Out with it."

She looked away. "I find it necessary to relieve myself."

Without a word, Jack went to the other side of the room. In the corner beside the fireplace, he moved a board on the floor to uncover a hole. It opened to one of the animal stalls below, where a fresh pile of straw had been laid. He used this makeshift latrine when he stayed here. Selena would have to use it as well.

Beside the hole he'd stored a reed screen in the interest of privacy. He unfolded it, and motioned to Selena.

She didn't budge.

"'Tis the only way," he said.

"But . . ."

He felt a momentary pang of sympathy, which he ruthlessly repressed. She didn't merit his sympathy. "Trust me. I'll not harm you," he said. "It would ruin my plans."

Her sigh seemed resigned. No doubt conditions were far worse at Newgate.

Selena slipped behind the screen.

Jack sat on one of the mattresses and removed his boots, then lay down on his back with his hands laced behind his head.

What would he have given ten years ago to be alone in a room like this with Selena? His fortune, to be sure. Dear God, how he had wanted her. It hadn't been mere boyhood lust, either. She'd owned his heart, with her wild eyes and throaty laugh. He would never forget the first time he kissed her.

They'd been out in the fields beating the brush, scaring up prey for the birds. Selena's skirts got tangled in some blackberry briars and he'd tried to release them, managing only to entangle himself. Eventually they'd given up and just sat in the briar patch, eating blackberries until their lips and fingers were stained purple. They'd been laughing over some silly joke, and then suddenly they were kissing. Selena's lips were warm and sweet with the juice of the berries. For him, it had been the kiss to which he compared all others. For her, just a lark.

He'd be wise to remember that she'd never cared for him the same way he'd cared for her. If she had, he never would have left Lockwell Hall. He would have put up with anything, no matter how deplorable, just to stay near her.

Selena emerged from behind the screen, and Jack rose abruptly. He filled an iron kettle with water from a jug and hung it on the arm over the fire. He pulled the screen in front of the fireplace and retrieved a basin from the cabinet in the corner.

"It's warm here. If you care to bathe, there is a basin in the cabinet in the corner." He laid a clean shift, a plain brown gown, and a pair of woolen stockings on the mattress. "I've brought some clothes for you, as well."

Jack left her, and went out to fill the water jug and collect some wood for the fire, making certain to lock the door behind him.

He took his time, and when he returned, Selena was dressed in the clothes he'd brought her, her damp hair trailing down her back.

She put the cassock back on and faded deep into the shadows.

Jack emptied the basin and retrieved some fresh linens from the cabinet, retreating behind the screen. He filled the basin with steaming water before stripping off his shirt and hanging it on a hook beside the fireplace.

He dipped a square of linen into the hot water and pressed it to his face, luxuriating in the heat. While at the falconry in Montainville, he'd missed the ritual of frequent bathing.

Had he washed every day, he would have drawn undue attention to himself. With the exception of the nobility, the French looked upon cleanliness with suspicion.

But the physician who'd treated his recurring childhood

fevers, the ones that had caused his limp, believed daily washing held many benefits. It became a habit Jack continued throughout his life.

He soaked the cloth again, scrubbing the fatigue and travel dust away, trying to ignore the fact that Selena sat somewhere beyond the screen.

Selena sucked a silent breath through puckered lips as the silhouette of the man's body emerged on the screen, converging swells and angles. Her eyes followed the linen as it traveled from shoulder to shoulder, down one well-muscled arm, over a broad chest, down the other arm, across a narrow waist . . .

When he shed his breeches, she wanted to turn away but found she could not. Watching him undress proved an oddly fascinating spectacle.

She'd seen only two men unclothed. One was her husband, whose forearms were covered with such thick, dark hair, she couldn't help but liken him to a bear. She'd seen him completely undressed just once during their marriage—on their wedding night. The other times he'd not bothered to doff anything more than his breeches.

The other man was Canby. He'd been changing out of his proper clothing into more practical garb in the falconer's shed, and she'd accidentally walked in. She'd been curious, of course.

But Canby, with his lean, lithe torso, looked nothing like this. This man reminded her of a painting Canby had once shown her of the Greek god Zeus astride a mighty throne on Mount Olympus, a bolt of lightning perched on his thigh . . .

A bolt of lightning?

Lord help her! She turned her face to the corner, chastising herself for such wicked thoughts. She had no cause to be watching this stranger. No cause to consider his . . . lightning bolt.

The problem was that he didn't *seem* like a stranger. There were times he struck her as a shadow of someone she knew. If she could just see him, touch him, perhaps she could figure it out. His gruff manner aside, she felt safe with him.

Perhaps because he'd been dressed as a man of the cloth when she'd met him.

Or more likely because her time at Newgate had done something to her reasoning. Taken her common sense. Her instincts.

Her sense of propriety.

She squeezed her eyes tight, trying hard not to peek.

CHAPTER 6

"She's escaped? From *Newgate*?"

In her surprise, Charity knocked over the inkwell on her desk. A black stain crept across the letter she'd been composing—the one expounding her joy at Selena Hewitt's incarceration.

"I'm afraid so." Sir Ambrose Hollister plucked an olive from a crystal dish on a tray beside his chair and held it between his fingernails, examining it.

"When?"

"Yesterday afternoon, as near as anyone can tell." He popped the olive into his mouth.

Charity removed an embroidered handkerchief from her sleeve and used it to mop up the puddle of ink spreading across her desk. "Shit."

Sir Ambrose tisked. "What the world doesn't know about the proper, perfect Duchess of Canby. Seems she does, in fact, make mistakes. And then she swears like a Hessian soldier."

"Shut up, Ambrose. What else did you hear about the Hewitt woman's escape?"

"Just that a priest had visited her earlier in the day."

"A priest?" Charity stood up and threw the soiled handkerchief on the desk. "I doubt even a priest can save that woman's soul."

He regarded her through narrowed eyes. "Why do you hate the girl so much?"

"She killed my son. Isn't that reason enough?"

Ambrose shrugged. "You and Canby barely spoke to one another."

"That wasn't my fault."

"Of course not." Ambrose snorted. "In any event, what does it matter if she's escaped? She's already been convicted of the crime. Canby is officially dead. Nothing stands in Randolph's way now."

Charity stalked to the other side of the room, as far away from Ambrose as she could manage. The man was an ever-present headache.

From the night he and her late husband Kellam met, they had been inseparable. Cut from the same cloth, they gambled against each other incessantly, putting no limits on their wagers. Thousands of pounds, properties, businesses, horses, dogs.

Her.

When she'd refused at first to take Ambrose as a lover, Kellam had given her so many bruises, it had hurt to wear clothing. Her husband made it clear she was his property, to be bought, sold, or wagered as he saw fit.

Charity had long ago convinced Ambrose to take a younger lover, but if word of that vulgar wager, along with Kellam's other peccadilloes, ever got out, the scandal would ruin her. Ambrose used this knowledge to his every advantage, garnering favors, borrowing money, making use of their homes and carriages.

To add to matters, Kellam had won controlling interest

of Ambrose's shipping company, Two Moons, in a card game the night before he died. Ambrose never had a chance to win it back. Thus, Two Moons was part of the duchy when Kellam died.

Lord Popper would never agree to sell it back. It was much too lucrative a business. But Charity might be able to convince Randolph to sell. And if she did, Ambrose had promised to pay her handsomely. But more important, he'd promised to get out of her life forever.

"Do you want Two Moons Shipping returned to you or not?" she asked.

"You know I do." An edge of tension crept into his voice.

"Then you'd better hope she's caught," Charity said. "Anything could influence the decision on whether or not Parliament hands Randolph the duchy—including the fact that the woman responsible for the previous duke's death is gone."

"You're making too much of this."

"Perhaps so. But Randolph's successful bid for the duchy is the only chance you have of ever taking possession of Two Moons again."

"If we don't do something soon, I'll go insane," Selena said.

Three days had passed since they'd arrived, which Selena measured by the light and dark through the latrine hole. Without it, she would never have been able to mark the passing of time.

Black cloth, nailed into place, covered both windows. They burned no fire in the daylight, so the room grew numbingly cold at times. And it was, of course, perpetually dark.

Selena imagined this was what it would be like to live in a tomb.

She'd taken to wearing the cassock over her clothes for

warmth, but also because it matched her increasingly darkening mood. Now she paced the short length of the room,
the robe dragging on the floor behind her.

"What do you propose? Shall we parade you about the
nearest town?"

Selena glared at him. Not that he could see her in the
dark from across the room. In fact, he'd done his best to
stay as far away from her as possible. And yet, there were
times when he seemed to anticipate her every need.

Selena slid into a chair at the little table and warmed her
hands near the lamp in the center of the table. She gestured
to the other chair. "Why don't we talk?"

Taut silence seeped from the dark.

"I don't understand," she said wearily.

"What?"

"I don't understand why you took me out of Newgate.
Why you brought me here when you obviously dislike
me."

"Dislike you?"

"Yes. You avoid me completely, except to hurl sarcastic
remarks at me from dark corners. You obviously don't care
for me. So why did you bother to rescue me?"

He rose from his mattress and crossed the room, sliding
into the chair across from her. The light of the lamp grazed
his fingers and his arm to the elbow, but his face remained
steeped in shadows.

"I do not dislike you."

She stared at his hands, her attention captured by the elegant curve of his fingers. His hands looked gentle.

"If you'd like to talk, go on," he said. "What do you
want to talk about?"

"Who you are. Where we are. Why I am here. When we
are leaving. Whatever you want to talk about."

He stared at her from across the table. She'd only ever
caught quick glimpses of his eyes, as they always seemed
to be shadowed by his hair or a hat. But now they glittered
in the dim light.

The image of a falcon's keen gaze flashed in her mind before he lowered his head.

"I'd like to talk about you," he said.

"About me?" She shrugged. "There isn't much to say. I have, or rather I *did* have, a very simple life."

"You are a falconer."

"Yes, as my father and grandfather were before me. My father never sired a boy, because my mother died shortly after my birth. But I was lucky. He entrusted his knowledge to me." And to Canby, she thought, remembering how the two of them worked side by side, the young duke learning by assisting with the birds. He'd felt like a brother to her at first. And then later, her other half.

"He was a good man."

Had he read her mind again? "Canby?"

"Canby?" he seemed startled. "We were talking about your father."

"Oh, yes. My father. You knew him?" she asked. It would certainly explain why he'd taken her out of Newgate.

"The way you speak of him, he could have been nothing but a good man."

"He was." Her mind filled with images of him. She'd hardly had time to miss him before all this began.

"Are you married?" he asked, his voice tight.

"I was."

"And?"

"And he didn't care for falcons. He didn't want me to return to Lockwell Hall to take my father's position."

"But you did so, despite his objections?"

"Yes."

"What did he do?"

She lowered her head. Her husband had made his disapproval more than clear, but it hadn't mattered. She would have endured anything in order to get back to her birds. "Eventually, he let me go."

Silence. And then, "Where is he now?"

"He died shortly after we parted."

"I'm sorry."

"Don't be."

He seemed to hesitate. "Are there children?"

A knot formed in her chest. "No." At least none that had lived past two days' time. Memories of her baby, born far too early, haunted her still. A child would have been the only good thing to come out of her marriage.

The man stretched his hand out to her, their fingertips touching before he seemed to realize what he was doing. He jerked his hand away.

"You weren't much of a wife, were you?"

"He wasn't much of a husband."

"Did you . . ." He cleared his throat. "Did you love him?"

"No."

"Then why did you marry him?"

His intensity caught her off guard.

"Because the man I loved didn't love me." Her words rung out into the smoky air, lingering in her ears in the short silence that followed.

"Who?" he said, in a voice like wheels on gravel.

She searched for him in the darkness, unable to make out anything but a dim silhouette. A priest behind a veil of shadows.

Should she confess her secret? That the falconer's daughter had been in love with her lord? She couldn't. Even after all this time, the memory of Canby's betrayal still hurt her too deeply.

She'd been hoping he'd come to her that day—his twentieth birthday. She'd made a new gauntlet for him, detailed with his family crest and initials.

She wondered, too, if he'd found out about her father's intentions to marry her off to a blacksmith. What would he think? Would it make him crazy to think of her with another man? If his feelings were anything like hers, it would. But other than a few stolen kisses, he'd never shown anything more than abiding friendship.

When she heard him ride up to the cottage, she stood

just inside the door, pressing her fist against her breast-bone, unable to control the wild beating of her heart. He knocked, and she pulled the door open immediately.

Her breath caught in her throat. The sunlight at his back turned his hair a dozen shades of amber. He shone like gold.

Selena wanted him more than anything she could imagine.

"Canby, happy birthday! Would you like to come in?" She stepped aside, holding the door open for him. As he passed her, the smell of crisp autumn leaves enveloped her.

"Is your father here?" he asked.

"No, he's at the mews if you want to see him."

"It's not him I want to see." He removed his hat and un-buttoned his coat.

Selena watched him, trying hard to keep her heart from showing in her eyes. They'd always been friends. Close friends. They'd shared all of their secrets, and even a few kisses growing up. But when had she fallen in love with him? She couldn't say. She only knew it felt like she'd loved him forever.

He stared at her with a strange look on his face.

"What is it, Canby?"

He twisted his hat in his hands. "Selena, you know I care for you deeply."

Her cheeks warmed. Did he suspect her feelings? "And I you."

He shook his head. "Not merely as a friend. I . . . I want to ask you for a birthday gift. Something I probably have no right to ask. But . . ."

Her heart leapt in her chest. He *had* come here to save her from her impending marriage! "What is it?"

Canby took a deep breath, and looked into her eyes. He removed his ring and slipped it onto her finger. Her hands trembled in his.

"I want you to be my mistress."

Selena blinked. "Your mistress?"

"Yes." He spoke quickly, as if in a race with her thoughts.

"Selena, you will have the best of everything. I'll build a house for you. Big and beautiful, and nearby of course. Or you could live in London if you wish. We'll have a grand time, I promise."

Shock numbed her. She spoke, but could hardly feel her mouth move. "I . . . I don't know what to say. Your mistress?" She looked down at his ring, so heavy on her finger. The citrine eye of the falcon winked up at her. "I suppose that's a wonderful offer for a falconer's daughter. The best I can expect, considering my lack of refinement."

"Selena, it isn't like that."

But she knew it was. She'd been foolish—oh, so foolish to expect he'd ask her to marry him. Dukes did not marry falconer's daughters.

She shook her head. "I know, Canby. It's a fine offer. But I am afraid I shall have to decline."

He hooked her chin with his finger and tipped her face up to meet her gaze. She pushed her emotions back, deep inside. She could not let him see . . .

"Selena, I would ask you to marry me, but I don't want—"

She knew exactly what he didn't want. Scandal. Shame to his family. Ridicule.

She interrupted him. "I know what you want . . ." She looked away, couldn't finish. "That is, I'm already getting married."

His hand dropped to his side. "You're getting married?"

She nodded. "In three weeks' time. I should have thought your mother would have told you."

"My mother? What does she have to do with it?"

"She introduced the man to my father and suggested we'd make a good match. I met him a month ago."

"Do you love him?"

"No."

"Then you cannot marry him."

A spark of anger lit in her chest. "You'd rather I be *your* mistress than *his* wife?" She shook her head. "I want a respectable life, Canby. I want children. I don't want to be anyone's mistress."

The look on his face proved he had not expected to be rebuffed. He backed toward the door. "Well, I suppose there is nothing more to say, then."

"I suppose not." She slid his ring from her finger and held it out to him, but he didn't take it. He simply walked away, out of her life, without so much as a backward glance.

It was the last time she ever saw him.

"Whom did you love?" The man's question drew her out of the past and back to the cold, dark room. He stared at her from across the table, his eyes blazing in the lamplight. Selena felt suddenly uncomfortable under his scrutiny.

"It doesn't matter." She rose, pacing again. "May I ask a question now?"

"You may. But I won't promise to answer it."

She stopped before him. "What is your name?"

He exhaled. "Jack," he said. "My name is Jack."

He hadn't planned to reveal his name, but her question took him by surprise. Did she suspect his true identity?

She couldn't. The things she'd told him . . .

The man I loved didn't love me.

Could that man have been *him*?

"Jack." She repeated his name. "I once had a falcon named Jack. He was a capricious fellow. I was never quite certain he would return to me when I sent him off."

Jack smiled. He remembered that falcon. In fact, the bird eventually did fly off, but stayed close enough to home so that, every now and then, he and Selena would hear its bell or catch a glimpse of it in the trees.

"The uncertainty of wild things," he said.

"How true," she said. "When the birds leave my arm, the only thing that binds us is our trust in each other. I consider it a gift each time they choose to come back."

Jack understood completely. He'd worked with all kinds of animals since childhood—horses, hounds, livestock. All of them could be tamed in some way. But birds of prey could never be tamed. They worked *with* a falconer rather than *for* him. They were not pets or servants, but hunting partners.

"Their wanderlust is part of their intrigue," he said.

"What about you?" Selena asked. "Do you have wanderlust? Are you a traveler?"

"I suppose so. I don't find any particular joy in it, but as Aristotle says, 'We are what we repeatedly do.'"

A strange look flitted across her features for just an instant. Then she motioned with her hand. "Is this your home?"

"No. It's merely a place to come." Jack crossed the room and knelt before the fireplace. If his hunger was any indication, it had to be close to dark by now. The smoke from the fire would no longer be visible from the road.

"When?" she said.

"When what?"

"When do you come here?"

He removed a flint and striker from a box and laid a square of charred linen atop a pile of peat in the fireplace. "I come here when I have nowhere else to be."

He could feel her watching him as he built the fire. Their conversation had created an intimacy between them that hadn't existed before. An intimacy he was much too tempted to nurture. It would be so easy to confess who he was. To find out whom it was that she'd loved so long ago.

But he was afraid. Because if by some miracle of God it was *him,* he wouldn't be able to hold back. He would tell her everything. And he couldn't have that.

He didn't *want* that.

If she told anyone, a single soul, who he was, his life could be in danger. He'd made many enemies during his years as Jack Pearce. And there were at least a dozen people who'd pay handsomely to get their hands around the neck of the Falcon, if they could ever discover who he was.

For that same reason, knowing his identity would put her in danger, too. For both their sakes, it was time to widen the distance between them once again.

But he still hated himself for what he was about to do.

"I hide from the authorities here," he said. "You see, I am a criminal."

"Why, exactly, did you rescue me?" she said quietly.

His throat tightened. He reminded himself that his lies were for the best. If his words frightened her, all the better. "Rescue you?" He laughed. "My dear, you are mistaken. I plan to ransom you."

Now she laughed. "Ransom me? To whom?"

"To the Markley family, of course. I'm sure Lord Randolph will pay handsomely for the return of the woman who killed his brother."

"You bastard," she whispered.

He turned back to the fire, trying to convince himself he didn't give a damn what she thought of him.

"The Hewitt woman has to be found. There are members of Parliament who wish to interview her before making their final decisions." Charity picked at the food on her plate as she awaited her son Randolph's reaction.

It was typically underwhelming.

"Hmm." He moved food about on his plate, engineering a bridge over a river of gravy with a plank of beef.

"We should issue a reward for her capture," Letitia suggested. "Money is the only true inspiration."

"I thought that was love," Randolph said.

"Don't be a gull," Letitia said.

"Unfortunately," Charity thought out loud, "all of us combined don't have the sort of money that would set the people of England into action."

The yearly jointure she received from the duchy since

her husband's death was hardly enough to keep her in fashion, much less offer a reward.

"What about Sir Ambrose?" Letitia asked.

"Absolutely not." Charity would not be beholden to that man for one more thing. If he provided the money, she would be the one to pay somehow. Besides, she didn't think he even possessed the kind of wealth necessary for this endeavor.

"Our only option is to get the money from Lord Popper," Charity said. "I could go to him myself, but past experiences have proven my lack of influence over him. And unfortunately, Randolph, you have even less a chance. So how do we convince him to part with several hundred pounds?"

"What about Ethan?" Randolph muttered to his plate.

Charity looked up, startled. Sometimes she wondered if Randolph had a brain in his head. And then there were times like these. Times when he surprised her.

Her lips curled into a smile. "Perfect."

How could her instincts have been so wrong?

Selena lay on her back on the straw ticking as the last of the fire glowed in the grate. The room had already grown uncomfortably cold. On the other mattress, Jack snored softly. She hadn't closed her eyes for a moment.

Time was of the essence now.

The initial shock she felt when Jack announced his intentions had quickly abated. In the blink of an eye, he'd gone from rescuer to ransomer. Hero to villain. Mysterious to sinister.

Selena felt a deep regret. There was something so familiar about Jack. She couldn't place exactly what it was, but something . . . An intangible connection charged the air around them.

She'd felt it when his fingers touched hers, and especially when he'd finally looked into her eyes. For as brief as that connection was, a spark had flared. She couldn't deny it, but she couldn't let it affect her, either. Her life was at stake.

Thoughts tumbled through her mind. How? How could she get out? Jack rarely left her alone. When he did leave the room, he locked the door behind him.

She could possibly break a window, but she had no idea how far up from the ground the windows were. Could she jump? Even if she could, Jack was bound to catch her. It was clear she would have to get the keys to the door, which Jack kept with him at all times.

One unwelcome thought persisted: She might have to harm him—or kill him—to get the keys.

Jack had a knife hidden in his mattress. She'd seen him remove it from the scabbard and test the blade against his thumb when he thought she was asleep. She would use that.

But how would she get to it? How would she get to *him*? She couldn't possibly overpower him.

He was too big.

She would somehow have to take the knife and attack him while he slept—the only time she could get close enough to him to do it.

She rolled onto her stomach, listening to the soft snores drifting from Jack's mattress.

CHAPTER 7

Ethan slid from Lady Mildred's bed and dressed quickly by the light of the moon.

All was quiet. Lord and Lady Shelbourne had gone out for the evening, leaving Mildred to seek whatever entertainment she might.

Which turned out to be him.

He slipped from Mildred's quarters, not bothering to say good-bye. He would be back. Despite her youth and equine looks, Mildred was a surprisingly accomplished lover and, more importantly, an excellent source of information. She frequently visited her father's offices at the wharf, and was pleased to gossip incessantly about what went on there.

Ethan passed through Shelbourne's elegant gardens on his way to the stables. Normally he would ride to his club for a bit of food and gaming. Tomorrow, however, he had an early morning meeting with Lord North to discuss the situation in Montainville.

Ethan sighed. Jack's absence from that mission had hurt the operation, perhaps irreparably. He'd received only one missive from Ned McQuirns, and the information it contained was all but useless. He needed Jack to return to France.

To cap off what would surely prove a difficult day, he was to meet his aunt at Lord Popper's offices. He could only imagine what that meeting would bring. For one thing, Lord Popper always eyed him as if he were a shank of roasted lamb.

Ethan urged his horse on through the night, forcing his thoughts in a more pleasant direction.

Tomorrow night at this time, he intended to be at home in his very own bed, alone.

Selena waited until Jack's breathing had become deep and even before rolling off her mattress and crawling toward his.

She'd decided to act. She had no idea when he planned to ransom her, but she was determined to escape before he had the chance.

The knife was hidden in a slit on the side of the mattress closest to the wall. She crept closer. Jack sprawled over the mattress, his feet dangling off the edge. He still wore his boots.

She would have to get over him to retrieve the knife. She stopped for a few moments to listen, counting his breaths, shoring up her nerve.

When she was certain his sleep was deep, she rose to her feet, hiking her skirts up to her waist. As softly as she could manage, she stepped onto the mattress.

Jack didn't stir.

Selena took shallow breaths. For a moment she feared she'd faint. She stepped over him, her foot landing between his hip and the wall, straddling him.

She bent over, holding her skirts with one hand and groping along the edge of the ticking with the other. Her fingers located the slit, but before she could get the knife, Jack's hand swept out, catching her legs.

Her knees buckled and she landed hard on top of him.

Jack rolled her over and pinned her beneath his body, nearly suffocating her. She lay perfectly still beneath him, not daring to move.

"What are you doing?" His voice was harsh.

She did not answer. Could not. Fear paralyzed her. If only she had gotten to the knife.

She wondered what he would do. Beat her? Kill her? But he did neither of the two.

Instead, he lowered his head and kissed her.

Her heartbeat quickened, but not completely from fear. Jack's lips were soft—the opposite of what she would have expected when the rest of him was so hard—and his beard tickled her chin.

The kiss was light. Gentle.

A curious sensation washed over her, but before she could identify it, Jack pulled away.

He sat up abruptly. "What are you doing in my bed?" The familiar gruffness had returned, shattering the strange, warm intimacy of the last few moments.

Her voice trembled a bit. "I heard a noise. It frightened me."

"Stay here."

He rolled off the mattress and she heard him move first about the room, and then out the door. The key grated in the lock, and she knew he'd gone to check the barn below.

She reached into the slit to get the knife, but it was gone.

It was just as well. If she'd taken it, she would have worried that he'd find it missing before she had a chance to use it. If she expected to overpower him, she'd have to catch him when he was vulnerable.

But his kiss had shown her she had a different weapon. There was no doubt in her mind that Jack was attracted to her.

She would never have dreamed it from the way he avoided her, but she could use it to her advantage. It might be the only way to get him on the bed, vulnerable, and put her in reach of the knife at the same time.

Unfortunately, she'd never been much of a seductress. There had simply been no cause for it. The only man she'd ever truly been interested in was Canby, and she had never had the nerve to be obvious about her desires.

Suddenly Selena wished she were more familiar with feminine wiles. How did a woman go about attracting a complete stranger?

While she mulled over this question, Jack returned to the room and lit the lantern, placing it on the table and stepping away from the light. "I didn't find anything. Perhaps it was an animal, or the wind?"

"Perhaps."

Selena went to the table, and Jack moved toward the mattress. She stepped toward the mattress, and he went to the fire. She bit her lip in frustration.

How was she ever going to seduce him from across the room?

Daylight filtered up through the hole. If Jack had to guess, he'd say it was midmorning.

Three more days until he and Selena would travel to Bristol to meet the boat.

He would be both disappointed and relieved.

In truth, he never expected the reaction he'd had to her. All the emotions he harbored, the ones he fought so hard to forget, had returned with a vengeance when he kissed her.

He couldn't help himself. The feel of her against him, skin to skin, was more than he could bear. She was so soft, so warm.

He could feel her heart beating against his chest, and he knew she feared him. He felt as if he were betraying her by not revealing his identity.

Perhaps one day he would. When his mission in France was over, he could find her in Amsterdam. Tell her who he really was.

Impossible.

He could never give up his work for the Crown. What he did was meaningful—far more meaningful than his life as a duke would have been. Lord North relied on his information to make crucial decisions about the protection of England. The Falcon would not fail his country.

He watched Selena surreptitiously from behind the screen.

She sat in the lamplight at the table, unbraiding hair that was darker than midnight. When she had finished, it hung down her back and cascaded over her shoulders in ebony waves.

She'd finally removed the cursed priest's robe. Why he'd wished for that, he had no idea. Now he was all too aware of the enticingly snug fit of the bodice of her gown. His mind flitted back to the feel of her breasts pressing against his chest . . .

He emerged from behind the screen, averting his eyes.

"Have you a hairbrush?" she asked.

"No," he replied, discovering that his mouth had gone dry. "But I may have a comb." He rummaged through the bag containing his precious few personal items. Indeed, he had a comb.

He took great care not to allow their fingers to touch as he handed it to her. He didn't think he could manage any contact.

Selena pulled the comb through her hair. "Mmm. This feels lovely."

It looked lovely. He swallowed.

Her movements worked like a gentle vise on his gut. The muscles of his stomach tightened with each stroke of the comb's teeth through the silken waves.

The lamp on the table cocooned her in a circle of hazy yellow. Her shadow on the floor doubled the sensual image as she tugged the comb down the length of her hair with maddening slowness. Her eyes were closed, her lips parted slightly as she released a contented sigh.

Jack's fingers burned with desire. The desire to tangle

her tresses around his fingers, bury his face in them, wrap them around his hands. He wanted to get caught in them like a fly in a spider's silken web.

He wanted to see them fanned out on a pillow in a huge, soft bed. From there it was but a tiny step to envisioning her as his lover, gasping beneath him with abandon . . .

She gathered her hair over one shoulder, mesmerizing him as she plaited it into a thick braid, her fingers executing a delicate dance among the dark locks.

A familiar ache built in his groin until he forced himself to look away. Like a voyeur who had witnessed an intensely intimate act, he was both aroused and ashamed.

He closed his eyes. Clenched his jaw. Dragged his hand over his face. Lord help him, she was only combing her hair.

Damn it. That one small kiss had opened a floodgate.

He strode to the bench beside the door and busied himself with the basket of food. Perhaps some breakfast would take the edge off the gnawing hunger that had suddenly grown in his belly.

When Selena had finished with her hair, Jack carried the basket to the table and removed several apples, a loaf of dark bread, and a wheel of cheese.

Selena rubbed an apple on her sleeve and bit into it. Juice ran down her chin, and she wiped it off with the back of her hand.

"Delicious." Her lips glistened.

Jack licked his.

She took another bite, chewing slowly, as if savoring the tart fruit.

A small groan caught in his throat.

"What?"

"Nothing. I must get more wood for the fire." He stood so suddenly, with such force, his chair clattered backward to the floor.

His face burned. He righted the chair and strode to the door, slamming it behind him.

* * *

Selena glanced at the tall stack of wood in the corner, and smiled. She could hear Jack pacing just outside the door.

Unwittingly, she'd found his Achilles' heel.

She'd felt his stare as she combed her hair. Canby had once told her how the sight of a woman with her hair unbound could drive a man insane with longing. He'd also explained the lure of a woman's lips, and the thoughts a man might have when watching a woman eat.

At the time she'd thought him ridiculous. Now she was grateful for those insights.

Dare she hope she could seduce Jack? Trick him into taking her to his bed? It was the only place he'd be off-guard and near the knife at the same time.

She would have to double her efforts.

There *was* one thing . . . one risky gambit. It would take courage. Audacity, even.

And if it didn't drive Jack to drag her to his bed, she would be out of hope.

CHAPTER 8

Ethan arrived twenty minutes late for the meeting with Aunt Charity and Lord Popper.

The duchess looked her usual self, fashionable and demure, as she waited for him on an uncomfortable-looking settee in Lord Popper's outer office.

He marveled again at how deceiving looks could be.

"Ethan. You're late."

"I'm sorry. I had some urgent business to attend to."

"No doubt it involved some poor, unsuspecting female."

Actually, it had involved a rather hard-nosed Lord North, who wanted to know why intelligence from Montainville had recently slowed to a trickle.

He laughed. "You know me too well."

"Yes, I do." She extended a gloved hand and he took it, bending to kiss the air above her fingers.

"To what do I owe this great pleasure, Aunt?"

Charity patted the settee. "Come, sit. I need your help."

"With Lord Popper, I presume."

"Naturally."

He perched on the edge of the couch, attempting to re-work his grimace to an expression of mild curiosity.

"I know you and Canby were close," Charity said. "I know you were more than cousins. You were friends."

"Yes, we were."

"I saw you at the trial. As you know, Selena Hewitt was sentenced to spend the rest of her life in prison."

"Of course. It is common knowledge."

"Well, she's escaped from Newgate."

"Escaped! When?" He hoped his surprise seemed genuine.

"A few days ago." Charity bowed her head. "It's a travesty, Ethan. I extended all courtesy to her, inviting her to take her father's position at Lockwell Hall after he died. I'm afraid I cannot bear this turn of events."

"I thought Lord Popper invited her back."

The duchess looked ready to faint.

Ethan patted her hand. "Rest assured, she'll be caught."

"But that's just it! I fear she won't. I cannot sleep or eat, knowing the woman who murdered my son runs free."

Ethan didn't like where this conversation was headed. "Now, Aunt Charity—"

"Please, Ethan. No amount of talk will soothe me. She must be caught, or I am afraid I shall never have a moment's peace."

"I don't know how I can possibly help you," he said.

Her expression softened. "I want you to convince Lord Popper to hire someone to find her."

"Hire someone?"

"Yes. To bring her to the steps of Newgate."

"Whom would you hire?"

The duchess leaned in. "There's a man. Sir Ambrose has heard his name bandied about the docks. He's well known for this sort of thing, but his fee is three hundred pounds."

"Three hundred pounds? That is quite a sum."

"And well worth it, from what Ambrose gathers."

"What is this man's name?"

"Samuel Kincaid."

Ethan knew the name well. In fact, Jack had been involved in several altercations with him, including one at a pub called the Green Dragon. Kincaid and his men had been on the trail of one of Ethan's operatives. Jack stepped in, and had nearly been stabbed to death for his efforts.

Kincaid was a rogue of the worst sort. But unfortunately the duchess was right about one thing—if anyone could find Selena, Kincaid could.

"This is a perilous game, Aunt Charity. You know nothing about this man."

"What is there to know? As long as he takes Selena Hewitt back to Newgate, I don't give two shakes what kind of man he is."

Ethan shook his head. "I'm afraid I cannot do this, Aunt Charity."

She raised a brow. "Why not?"

"Because it's dangerous. And because I don't happen to agree with Selena's conviction. I don't think she murdered anyone."

His aunt's face turned stony, and Ethan knew he was in for a fight.

"My boy, it is quite admirable to stand up for what you believe. But in this case, I pray you relent."

"I cannot."

She sighed. "Oh, dear. I thought you were smarter than this."

He regarded her, not without some wariness. She could be a brutal opponent. As he suspected, her ammunition was fierce.

"I understand you've been courting the Shelbourne girl. What is her name—Mildred?"

"Yes."

"Lady Shelbourne is a very close friend of mine. Almost like a sister, really. She might be quite interested to hear you were spiriting a certain port master's wife into the maze at

Vauxhall just two nights ago." She gave him a pointed look.

"Aunt Charity—"

"I need your help, Ethan."

And *he* needed the information Lady Mildred supplied. Desperately. He rubbed the back of his neck.

His aunt smiled. "Will you help me convince Lord Popper to release the money from the estate to pay for Mr. Kincaid's services?" she asked.

Ethan knew he'd been soundly defeated. He sighed. "Shall we inform Lord Popper we're here?"

Lord Popper, who'd been appointed to manage the duchy's assets and holdings when her husband died, had been a nettle in the fur of Charity's contentment ever since.

Initially, he was to handle things until Canby's twenty-first birthday. But when Canby disappeared, Lord Popper had continued on until a new duke could be named.

He was a pompous, odious bag of wind who never bothered to hide his contempt for her. One of the few people in London society who didn't treat her with deference and respect. And he hadn't given one inch to her or Randolph's requests—a circumstance that left Charity a frustrated and relatively ineffectual *grande dame* of the *ton*.

And they would never be rid of him unless Randolph became duke.

Damn Selena Hewitt.

How the woman had managed to escape Newgate in the first place was a mystery. Charity privately admitted to a grudging respect for her in that regard. Nevertheless, she had to be caught.

Lord Popper would most likely refuse Charity's own request for money. But she doubted he would refuse Ethan. Charity long suspected Lord Popper of secretly lusting after her nephew.

She could hardly blame him. Ethan was devilishly handsome, and attracted many admirers of both sexes. With some amusement, Charity watched the old peacock preen before Ethan.

"We'll require at least three hundred pounds." She laced her fingers on her lap, giving Lord Popper a challenging look. "One hundred now to secure Mr. Kincaid's commitment, and the rest upon the return of Selena Hewitt to Newgate."

"Three hundred pounds?" He tisked. "With all due respect, Your Grace, you cannot expect this estate to put out so much money to search for one small girl."

"She isn't small, and she isn't a girl. She's the woman who murdered my son."

Lord Popper, seated behind a table stacked with papers, raised a brow. "So the *jury* has concluded. However, it isn't my responsibility to bring the woman to justice. It is my responsibility to manage the duchy's funds with prudence and frugality until such time as my duties are, by order of Parliament and His Royal Highness, handed over to another party." He smirked. "Might I suggest that you pay this Kincaid fellow with the money from your jointure?"

Charity sighed. "You know exactly how much I receive from the duchy as jointure, and you know it isn't enough to cover my whist bets, much less pay for Mr. Kincaid's services."

"Perhaps you can impose upon Sir Ambrose? Lord knows he's taken advantage of *you* more than a few times."

Charity ignored his dig. "Why must we be at constant odds? The coffers are full to overflowing. You've done incredibly well for the duchy. Why, your management of Two Moons Shipping alone has garnered a small fortune. The estate will never miss such a meager amount."

"I'd hardly call three hundred pounds a meager amount."

"Why, nearly twice that is spent each year on the mews, and those horrid birds."

"Falconry has been an honored tradition of the Markley family for centuries. The upkeep of the birds and mews is of the utmost importance," said Lord Popper.

"The search for Canby's killer is of the utmost importance," Charity retorted.

"It certainly is. To you and Sir Ambrose and Lord Randolph." Lord Popper picked up a quill and ran the feather beneath his chin, his gaze locked on Ethan.

"Make your point," Charity said, her cloak of civility wearing thin.

Lord Popper drew up. "I understand a few members of the House of Commons wish to speak with Selena Hewitt before the vote. The only reason you want to find her is because you're worried that Parliament won't install Randolph as duke unless she's in custody."

Charity's expression turned stony. "*You* are the one who should be worried, Lord Popper. As soon as Randolph claims his rightful title, you'll lose your fat yearly commission, won't you? That, and whatever else you secretly stuff into your pockets."

Lord Popper's face went crimson. "Do you mean to imply that I am dishonest? You'd do best not to throw stones. Perhaps your jointure is depleted because you used it to bribe the jury and the judges. That trial was a mockery."

Charity gripped the edge of the desk, rising unsteadily to her feet. "Do you accuse me of perverting justice?"

"*Accuse* you? No. I state, outright, that you—"

"Lord Popper, please," Ethan interrupted. "Be very careful what you say. You're leveling serious charges at a member of English society who is considered in many circles to be a moral compass."

Lord Popper closed his mouth and smoothed his neckerchief.

"I will not stand accused of such heinous behavior," Charity said breathlessly. "You've crossed the line, Lord Popper. And this time, *there will be repercussions.*"

Lord Popper paled.

Ethan took her by the arm. "Aunt Charity, I'm certain Lord Popper is simply distraught over the undue scrutiny he's received of late, as manager of a duchy in turmoil. I'm sure he'd gladly open the accounts to pay for Mr. Kincaid's services."

Lord Popper examined his hands, now folded over one another on the table. "I suppose the estate could pay the initial one hundred pounds toward the endeavor."

"One hundred?" Charity said, enjoying Lord Popper's rare display of deference. "I don't know . . ."

Ethan shot her a look of warning. "Lord Popper," he said. "If the estate were to offer two hundred pounds, my aunt would be most grateful."

"But of course," said the older man quickly. "Two hundred."

The duchess eased back into the leather chair. "How kind, Lord Popper. Thank you."

Lord Popper scowled at her, and she bestowed him with a triumphant smile as he summoned his assistant to write a draft for the amount.

In a matter of minutes, Ethan escorted her from the office, check in hand.

"I only hope you understand the devil you're about to conjure," Ethan said.

A hand snaked out over the table and grasped the coin that lay beside Samuel Kincaid's empty mug. Quicker than a blink, a knife appeared in Kincaid's hand. He plunged it into the back of the pilferer's hand, pinning it to the table.

The would-be thief howled in pain. Kincaid grabbed him by the hair and pulled him closer. "Never touch what's mine."

Kincaid removed the knife and wiped the blood on his shirt before replacing the blade in its scabbard on his hip.

The thief bolted for the door, cradling his injured hand against his side, leaving a trail of blood in his wake.

"Now. What's yer business with me, Mr. Smith?" Samuel Kincaid tipped his chair back on two legs and propped a booted foot up on the table of the pub in Tunston that served as his place of business. All about them, men and women engaged in an endless variety of illegal activity.

The face of the man seated across from him remained emotionless throughout the incident, but his white-knuckled grip on the handle of his mug betrayed his unease. "I need you to find someone." He leaned in. "He is an operative for the Crown. A spy. I hear you've tracked them in the past."

"One or two."

"He goes by the codename 'Falcon.'"

Kincaid narrowed his eyes. "He is in France. I don't work in France."

Smith, who looked vaguely familiar, shook his head. "I have reason to believe he's in London as we speak."

"Do you want me to kill him?"

"No. I need information from him. He must be taken alive."

A trickle of disappointment dampened Kincaid's enthusiasm for this pursuit. He despised the British government with every beat of his Scots heart and welcomed any opportunity to harm it.

"How much?" Smith asked.

"Six hundred."

"Six! I understood you charge three."

Kincaid shrugged. "The Falcon is no ordinary man. He's a master of disguise. Tricky. And he's dangerous. Six."

"You must be insane."

Kincaid pushed away from the table and turned to leave.

"Wait!"

He turned back.

Smith's face had gone crimson. Beads of sweat populated his forehead. "Two and a half now, two and a half later."

Kincaid sucked a bit of meat from between his teeth. He took his seat again. "A'right. Five."

Smith's shoulders relaxed. "Good. Here." He removed a leather purse from the groin of his breeches and counted out two hundred and fifty pounds. Atop the pile he placed a slip of paper. "You may reach me here."

He looked ill as he pushed the pile of gold coins toward Kincaid.

Kincaid motioned to one of his men, who collected the money and disappeared. "I will find him."

"Quickly, please." Smith finished his ale and started for the door. He turned back. "One more thing. His real name is Jack Pearce."

"Pearce?" The name hit Kincaid like a cannonball. Jack Pearce had foiled several of his attempts to capture a lucrative mark. As a result, Kincaid had lost more money than he cared to think of.

He'd also gained a nasty scar on his leg, a permanent reminder of that debacle. His mouth turned up in a grin that looked more like a grimace. If he'd known the Falcon was Jack Pearce, he would have agreed to hunt him down for free.

"Will you please heat some water? I'd like to bathe." Selena's voice quavered just the slightest bit with her request.

Nervous, Jack thought. Afraid to be in the same room with him, completely unclothed. He could hardly blame her after he'd forced that kiss on her. She probably feared he would attack her. Though it might prove damned near impossible, he'd not make that mistake again.

Besides, while Selena might be nervous at the thought of undressing in the same room as him, he was positively terrified of it. He tamped down a traitorous burst of arousal and considered denying her request. Why tempt fate—and his own shaky self-control?

To deny her, though, would be terribly unfair. Soon she'd be on a ship, sailing toward an unfamiliar land, unable to wash for God knew how long. He should give her this small comfort, at least, no matter how uncomfortable it made him.

He carried the jug to the fireplace and filled the iron pot, moving the arm so it hung above the fire. Water spilled over the edge and sizzled on the burning logs. He pulled the screen from the corner, unfolding it in front of the fireplace.

"Thank you," she said.

Jack expelled a breath, keeping his eyes to the ceiling and his thoughts on hawking as she sidled behind the screen.

When he was certain she wasn't looking, he moved a floorboard beneath which he kept a cache of money, a coded list of all the English operatives in France, and a couple of pistols in case of an emergency. He removed one of the pistols and replaced the floorboard. The gun was in need of a cleaning. He didn't expect any trouble between now and their departure the next morning, but he wanted to be prepared just the same.

As he dismantled the pistol, he studiously avoided looking at the fire, the screen, and everything near it, until a flash of white caught his eye. The chemise he'd given Selena hung over the screen.

Never had he seen anything so beguiling.

Oh, he'd seen undergarments aplenty. Lacy, frilly, soft. Rich, seductive, clinging. All of them much fancier than the plain white cotton thing hanging there. But God help him, none had ever given him such a thrill.

Because none of them had ever touched Selena's skin.

Jack attempted to concentrate on cleaning the pistol, but his attention repeatedly roamed to the garment flung so recklessly over the screen. He tried to forget that Selena was naked just footsteps away, and the only thing separating them was a curtain of reeds no thicker than a shilling.

The fire suddenly flared, illuminating the screen. Behind it, Selena's bewitching silhouette danced against the flames like Satan's mistress. The outline of her breasts, the curve where her waist met her hips, the smooth line of her thighs beckoned him through the screen.

Jack bit his cheek as he hastily reassembled the pistol and tucked it into his waistband. He raked his fingers through his hair.

Damn, he needed a walk.

* * *

The door slammed shut, leaving Selena momentarily stunned.

Her attempt to seduce Jack hadn't brought him nearer, it had driven him away!

She almost felt insulted, until she realized that his actions suited her true purpose far better. If she hurried, she could get to the knife and wait by the door for him, winning the element of surprise.

She hastily dried herself and pulled her clothing on, saying a small prayer of thanks that Jack had given her a gown with few buttons. Then she stood completely still, listening.

No sound. No scrape of boots on the wood floor outside the door. No creak of the ladder.

She tiptoed to Jack's mattress, felt for the slit, and retrieved the knife, testing her grasp on the handle.

Hurrying now, she placed a tinderbox, two apples, and some cheese in the center of a square of linen, tying it into a bundle. Anything else she might need she could get from the woods. Provided she could get that far.

Pressing her ear to the door, she listened again.

Nothing.

Perhaps she wouldn't have to hurt him after all. If she could get out before he returned . . .

She took the handle of the dagger in her palm and jammed the tip into the lock, twisting it this way and that. It wouldn't budge.

She scratched at the wood on the doorframe. It was soft, rotted with age, chipping easily away beneath her fingernail. She pried quietly at the frame with the tip of the dagger, liberating finger-sized chunks of wood with each stab. When the piece of frame that housed the door lock was nearly gone, she pushed against the door with her shoulder until it gave way.

It swung open, the squeak of the hinges as loud as a

baby's cry. Selena's heart squeezed painfully in her chest. On trembling legs, she stepped out of the room.

The loft was as dark as when Jack had brought her here. She dropped to her knees and crawled across the floor, searching for the ladder. She listened again. Nothing.

As if descending into water, she held her breath until her bare feet touched the hard-packed earth below. She gained her bearings quickly, her gaze darting about the darkness.

She made for a large opening illuminated by a full moon. Beyond it, the countryside beckoned like Canaan. A breeze drifted in, the fresh night air filtering through the stale animal odors. She was free!

Or nearly so.

She passed through the barn doors to the outside, and pressed her back up against the rough stone. A line of trees stood just twenty paces away, across an overgrown stretch of land well lit by brilliant moonlight. Crossing it, she would be as visible as if she were strolling through Hyde Park in the middle of the afternoon.

She held her breath.

Just as she was about to take off, she heard the scuff of boot heels on the hard-packed floor of the barn, followed by the creaking of the ladder.

Selena's belly lurched.

She sucked shallow breaths through her mouth. Her heartbeat thrummed in her ears, and she felt an incredible need to relieve herself.

In the trees, an owl hooted as if it were calling her.

She pushed away from the wall and darted out into the tall grass.

Jack paused on the bottom rung of the ladder.

A noise outside the barn caught his attention. It could have been an animal, but Jack's sixth sense, borne of countless situations like this, told him otherwise.

He slowly released his grip on the ladder's rungs and edged toward the open barn doors. Keeping low, he moved into the moonlit night with the stealth of a tomcat hunting a shrew.

A dark figure crossed the grass. A familiar figure.

"Ethan?"

"Jack. I tried to signal you, but there was no answer."

"What happened? Is anything wrong?"

"I've come straight from a meeting with your mother and Lord Popper. Your mother intends to hire Samuel Kincaid to find Selena and take her back to Newgate."

"Hell's teeth." Jack paced before the door of the barn. "Why would she go to such trouble? It certainly isn't for love of my memory."

"She wants Randolph installed as duke, and rumor has it that unless the MPs can question Selena, they won't vote favorably for the writ."

"How did she come to hear of Kincaid? He's not the sort she'd meet at a soiree."

"Sir Ambrose gave her Kincaid's name. She says he'd been suggested to them by someone at the docks."

Jack shook his head. "Couldn't you put her off the idea?"

"I tried. But she threatened to put an end to my contact with Lady Mildred Shelbourne. If that happened, it would staunch the flow of information about her father severely, and I need to be close to him."

Jack ran through his options in his mind. "Selena and I will have to leave tonight for Bristol. As soon as Kincaid puts his men on this, it will be too difficult to travel. And if he begins his search from Tunston . . ."

"He's only a few miles away from here."

"Exactly. Much too close for comfort."

"When does Selena's ship depart?" Ethan asked.

"Two days. As soon as she's on it, I'll head back to Montainville."

"Good. We need you there as soon as possible. There may be a problem."

"What problem?"

Ethan withdrew a small square of paper from his waist-coat pocket. "Read this. See if you can make any sense of it, because I can't."

Jack took the paper from Ethan. "It's too dark to see."

"Do you have a candle?"

"Yes. Upstairs."

Ethan waited. When Jack made no move to go, he said, "Do you intend to get it?"

The thought of Selena outlined by fire sent an involuntary rush of lust coursing through Jack's body. The last thing he wanted to do was go back up there. He sighed. "I'll be back."

Jack reluctantly climbed the ladder. Selena had to be finished with her bath by now.

He fished the key from his vest pocket, taking a moment to collect himself. As he bent to insert the key into the lock, his elbow brushed the door.

It swung slowly open.

CHAPTER 9

Jack squinted at the lock. It looked as if the doorjamb had crumbled away around it. It took a moment for him to realize what had happened.

"Ballocks!"

A quick search of the room confirmed what he had suspected. Selena was gone.

How had she managed it? The only thing sharp enough to gouge out the doorframe was . . .

Damn.

Jack strode to the mattress and fell to his knees, working his hand into the slit.

His knife was gone.

He pounded the mattress with his fist. How bloody stupid of him to leave her alone. He knew what kind of a woman she was—quick, resourceful, determined. His story about ransoming her must have made her feel like a cornered animal. No wonder she'd run.

He cursed his poor judgment. He never should have left her alone. But the truth was, if he hadn't put some space between them, he might have done something rash. He'd left to save his sanity.

In any case, this wasn't the time for self-drubbing. Now was the time to use his knowledge and experience to find her and bring her back. Time was of the essence.

"She's gone," he said as he clattered down the ladder.

"What?" Ethan materialized from one of the old animal stalls.

"Selena has run off. Must've happened when I went for a walk."

"You took a *walk* while there was a prisoner in your custody?"

"She was hardly a prisoner. And she was . . . naked."

Jack could feel Ethan's grin in the dark. "She was naked and you voluntarily left?"

"I've got to find her," Jack said, ignoring Ethan's amusement.

"I'll help."

"No. She might recognize you. I have to do it alone."

"We could cover more ground together."

Jack considered Ethan's offer. Most people in Selena's position would head straight for a village. It would be the best place to find transportation, money, help. But Selena wasn't like most people.

He didn't think she would head toward a village if she could avoid it. She'd keep to the woods.

"I'll find her myself," he said. "And when I do, I'll take her straight to the docks at Bristol."

"Well, at least let me help you close this place up then."

Jack climbed the ladder, with Ethan close behind. The room seemed empty without Selena's presence to fill it.

He gave Ethan instructions to fix the door and close the hideout, then he gathered up the things he'd need.

As Jack descended the ladder, Ethan stuck his head out over the edge of the loft. "My horse is out there."

Jack stopped. "Damn. Where is it?"

"In the field."

* * *

Selena steadied herself against the rough bark of an oak tree, staring at the beast. Her stomach danced.

Before her was the perfect means to escape, standing there as if dropped from the heavens as a gift. She walked slowly toward it, but when the horse raised its head, Selena went scuttling back to the tree.

It was no use. This animal wasn't so much a gift as a cruel joke. Her fear simply would not let her ride it. She hadn't sat a horse since she'd been thrown as a child, suffering injuries that had nearly killed her.

She rubbed her arms, regretting now that she hadn't brought the priest's robe. She'd thought it would hinder her movement, but she hadn't imagined it would be so cold. She listened to the night, her ears searching for sounds of footsteps.

There was no indication yet that her abductor followed. For that was, indeed, what Jack was. Her abductor. Her enemy.

And to think, she'd actually come to like him.

Though his comments often bordered on cruel and she'd be hard-pressed to describe his face in detail, his presence had been, at times, comforting. She'd thought he was on her side. He'd made her feel safe, for the first time in a long while.

She could hate him for that alone.

Selena started off on the path ahead of her, silent as the eerie mist swirling in the shafts of moonlight filtering down through the trees.

The horse looked at Jack with disinterest, and went back to chewing clover.

He considered taking it to find Selena, but if she'd gone into the woods as he suspected, the horse might become more of a nuisance than an advantage. It was difficult to track a person traveling on foot from so far above the ground.

Jack rode the horse back to the barn. Selena would never return there. He and Ethan would have to take the chance that no one would pass by that night and discover the barn was not so abandoned after all.

Then he trudged in ever-widening circles around the hideout, looking for some sign of Selena. He knew it wouldn't be easy to find her. She'd always been an excellent navigator in the woods, with her keen sense of direction and well-honed instinct for the lay of the land.

When they'd gone hawking as children, they'd never bothered to bring dinner. Selena could make a feast of mushrooms, greens, and other delicacies of the wild. In a rainstorm, she'd find shelter. If they were thirsty, she'd find water. She moved like a deer, often leaving him far behind only to circle back and rejoin him a few minutes later.

He would have a devil of a time finding her.

But they weren't children anymore, he reminded himself. He was a grown man with plenty of tracking prowess. He also knew this area well. He'd traveled in and out of here in the dark a dozen times.

Being unfamiliar with the area, Selena would be forced to take things more slowly.

He would find her.

"It is exactly as you've predicted." Sir Ambrose spoke in funereal tones. "I've spoken to dozens of MPs, and they say the writ won't be issued unless they can first talk to the Hewitt woman."

Letitia threw her cards onto the polished table and shot to her feet. "It has to pass. It must!" She went to Randolph, who hovered over something at his desk. She poked him on the shoulder. "Stop playing with that toy and pay attention to Sir Ambrose."

Randolph looked up at his fiancée without a hint of

annoyance. "This isn't a toy, my dear. It is a model of the engine I've bought from Mr. Watt. We'll use it in the coal mine, if I can finally convince Lord Popper to allow me to build it here. You see, the engine converts steam—"

"For heaven's sake, Randolph," Letitia said, "don't you understand? If you are awarded the title of duke, you shall never have to ask Lord Popper's permission for anything again."

Randolph regarded her with patient adoration of the sort one would bestow upon a precocious child. "I understand. But if I could just convince Lord Popper of the benefits—"

Letitia made a strangled sound and stomped back to the card table.

Charity regarded the young woman with both pity and exasperation. At one time Charity thought Letitia would be just the sort of woman to pull Randolph's head out of the clouds. But lately, she wondered if Letitia would really be such a good match for her son.

Letitia wanted to be a duchess. And in fact, Charity had all but promised it to her to get her to accept Randolph's proposal of marriage. Letitia's family held quite a bit of clout in certain circles. Socially, it would be a good match.

In her own defense, at that time Charity truly believed Randolph would become duke. As the last remaining Markley heir, the title was rightly his. Unfortunately, without Canby's body or evidence of perfidy, Parliament wasn't of like mind.

Letitia's hopes, and indeed Charity's own, had been raised to new levels with the arrest of Selena Hewitt. Now with her escape from Newgate, it all seemed to be slipping away.

Charity's considerable influence could squelch naysayers in the House of Lords. But the House of Commons might prove problematic.

"Take heart, Letitia." Charity forced cheeriness into her tone. "Lord Popper has agreed to hire someone to hunt down Selena Hewitt."

Letitia brightened. "He has?"

"Yes. In fact, I've sent a message to a Mr. Kincaid this morning."

"Excellent," Ambrose said. "If the man is as good as I've heard, he'll have her back to Newgate in no time at all."

"I understand there's already a petition for Randolph's instatement being circulated in Fulcrom Parish," Letitia said, her voice filled with hope. "Randolph is fast becoming a national cause."

"Mother's doing, no doubt," Randolph muttered from his desk.

Charity smiled. "Sometimes popular opinion must be nudged in the proper direction."

Sir Ambrose nodded his approval across the card table, as if Charity should feel privileged to have it. He was so imperial, so self-important. So like her husband, Charity nearly shuddered.

Things simply *must* work out in their favor. She needed the money Ambrose promised her. But even more than that, she wanted him out of their lives for good.

Jack doubled back to the barn for the third time.

So far, he'd found no evidence of Selena's trail. He'd wasted hours looking for something, anything, that would tell him which way she'd gone.

He planted himself in front of the barn doors, going completely still, allowing instinct to commandeer his thoughts.

Had Selena gone to the north or the south? Which way made the most sense?

As it was dark when she escaped, she wouldn't have been able to use the sun as her guide. But perhaps the moon? The stars?

He closed his eyes, trying to put himself in her mind.

He'd searched outward in every direction save the meadow where Ethan's horse was tethered, assuming that if she'd passed that way, she would have taken the mount.

And then he remembered. Selena had developed a deep fear of horses when they were children, after being tossed by a poorly trained mount. If she hadn't conquered that fear, she wouldn't have taken Ethan's horse.

He set off toward the meadow, knowing that if he didn't pick up Selena's trail soon, she might be lost to him forever.

CHAPTER 10

Kincaid downed a fourth mug of ale in celebration of the only lead he'd received on the whereabouts of Pearce. He'd begun to doubt the man was really in England, until he'd gotten a tip from a coach driver who, after a bit of persuasion, admitted he'd been in the Falcon's service.

Kincaid had returned to Tunston to regroup and recruit more men when he received the request to find Selena Hewitt.

The thought appealed to him. He'd never been hired to bring in a woman before. And it seemed almost fitting to be hunting a Falcon and a falconer at the same time.

He eyed the half-dozen men who surrounded him at the pub's table. "A'right, you bags of shit. Let's go hunt some birds."

"I will ask you again. What in the hell is going on in Montainville?"

Lord North glared at Ethan through a haze of pipe

smoke as he studied the lay of billiard balls on the table. The two often met to discuss the business of the Anti-British Activity Committee over a friendly game in Lord North's billiards room.

"I am trying to discern that very thing, sir. The intelligence I've received has been difficult to decipher."

Lord North frowned. "It isn't like the Falcon and the Fox to be so inattentive to their duties."

"No, it isn't." Ethan hit a ball into the leather basket at the side of the table. "But I'm not terribly concerned. By all accounts, the delegation from the colonies will not arrive in Versailles for some time yet."

"Nevertheless, I expect you to get the situation under control," North said as he took his shot. "I do not need to tell you how vital that contribution is to the Crown."

"I understand completely, sir," Ethan said.

He only hoped Jack did, too.

A bitter wind drove Selena to seek shelter.

She would have welcomed a fire, but she'd already lit one that afternoon to cook a small hare she'd trapped. She doused the flames as soon as the food had cooked, although the temptation to warm herself was great.

Fires were dangerous. They put smells on the breeze, light in the darkness. They created a false sense of security.

Walking might have helped to warm her, but the woods had become so thick that no light could filter through. She'd spent an hour or so bumping into trees and tripping over roots before she decided it wasn't worth the risk of breaking an arm or ankle.

Now she huddled in the thick branches of a fallen fir. Her spirits sagged. What had been the point of escaping? She had nowhere to go. She should have planned things out before she'd left, but hadn't dared to hope she'd actually get away.

The important thing was that she was free. She could take the opportunity to go anywhere. Everywhere. All the places Canby used to tell her about. The places in his books.

Rome, Venice, Paris, Brussels—the cities of great artists and composers.

Selena used to love listening to Canby read of them, and they imagined they'd go there together, someday. They'd hold hands and walk along the Seine. Drift upon the canals of Venice in a gondola. View the great cathedrals of Italy.

"We'll have a grand time," he'd said as they sat side by side, their backs to the wall in the falconer's shed. His head was pressed to hers, his breath warm on her cheek as they examined the book that was open on his lap.

"Here, give me your hand." He took it in his and used her finger to trace the route they would take across Europe. "We'll dance in every city. You'll wear the finest gowns, and I'll find someone who can fix this limp."

But those were just childish fantasies, and she was, at the present, rooted in a horrible reality.

Canby was dead. She had no money, no maps, no knowledge of the world outside of the woods and villages that surrounded Lockwell Hall. She was lost, and scared, and completely alone.

There wasn't a soul in the world who gave a tinker's damn about her. What was she to do, live in the woods for the rest of her life?

She nearly gave in to her despair, until she realized her situation wasn't completely hopeless. She had a small cache of money hidden in her sewing box at home. It wasn't much, but it might get her to Scotland. Her father had often talked of the beauty of that country, and the open land so perfect for hawking. Returning to the estate would be dangerous, but at least it would give her a chance to make sure her birds were taken care of.

If they weren't, she'd set them free. She knew it would be far easier for them to survive without her than it would be for her to survive without them.

* * *

Jack's confidence flagged.

Selena's ship left Bristol in two days, and he still hadn't caught up with her. A short while ago he'd been close enough to hear her moving through the forest, but then he'd lost her and hadn't seen one sign, not one broken branch or overturned stone, in hours.

Only one meal remained in the sack he brought. He sat on a log to eat it before backtracking to where he'd last seen evidence of Selena's passing.

Around him, the chirps and scuttles of wildlife echoed through the trees. A faint odor lingered at the edge of his senses. He swallowed the bread he'd been chewing and sniffed the air.

Ashes.

There had been a fire in this clearing.

Jack stood, observing his surroundings with a critical eye. He walked through the clearing slowly, examining the dead leaves on the ground until he came to a spot where they seemed to have been disturbed. Beneath the leaves, the dirt was loose. He kicked it away with the toe of his boot to reveal a small circle of gray silt.

Jack kneeled down and rubbed the ashes between his fingers. Cold, but not yet damp. A half a day old, he would guess. Beside the ashes, the bones of a hare had been buried.

He stood, closing his eyes, breathing, listening. Selena was close. He could feel it.

When the sun was high, Selena stopped to rest and pick the leaves and branches from her dress. She rebraided her hair and washed her face and hands in a stream, ignoring the rumblings of her stomach.

A few times she thought she'd heard noises behind her. Twigs snapping. Leaves rustling. Now those sounds were drowned out by the louder noises of travelers—the squeak and rumble of coach wheels, the clop clop of horses' hooves.

Selena straggled out of the woods and onto the road,

momentarily disoriented by the light and open space.

A wagon clattered up behind her. She kept walking, head bent, eyes to the ground.

"Ye need a ride, missy?" the driver shouted over the clamor of the wagon's wheels.

Selena shook her head.

"Ye be goin' to Tunston?"

Tunston! She was closer than she had imagined to Lockwell Hall. If she started from the town, she'd have a fair idea how to get home. By road it would take a few hours, at most.

"Missy! I said, ye be goin' to Tunston?" The driver's nag hobbled beside her now, drawing flies from all corners of the earth.

Selena swatted them away. "Yes."

"Be needin' a ride?"

Her feet ached, and she was sorely tempted, but she didn't need anyone asking her questions. She'd make it to Tunston by foot. "Nay. Thank you."

"Suit yerself." The wagon driver slapped the nag's flanks with a whip, eyeing Selena as he pulled past.

A pumpkin bounced off the bed of his wagon and rolled to a stop at her feet. Her stomach grumbled again.

Wonderful. Why couldn't the wagon have been filled with hams?

Jack touched the footprint in the mud beside the stream.

She'd been there just a short time ago. And by the looks of things, she was headed straight toward Tunston, a well-known haven for all sorts of unsavory characters, including Samuel Kincaid.

Selena had no idea Kincaid sought her, nor what kind of danger she was in. Kincaid was brutal. Pitiless.

Jack had to find her first.

He stepped up his pace, hoping to reach her before she reached Tunston.

* * *

A hawk circled above, as if keeping watch over her.

Selena considered it a good omen, thinking again of her own birds. Had they been hunting? Had they even been fed? The mews would surely need cleaning, and—

She stopped herself. She'd clean no mews. Not at Lockwell Hall, anyway. She would have time to do nothing more than retrieve her money and check on the birds. But at least she would get to see them one last time.

She'd just rounded a curve where a field opened up beside the road when she heard the shouts.

A cloud of road dust plumed up behind a pair of riders, swirling out into the open field to cover the tall grass with fine brown grit. There was purpose in the hoofbeats. She could feel urgency in the vibration beneath her feet.

One of the riders pointed in her direction. Selena looked over her shoulder. Something moved in the trees. An animal?

The horsemen charged toward it.

Selena had no desire to be caught between hunters and their quarry. She changed direction, heading back toward the protection of the trees.

"Halt, woman."

The voice, and the fact that it came from so close behind her, startled her. She turned to discover that one of the riders had moved ahead of the other. He shouldered a rifle and pointed it at her head.

Too late, Selena realized that she was their quarry.

"Selena!"

Jack called out to her, but he was too far away, his voice drowned out by the pounding of horses' hooves. He'd almost broken through the tree line when he heard the shot.

He watched in horror as Selena's body crumpled to a

heap on the ground, just footsteps from the cover of the woods. One of the men on horseback reined up beside her motionless form.

Jack opened his spyglass. He recognized the shooter immediately as one of Kincaid's men. Kincaid himself was just moments behind.

Though Jack couldn't hear what they said, he could tell by their voices that they were arguing. Selena lay gray and motionless at their horses' feet, blood pooling on the ground beneath her shoulder.

Fear for Selena's life urged Jack forward, but reason pulled him back. If he showed himself now, Kincaid would shoot him before he could reach Selena's side. He needed to get closer while still under the cover of the trees.

He crept toward the clearing, watching.

Selena rolled onto her back, and he was close enough now to hear her groan with the effort. As he was about to step out of the trees, two more riders veered from the road and into the field, barreling straight for Selena and Kincaid.

Jack ducked back into the brush as two menacing-looking thugs joined Kincaid and his partner. The four of them encircled Selena with their horses, making it difficult for Jack to see her.

"Is it her?" asked one of the men.

"Must be," Kincaid said. He nudged Selena with his foot. "You the falconer's daughter?"

She said nothing. Whether it was because she couldn't or wouldn't, Jack did not know.

Kincaid kicked Selena's leg and she whimpered. Jack fought the urge to leap out of the forest and rip the man apart with his bare hands.

There were four of them, each with a rifle. He was one man with a pistol. It didn't take a fortune-teller to see the outcome.

"Woman. I asked if you were the falconer's daughter."

"Yes." Her voice was hoarse, but unbroken.

The men nodded and slapped each others' backs.

"We should get 'er to a doctor," one of them said. "She don't look well."

"She shouldn't have been *shot* in the first place," Kincaid spat. He backhanded the man who held the rifle. "I pay you all well to follow my orders. I said, no shooting."

Kincaid dismounted and kneeled beside Selena, stroking her cheek with the backs of his fingers. "She's a beauty, eh?"

"Why don't we take her to Lockwell Hall? It's closer," said another of his men.

"We could kill her," said the last. "It'd be a damned sight easier to take her anywhere dead."

"No," said Kincaid. "We won't kill her. But we won't waste time taking her to a physician, either. We'll take her to Newgate, as requested. If she happens to die on the way, so be it."

Jack's instincts rebelled against his inaction. He was so close. He had to get to her. But how?

His mind ran through a thousand scenarios, each ending the same way: with him lying dead in the field and Selena in prison.

In the end, logic prevailed over emotion. He'd do more good for Selena, have a better chance of saving her, if he stayed alive. But he needed help.

He needed Ethan.

Kincaid rode toward London, his men behind him, an unconscious Selena Hewitt draped over the saddle in front of him. She'd passed out as soon as he picked her up to put her on the horse. Blood from the gunshot wound on her arm dripped onto his boots.

A bit of blood never bothered him, especially when he'd been paid to spill it. And he usually didn't care one way or the other if he brought in a bounty dead or alive. But this one was different. She intrigued him.

She was a falconer. A woman captivated by the hunt and the hunter, unafraid to witness the beauty of a kill. Under different circumstances, she might have been the perfect woman for him.

He stroked the enticing curve of her bottom, letting it warm the palm of his hand. He wished she were conscious. A bloody shame Hervis had shot her.

If she awoke before they arrived at Newgate, perhaps he'd have a bit of fun with her.

CHAPTER 11

A pink glow filtered up from the horizon as Selena slipped silently through the door of the mews. All fear and heartache dissolved in the warm, musky air.

She closed her eyes, listening to the quiet rustlings of the birds. Though it was still too dark to see them clearly, she imagined each one's markings and mannerisms as they rested on block or perch.

The eagle she called Holly, raised from a fledgling. The peregrine, Midnight, whose keen eyes reminded Selena of her father's.

And her favorites, the cast of hawks. Diana and Orion, with their chocolate wings and cream-colored breasts. It had always fascinated her that hawks mated for life, as if they were reincarnations of time's most steadfast lovers. Dido and Aeneas, Troilus and Cressida, Lancelot and Gweneviere taking wing.

She left the mews and traveled along a narrow path that led to a well-kept cottage—her home for most of her life. The leaves had been swept from the porch, the firewood stacked in a neat pile. Smoke drifted from the chimney.

She pushed the door open. A man sat in her favorite chair in the sitting room. When she entered, he turned to face her.

"Father!"

He smiled. "Selena, my girl."

"Father, I've missed you so much."

He held out his arms and she moved toward him. With each step he grew farther away. Selena quickened her pace, but the faster she ran, the farther away he seemed . . .

"Father!"

Selena bolted up in bed. Or rather, the lumpy pile of blankets that served as a bed. Pain seared her arm. Black clouded her vision.

"Shh, child." Gentle hands pressed a cloth to her forehead.

It had all been a dream.

She hadn't seen the birds. She hadn't seen her father. She hadn't been home.

"Where am I?" she whispered. Her throat burned with the effort.

The woman with the cloth, a nun, took Selena's face in cool hands. "Newgate."

Tears filled Selena's eyes. The nun's face blurred and doubled.

"Would you care to make a confession? I can fetch a priest."

"Jack?" Selena whispered hopefully.

The nun looked confused. "Who is Jack?"

Selena sobbed. God would not be with her today.

"Shall I fetch a priest?" the nun asked again.

"No."

"Are you certain, child?" The nun stroked her cheek. "You're meant to hang tomorrow."

CHAPTER 12

"Tomorrow?" Jack clutched Ethan's arm.

"Aye, tomorrow. They didn't want to risk having her escape again. The citizens of England demand a hanging."

"Damn it. We should have intercepted Kincaid and his men before they reached Newgate. It's my fault. I should have been faster."

"You were on foot. How could you possibly have arrived before them?"

Jack felt as if he might puke. "How will we stop the hanging? How will we get her?"

Ethan's expression was grim. "I'm afraid we can't. She's in a cell by herself. Extra guards have been posted on the request of Sir Ambrose and your mother."

"Sir Ambrose? What would he care?"

"Apparently your mother has promised that Randolph will sell Two Moons Shipping back to Ambrose once he's installed as duke."

"Will he be?"

Ethan shrugged. "Popular opinion has swayed Parliamentary vote on more than one occasion. The people are calling for Lord Randolph to be named the Duke of Canby. There are now dozens of petitions circulating, and even the members of Parliament who were so anxious to question Selena about your murder have acquiesced."

"This reeks of Mother's scheming."

"Without a doubt. But that doesn't change the fact that it will happen."

Jack dropped to his knees, feeling as if he were trapped in a swirling eddy. "We've got to save her. We'll have to take her off the wagon on the way to Tyburn. It's a long enough ride from Newgate to the gallows—"

"Jack. We can't." Ethan put a hand on his shoulder. "The line of guards will be impenetrable, the odds unbeatable, especially when we have so little time to plan."

Jack buried his face in his hands.

"I know you believe you owe her your life," Ethan said quietly. "I'm sorry."

Jacks swiped the tears from his cheeks with his fist. He'd been so stupid. If he hadn't helped Selena escape, she'd have spent the rest of her life in Newgate, but at least she would have *lived.*

And if he'd told her who he really was, she never would have tried to escape the barn. Never would have been shot and captured by Kincaid and his men.

If only he could undo what he'd done.

He couldn't. But he could undo what *she'd* supposedly done.

"I have to save her, Ethan," he said, his voice hoarse with emotion. "I love her."

Ethan's look of surprise quickly turned to one of sympathy. "You must face facts. We cannot save her. Not now."

Jack raised his head. "There is one way."

"Tell me."

"We must stage a resurrection."

* * *

Letitia and Charity walked arm in arm through Vauxhall Gardens, stopping briefly where the well-heeled gathered. Below an ornate balcony upon which an orchestra played, an opera singer performed an aria by Millico, her sweet, high voice carrying on the breeze.

Charity gave a regal nod to the Duchess of Devonshire. Lord, how she loved all of this.

Letitia wore a delicate pink blush high on her cheeks. To others, it might be mistaken for the blush of love. But Charity knew it was the flush of success, for Letitia would soon be a duchess.

The young woman patted Charity's hand, apparently forgiving all to the woman who had enough power left to make everything right. "I cannot thank you enough, Your Grace. I know Randolph will make an excellent husband, and an excellent duke."

"And you will be a charming duchess, my dear."

"Well, I am certain I shall rely on your ingenuity and advice to guide me."

"And it shall be given, as you wish."

They walked in amiable silence for a while, Charity lost in thoughts of better days to come. They would plan the wedding for the start of the Season.

She was so close to having everything. With Selena's hanging and Randolph's appointment as duke, Charity would soon possess a small fortune, her own home in London, and best of all, freedom from Ambrose. Her life would be better than it had ever been.

As she and Letitia left the gardens, a beggar woman stared at their fine gowns with a look of hungry longing.

Charity offered her a benevolent smile. She couldn't blame the poor woman for envying her. After all, there were precious few people who wouldn't give their left eye to be part of her world.

* * *

He was a moth emerged from a cocoon.

Stripped of all disguise, beard shaven and hair shorn, Jack Pearce was all but gone. He stood in the middle of the dressing closet in Ethan's London home preparing for the final transition—the one that would take him from spy to duke, from chosen life back to forsaken.

His bare face and freshly scrubbed skin left him feeling profoundly vulnerable.

"You'll have to wear my clothes," Ethan said, rooting through a wardrobe. "I hope they fit."

Jack shrugged. He didn't give a damn about clothes. All he wanted was to save Selena from the noose. "What time is it?"

Ethan pulled a jacket from the wardrobe. "Don't worry. It's hours to dawn, and the prisoners don't arrive at Tyburn until well after noon."

Ethan helped Jack dress and powder his wig as best he could by himself, not wishing to involve any servants in the transformation. The less who knew of this, the better.

"There," Ethan said, turning him toward a full-length dressing mirror.

Jack stared at his reflection. He hardly recognized the man in the mirror—the hollow aristocrat. He thought he'd left that man behind for good six years ago.

"Here," said Ethan. "I sent a footman to fetch this from your town house." Ethan handed Jack a cane. The gold handle was the shape of a falcon's head.

All the insecurities and awkward self-consciousness of his youth, the part of him he thought he'd left behind, seemed to surge from the cane into his body. The resurrection was truly complete.

"Welcome back, Canby," Ethan said. "Now, let's pay a visit to Lord North."

* * *

"Time ta meet yer maker!" The night guard ran his stick against the bars of the cells, each of which held a single prisoner slated to die at Tyburn that day. It was the first and last time any of them had had a cell all to themselves—a one-day privilege of the condemned.

Selena lay on her blankets, closer to death than any of them. Her fever had grown more severe overnight, leaving her weak and near delirium.

She opened her eyes, unable to imagine that this would be the last dawn of her life.

She struggled to sit. The gunshot wound on her upper arm throbbed, though the bleeding had ceased sometime during the night. Her throat was as dry and scratchy as a woolen sock.

She stumbled to the bars and gripped them to keep from falling over. "Guard. Water."

The bars seemed to writhe beneath her fingers. She snatched her hands away. Perhaps she ought to lie down again.

The blankets seemed miles away. She would never make it. She sank to the floor, closing her eyes.

"Get up."

The scrape and clank of the cell door was unbearably loud. She covered her ears with her hands.

The guard hauled her to her feet and dragged her out of the cell, screwing a set of shackles around her hands and feet, binding her to the line of prisoners heading for the gallows wagon.

Some stood tall, ignoring the begging and crying, the desperate fear of their less stoic brothers. Selena, the only woman on the line that day, allowed herself to be pulled along, all of her efforts concentrated on staying upright. Pain seared her arm.

Two deputies led the prisoners out through a side gate to a long, freshly painted wagon parked on the street. It was surrounded by dozens of guards in green coats and tricorn hats, who would walk beside the wagon the whole way to Tyburn to prevent escapes, and also to make sure the overeager crowd didn't cheat the hangman out of his work.

"In you go," said one of the guards, leading the first prisoner to the wagon. A ramp was laid in the back, and the prisoners, eight in all, shuffled up to it in their chains.

As the wagon rolled out of the yard toward Saint Sepulchre's, the bells of the church tolled. The mournful sound hardly penetrated Selena's conscience.

The pain in her arm erased all other thoughts save the one that said death might not be such a terrible prospect after all.

Unable to hold her head up any longer, she leaned against the man beside her. He pushed her away.

"Yer wrinklin' my weddin' clothes," he said.

The garments had seen better days. Perhaps the man had, too, although by the sad look on his face, Selena wouldn't have placed a wager on it.

She looked at his feet. They were bare.

"No sense in wastin' a perfectly good pair of shoes," he said. "Jailer'd only get them after the hangin'. Me wife don't have the money to buy them back."

Selena nodded. It was the best she could manage.

It all seemed like a dream. A horrible, unnatural dream.

Canby and Ethan waited in a small drawing room at Lord North's home on Downing Street. Canby stared nervously at the clock on the mantle. Five-thirty.

It had taken almost half an hour to convince the houseman to let them in, and another twenty minutes already waiting for the prime minister to make an appearance.

The sun had risen by the time Lord North, his cumbersome eyelids puffy with sleep, stepped into the drawing room. He hardly glanced at Canby, but his look of groggy annoyance changed to one of concern the moment he saw Ethan.

"Gray. What brings you?"

Ethan bowed. "So sorry to bother you at such an ungodly hour, sir, but I have an urgent request. I have knowledge that one of the people to be hanged at Tyburn today goes to the gallows an innocent."

"Indeed? Who?"

"The woman. Selena Hewitt."

Lord North raised his eyebrows. "Selena Hewitt? The young woman convicted of murdering the Duke of Canby?"

"The same."

Lord North expelled a huge breath. "You cannot be serious, Gray. A jury has convicted her. The family clamors for her neck in a noose. So does the public, for that matter."

"But she is wrongfully accused, sir."

"And you conclude this how?"

Canby stepped forward. "Because *I* am the Duke of Canby."

The prime minister squinted at him. "You say?"

"I am John Markley, the Seventeenth Duke of Canby. As you can see, I am very much alive."

"Good heavens." Lord North staggered to a chair. "Do you know the implications of such a statement?"

"I'm sure there are many," Canby said. "However, at this moment I only care about one. We must spare Selena Hewitt from the gallows. She's committed no crime, sir."

"Have you any proof you are who you say?" Lord North sputtered. "You could be anyone. If you are the Duke of Canby, where in the devil have you been all these years?"

"I—"

Ethan interrupted. "He's been locked away in a French prison, sir. A case of mistaken identity. Kidnapping. A very long and complicated story."

"And he just happens to reappear on the day of the woman's hanging?" Lord North propped his elbows on his knees and buried his face in his hands. "This all sounds so preposterous. Unbelievable, really."

"He *is* the Duke of Canby. I give you my word," Ethan said. "You must stop the hanging."

"I'm not certain I can do that. Without solid evidence—"

"You'll have it, sir, eventually."

Lord North rubbed his chin. "This could take weeks to sort out. I simply cannot stop the wheels of justice on the basis of the word of a man who shows up out of nowhere—"

Ethan cleared his throat. "Sir, if we may speak with you in private . . ." His gaze drifted to the manservant standing silently in a corner.

Lord North waved him from the room. When the door had closed, he turned to his visitors.

"Sir," said Ethan in a quiet voice, "I think there is something you should know. This man is not only the Duke of Canby. He's also the Falcon."

Lord North's eyes grew wide. "The Falcon? But I thought the Falcon was in Montainville."

"He came back to free the young lady. He *is* the Falcon, and he *is* the Duke of Canby. For obvious reasons, we cannot allow anyone to connect the two. So you can see what sort of dilemma this presents."

"Dilemma. Yes." Lord North stared at Canby as if he'd witnessed the raising of Lazarus.

"We'll come up with a suitable story to give the public and the papers. But in the meantime, you cannot let Selena Hewitt hang for a crime she did not commit."

Lord North glanced down at Canby's walking stick and shook his head. "I'll see what I can do."

The wagon rolled slowly through the crowd, stopping only twice on the way to Tyburn—once at Saint Sepulchre's, where each of the condemned was handed a small bouquet of white flowers, and again at Mason's Arms, a pub where the prisoners were offered a final draught of ale to toast their lives and numb their senses.

Selena was too weak to leave the wagon, so she was chained to the bench while the others went inside. One of the guards, a barrel-shaped man with kindly brown eyes, fetched a mug of ale and brought it to the wagon.

"Here ye go, missy," he said, raising the mug up to her.

"No ale for the Duke Killer!" someone shouted.

"Let her drop without it!"

"Why waste good drink on the likes of 'er?"

"Ah, stifle!" the guard shouted back. "There are plenty of others who done worse." He passed the mug over the side of the wagon. The crowd hissed.

Selena gave the guard a grateful smile.

"Be strong, missy," he said. "Th' Lord'll have ye soon."

Selena could no longer fight her exhaustion. She couldn't fathom how she'd ended up here. People yelled profanities at her, some pelting her with rotten food and rocks. She curled into a ball and huddled on the floor of the wagon until the rest of the prisoners were brought out from the pub.

The man in the wedding clothes shouted, "I'll buy ye all a pint on th' way back!"

A cheer went up for the joke that had now become a hanging-day ritual.

As the wagon approached Tyburn, the crowd swelled. Thousands of faces peered up at her. Hawkers worked the crowd, selling pies, flowers, and speeches from the condemned, including a confession from Selena that she had supposedly written herself.

When she caught her first glimpse of the gallows, waiting in the distance like the gates of hell, she closed her eyes.

A footman spread a blanket over the rough planks of wood that served as seating for the audience at Tyburn. At least, for those who could afford seats at the spectacle.

Thousands—nay, tens of thousands—stood in the fields surrounding the gallows.

Charity sat gingerly, taking care not to wrinkle her gown. It was new, bought on credit in anticipation of the money she'd receive soon from Ambrose.

The sun warmed her shoulders chasing away the chill from the air.

"I cannot believe we'll finally be done with all this rot," Letitia said, her voice mirroring the excitement of the crowd.

Footmen flanked Charity and Randolph and Letitia on all sides, serving as a buffer between them and the sweaty mass of onlookers around them.

Ambrose had offered to buy spots for them in the gallery directly beneath the hanging beams, but Charity had refused. She didn't want to be quite that close to Selena.

If she thought about it, she might interpret this reluctance as guilt. But she had no need for self-examination. Nor for guilt.

She'd done what she had to do for Randolph. If Selena Hewitt was made to suffer for it, so be it. She wouldn't shed any tears for the woman who had all but stolen her eldest son from her.

Charity put a pair of opera glasses to her eyes and scanned the crowd, smiling.

It was a lovely day.

The wagon stopped before a gallery of people who'd paid a fine price to see the condemned up close. To hear their final speeches and confessions. To hear their necks snap beneath the rope.

One by one, the prisoners were led from the wagon to stand before the crowd, offering final words, begging for God's forgiveness. All pretense of bravery had fled.

"I'll pray for your soul," the stocky guard said quietly as he unlocked Selena's shackles. He stood beside her in the wagon as she waited.

A group of men in dark clothing gathered beneath the nooses. "Who are they?" she asked the guard.

"Physicians," he said. "They're waitin' for the bodies that've been sold for dissection. For some, 'tis the only way to provide for their families."

Selena's head swam.

Physicians waited for her body. The hangman waited for her clothes. Clergymen prayed for her soul. In a matter minutes, she'd become mere parts for the business of others.

The man in the wedding suit cried during his speech, and struggled against the hangman as he bound his wrists. "You'll not take me. Not like this!" he sobbed. His words were drowned in the cheering of the crowd.

The hangman fitted the noose around his neck and pushed him up the ladder. Below him a woman wailed, wringing her apron with red, work-roughened hands. Perhaps it was his wife.

Selena turned away, refusing to watch his demise. A roar went up, and she knew he was gone.

She felt the tap of a stick against her back.

"'Tis your turn, missy," said the kindly guard.

Selena's vision blurred. She rose to her feet, her knees shaking so badly she feared she'd collapse and fall head-first over the side of the wagon. The guard lifted her out.

The crowd chanted. "Duke Killer. Duke Killer. Duke Killer."

"Would you care to make a speech?" the guard asked.

Selena shook her head. Had she wanted to, she didn't believe she could force a word from her mouth.

"Speech!" the crowd roared. "Speech! Speech! Speech!"

She bent over and vomited.

A cheer went up.

The guard led her to the base of the ladder. "Don't worry." He jerked his head toward the hangman. "He's good with a rope. It won't take long."

Selena stared at the hangman, dressed in black from head to toe. His image doubled, then tripled. The guard took her hands behind her back and the hangman tied them. Pain shot like fire through her arm, and she nearly fainted.

This was the end.

The crowd's yelling and cheering dropped to a dull roar. Selena looked up. The bare feet of the man in the wedding clothes dangled overhead.

She whispered a prayer for her birds, and one for herself as well. Then she vowed to face her fate with dignity and courage.

She closed her eyes and put one foot on the ladder.

CHAPTER 13

"Halt! I command you to halt these proceedings immediately!"

Selena opened her eyes.

The crowd parted as two men pushed through to the gallows and handed the hangman a rolled parchment.

Selena recognized one of the men, the one with the auburn hair, as Ethan Gray. The other, the one in blue with the limp . . .

Dear God, could it be?

Canby.

Selena collapsed beneath the gallows. The fields of Tyburn erupted. Word that the hanging of the Duke Killer would not proceed spread rapidly from its epicenter.

Canby gathered Selena up from the ground, alarmed at how hot her skin burned against his hands.

"Make way for us," he ordered one of the wagon guards who stood nearby.

The guard looked incredulous. "And where would ye take 'er? In case ye haven't noticed, we're surrounded."

The guard spoke the truth. Hundreds, perhaps thousands, of people blocked any conceivable retreat. Canby climbed the ladder partway and looked over the sea of bodies.

"There!" he yelled to the guard over the din. "We've got to get across the field to the inn."

Several guards surrounded them, arms linked, while two others set about knocking spectators out of the way. People screamed obscenities, hurled putrid vegetables, and pulled at their clothing. Canby wrapped his arms protectively around Selena as the guards fought their way through the hostile masses.

As the horror of what had almost happened set in, he shuddered violently. He'd almost lost Selena once again—this time not to another man, or to their class differences, but to a length of rope about her neck.

He gathered her close, burying his face in her hair. "I'll not let you go again."

Charity watched the drama unfold through a pair of mother-of-pearl opera glasses.

The Hewitt woman disappeared from view. Two men stood beside the platform, talking with the hangman and the guards.

Good heavens. Was that *Ethan*?

The din was unbearable. Charity put her opera glasses in her lap and covered her ears. Through the crush of bodies she could see Sir Ambrose fighting his way toward them.

"Where did Selena go?" Randolph asked, his typical look of passive indifference replaced by one of genuine curiosity.

Charity gave Ambrose a questioning look. He leaned in, pressing his lips to her ear. "Your bloody nephew arrived with another man. Somehow, they stopped the hanging."

"What!" Charity stood on tiptoe, looking out over the sea of heads, trying to catch another glimpse of Ethan. He was surrounded by a circle of guards moving slowly away from the gallows platform. She held the opera glasses to her eyes.

The man in blue carried the Hewitt woman in his arms. He was tall, dressed in fine clothing. With his long legs and broad shoulders, he reminded her of Kellam.

And he walked with a limp.

The world faded to dark. Charity's legs fell out from under her, and she plunked onto the bench, hard.

"What? What did you see?" said Ambrose, grabbing the opera glasses from her hand.

"A ghost."

"I don't care what you must do, just get us to that inn." Charity fought to control the numbing hysteria filling her chest, raising her voice three octaves.

"We'll never make it through all these people," Ambrose said. "We will have to wait."

"*You* wait. I'm going to the inn."

Charity pushed and elbowed and scratched her way through the gallery to the door of the inn, with Ambrose, Randolph, Letitia, and several footmen trailing far behind.

Two guards bearing rifles stood watch at the door, one of whom looked like the guard who'd stood with Selena on the wagon.

"Let me pass, please." Despite the polite phrasing, it was not a request, but an order. Unfortunately, the thick-headed Newgate guard failed to understand that.

"Sorry, mum," he said. "We're to keep everyone out except the physician, and I don't think ye be him."

"Of course I'm not the physician. I am the Duchess of Canby. I have reason to believe my nephew, Ethan Gray, is within."

"Forgive me, Yer Grace." The guard bowed.

Charity pulled up to her full height. "You are forgiven. Now, if you'll step aside . . ."

The guard's ears went pink. "With respect, Yer Grace, we cannot. We have orders from Lord North his very self."

Charity struggled to retain the precious little patience she had left. The problem with most common folk was that they simply did not understand their place. Or more to the point, hers.

"Is Ethan Gray inside?"

"Aye."

"Please inform him I would like to speak with him immediately."

The guards shared a look. The Newgate fellow shrugged, and the other opened the door a crack and disappeared inside.

Sir Ambrose and the rest of Charity's entourage straggled to her side, drawing speculation from the crowd. People squeezed ever closer in an attempt to discover what was happening, leaving the other poor souls hung at the gallows with nary a fraction of the attention they deserved.

The second guard reemerged from the inn. Ethan followed.

"Ethan, thank goodness." Charity clutched him to her and whispered in his ear. "Is he in there? Is it really Canby?"

Ethan pulled away. "Aunt Charity, Randolph, Letitia. You're all putting yourselves in great danger here. As you well know, these events can become quite violent."

"Then allow us to come in."

"I cannot." He looked tired.

"I want to see my son," Charity pressed. A feeling akin to hysteria welled within her.

"Your son?" Ambrose crowded close, giving her a searching look. She pushed him away.

"We will sort this all out, Aunt Charity. I promise," Ethan said. "But not now. We must see Mrs. Hewitt through this ordeal—if indeed she survives. She's been shot, and is badly wounded."

"Shot? By whom? Ethan, you must—"

Her nephew held up a hand. "Sir Ambrose, please escort my family home. Aunt Charity, I assure you, all will be resolved as soon as it is possible."

Charity seethed. But it was clear by the stubborn set of Ethan's jaw that he would not relent. It was a look he'd inherited from Charity's brother. A look she knew all too well.

Her head pounded. What was one to do when it seemed one's dead son suddenly reappeared? There simply was no precedent.

She didn't want to leave. Not if there was any chance at all that Canby was behind those doors.

Truthfully, though, things seemed a bit surreal there. All about her, toothless, barefoot commoners leered at her and her family. One woman had the audacity to reach out and touch her necklace! It all had begun to take on a sinister feel.

Letitia's eyes shifted nervously about the crowd, as if she were waiting for someone to leap at her. Sir Ambrose pulled incessantly at his neck stock. The only person who seemed unaffected by it all was Randolph.

Ethan folded his arms over his chest.

"Very well," she said. "We'll be waiting at Lockwell Hall."

"What do you mean by all this?" Ambrose sputtered. "You mean to say Canby is *alive*?"

Ethan motioned to one of the guards. "Will you please see the duchess and her party safely to their carriage?"

Charity gave her nephew one last furious look before the guard escorted them away.

"I must remove the arm."

"No."

"But the skin has gone putrid. If I leave the arm, she'll die."

Canby stared down at Selena, willing her to take each breath, to open her eyes. He would not let her lose a limb because he'd been too much of a coward to prevent her from being shot in the first place.

"You must try everything in your power to save it," he demanded.

By all accounts, the doctor who hovered over Selena was the best London had to offer. If anyone could spare her arm, he could.

"I understand your concern, Your Grace," the doctor said. "But—"

"Please."

The doctor shook his head, and sighed. "I suppose I could cut the affected skin away. If she lives through it, she'll have a mighty scar."

"Better a scar than a missing limb."

"Very well. But I'll need another physician to assist me."

"I'll send for one immediately."

In less than an hour, the other doctor had arrived, Selena's case was presented, and the two set about preparing her for the painful procedure.

"Why don't you retire to your room, Your Grace? Get some sleep. This will take quite a while."

"No, I want to stay."

"It will be a bloody affair," the doctor warned.

"I don't care. I will stay."

"As you wish."

Canby smoothed the hair from Selena's brow and settled in beside her.

The doctors readied their fierce-looking instruments. The hole in Selena's arm was the size of a walnut, ugly and dark. Canby closed his eyes, sending all his strength into her.

Each slice of the knife to Selena's skin cut into Canby's heart. Even in her unconscious state, she groaned with pain. Blood poured from the wound, soaking rag after rag, pooling on the sheets beneath her.

"We must cauterize the wound, Your Grace," said the first physician. "'Tis the only way to stop the bleeding."

Canby clenched his teeth. He'd seen such a procedure before. It was a horrible thing to witness, but he knew there was a good chance it would work. He nodded to the physician.

The doctor heated a short length of iron with a wooden handle in the coals of the fire until it glowed red. He let it cool for only a few moments before approaching the bed.

"Are you certain you don't wish to wait outside, Your Grace?"

Canby shook his head. He gripped Selena's hand tightly and raised it to his lips, kissing the palm.

One physician removed the blood-soaked rags that covered the gaping hole and held Selena's arm, while the other applied the iron. It hissed when it met the wound. Steam rose over the bed.

Selena screamed.

Canby pressed a kiss to her hand, wishing he could change places with her. The sickening smell of burning flesh overcame him. His stomach heaved.

By the time the procedure was complete, Canby was numb. He only wished he could say the same for Selena. The pain she would endure when she awoke he wouldn't wish on a Frenchman.

But the decayed flesh was gone, and the bleeding had almost stopped. One of the doctors packed the wound with a poultice of shepherd's purse and comfrey and bound it tight with a clean strip of linen.

"We've done all we can," said the first doctor. "I'll leave a draught for the pain. If her fever does not subside within the next two days, come for me."

"Thank you," Canby whispered, his gaze never leaving Selena's face. He realized now how ridiculous he'd been to think he'd be able to remain distant from her.

Their lives were hopelessly connected, whether he liked it or not.

"I hope she lives," said the doctor, his tone grim.

Canby wiped a tear from his cheek with the back of Selena's hand. "She will."

CHAPTER 14

That she was alive was, in itself, a miracle. That she was on her way back to Lockwell Hall to see her birds was even more incredible.

That she was sitting across from Canby was . . . unfathomable.

It hadn't been delirium. Canby had parted the crowd at Tyburn and snatched her from certain death. And while her conviction had not yet been overturned, she was free on Ethan Gray's assurance to Parliament that Canby truly was the long-lost duke.

Since she'd opened her eyes at the inn a few days ago, Selena hadn't been able to keep from staring at Canby's face. His eyes. His chin. His smile. All so familiar, yet so strange as well.

The pain she suffered upon waking couldn't touch the joy of discovering that Canby was alive. As he sat beside her bed, he kept urging her to sleep. But how could she? Her sweetest dreams were nothing compared to reality.

"Does it hurt?" His voice was deeper, richer than the last time she'd heard it. It was music.

"My arm? It hurts like the devil. But it's much better than it was a few days ago. It seems to be healing quickly."

"Nonetheless, I shall have the physician visit you as soon as possible." Concern was so clear in his eyes. Those eyes that had changed so much. Hardened.

"Canby, what happened? Where were you all these years?"

"Shh. There will be plenty of time for questions later. You should rest."

"I cannot. Every jolt of the coach sends a pain through my arm."

"Perhaps we should have spent another day or two at the inn. We could stop somewhere," he suggested.

"No. Please. I want to see my birds."

"Of course." He smiled.

They said little as the coach bumped closer to Lockwell Hall. What would become of her? Her apprehension grew by the mile.

One thing was clear. She couldn't stay there. The Markley family had accused her of murder. That anyone who knew her could believe her capable of such a thing both shocked and saddened her.

She'd always had something of a rapport with Lord Randolph. They were never close like she and Canby, but he seemed like a decent man. She didn't understand how he could have thought the worst of her.

On the other hand, Canby's mother had never shown her any kindness.

If left up to the duchess, when Selena's father had died, the falconry at Lockwell Hall would have died with him. But Lord Popper had written to Selena's husband to ask if she wished to return and take her father's place. Her husband forbade her to accept the position, threatening to leave her if she took it.

Selena never hesitated.

She'd missed her birds and her home too much. Though it had cost her her marriage, it wasn't a high price to pay for the peace she craved. The peace she only seemed to feel in the place where she grew up.

Now she wondered if she should have stayed away.

"Don't worry. I'll keep you from their clutches," Canby said, guessing at her thoughts. "We'll put you in a room on the fourth floor."

"Fourth floor?"

"Yes. Away from the family wing."

"But I'm going to stay at the cottage."

Canby looked surprised. "I cannot care for you there. You need to be nearby."

"Please, Canby, I can't stay under the same roof with your mother. You must understand."

He gave her a thoughtful look. "Very well. I'd wager you could live at the cottage forever without setting eyes on her."

Selena shook her head. "I won't be there forever. I only wish to visit the birds. Make sure they're well taken care of. Then I'm going to leave."

"But you can't. Who will take care of them?"

She smiled. "You will. Or have you forgotten how?"

He looked down at his hands. "I remember. But you cannot leave until your arm is healed. Agreed?"

"I don't know." Her chest ached. Lockwell Hall was the only real home she'd ever known. Now it would never be the same. "I cannot stay, Canby."

He was quiet for a moment. "I don't know when this all will end," he said. "I don't know how long it will take for my title to be restored, and for you to officially be free. But I had hoped you'd stay on for a while. I feel as if your injury is my fault."

"How could it possibly be your fault?"

Canby looked away.

"I suppose I could stay for a little while," she said. "If only to talk to you again. Find out where you've been."

"Good. I'll take you directly to the cottage and settle you in."

"Canby, you needn't coddle me. I'm sure your family will want to see you as soon as possible. They are bound to have plenty of questions for you."

"No doubt."

She studied his face. He looked weary of the whole business already. Though she hadn't seen him in many years, she still felt as if she knew him.

He was hiding something; she was sure of it.

They soon passed the elegant, white, seventy-room manse that was Lockwell Hall. With its colonnades and sweeping marble stairways rising from pristine gardens, it looked as if it were built for a Greek god.

The carriage rumbled past the stables and down the lane, pulling up before the falconer's cottage a few minutes later, just as dusk blanketed the countryside. Canby offered a hand to her as she stepped off the coach.

His touch was warm and light. Sparks spread through her belly—the same kind of sparks she'd felt the first time he kissed her in the berry patch. She tugged her hand from his. Such memories served little purpose. Now, just as then, Canby could never be hers.

Selena stared at the cottage. It certainly didn't resemble the welcoming home of her dream. The woodpile sat as high as when she'd left. Leaves carpeted the stone walkway to the door, undisturbed by a broom. Not a trace of smoke curled from the chimney.

And sadly, her father would not be waiting within.

"What's wrong?"

She forced a smile. "I just . . . my arm hurts."

"Let's get you inside."

"I want to see the birds."

"In a few minutes. Come." He led her to the door and pushed it open.

All was the same as when she'd left.

Broken crocks littered the floor near the pantry. The few

clothes she owned were strewn about the floor. The small
workbench where she and her father had fashioned leather
hoods, gloves, and jesses when the shed was too cold for it
lay overturned.

"My God, what happened here?" Canby kicked debris
from underfoot as they entered.

"They searched through my things, and they weren't
careful about it."

Canby's features grew dark. "Looking for evidence of
my murder."

"They found it," she said. "Your ring."

As soon as the duchess's men discovered it tucked away
in a drawer, they dragged her from the cottage without allowing her a moment to collect herself or right her home.

Canby picked up a kitchen crock and placed it on a
shelf above the window. "I didn't think you'd have kept the
ring."

"What else would I have done with it?"

He shrugged. "Sold it, perhaps."

"You think money would have meant more to me?" she
asked, hoping the hurt wasn't too obvious in her voice.

He regarded her for a few moments. "I suppose not."

They spent a few minutes silently picking up.

"Where did you go?" Selena finally said quietly.

"You would never believe me if I told you." He kicked a
broken pot. "I shall have someone come to take care of this
mess immediately. In the meantime, why don't we go to
the mews?"

Selena all but flew over the path, ignoring the pain in
her arm, even forgetting that Canby followed her.

When they arrived at the mews, Selena hesitated. What
would she find when she opened the doors? She took a
deep breath, and entered.

The building was set up much the way a stable would
be. Each bird had its own enclosure with a separate door,
save the pair of hawks, who shared a larger space together.

Along the row of enclosures ran a narrow aisle. Selena

moved from mew to mew, starting with the injured eagle. Her arm was too weak to support the birds, so Canby held them on a gloved hand as she checked weight, condition, and feathers to assess their health.

Though it appeared they hadn't been flown since she'd left, they were apparently well fed and the mews were clean.

Selena and Canby left the building and walked around to the weathering area—a large, open circle where several branches and stumps implanted in the ground served as perches for the birds. It was a place for them to dry their feathers after a bath and warm themselves in the sun. This space had been kept well, too.

Selena collapsed onto a log with relief. "Nothing amiss."

Canby held out a hand. "You've got to be exhausted. Come. Let's get you back to the cottage."

"I don't want to leave them."

"You need rest. Tomorrow we'll take them hunting if you feel well enough."

She took his hand as they started back toward her home. "Won't you have too much to do? I'm sure one can't simply reappear from the dead without consequence. Without explanation."

"I've said all I care to say on the matter for the moment."

"But you can't leave things this way. Everyone will want to know what happened to you. They will want to know where you've been."

"I've told everyone who needs to know."

"You haven't told me."

They stopped before the cottage door. "You should get some sleep."

"Tell me what happened the day you disappeared," she pressed.

"Your wedding day?" he said, his voice tinged with bitterness.

"Do you plan to be angry with me forever because I

wouldn't agree to be your mistress?" she asked with equal asperity.

He sighed. "Let's go in."

Canby righted a small table and two chairs and set them up beside the stove while Selena found a battered kettle in the mess on the floor.

Canby ducked out the door and returned carrying an armful of wood and a bucket of water. He poured some water into the kettle and set about lighting a fire in the stove.

Selena watched him closely. Where had he learned to perform such a domestic act?

"Tea?" he asked.

She sensed he was using these mundane activities to put her off. No matter. She could wait. "Tea would be very nice. Thank you."

Canby searched the contents of an overturned cupboard and found a small sack of tea. "Not terribly fresh," he said, "but it will have to do."

He retrieved two unbroken teacups from the mess and set them on the table, filling them with the steaming amber liquid. By the time he finally came to sit beside her, it was clear he had changed in more ways than one.

She waited, sipping her tea in silence, aware that to press him would get her no answers.

Finally, he spoke. "I don't remember much about my abduction," he said. "As I rode my horse through the thick woods beside Argus Pond, I suddenly felt a pain in the back of my neck. I awoke aboard a ship on the English Channel. We arrived in France at night, and I was taken to a prison." His voice was flat, emotionless.

"A *French prison*?"

"Yes. I was kept there until they released me a few weeks ago. It took me a while to get back to England. I had no money. Nothing. I arrived on Ethan's doorstep the night before the hanging."

Selena rubbed her temple. "Canby, this doesn't make

any sense. Why? Why would these people have taken you in the first place?"

Canby shrugged. "I've come to believe it was a case of mistaken identity. I was never told why I was there." He stared into the depths of his teacup.

"Did you learn to make tea in prison?" she asked quietly.

She'd caught him off guard. His eyes revealed *that*, at least. But his look of surprise was short-lived. His expression quickly turned neutral.

"You don't believe me?" he said.

She regarded him intently. The story was incredible. So incredible she could hardly believe it was true.

"I trust you, Canby. You've never lied to me, ever." She took a sip of her tea. "I suppose it was a lucky thing for me that you were released just then."

"I vow it was," he said. "Now it's your turn to answer some questions. How did you escape from Newgate?"

Selena's thoughts leapt to Jack, her mind straying willfully to his kiss. Her cheeks heated.

She wondered briefly what had become of him, until anger swept curiosity aside. She hoped he was walking in circles in the woods, still looking for some sign of her.

"It wasn't a well-planned event," she said. "More like a divine intervention. An opportunity presented itself, and I took it." Why she didn't tell Canby about Jack's rescue and ultimate betrayal, she didn't know, but she felt a sense of protectiveness for him she couldn't explain. She wanted to keep him to herself. For a little while, at least.

Canby raised his eyebrows. "Where did you go?"

"I was . . . in the woods for a while. I should have stayed there, I suppose."

"Maybe." Canby drained the tea from his cup. "But if you had, we wouldn't be sitting here now."

She smiled. "True. And I'm glad we are."

"I am, too."

They simply looked at each other for a long moment. Selena caught a glimpse of something new, and yet familiar, in Canby's eyes. Before she could pin it down, he looked away.

"I'd best return to the house," he said. "It's time to allow my mother to interrogate me."

"You'd better get used to it. She won't be the only one."

He smiled. "I'll send someone immediately to help you put this place to rights."

He walked to the door, stepping over the pieces of her old life along the way. She could hardly believe that life was gone. Well, most of it, anyway.

"Canby?"

He turned, his hand still on the door latch.

"Yes?"

"Thank you."

Ethan's contact, the youngest son of a marquis who preferred adventure to his father's woolen trade and went by the codename "Badger," looked supremely uncomfortable in his formal attire.

"Why couldn't we meet somewhere a bit more hospitable?" he complained. "I don't do well at these things."

The two stood off to the side of the orchestra, assured no one could hear their conversation above the music.

Ethan laughed. "Sorry. I'm escorting Lady Mildred tonight, and will be tied up with other matters all day tomorrow. What did you find out?"

"The shipment of weapons originated in Birmingham. Most of the guns were loaded onto a ship bound for Africa, as the order claimed they would be. But some were crated and sent to a warehouse at the docks. Word is, they're bound for the colonies."

"Which quay are they housed at?"

Badger's face turned red. "I haven't been able to get that far."

Ethan frowned. "We've got to find them before they're shipped. Need some help?"

"Whom did you have in mind?"

"Myself, of course."

"You! That's a rich one." Badger grinned. "There aren't many ladies to charm at the quays. At least, not the type you're accustomed to."

Ethan held his annoyance in check. "I'm capable of much more than charming ladies."

"I'm sure," Badger said, insipid grin still in place. "Why don't you tell that to her?"

Ethan looked over his shoulder to find the horsy Lady Mildred galloping full-speed toward him, dance card fluttering on the ribbon tied about her wrist. She had an equally homely friend in tow, and the two giggled absurdly behind their fans.

Ethan gave Badger an evil grin. "Lady Mildred, perhaps we should introduce our friends."

True to Canby's word, a small army of servants arrived shortly after he'd gone, followed by Lockwell Hall's private physician, Dr. Newell.

The doctor checked Selena's arm and changed the bandages on the wound while the servants quickly reassembled the cottage, righting furniture, sweeping broken crockery away, replacing the linens.

In short measure they were gone, leaving her with no more than a few lingering looks of curiosity.

The silence was peculiar.

After weeks of chaos at Newgate, two days on the run from Jack, and the delirium after she was shot, the quiet of the cottage was almost disturbing.

She wished Canby hadn't left.

He shouldn't have left her.

If he'd had a choice, he would have stayed with Selena in the falconer's cottage all night. But the specter of Lockwell Hall loomed large in his thoughts. He had to face his demons—and his mother.

The dust of Tyburn still lay upon the clothes Ethan had lent him, and had settled on his skin, much as the horror of the place had settled into his dreams.

He hurried through the Great Hall, giving little notice to the changes implemented in his absence. Lockwell Hall hadn't been his home, merely a place he'd slept until he was old enough and wise enough to leave it.

As he mounted the stairs to his quarters, Canby thought about the falconer's cottage—Selena's cottage—and the memories it stirred.

He'd spent many days there, protected from his mother's unrelenting obsession with moral perfection, and from the ghosts of his father's moral indiscretions.

Canby never knew exactly what had happened between his mother and father, but he sensed it was an ongoing battle between corruption and self-righteousness that had left lasting scars on them all. As the battleground, Lockwell Hall was haunted by the specters of all his childhood apprehensions.

Compared to the cottage, Lockwell Hall was cheerless at best.

As he reached the top of the staircase, a voice stopped him cold. "It was you, after all."

He turned. "Mother."

She looked the same as she had in the courtroom—stately, beautiful, unyielding.

"I would see you in my quarters." Her tone invited no debate. No denial.

Nor did it hold any pleasure.

"I shall meet you there in half an hour," he said.

Charity gripped the newel post at the bottom of the railing. It was all she could do to remain standing as Canby limped up the stairs.

Dear God, he was alive! Her son, her firstborn.

She ached to call him back. By the look in his eyes, though, nothing had changed. He still hated her as much as he always had.

She'd done nothing but try to protect him when he was a boy. But he never could see that; he'd been blind to anything but those damned falcons. And of course, Selena.

And now he appeared on the eve of Randolph's investiture—on the eve of her own freedom—like the ghost of things past, just in time to ruin everything.

And looking more like Kellam than was conceivable.

The bitterness she'd swallowed for so many years seethed to the surface, putting enough strength back into her legs to climb the winding staircase to her apartment.

Canby's suite of rooms had remained virtually unchanged. A half-finished chess game stood undisturbed on the table beside the window. Books on art and philosophy rested neatly beside the bed. The quill and ink he'd used to send the final missive to Ethan—the one accepting the mission in France—still sat on his desk.

A sharp knock at the door produced Steeples, the valet who'd served his father and, in turn, him.

"Have I you to thank that my rooms haven't become a haven for mother's spare gowns?"

Steeples bit back a grin. "Yes, sir. I suppose you do."

"Thank you, old man."

Steeples looked at the floor. "It's good to have you back, Your Grace."

"Well, it remains to be seen if it will actually be good to *be* back. Tell me, Steeples, why did you stay on?"

"Lord Popper requested it, in the event you should ever turn up. I hadn't much to do besides keep this room intact, but for a man of my years, it was a good offer."

"Did Lord Popper really believe I'd return?"

"I don't think so, sir. But the idea irritated the duchess."

"Ah. Well, I shall have to thank Lord Popper, anyway, for keeping you around."

With Steeples's assistance, Canby washed and changed into wine-colored breeches, a brocaded vest, and an ever-green coat. If he'd thought Ethan's clothing ill-fitting, the garments in his own closets were even worse. Besides being hopelessly out of fashion, it was impossible to button them. He hadn't realized how thin he'd been back then.

He adjusted his wig and tried several suitable expressions in the mirror. It was imperative to show no vulnerability when in the presence of his mother. Especially now that he had so many secrets to guard.

He reminded himself that he was no longer a boy, no longer subject to her fits of pique, but he knew that wasn't true. Everyone was subject to them, including him.

No, especially him.

She would find a way to penetrate his carefully constructed armor. It was her special gift.

Regretting the fact that he'd revived his limp, he took his cane from the corner and headed for the dragon's lair.

His mother remained seated in a hideous gilded, swan-shaped chair. He remembered the chair well. It was the one she'd been sitting in when she told him of his father's death, and announced that he would be the new Duke of Canby.

Beneath her arm, a tiny dog trembled. Canby's heart went out to it.

"I must admit, you've managed to surprise me," his mother said.

"No easy feat, if I remember correctly."

She smiled. "I've missed you, my boy."

"You don't really expect me to believe that, do you, Mother?"

"You doubt my word?"

"You have a history of lying to me."

Charity's expression grew dark. "'Tis a history that is purely imagined on your part."

They stared at each other across a sea of Persian carpet, woven in shades of green and blue.

Canby looked away first. It wasn't worth his time to argue about the past. Besides, he had no idea of the extent of his mother's power and influence these days. Before he burned any bridges, he needed to gather some intelligence.

He didn't want to admit that simply standing in Charity's presence made him feel like a frightened, feeble boy again.

"Where have you been?" she asked casually, as if he'd been gone for a week rather than six years.

"In a French prison."

She waved her hand. "I've heard the stories Lord North's secretary released, and I'm sorry to say, I don't believe them."

"No? Why not?"

"Look at you. You're hardly the picture of a deprived prisoner, are you? Now, where have you really been?"

"Do you doubt *my* word?"

"*Touché.*" She patted the dog's head. "Perhaps one day you'll tell me?"

He said nothing.

"Well, I suppose the important thing is that you are back. And to show how grateful we are for your return, I've already begun to plan a grand celebration."

"I wish you wouldn't."

"Oh, but I must. It's only proper." Charity laughed. "You never were much for social gatherings. No matter, I'll be sure to set up a chair in the corner for you. Or will you be off flying your dreadful falcons like you did when you were a boy?"

Canby answered her with silence.

Charity's smile faded. "Speaking of falcons, what of the Hewitt woman?"

"What do you want to know?"

"Where is she?"

"At the falconer's cottage."

"So, she's returned as well." Charity set the trembling dog on the floor. Abandoning the chair, she wandered to the window. It was dark, but she looked out anyway, as if searching for something in the blackness.

"She's returned, and I think she deserves some sort of compensation for the ordeal you've put her through. At the very least, she deserves an apology."

"She'll not get it," his mother said. She turned to him. "She's a thief. She had your ring in her possession."

"That's because I gave it to her."

She blinked. For anyone else, it would have been just a blink. But for Canby, it was a coup. It wasn't easy to shock her.

"For heaven's sake, why?"

"Because I cared for her. She was my friend."

"Your *friend*?" Charity sighed. "Honestly, Canby. You and your father. Always tempted by inferior women. Really, couldn't you have found a more appropriate mistress?"

His fingers curled into a fist. "She wasn't my mistress."

She raised her eyebrows. "Forgive me for assuming." She wandered to her desk and ran a finger over the white lacquered finish. "So, what are your plans?"

"I thought I'd dine in my rooms tonight, and then—"

"I meant, what are your plans for the estate? What are your plans for the future?"

"I know what you meant. I'm simply not prepared to discuss it at this moment."

"Will you take your seat in Parliament?"

"That's the least of my concerns right now. Besides, my title hasn't even officially been restored. I've got to prove I am who I say."

Charity crossed the room and stood before him, reaching out a hand. For an instant he thought she might touch him, but she didn't. "All they'll need is one look and they'll know who you are. You're the spitting image of your father."

Canby's throat squeezed shut. "Is that why you've always hated me?"

His mother's hand dropped to her side. "Well. Would you like me to join you in your chambers for supper?"

"Not tonight."

"Canby . . ."

"Let's not pretend, Mother. We've never been kindred spirits. I think we would both agree that the less time spent in each other's company, the better."

She turned away. "Very well. But your brother is to return from London in the morning. I suppose we should all meet for breakfast. We need to discuss the front we'll put up."

"You haven't changed a bit. Ever conscious of how the world will look upon us."

"If you expect to have your title returned, you'd best be conscious of it as well."

It was too dark to visit the mews again, Selena thought with regret. Besides, her arm throbbed terribly. She'd never be able to hold the birds by herself. She needed Canby.

She drove that thought from her mind. She'd never needed anyone. At one time she thought it might be nice to have someone to love. Someone to talk to and live with. Children to fill the house with laughter.

But wanting was different than needing. And right now, the only thing she *needed* was a distraction.

Though a fire crackled in the grate, its warmth could not remove the chill she felt when she thought of all she'd been through. The men ransacking her home. The trial. Newgate.

Jack.

A curious mix of emotions washed over her when she thought of her time with Jack. In some ways she'd felt more at ease with him than she did with Canby.

With Canby she was ever conscious of their differences. His wealth and sophistication. Her own lack of refinement.

He'd taught her about many things—art, history, philosophy. She loved him for that.

But when Jack had kissed her, she considered, just for one brief instant, possibilities she could never consider with Canby.

Canby carried a burden with the title of duke, along with plenty of familial distress, and he needed a woman who could help shoulder that burden. She realized now, it wasn't her. She wanted a peaceful life of hawking and hard work.

That was why, no matter how much she cared for Canby, she couldn't stay on as falconer of Lockwell Hall. She could no longer find the peace she craved there. She would stay only until she was cleared of committing any crimes. Long enough to heal, and long enough to renew her friendship with Canby.

There were so many things she wanted to tell him. All the little things one thinks about after a person has died. So many times she'd wished for just one more day with him, and now she had it. It was a rare gift.

Sadly, it was a gift she wouldn't enjoy for long.

Dinner lay in Canby's stomach like musket balls. The wine he'd overindulged in left a sour taste in his mouth.

He tossed and turned, unable to find comfort on the massive featherbed. He wasn't accustomed to such luxury anymore.

And he couldn't stop thinking about Selena.

He didn't like the idea of leaving her at the cottage alone with an injured arm. He should have sent a maid to spend the night with her. Now all the servants were abed.

He supposed he could wake one.

Or he could go himself.

He rose and dressed hurriedly in the dark, relying on memory rather than sight to get him to the stables.

The grooms slept, too, so Canby lit a lantern and saddled his mount himself. Horses nickered softly in their stalls, and he gave them each a treat. He'd always had a special affinity for animals, which Ethan had used wisely when assigning him to missions.

He'd posed as a breeder of hounds, a master of livestock, a groomsman, and now a falconer's assistant. In all those positions, he'd been amazed how gentlemen considered their servants invisible. Information came easily to a servant.

With a pang of regret, he wondered if he'd ever be able to take another mission once the one at Montainville was finished.

His extended absence displeased Lord North, but nothing could be done at this point. Even if Canby had wanted to, he couldn't return to France right now. Not when all the eyes of England were upon him.

Canby mounted his horse and set off down the lane. It seemed to take forever to get to the falconer's cottage. A lifetime.

When he arrived, he almost turned the horse around.

He had no right to offer Selena protection. Not when he was the very person she needed protection from. But of course, he couldn't stay away.

She answered his knock immediately.

"Canby." She didn't bother to hide the relief in her eyes. "I'm glad you're here."

He crossed the threshold and she stepped into the circle of his embrace, wrapping her arm about his waist.

"I've missed you so." She pressed her cheek against his chest.

"Shh. All is well. I won't leave you." He stroked her unbound hair, reveling in the silky feel of it between his fingers.

She allowed the intimacy for only a moment, but the damage was already done. Every feeling of arousal, desire, hunger he'd ever felt toward her multiplied a thousandfold. He couldn't deny it. She was in his blood forever.

He took her face in his hands and tilted her head, capturing her lips with his. She made a small noise of protest, but her eyes closed and her uninjured arm left his waist and crept up around his neck, pulling him deeper into the kiss.

They drew one another in, moving, touching, stroking, sighing. He kissed her neck, dipping his tongue into the grotto of her collarbone, tasting her. He placed her hand over his heart so she could feel it beating. "I want to make love to you."

CHAPTER 15

Canby's heart drummed beneath her palm. Her own heartbeat pulsed in her ears. They beat in time with one another, as it seemed they always had. They were two parts of a whole.

But they did not belong together.

She pulled away from him. Canby's injured look only added to her own pain.

"We're not children, Selena. I see your desire. Why won't you give in to it?"

Why, indeed? Before he arrived, she'd wanted nothing more than to be with him. But now that he was there, she realized that making love to him would only hurt them both. No matter how much she loved him, she would be leaving him soon. She had no choice. She could never find peace there. And she would certainly never find it in the arms of a duke.

"Canby, there is enough scandal surrounding us now. More gossip won't help your cause, or mine. You shouldn't be here tonight."

He pulled her to him and tipped her head up so she looked into his eyes. "I don't give a damn what anyone else thinks. I never did."

The pain and longing were so clear in his eyes, it took all of Selena's power to look away. "A tryst between us would be scandalous. Should anyone find out, it could make it difficult for you to reclaim your title."

"I don't care, Selena. I want you. I need you."

She gave a frustrated sigh. "You never did think about consequences. Remember when you fell over the cliff?"

He gave her a reckless smile, and her heart leapt in her chest. "I remember it well."

"Just as that mistake could have meant your demise, so could this."

He touched her lips with his fingertips. "This," he said softly, "could never be a mistake."

His mouth claimed hers, stealing her breath with the passion of his kiss. His hands roamed over her body, leaving a trail of fire wherever he touched, paralyzing her with desire.

He skimmed a fingertip over her breasts, tracing the curves and valleys along the edge of her chemise, teasing a nipple through the thin cotton bodice of her wrapper.

She pushed him away, though she wanted—nay, ached—to bring him closer. What had made her think they could spend a quiet, companionable evening together? "Canby, I cannot. The thought of being with you scares me too much."

"Why does it scare you?"

"Because of who you are."

He grew very still. "Who, exactly, do you think I am?"

She moved out of the circle of his arms. "My master, of course. While I live at Lockwell Hall, I am your servant."

"That isn't true."

"Yes, it is," she said quietly. "Your family paid my father, and now you pay me. If I were to stay here and become your lover, I'd be your paid mistress. Little more than a prostitute, really."

He took her hands. "You are paid for your services as falconer, for which you earn every bit of your wage, and more. You would be free at any time to end our affair with no consequence to that. Except, perhaps, my broken heart."

Somehow, she didn't think it would be *his* heart that would suffer.

Selena suddenly felt very weary. Her arm ached. Her head ached. It had been a long day.

Nay, it had been a long six years.

She wanted Canby so much. Her will grew weak, but her reason did not. She had to put him off until she left. Somehow, she had to do it without hurting him more.

She took his hand. "If you truly want this, then let us wait. When the shock of your return subsides and the scrutiny has lessened—"

"You want me to wait?" He gave her a dispirited laugh. "I suppose waiting more than half a lifetime hasn't been long enough?"

"If this is truly meant to be, a little more time won't mean anything. Besides, my arm . . ."

Canby let his hands fall to his sides. "You're right, of course. I am so sorry. I wasn't thinking." He reached out to touch her hair. "We shall wait."

"Will you return to Lockwell Hall tonight?"

"Yes." He brushed her forehead with a kiss. "But tomorrow we are going hawking, in plain sight of the gossips and my mother, and anyone else who cares to look. A man cannot be faulted for wanting to spend time with his falconer."

"Where are your parents?" Ethan asked, trying to escape Lady Mildred's iron grasp as they wrestled on the dreadfully uncomfortable settee in Lord Shelbourne's London home.

"Don't worry," Lady Mildred giggled. "Mother's in the country. My father meets with a few other men every

Thursday evening for supper and cards. He's gone for hours."

"Really? Where do they meet, White's?"

"Good heavens, no." Lady Mildred closed the space between them. "They meet at an inn on Hampstead Heath. I heard him talk about it once."

"Hampstead Heath? That's rather odd, isn't it?"

Lady Mildred shrugged. "It keeps him out late, which is my only concern. Now, shall we retire to my quarters?"

"Need you ask?" Ethan bestowed upon her the customary wicked grin, although he would much rather have gone home and climbed into bed with a good book.

Canby rose, bleary-eyed, at the fashionable hour of eleven. After he'd left Selena's cottage the night before, he'd spent some time at the mews.

His frustration cooled in the presence of the birds, and he remembered how he'd always found acceptance there as a boy. Selena's father showed respect for his abilities, but did not fawn. Did not want anything from him.

As Steeples helped him dress, Canby thought about what Selena had said about them waiting for the proper time.

Of course she was right. To begin something with her now would help neither of their causes. But he wanted her. His gut ached with it. His mind reeled with it.

The image of her unclothed behind the screen at the hideaway was burned on the inside of his eyelids—he saw her every time he closed his eyes.

He'd wanted her before, but now desire consumed him. Thoughts of her filled his dreams, and every waking hour as well.

It was damned dangerous.

His mind should be fixed on other matters, such as when he'd be able to return to Montainville. His duty to the Crown should be first and foremost in his mind.

In the past he wouldn't have doubted Ned's abilities there in the least. But Ethan's news of the strange messages from his partner, combined with Ned's odd behavior that last day, gave Canby pause.

Somehow very soon he'd have to find his way back to France. When things cooled a bit, it wouldn't be difficult. People would expect him to want to escape the frenzy spawned by his return. It would only be natural. But he couldn't leave until his title had been restored. Until he knew Selena was inarguably free.

Canby grabbed his cane and headed to the breakfast room, anticipating an afternoon of hawking with Selena. He did not, however, anticipate the ordeal that breakfast would prove to be.

The dining room resembled a battlefield.

People sat shoulder to shoulder on either side of the table, squared off across trays of cold meats and sweet-breads. The hostility was as thick as clotted cream.

On one side, Canby's mother and Sir Ambrose Hollister regarded him with an expectant air. His brother smiled with what appeared to be genuine affection, while Letitia stared in sullen disbelief.

"Canby, my boy," Sir Ambrose boomed, rising to his feet along with the rest of them. "How wonderful to have you back."

Canby suppressed a look of repugnance. The two had rarely been civil to one another. As one of his father's clos-est cronies, Canby knew Sir Ambrose rather well. His gross disregard for those weaker in body and mind had often left Canby disgusted. He'd found himself a target of Ambrose's derision on more than one occasion because of his limp.

Why his mother had continued to associate with the man after his father had died was a complete mystery.

"Dear brother, welcome home."

"Thank you, Randolph. It's good to see you again."

On the opposite side of the table, Ethan sat between Lord Popper and a man wearing a sash identifying him as an envoy to the Crown.

Popper wore a solemn expression. When Canby glanced his way, he affected a halfhearted bow. "Your Grace."

"That remains to be seen," said the gentleman with the sash.

Ethan gestured to him. "This is Lord Casterbridge, secretary of domestic matters for His Majesty."

Lord Casterbridge gave Canby a curt nod. "I am sent to inform you that His Majesty requests an audience with you in two days' time, to ascertain that you are who you claim to be."

"But of course." Canby wondered how, exactly, the king would determine that, considering they hadn't seen one another face to face since Canby was thirteen.

"There are a number of members of Parliament who would like the same privilege," Lord Popper interjected. "They'd like to meet with you before the vote."

"And they shall have ample opportunity," his mother said. "As soon as his family has given him the proper welcome."

"Certainly, Your Grace," Lord Casterbridge said, affecting a bow of sincere deference in Charity's direction. "No one wishes to interfere with your joyous reunion."

Joyous reunion?

Canby choked back a laugh.

He took his place at the head of the table, as was expected.

"Ethan, I didn't expect to see you here today," Canby said.

"I escorted Lord Casterbridge, at Lord North's request." Ethan gave Canby a pointed look. "I also wanted to check on Mrs. Hewitt, as the both of you *are* officially under my sponsorship."

"Certainly. We shall make for the falconer's cottage as soon as we've had breakfast."

Sir Ambrose gave Canby's mother a sideways glance.

The duchess cleared her throat. "We had rather hoped to spend some time discussing your intentions for the duchy now that you've returned."

Lord Popper's face grew red. "Isn't that a bit premature?" He turned to Canby. "If you'd like, I can continue on with the administration of the estate for a while. Assist you in any way you deem necessary. Why should you burden yourself with the tedium of everyday affairs so soon after your return?"

"Why shouldn't he burden himself?" his mother sniped. "If you'd had control of *my* estate for the past twenty years, I would be quite anxious to take hold of it. And I would check the records very carefully."

"I take offense at that statement, Duchess." Lord Popper sprung from his seat and threw his napkin on the table. A fork upended on his plate, spattering poached quail's egg across his waistcoat. His previously red face deepened to an unattractive shade of crimson.

Randolph tucked into his meal, oblivious to the tension around him.

"Oh, dear. Perhaps we should have someone examine the records of the duchy?" Lord Casterbridge suggested, a note of anxiety in his voice.

"I hardly think that necessary," Sir Ambrose said quickly. "The duchess merely meant to suggest that her son may want to familiarize himself with the duchy's holdings. Isn't that right?"

Charity blanched. "Absolutely. Lord Popper is as honest as a day."

Charity and Sir Ambrose exchanged a quick look, and Canby wondered what they were about. He'd never known his mother to allow anyone to put words into her mouth.

"I am sorry to say, Canby, that there are those in Parliament who would challenge your identity for political gain," his mother said. "But I promise I will do my best to persuade those dissenters to act as quickly as possible on your behalf."

"With what gain to you?" Lord Popper muttered under his breath.

Canby wondered the same. His mother's influence was never offered without strings.

"Canby, I'd hoped to speak with you, as well," Randolph said, startling them all into silence. "I've drawn up some plans I'd like to show you . . ."

Letitia gave her betrothed a pleading look, but Randolph's smile never faltered.

Canby suddenly decided he'd had enough of the cryptic conversation and meaningful looks. He no longer wished to be the spoils of this horrid little war.

Including the time he'd spent at the inn with Selena and the physicians, he'd been back for less than a week. Already people attacked him from all directions, wanting something.

"Mother. Randolph. Letitia. This 'joyful reunion' has been interesting, but I must be off to the mews."

"Of course," said Randolph, always the affable one.

Sir Ambrose looked like a fisherman watching his dinner swim away.

"Lord Casterbridge," Canby said. "Please inform His Majesty that I will be honored to present myself to him whenever he may so request."

Lord Casterbridge nodded. "I shall leave the particulars with your valet."

"Very good. Have him arrange for a carriage to take you back to London, as well. Ethan, shall we go?"

Canby waited outside the stables for his cousin. His horse shuddered beneath him, as anxious as he to be off.

By the time he'd escaped the confines of Lockwell Hall, he could hardly breathe. The ill fit of his clothing and the strange maneuverings at the breakfast table combined with near-lethal results.

All that could save him now was a few hours in the fresh air, hawking with Selena.

Before long, Ethan's mount had been saddled and they started up the lane for the falconer's cottage. When they were well away from the stables, Canby spoke.

"Have you heard from the Fox?"

"Not lately."

Canby frowned. "I wonder if De Ligiers will not hawk with him."

"Could he have run into trouble? Perhaps he means to abort the mission."

"No. We have a clear code for such a situation. The note you gave me at the barn indicated nothing of the sort. If he meant to abort, I would know it."

"As well you know, the connection with De Ligiers is crucial. He is our most reliable link to King Louis's committee on foreign affairs. I can't have this confusion." Frustration laced Ethan's words.

Canby couldn't imagine what had gone wrong. Ned's missive contained nothing of value. "Perhaps there is nothing new to report."

"Perhaps," Ethan said. "But if we don't receive word from him soon, we're going to have to get another operative to Versailles somehow, and at this point that could be dangerous."

"I'm sorry, Ethan. I know I've put you in a difficult position," Canby said. "I will return to France as soon as I possibly can. But I cannot leave here until my title is restored. Until Selena is cleared."

Ethan nodded. "I'll push Lord North to schedule the vote on the issue as soon as Parliament resumes next week. Until then, I need your help with another matter."

Selena's home came into view, and Canby slowed his horse. "What is it?"

"I've received some information from the quays. Several shipments of arms bound for Africa have been skimmed. The guns removed from these shipments have been crated and hidden in a warehouse by the docks. We have every reason to believe they are bound for the American colonies."

"What do you want me to do?"

"I need to know where they're being stored, who paid for them, and who is secretly shipping them to the colonies."

"Any leads?"

"While you're in London, pay a visit to the Green Dragon. One of the port master's assistants, a Gerald Quimby, all but lives there. He might be of some use. But be careful. Kincaid and his men have been about."

Canby nodded.

"Also, see what you can find out about Lord Chadwick. Apparently he and Lord Shelbourne, along with two other men as yet unidentified, hold frequent meetings at an inn on Hampstead Heath."

"How do I get to him?"

"He's holding a small soiree. Unfortunately, I cannot attend myself, as I have a meeting with one of my sources."

Canby glanced in his cousin's direction and grinned. "What's her name?"

Ethan frowned. "Why does everyone assume all of my intelligence efforts pertain to women?"

"Don't they?" Canby laughed. "Face the facts, Ethan. Your expertise has shifted from the battleground to the bedroom."

Canby reined in his horse at the stone walkway leading to Selena's door. He knocked, but there was no answer.

"I'll take care of the horses," Ethan said. "You go find her."

Canby knew his cousin meant to give him some time alone with Selena. He followed the path to the mews, reveling in the sounds of the woods. He caught sight of a bright red bird flitting through the trees, and watched it disappear into the canopy of leaves overhead. On the path before him, another movement caught his eye.

Selena.

My God, but she was spectacular. A faerie arisen from the forest floor. The hard days behind her had done nothing to diminish her beauty. Her hair shone in the sunlight; her steps held graceful purpose.

Her injured arm was bound to her side like a broken wing. Flung over the opposite shoulder was a leather hawking bag.

Canby quickened his pace, hoping to catch her before she entered the mews.

He was almost close enough to touch her when a soft noise beside his ear—*ssshht*—stopped him short. He reached out and grabbed Selena by the waist, yanking her back against his chest.

Selena gasped, startled by his touch. The falconer's bag fell to the ground at her feet, its contents scattering on the path.

"Look," he whispered. In the tree in front of her, just inches from her nose, an arrow quivered with the force of impact.

CHAPTER 16

Canby pushed Selena to the ground and covered her with his body.

Ssshht.

Another arrow met the tree, its red-and-yellow fletching blurred from quavering.

"Stay down." Canby rolled off her into a crouch and plunged into the woods, keeping his head low. He made as much noise as he could, warning the shooter of his advance.

Even more than catching the bastard, he wanted to chase him away from Selena.

His efforts were rewarded by a thunderous retreat. Canby gave chase, but turned back when he heard Selena calling him. What if there had been more than one shooter?

He charged back through the brush, nettles snagging at his breeches, until he reached her.

She sat up on the path, holding her arm, eyes focused on the arrows sticking out of the tree.

"Who shot them?" she asked, breathing hard.

Canby helped her to her feet and snapped the shafts of

the arrows from the tree. "I don't know. But I have every intention of finding out."

"I won't leave you alone tonight," Canby said. His tone brooked no argument, but she would not have argued anyway. Her nerves were thoroughly rattled, and she no longer believed she was capable of defending herself.

She wanted to cry.

She'd never felt so helpless. Even as a child, she'd always had faith in her own ability to take care of herself.

"Your arm," Canby said. "Is the pain bad?"

"No."

"You're lying. You're pale as King Richard's ghost."

"I will be fine, Canby. Really. I just want to get to the mews."

He helped her gather up the leads and glove that had fallen out of the falconer's bag, and they proceeded the short distance to the squat wooden building.

"Shall we take the cast of hawks?" she asked. "I think they're ready to hunt."

"Are they the same ones you had when I was here?"

"Yes, Diana and Orion. They've mated quite well. I trained two of their offspring from fledglings."

Ethan arrived just as they emerged from the mews with the birds.

"Mrs. Hewitt, I trust you are well?"

She gave him a genuine smile. "Selena, please. And yes, I am well, thank you."

"No, she's not," Canby said. "We were shot at on the path. Two arrows. Yellow-and-red fletching."

"No doubt it was a poacher's stray," Selena said with a dismissive shake of the head. "I've come across several of them recently. Times have been hard, and families need meat."

Ethan frowned. "Perhaps you should come to London for a while. You may stay at my home for a few days."

"You'd be safer there," Canby agreed. "I can escort you myself."

"Nonsense," she said. "Let's forget about all that and go hunting."

They caged the birds and Canby carried them through the woods until they arrived at Selena's favorite field.

She hadn't taken any of the birds hunting there for a while, and it was bound to be teeming with prey. They released the hawks and spread out in the field, beating the grass with sticks to stir up quarry, laughing like children when Ethan's foot got caught in a rabbit hole.

The sun hung low and red in the October sky by the time they'd finished the hunt. The falconer's bag contained several plump rabbits and a grouse, and the hawks were hooded and caged, no doubt exhausted by the day's work.

Selena was exhausted, too, but more content than she'd been for many months.

Ethan had left an hour or so before, so it was just her and Canby now. They lay side by side in the soft grass of the meadow, tall stalks of long-ago wildflowers illuminated in the gloaming.

Selena stared up at clouds aflame with the setting sun. "Canby, I want to apologize for . . ." She took a deep breath. "I'm sorry I married another. I hope I did not hurt you too deeply."

He was silent beside her.

"It seemed to be the sensible thing to do at the time." The explanation sounded weak, even to her own ears.

"What was he like?" Canby asked quietly.

A flood of memories engulfed her, none of which she cared to repeat to him. How could he ever understand?

"He wasn't a tender man."

"Did he strike you?"

She couldn't look at him. "I suppose I wasn't the most accommodating wife."

Canby reached out across the grass and took her hand.

In a voice heavy with emotion, he said, "Don't you ever believe you are anything less than perfect. Or that you deserved one moment of the hell he put you through."

Her chest grew tight, making it difficult to breathe. She willed herself not to shed one more tear over things best forgotten.

Canby rolled over onto his side and propped his head up on his elbow. "Are you cold?"

"Yes. And hungry. And thirsty. And so, so happy to be here with you."

He smiled down at her, the look in his eyes changing from concern to desire.

Even before he kissed her, her body responded, melting into the ground. The blades of grass beneath her felt like tiny fingers tickling her skin. The breeze whispered in her ear.

Just one kiss. Just one kiss.

The smell of cedar and sun washed over her as Canby leaned in.

His kiss was softer than she'd expected. Intense but not urgent. He moved his lips over hers, stroking, nibbling, tasting. She opened to him and the tip of her tongue met his. Tiny shivers of excitement cascaded out to her fingers and toes, and back in again, washing her with breathless expectation.

She touched his face, tracing the fine stubble of beard that had sprung up along his jaw until her fingertips tingled.

Canby caught her hand and laced their fingers together, stroking her thumb with his, coaxing a satisfying chill that had nothing to do with the breeze.

He pulled her to him gently, taking great care not to aggravate the pain in her arm. So typical of the care he showed her in everything he did.

If only she could have him. *Truly* have him.

Exploration turned gradually to passion and he released her hand, stroking her back, the swell of her hip, the curve of her breasts. The heat of his hand seeped through the thin wool of her dress. She imagined that heat against her bare skin, searing her in other places . . .

She tore her lips from his, burying her face in his neck. "Canby, we must stop before I cannot."

"We don't have to. There is no one to see." He tilted her chin up and looked into her eyes. "I will be gentle, Selena. I'll take great care with your arm."

She lowered her eyes. "We'd be starting something we cannot continue. Not . . . now."

Not ever.

He groaned and rolled onto his back, covering his face with his hands. Selena struggled to her feet.

"I am sorry, Canby. I shouldn't have kissed you."

"It was I who kissed you," he said. "And I'm not sorry in the least. If nothing else, it's given me a taste of what's to come."

As they walked through the darkening woods, Selena offered up a wish to the single star she could see. She wished for the strength to resist the force that kept drawing her and Canby together.

"Canby doesn't care for you," Charity stated as she scrutinized the contents of her dressing table.

"So what?" said Ambrose. "He doesn't care for you, either."

Charity tamped down a twinge of hurt at Ambrose's words. "It's going to make things difficult for me," she said. "I could have persuaded Randolph to return controlling interest of Two Moons to you with no hesitation. But Canby . . ."

Ambrose poured a glass of port and stretched out on her bed, his boots leaving a streak of mud on her satin coverlet. Although they hadn't been lovers for years, he continued to make himself at home in her boudoir.

Just one more thing she wouldn't miss about him.

"What are you getting at?" he asked.

She pasted a black velvet beauty mark, one shaped like a butterfly, on her cheek, examining the effect in a silver hand mirror.

"There are several MPs who are still hesitant to return Canby's title. They want answers. They refuse to blindly accept his absurd story about the French prison."

"And?"

"And I'm going to have to call in quite a lot of favors in order to fix this situation."

"So what do you want from me?"

Charity batted her eyelashes at herself in the mirror. "I want more."

Ambrose sat up. "More what?"

"More money, of course." She laid the mirror on her lap and turned to face him. "Instead of a single payment, I want an interest in Two Moons Shipping."

"No."

"Very well, then. We shall forget everything. Canby can retain controlling interest of Two Moons."

It was a bluff, but it seemed to hit the mark.

Ambrose's face went white. Charity picked up the mirror, suppressing a victorious smile. Until Ambrose's hands encircled her neck.

She went still.

"You greedy whore." Ambrose squeezed, ever so slightly. "Do not so much as jest about your intentions. You will do whatever necessary to return Two Moons to me, and you'll do it quickly."

He squeezed tighter. Charity dropped the mirror and clawed at his hands.

"For your efforts," he said, the tone of his voice conversational, "you will get exactly what I promised you, and not one penny more. Do you understand?"

"Yes," she croaked.

Ambrose released his grip, and Charity gasped for breath, rubbing the feel of his hands from her neck.

Oh, she understood perfectly. Sir Ambrose Hollister

was insane. Perhaps even more insane than her late husband had been.

"I don't want to do this," Selena said as Canby carried a pack of her things toward Lockwell Hall.

"You have no choice. I must go to London, and I don't want you alone in the cottage while I'm gone. You have no protection there."

"Can't you send someone to stay with me?"

"Everyone is busy preparing for the ball my mother has planned. There are no servants to spare. When I return, I'll hire someone, but until then, you must stay at the house."

"But your mother—"

"Has no say in this matter. Besides, you'll not even see her. I've installed you in a beautiful apartment far from the family's quarters. I've instructed the servants to give you anything you ask for. You'll have everything you need until I return."

"But what about the birds?"

"I'll have someone escort you once a day. You're not to go to the mews alone."

One look at her face, and he softened his tone. "I'm not trying to be cruel, Selena. I just want to protect you. You'll be safe at the house."

As safe as a rabbit in a den of wolves, she thought.

"Are you sure you don't want to go with me, and stay at Ethan's house?" Canby asked.

"No. I want to make sure the eagle's talon is healing properly."

"I'll only be gone for three days," he said. "When I return, we'll go out for a hunt together."

Selena's heart beat faster at the memory of the last time they'd gone hunting together. There was no doubt that in one way, at least, she *would* be safer while he was gone.

She sighed. "The moment you return, I'm coming back to the cottage."

He smiled. "Whatever you wish."

They walked in silence, their breaths creating elusive puffs of condensation. She slid a glance in Canby's direction, admiring his profile. He was lost in thought, his brow wrinkled in an appealing furrow.

"Why does the king want to see you?" she asked.

"Most likely to assuage his curiosity. I hope he'll be able to persuade Parliament to act soon on this whole matter. The sooner my title and your freedom are restored, the sooner we can get on with our lives." His voice held an undercurrent of suggestion, and she knew exactly what he implied.

The sooner their lives returned to normal, the sooner they could be together.

Her stomach fluttered. It was impossible. It wouldn't happen. And yet her mind could not leave the thought alone.

The lane took them past the stables and eventually led them out of the woods and onto a perfectly tended lawn. Selena gazed up at Lockwell Hall, looming over them like a fairy-tale palace.

The sight of it served to reinforce her belief that she and Canby had as much business being together as a falcon and a hare.

"I cannot believe he'd bring *that woman* into this house." Letitia stood beside Charity at the window in the library as Canby and Selena Hewitt crossed the lawn.

Charity's future daughter-in-law would stay out in the country with them until the social season surrounding Parliament began in London.

She took Letitia by the shoulders. "Come away, my dear. It will do you no good to dwell on this. We should concentrate on happier thoughts. Your wedding plans, perhaps?"

The pained expression on Letitia's face wearied Charity almost unbearably.

"Can we not *do* something about this? I do not want that woman under this roof," Letitia complained.

"Unfortunately, it isn't your roof. Nor is it mine, or Randolph's. It's Canby's."

Letitia's eyes filled with tears.

Charity steered her away from the window and toward the door. "Why don't we take a rest from the wedding plans? You go up to your rooms and lie down."

Letitia sniffed. "I believe I'll do that."

She kissed Charity's cheek and trudged from the library, a pale, powdered picture of misery.

Charity shook her head. Letitia was beautiful, her reputation was impeccable, and her family owned a lovely little villa near the ocean that Charity thought she might enjoy visiting once or twice a year.

The girl had so many social advantages. What did it matter if she would never hold the title of duchess? There were any number of ways she could raise her import in society. But sadly, Letitia lacked resourcefulness.

All the beauty in the world could never make up for this shortcoming, and Charity wondered if it had been truly wise to push for a union between Letitia and Randolph after all.

The girl wasn't anything like herself. Resourcefulness was something Charity had always possessed, in abundance. Her doting father used to love to tell the story of how, when Charity was just seven, she made an impassioned plea to dozens of riders lined up for a fox hunt, convincing them that the animal's life should be spared. The hunters had ended up playing Pharo the whole weekend, instead.

Right now, Charity needed that resourcefulness greatly. Things had not gone according to her plans. She'd been so close to installing Randolph as duke. To winning the independence she craved. The outcome had been as certain as London fog.

But now that Canby had returned, everything was speculative.

She would have liked to believe that if things didn't

work out with Ambrose, Canby would take care of her. But she hardly knew her son, and couldn't count on receiving any measure of pity or generosity from him.

The only way to absolutely secure her own future was to get Canby's rightful title restored, and get him under her thumb. It would hardly be easy.

Damn him for returning at such an inopportune moment.

Charity had no idea where he'd been, but it wasn't in a French prison. No one believed it. However, it did make for an exciting story, and God knew that was what the people wanted.

Someday she'd find out what truly had happened. But until then, she simply had to concentrate on getting him under her control.

Which would require getting Selena away from him. From her. From all of them.

Once she had control, she could make everything right again.

"What do you think?"

"I've never seen a place so beautiful." Selena gaped at the rich carpeting and gold-gilt furniture in the apartment where she'd be staying.

Canby handed the few belongings she'd brought to a maid, who disappeared into the bedroom with them. "It will do for now," he said.

"Canby, I cannot stay in this room."

"You can. You will."

He looked as if he wanted to come to her, to touch her, but she knew he wouldn't. Not here.

"Try to enjoy yourself. There are many things to do." He pulled open a door, which slid away into the wall. Behind it sat an ornate porcelain bathtub, awash with painted roses.

She stared at the tub and thought about the bath she'd taken at the hideout.

Her face grew warm.

Canby watched her, an expression of raw desire darting across his face. He turned away, closing the door to the bathing room.

"There is a library downstairs. Do you still enjoy reading?"

"Of course. But I haven't seen a new book in ages."

Canby had taught her to read when they were children, and he'd brought her all kinds of wonderful books whenever he'd seen her. She'd reread those volumes over and over, until the corners were ragged and the covers half off.

How she wished for those careless days again. Her chest grew tight.

Canby reached out, then let his hand drop helplessly to his side. "Please don't worry. No one will bother you. If they do, they will have to answer to me."

The maid reappeared, bobbing her head in his direction.

"Be sure Mrs. Hewitt has everything she needs," Canby said to her. To Selena he said, "I must be on my way, but I will return soon."

Selena forced a smile. "I will be fine. Thank you, Your Grace."

A short while later she watched from her window as his coach grew small on the long drive, wishing with all her heart that she were anywhere but in that beautiful room.

CHAPTER 17

In the privacy of his bedroom, in the tastefully furnished London town house on Saint James's Square, the Duke of Canby turned into Jack Pearce once again.

And Jack Pearce turned into the Falcon, in the guise of a wizened old man.

A lady's pannier served as a hump for his back, which he wore beneath clothing he'd bought for two crowns from a beggar near Covent Garden. The odor of the garments nearly gagged him, but that was an essential part of the disguise. If no one wanted to come near him, the chance of scrutiny would be greatly reduced.

Small strips of soft pigskin, applied with hide glue to his forehead and at the corners of his mouth, created a wealth of wrinkles. Using a handful of ashes from the hearth bucket, he dirtied his face and neck and hair. A pair of tattered gloves completed the disguise, covering youthful-looking hands.

In the foggy dark of a London night, smelling as he did, he doubted anyone would approach him voluntarily.

He left the house through the servants' entrance.

Slipping unnoticed through alleys between looming warehouses, he made his way to the quays, where merchant seamen, dockers, prostitutes, and thieves were thrown together in a volatile stew to gamble, scheme, and fight.

Ethan had told him the arms stolen from a shipment bound for Africa were stored in one of these warehouses. He intended to find out which one.

Jack anticipated no problems. His was a relatively simple task, and would serve to keep his skills sharp until he could get back to France.

He prowled the waterfront, avoiding gangs of stevedores who might look to have a bit of sport with an unfortunate old man. At last he arrived at his destination.

The pub's door flew open as two sailors staggered out. Raucous laughter seeped from its bowels. Even the light that spilled out onto the wet street looked grimy.

The Green Dragon.

It was said a man shouldn't enter there without two things—a knife in his boot and a verse for his gravestone—in case he didn't get to the knife in time.

Jack had never seen a man killed there. But he had seen one blinded for life, and another whose legs were broken in half at the knees. He himself had almost been stabbed to death there by Samuel Kincaid, and had the scars to prove it.

He took a deep breath and entered.

The floor of the place was slick with spilt ale and spittle. Tables lay overturned; benches were nonexistent. They'd long since been broken in the numerous brawls.

No one gave him a second glance as he pushed through the horde of sweat-damp bodies. In a corner near the back, Jack spotted the man he was looking for.

Gerald Quimby, one of the port master's assistants, ogled a prostitute in torn green satin and dirty lace. Ale sloshed over the sides of his cup as he bent to peer down her bodice. Jack sidled up beside them.

"Guv'nor."

"Go away."

"Please, guv'nor. Help me."

"Bugger off." Quimby elbowed him hard in the chest.

Jack made a feeble whimpering sound.

The whore looked at Quimby with disgust. "Why did you have tae do tha'?"

"What? He's jus' a smelly ol' bastard."

"So are you," the whore returned.

Quimby laughed. Ale soaked his already stained shirt. "A'right. Here." He handed Jack a farthing.

The prostitute gave Quimby a toothless smile.

"I thank you, guv'nor," Jack said. "But it be information I'm needin'."

"Information? What do I look like, a bloody schoolmaster?"

He and the whore burst into laughter.

Jack pressed on. "I hear there be a very special cargo bound for the col'nies. Can ye tell me where she be?"

Quimby stopped laughing. "I don't know what yer talkin' about."

"I think ye do."

"Go away." Quimby pushed him.

"I can't. Newcomb sent me."

Quimby's hand began to tremble.

Jack wasn't surprised. Thomas Newcomb was a ruthless customs officer who controlled most of the illegal activity at the docks. Quimby owed Thomas Newcomb nearly a hundred pounds—Newcomb's cut of bribes and rake-off Quimby had conveniently forgot to hand over. Money that would soon be taken out of Quimby's flesh.

And Quimby's flesh didn't look as if it was worth a hundred pounds altogether.

Quimby waved the whore away. He stared at Jack intently. Jack met his stare, hoping his disguise held up. The fact that the man had drunk his share of a barrel helped, as did the dim light in the pub.

"Newcomb sent ye?"

"Aye. Said if you helped me, it might lighten his mood."

Quimby cleared his throat. "I'll see what I can do. Meet me at the Northside quay tomorrow night."

Jack nodded. "Much obliged. Newcomb will be, too."

Quimby's shoulders sagged. "I hope 'e will."

Something in the way the old man moved caught Kincaid's eye. He was too agile as he threaded through the crowd. Too quick to duck swinging elbows and flying fists. The old man wasn't old.

The old man was Pearce. The Falcon.

Kincaid knew it like he knew the feel of his favorite whore's tits.

The disguise was a good one, and if Kincaid hadn't been searching for a man skilled at changing his appearance, he probably wouldn't have given the old man a second look. But the money on the Falcon's head, as well as his own thirst for revenge, had made his vision much sharper.

Kincaid hunkered down in a corner and watched. A quarter of an hour later, when the "old man" shuffled out of the Green Dragon, Kincaid followed.

Once Pearce took to the alleys, it was more difficult to stay with him. Kincaid left as much space between them as he could risk without losing his track. He wished he could close the distance between them, come up behind Pearce, drag a blade across his throat . . . finish what he'd begun a few years back, when Pearce had interfered with his business.

Kincaid had been on the trail of an operative for the Crown, a man known as the Hare. He'd been paid well to kill him—a task Kincaid relished.

Kincaid had the man trapped inside the Green Dragon, with his men covering any possible escape, when Pearce had appeared out of nowhere. He and Kincaid faced off, both of them emerging with permanent reminders of the night.

At the time, Kincaid thought the altercation was related to a smuggling deal gone bad. Now he knew differently. Pearce, the Falcon, was protecting one of his own.

Kincaid followed Pearce through the rough quayside neighborhoods and into the heart of London, to Saint James's Square.

What business did Pearce have here?

Kincaid watched as the "old man," his step now strong and quick, entered a town house through the servants' entrance.

The neighborhood was quiet save the footsteps of the lamplighter. Kincaid became one with shadows, settling in to watch the house into which his quarry disappeared.

Jack removed the pigskin wrinkles from his face, washed his hair, and donned a dressing gown. Then he sealed a hundred pounds into an envelope and addressed it to Thomas Newcomb, courtesy of Quimby.

The poor port master's assistant had unwittingly given up so much valuable information to operatives of the Crown in the last several months, that a hundred pounds was a mere pittance to pay to keep him in one piece. Jack had no doubt he'd be used well in the future, too.

He rang for Steeples. As far as the old valet knew, he'd never left the house.

"Yes, Your Grace?" Steeples had entered noiselessly, and Canby thought he might have made a good spy when he was younger.

"Good evening, Steeples. I need this envelope delivered, and I wondered if I might send you on a small mission."

"A mission, sir?" Steeples blinked. "What sort of mission?"

"It would seem that I mistakenly discarded an invitation to Lord and Lady Chadwick's supper party tomorrow, and had really hoped to attend. So you see, I'm in an awkward position."

"Say no more, Your Grace. I should have no problem recti-fying the situation. 'Twould seem all of London craves the presence of the famed Disappearing Duke at their soirées."

"How lucky for me," Canby said. "Well, if I should find myself reinvited, I would be very grateful."

Steeples nodded. "It will be done."

"Thank you, Steeples. Now, if I might have a brandy and some quiet . . ."

"Of course, sir." Steeples poured a glass of brandy, hung up Canby's jacket, and turned down the bed before he excused himself. In the morning he'd go straight away to Lord Chadwick's to charm an invitation from the housekeeper.

Canby knew it wouldn't be difficult to obtain. Since his reappearance he'd gained some notoriety. The invitations to parties, balls, and suppers poured in by the dozens.

Until now, he hadn't accepted any. He had no desire to trot himself out as entertainment. But this particular party would serve multiple purposes.

First, it might yield some useful information for Ethan. Just knowing the arrangement of Lord Chadwick's home could aid in future endeavors.

Second, it would be a small party. Not nearly so unbearable as a ball or court event. He would be able to make contact with some of the members of Parliament likely to be the most uncertain about reinstating his title.

And last, his cousin Frederica, Ethan's sister, would be there as well.

At the thought of her, Canby smiled. He could hardly believe she was old enough to attend such events. The last time he'd seen her, she was a freckled sprig of a girl with boundless energy and a shocking vocabulary.

From what he'd gathered from Ethan, not much other than her appearance had changed.

He drained the last drops of brandy from his glass and headed for his bed. Tomorrow would prove a trying day. He would meet with the king, attend his club, and then head to the soirée at Lord Chadwick's, followed by his rendezvous with Quimby at the Northside quay.

If by some miracle he should make it through all of that, the next day he would be on his way home.

Canby stared into the fire, thinking that it was a curious thing: When he thought of home, it wasn't Lockwell Hall that came to mind. It was Selena.

Just Selena.

The room was too warm, and the bedclothes—rich embroidered linens and a thick, watered silk coverlet—weighed upon Selena like deep water. She missed her well-worn quilt.

She missed the cool night air that sneaked in beneath the door and around the loose windows of the cottage, and the sounds of the owls in the trees.

She missed Canby.

Throwing the covers off and slipping out of bed, she wandered restlessly about the room, touching this, studying that. A gargoyle carved out of green stone. An ugly porcelain dog with gold-painted ears. Flowers made of paper. The rich collected such frivolous oddities.

She examined each embellishment twice, still wide awake.

Perhaps she would read something. She remembered a few philosophy books Canby had loaned her that had nearly put her to sleep.

A quick search of the apartment unearthed no books. Did she dare raid the library downstairs? She chewed her bottom lip. It was unlikely anyone else would be awake at this hour.

She donned the slippers and quilted satin wrapper laid out by the maid, feeling like a fish out of water. Or rather, a fish in a satin wrapper.

The hallways were still lit. Selena remembered the servants' stairs were to the left. She scuffled down the dark stairwell, praying she'd find the library before someone found her.

When she reached the Great Hall, she couldn't help but stop for a moment to examine the portraits of Canby's predecessors.

Lords and ladies in formal court dress posed with hounds, books, swords, and children—things that indicated their most passionate interests. More than a few of them were painted with falcons on their arms, a testament to the enduring appeal the sport had held for the family over the centuries.

She rounded the staircase, suddenly finding herself before a familiar face. Kellam Markley, the Sixteenth Duke of Canby.

Canby's father.

He struck an imposing figure, mounted on horseback beneath a banner bearing the Markley crest—a moon and a falcon. But his dashing smile failed to warm the depths of his ice blue eyes.

A chill chased up Selena's spine. She hastened from the Great Hall with the inexplicable feeling that Kellam's gaze followed her.

She hurried toward the back of the house, passing both closed doors and dimly lit, richly appointed rooms. Some of them seemed bigger than the whole of her cottage.

Large drawing rooms. Small drawing rooms. Salons. Conservatory. Study.

The last set of double doors was closed. This had to be the library. Selena had never been past the kitchen before, but she knew the library overlooked the south lawn. Canby used to talk about watching her and her father fly the hawks from the room's great windows.

She pushed the doors open slowly. Relief washed over her. She'd made it.

The room was fully lit. She stepped inside to find shelves and shelves of books—so many more than she had expected.

Unfortunately, also unexpected were the rows of ladies and gentlemen staring back at her.

CHAPTER 18

A cluster of chairs surrounded a slight Oriental man, his face painted white, obviously engaged in some sort of late-night entertainment.

Selena could think of no happier circumstance than to die at that very moment.

"Well, well." The Duchess of Canby peered at her over a huge blue-and-gold fan. "Come in, my dear. Make yourself at home."

The ladies and gentlemen tittered. Selena could feel the heat rising to her cheeks. The anger she felt toward herself for her own reaction only served to make them burn hotter.

"I'm sorry," she mumbled. "I did not intend to interrupt your evening."

"Nonsense." The duchess rose to her feet, cutting a striking figure against the backdrop of finely attired guests. "Do come here, Mrs. Hewitt."

Selena stood rooted in the doorway.

"Very well, I shall come to you." The duchess broke away from the group, the train of her gown brushing people's shoes in her wake. A tiny dog danced about her feet. Selena watched her approach with a mix of horror and fascination.

The duchess reached out, cupping Selena's chin in her fingers. "You've become quite the beauty, haven't you?" Her smile was icy. "How is your arm?"

"Much better."

"Very good. I suspect my son took excellent care of you." She looked about the room, as if noticing for the first time that her guests were enthralled by this exchange. "Forgive me," she said, her hand still gripping Selena's chin. "This lovely young woman is the falconer of Lockwell Hall, Selena Hewitt. She's temporarily residing in an apartment upstairs until the wound on her arm heals."

A murmur rose from the tables.

The duchess chuckled. "I am sure many of you are familiar with her name. Indeed, you may have seen her in the courtroom recently. Though she didn't look nearly so . . . healthy."

"I should leave," Selena's voice barely broke a whisper.

"You never should have come at all," the duchess said, too quietly for the others to hear. "But you're going to give me the courtesy of two more minutes."

She took Selena's hand and faced the gathering. The white-faced Oriental man watched with irritation, as if Selena had stolen the show.

"I would like, before all of you, to issue a public apology to this young woman," the duchess said. "She was wrongly accused of a crime, and while the circumstances certainly warranted our accusations, we acknowledge this egregious error." She turned back toward Selena. "My dear, will you ever forgive us?"

The guests leaned forward in their chairs, waiting for Selena's response. Lady Letitia sat in the front row, eyes narrowed. Selena fought the urge to bolt for the door.

The duchess squeezed her hand. "Well, my dear?"

"I . . . of course."

A collective sigh swept the room.

The duchess beamed. She leaned down and whispered in Selena's ear. "Well done. Now, excuse yourself and go."

Selena bowed her head. "If you don't mind, I really must . . . I must . . ."

"Oh, but of course. By all means." The duchess ushered her back over the threshold and closed the doors.

Selena stood in the fancy silk wrapper with her back to the oak doors, appreciating their solidity. Her legs had suddenly refused to hold her. Muffled laughter seeped out from the room.

Somehow she managed to make it back to the apartment, where she immediately began to collect her belongings. She'd rather suffer a hundred arrows than one night under this roof.

She returned to the cottage by moonlight.

The night noises soothed her nerves, and the smell of the forest cleared her nostrils of Lockwell Hall's perfumed air. Though she didn't feel strong enough to light a fire and spent the entire night shivering beneath her worn quilt, she was far more comfortable than she would have been beneath the rich, warm coverlets.

When the sun rose, she did, too. She shrugged into her rough brown wool gown and smoothed her hair, recalling the feeling of complete humiliation when Canby's mother had forced her to stand in her nightclothes in front of two dozen strangers.

Why did the woman hate her so?

Selena shook her head to clear it. It didn't matter what the duchess thought of her, as long as their paths never crossed again.

And they wouldn't. Selena would make sure of it.

If all went as it should, Parliament would vote on Canby's title in just a few days, so it was conceivable that she could leave there within a week.

A low-lying fog tangled in her skirts as she hurried toward the mews. At Lockwell Hall, she'd felt so far away from the birds.

It was no wonder Canby had always looked at her with envy when he'd walked her to the door of the cottage and headed back toward his home. At the time, she couldn't understand why he wouldn't want to go back to the warmth and comfort of his fine house. Now she understood perfectly.

There hadn't been any comfort or warmth there.

Retrieving a rake from the shed, she cleaned the hawks' mew first, handling them only briefly to check their weight and feed them. Her arm had almost healed, but she did not want to risk opening the wound again.

She moved to the eagle's mew next, treating the bird's talon with an herbal ointment known to draw out infection. But outside the falcon's mew, something didn't seem right. The bird usually greeted her with a short screech in anticipation of his meal. This morning, all was silent.

Selena pushed open the door.

The falcon lay on the ground in the corner, unmoving. Unnatural.

She sank to her knees beside the bird's lifeless body. One yellow eye stared up at her, unseeing and unsettled. Selena had seen that look before. This bird had not died a peaceful death.

With a trembling hand, she turned the body over. Beneath the left wing, lodged deep in the falcon's chest, was a small, pearl-handled knife.

It was fortunate she hadn't had breakfast, for her stomach heaved. She stumbled out of the mews.

"I'm sorry, sir, but the documents for that transaction seem to be missing." The bank clerk's Adam's apple bobbed like a cork on a river.

Ethan rubbed the back of his neck, doing his best to

hold his frustration in check. Everywhere he and his men went, they found the same thing. Documents, records, orders of purchase—all missing or illegible.

From Birmingham's gun quarter to the quays, it was all the same. Any information pertaining to the shipment of guns to Africa had been tampered with.

On the one hand, these circumstances indicated they were on the right trail. On the other hand, it irked Ethan to know that someone was a step ahead of them.

Perhaps he should have taken these efforts on himself earlier. Canby and Badger had hinted he'd become soft. That he was fit to work only in the bedroom, and had lost his ability to work in the field.

While it might be true that many of Ethan's recent endeavors had involved seducing women, he hadn't lost his edge. Had he?

"Let me speak with your superior immediately," Ethan told the clerk, with a bit too much venom. He knew it would be fruitless. There would be not one shred of information about the person who'd drawn the bank draft to pay the gunmaker in Birmingham.

Whoever had been obliterating this trail was far too clever.

CHAPTER 19

Canby's meeting with the king had gone well. Lord North's recommendation had made the visit an easy one, so His Majesty hadn't been keen on disproving Canby's identity. He asked only a few questions and assured his support before dismissing Canby with a wave.

But the king's support was only half the battle.

Though Canby had been out of society for quite a while, even he knew that he could not snub the peers of England; not if he wished to have any kind of accord in his life.

If he hoped to have his title restored quickly, he would have to reintroduce himself to the people who could make it happen.

His carriage pulled up at the doors of White's. Canby steeled himself. The last time he'd been here, he was twenty years old. Even then he'd realized that money and privilege had warped so many of these men, he could never hope to share any sort of camaraderie with them.

They gambled on anything. The births of babies. The deaths of dowagers. Who would fall asleep in Parliament first. How many toasts would be made at a certain supper.

Once they'd set a dog loose on a busy street, and bet on whether it would make it to the other side alive. The whole of White's patronage had gathered in the street to watch the wretched cur until it was trampled by a hackney cab.

There were some with such gambling addictions they'd wagered away their families' homes. Others spent more on the latest ridiculous fashions than a man of modest means would need to feed and clothe his entire family for a year.

Some were cruel to animals. Some were cruel to their wives. And others, like his father, were outwardly upstanding, moral men. But behind closed doors . . .

Canby feared the thought of becoming like his father more than anything. More than death.

He would do his duty here. He would stay for an hour and garner the support he needed from the MPs. Convince them he was the long-lost duke. Offer subtle promises of political and financial support.

Then he would go home and take a long bath, and wash the taint of them from his skin before the Chadwicks' party.

"By God, Canby. It's really you."

Having been at White's for three quarters of an hour, it wasn't the first time Canby had heard that exclamation. But it was the first time he'd been glad to see the man who issued it.

Lord Archibald Staunton was the only friend Canby had made in his short stay at Eton, until his illness had forced him home to Lockwell Hall.

"Staunton. How are you?"

"Damn well, old fellow. Especially glad to see you. I'd thought you were lost to us."

"As did I." Canby led Staunton to his table, by now accustomed to the stares and whispers around him. He couldn't wait to leave this place.

"I cannot imagine," Staunton said, shaking his head. "Six years in a French prison! How did you manage?"

"I vow I don't know. But when I thought of my beloved England, I knew I had to survive."

Staunton looked at him with such blatant admiration, Canby almost felt guilty for the lie.

Almost.

Then he looked about him. He was simply telling everyone what they wanted to hear. What he needed them to believe.

Staunton leaned in. "They're taking bets on whether or not you'll have the duchy back."

"What are the odds in my favor?"

"Rather good, I'd say."

Canby smiled.

"I understand you're going to Chadwick's soirée tonight," Staunton said.

"Do I detect a note of envy in your voice? I didn't think there was a Tory alive who'd envy a supper with Chadwick."

"Lady Frederica is going to be there," Staunton said wistfully. "Of course, she'd never notice me even if I were going. Not with Blackwood there," Staunton said.

"Who's Blackwood?"

Staunton looked at him as if he'd grown another head. "Josiah Blackwood, the ship's captain from the colonies."

Canby shrugged.

"Women cannot resist him. It would seem he was involved in some sort of scandal or tragedy so terrific it cannot be discussed in proper circles." Staunton snorted. "Of course, that makes him greatly sought after in proper circles."

Canby withdrew a gold snuff-box from his waistcoat. "What is he doing in England?"

"Stealing all the most beautiful ladies, it would seem." Staunton sighed.

Canby gave him a sympathetic smile. "I'll give Lady Frederica your most respectful regards."

"Thank you."

Canby rose. "Well, I really should be leaving. It was good to see you again, Staunton."

"Likewise." Staunton flashed an easy grin.

Canby made his way to the street, where his carriage waited for him, satisfied that he'd accomplished his aim. He'd proven his identity.

But he knew that wasn't the entire issue. The question still remained as to whether or not he was prepared to take responsibility for the political influence he would wield when the duchy was his.

In all truth, Canby wondered this himself.

"Are you ready, Your Grace?"

The footman held open the carriage door. Sheets of frigid rain fell on the servant's head, but he gave no indication of noticing it. His full attention was trained on the man within the carriage.

Canby hopped out of the vehicle and bounded up the steps between two other servants, who held an awning over his head as if he might melt in the rain.

One of the servants knocked on the door of Chadwick's home on Berkeley Square.

On the street beside the coach, the footman who had opened the carriage door stood in the rain, ramrod straight, eyes trained on him.

Canby knew the aging servant was supposed to wait until his master was in the house and out of sight before he could escape the rain himself. But it was ridiculous for an old man to stand in the drenching cold for no reason.

"Fowley, get in the coach, man."

The servant balked, obviously confused.

"Get in the coach," Canby yelled through the rain. "You'll catch your death!"

Fowley nodded, and disappeared into the vehicle just as the doors of Lord Chadwick's house swung open.

* * *

Kincaid's head snapped up.

Rain funneled from his tricorn down the front of his jacket. He paid it no heed.

That had been Pearce's voice. He'd know it anywhere. It was burned into his memory.

He'd finally found him. He'd checked out every other servant in the Saint James's house staff, with no luck. Apparently the Falcon had managed to garner a position as one of the footmen for the duke's coach. Now he only had to figure out which of the two was Pearce.

Kincaid waited until the duke had disappeared into the town house. Then he crossed the street and pounded on the door of the coach. An elderly servant peeked out.

"Are you Fowley?"

"Aye."

Kincaid pointed to the two footmen who still stood at the top of the steps, waiting for the rain to abate. "Which of those footmen bade you enter the coach?"

Fowley gave him a suspicious look.

Kincaid fished a pound note from his pocket and held it to the window. "Which footman?"

Fowley took the money. "It weren't a footman who told me. It were the Duke of Canby."

"The Duke of Canby?"

Could it be possible Kincaid had mistaken the duke's voice for Pearce's?

He couldn't have. Besides, the coincidence was too great. The Falcon entered the duke's town house. The duke sounded just like the Falcon. The duke returned from the dead at the same time the Falcon returned from France.

Kincaid couldn't believe he hadn't figured it out sooner. He reeled with the revelation.

Jack Pearce, the Falcon, *was* the Duke of Canby.

* * *

A servant in white-and-gold-livery ushered Canby into a high-ceilinged foyer adorned with a stunning chandelier.

Canby followed the servant to an intimate salon, where a small group of people clustered about a pianoforte. A sweet, clear voice drifted over them, reaching out to soothe Canby's frayed nerves.

He listened from the outskirts of the group until the song ended. In the ensuing silence, the servant cleared his throat.

"Presenting His Grace, the Duke of Canby."

The servant had announced him by his title. It was a good sign. It meant that, as of the moment, there was a fair measure of support behind him.

Canby smiled.

Lady Chadwick broke from the crowd and approached him, a gloved hand extended. He took it in his and bowed low, pressing it to his lips.

"Lady Chadwick. Lovely as always."

"Your Grace, what an honor! We're so happy to have you with us this evening." Her voice held the promise of endless questions, and Canby steeled himself.

"My pleasure, to be sure." He extended his elbow and escorted her back to the other guests. "Tell me, who is the lady with the enchanting voice?"

Lady Chadwick tittered. "Surely you recognize your own cousin, Your Grace?"

Indeed, it was Lady Frederica who stood beside the pianoforte, copper curls framing her delicate face, her eyes sparkling in the candlelight. Good Lord, his aunt and uncle were in trouble.

"Canby!" Freddie pushed through the crowd. "How wonderful to see you! I vowed I'd not believe you were alive until I saw you with my own eyes."

"Freddie, your singing has mesmerized me."

She laughed, and Canby bet the musical sound of it had bewitched as many young men as her singing had.

Lord Chadwick, whom Canby had always likened to a stuffed quail in both looks and personality, gave him a rigid bow. "Come. Meet the other guests."

An hour and a half later, after a few more songs from Freddie and a lively, if not completely on-key, flute performance by the Chadwicks' daughter, the party moved into the formal dining room.

Attention from the guests seemed to be equally divided between himself and the dashing Captain Blackwood. Canby hadn't had much of a chance to speak with the man—an opportunity he would have welcomed, if only to learn more about the political climate in the colonies.

He was disappointed to learn that they would not be seated near one another at supper, either. Canby was seated to Lord Chadwick's right at the head of the table. Blackwood was seated beside Lady Chadwick at the foot.

The distance between them discouraged any direct conversation. However, they were not so far away that Canby couldn't see the somber light in Blackwood's eyes—and the smitten expression on Freddie's face whenever she looked at him.

Throughout the interminably long meal, Canby watched with a mixture of amusement and concern as his young cousin attempted to charm the captain. He noted with some relief that Blackwood seemed immune to her considerable charms.

Beside him, Lord Chadwick droned on about the Battle of Culloden, and his three-hour incarceration as a prisoner of war.

"Of course, Lord Thorndyke's men moved in, swift as foxes, and had us all released in time for tea. Heh heh heh."

"Most excellent," Canby said. "I wondered, what do you know of Mr. Blackwood there? I confess that, having just come back to London myself, I don't know a thing about him."

Lord Chadwick shifted in his chair. He glanced down the table at the infamous guest. "I can't abide most colonists myself. 'Twas my wife's idea to invite him this evening, most likely at our daughter's insistence. Apparently he's got some sort of past—quite sad and romantic—that has the ladies swooning. Including, it would seem, Lady Frederica."

Canby watched his cousin flirt outrageously, without a hint of reaction from Blackwood. The man was a stone.

"What say you, Your Grace?" Lord Chadwick said brightly. "Shall we relieve the ladies of our presence and proceed to the billiards room for less refined conversation?"

"Absolutely."

The party split off, the men heading for the billiards room for cigars and brandy, the ladies to the drawing room to play cards and sip chocolate.

Freddie gave Canby an envious look as he followed the handsome captain from the dining room. Canby smothered a grin. He really must warn Ethan of his sister's obsession.

For his part, Captain Blackwood seemed vastly relieved to be away from anything remotely feminine. His smile relaxed, and he spoke easily with the other men, laughing and making bets on the billiards matches. After he'd won several games, Canby finally had the opportunity to speak with him directly.

"I suppose thanks are in order," Canby said, handing Blackwood a cigar. "Without your presence, I might have been the only entertainment here."

"Can't say I'm happy to oblige, Your Grace," Blackwood said with a grin. "I'd just as soon go unnoticed."

"If you don't mind my asking, what brings you here then?"

"Money, actually."

"I see. You've been *paid* to attend," Canby joked.

"In a manner of speaking. I'm here to convince Lord Chadwick to invest in a ship."

"What type of ship?"

" 'Tis a mere merchant ship at the moment. My own, actually. But with Lord Chadwick's help, she'll be outfitted for war."

"To use against the colonists?" Canby asked.

Blackwood nodded. "Someone must stop the scourge of privateers who have been attacking His Majesty's naval ships."

"Quite right. What's the name of your ship?"

"The *Christie*. She's moored at Saint Saviour's Dock at the moment."

"I shall have to take a look at her. One of my holdings is located quite nearby. Two Moons Shipping. Do you know it?"

Canby watched Blackwood closely, but the man's expression remained one of friendly interest only. "I've passed it on my way to port."

"Do you have cause to deal with importers and exporters, Captain Blackwood?"

"Of course. I never sail into or out of London without a full ship. On my return, I shall be transporting cloth and china. Our fine English ladies in the colonies crave all things from the homeland."

Lord Chadwick interrupted them. "Will you play, Your Grace?" He held out a cue stick.

Canby nodded to Chadwick, then turned back to Blackwood. "May I ask a favor of you?"

"Certainly."

"Be gentle on my cousin's pride."

"Your cousin?"

"Lady Frederica."

Surprise registered in Blackwood's eyes. "Lady Frederica is your cousin?"

"Indeed."

Blackwood smiled. "Rest assured. Her pride will be safe with me."

* * *

"A shipment of guns went out to Africa just two days ago," Quimby said, running his finger over entries in the port master's log book. The book lay open on an empty barrel at the dock where they'd agreed to meet.

Jack, dressed again as the beggar, held a lantern up so he could see.

"Was the shipment examined before it left? Did it include everything it was supposed to include?" Jack asked.

"It's marked as bein' inspected, but don't put much store in it. A handful of silver in the right palm's all it takes to buy that mark."

"What shipping company?" Jack said, scratching his belly. He couldn't wait to get out of the cursed smelly clothes.

"Two Moons."

Canby stopped scratching. "The shipment of guns to Africa left from the Two Moons warehouse?"

"Aye."

"Who paid to ship them?"

Quimby squinted at the book. "Can't say. There's ink spilt on it."

"Show me," Jack demanded. Quimby pointed to a black splotch in the book. There was no way to make out the name.

"What about the dockers. Have you talked to any of them?"

"Aye, at the pub. One of 'em was braggin' about makin' twenty quid for movin' a few crates from one warehouse to another."

"Did he say which warehouse?"

"Aye. Dresden."

"So the guns were moved from the Two Moons warehouse to the Dresden warehouse?"

"Aye. And hidden amongst cargo that's slated for the colonies." Quimby's eyes skirted about. "Are ye finished wi' me, then? I'd best get this book back to the port master's office."

"Go on."

Quimby hesitated. "You'll be sure ta tell Newcomb how I helped ye?"

Jack nodded.

Quimby looked vastly relieved. He tucked the ledger beneath his arm and hurried off.

Jack stood at the dock looking out over the Thames. Moonbeams converged and shattered over the lapping waves, scattering diamonds across the water.

He wondered if Ambrose had anything to do with all of this. Or worse, his mother.

For some reason, the thought that she might be involved in something like that disturbed him more than he cared to admit.

In his tenure with the Anti-British Activity Committee, Ethan Gray had learned to find the opportune moment in every situation.

This night at Lord Shelbourne's party, the opportune moment came during a salon game called Tiamet, named for the Babylonian goddess who'd been split apart by an arrow.

For the game, each guest chose half a tin shape—men from one box, women from another. The lights were doused, and the guests were required to use their tactile skills to find the other half of their shape.

Ethan himself had suggested the game to Lady Shelbourne, who'd gasped at the implications of such a risqué amusement, but who'd snapped at the bait like an eager trout after a fly.

So, as the servants snuffed the candles in the mirrored wall sconces, Ethan made certain he was near the door. In the good-natured chaos that erupted in the dark, Ethan ducked out of the salon.

He found the door to Lord Shelbourne's study locked, as expected. He removed the unusual silver stick pin from his lapel—the same one Lady Shelbourne herself had commented on, unaware it was a copy of the key to her husband's study. Ethan had taken an impression of it in clay after a late-night tryst with Lady Mildred.

Once inside, he went directly to Lord Shelbourne's desk, using the other end of the pin to pick the lock on the letterbox.

There were three letters within, none bearing the sender's name or address. Ethan unfolded one, uncertain of exactly what he was looking for.

The letter seemed mundane enough, but was unsigned, a suspicious circumstance in and of itself. He suspected something important was hidden within. He knew Lord Shelbourne had placed several of the gun orders that had been skimmed at the quays.

He had no more than a strong suspicion that the man was involved with the French as well, but in the past, his instincts had rarely been wrong.

A rattling at the door latch startled Ethan. He quickly closed the desk and crouched behind a nearby settee.

Footsteps, shuffling softly on the thick carpet of the study, headed directly for Lord Shelbourne's desk. The hinges creaked as it was opened, and again as it closed.

The footsteps retreated, the door latch clacked, and once again Ethan found himself alone in the study. He waited a few minutes before returning to the desk.

The two letters he'd left there were gone.

On the air, a faint scent lingered. It took a few moments for him to identify the pungent smell.

Tobacco.

Not cigar smoke, pipe smoke, or snuff, but the full dried leaf of it, uncut and unprepared. The sort that might be imported from the American colonies.

CHAPTER 20

Canby avoided the front entrance of Lockwell Hall, knowing that his family might be taking breakfast in one of the downstairs rooms. Instead, he entered through the kitchen and took the servants' stairs two at a time, all but running to Selena's apartment.

He stood before the door, breathing heavily, chastising himself for coming after her this way. Nothing had changed since he was a boy. She still held him in her power. And, he realized just then, he didn't mind that one bit.

He knocked at the door.

No answer. He was going to jump out of his skin. He knocked again.

No answer.

A chambermaid slogged up the hall with a bucket of water.

"Is Mrs. Hewitt in the bath?" he asked.

"No, Your Grace. She be gone."

"Gone?"

"Aye. I'm goin' to clean the room."

The maid pushed Selena's door open, and Canby followed her inside, taking a quick walk through the quarters.

Empty.

The few personal belongings Selena had brought with her—a hairbrush, combs, clothing—were missing as well.

"Where did she go?"

The maid looked up from scrubbing the floor in front of the fireplace. "Dunno, sir. The duchess asked me to come and clean the room well. Said Mrs. Hewitt wouldn't be stayin' here anymore."

A tiny spark of trepidation joined growing annoyance. His mother had chased Selena away. He'd lay money on it. And when he found Charity, she'd be the one to pay.

Charity stood alone on a stone terrace overlooking the formal gardens. A chill wind swept her light wool cape tight against her shoulders, but she hardly seemed to notice.

There was a faraway look on her face—a look he'd never seen before—and for the first time Canby realized his mother was starting to show her age.

In a moment of weakness, he felt sorry for her. It couldn't have been easy for her to live with his father for all those years. But then he remembered the way she'd pushed him out of her life, ashamed of the weak little boy with the limp, and any sympathy he may have had for her took wing on the wind.

"What happened with Selena?"

She startled at the sound of his voice. But by the time her gaze met his, she was herself again—cool and collected.

"I'm sure I don't know."

"She's left her apartment."

His mother smiled. "My dear, it never was *her* apartment, was it? Perhaps she realized she didn't belong here."

"I wanted her here. I brought her here to keep her from danger."

"For heaven's sake, what sort of danger could she possibly be in?"

"Someone shot at her in the woods, near the mews."

"Shot at her? Oh, dear." Charity turned back toward the garden.

"I want to know who is responsible for her leaving."

His mother sighed. "If you must hold someone responsible, I suppose it should be me."

"You chased her away."

"On the contrary. I apologized for accusing her of your murder."

He studied his mother's face. Guileless. A sure sign something had happened between her and Selena.

"I will find out what why she left. You know that, don't you?"

She stared out over the garden, saying nothing.

He turned to leave.

"Canby."

He stopped.

"I have a favor to ask of you." She turned to him. "Should your title be restored, I'd like you to return controlling interest of Two Moons Shipping to Sir Ambrose."

Her gall surprised him. She must have been truly desperate to broach the subject at such an inopportune time. It wasn't like her to commit such a gaffe.

"I will look into the situation," he said pointedly. "At the moment, however, I'm more concerned with what happened to Selena."

His mother's hand fluttered in a dismissive wave. "There are so many more important things to worry about. For instance, don't you wish to know how my efforts are faring to help you get your title back?"

"What do you want, Mother? My undying gratitude? My respect? Or something more useful. Money?"

She smiled. "For now, I just want you to return Two Moons to Ambrose. That's all."

"Well, for now all I want is to find Selena."

She sighed. "Someday you'll understand what it really means to be a peer of the realm. You'll understand your responsibility to England. When you do, you'll have to leave her. Do you really want to break her heart?"

"I understand my duty perfectly, Mother. And I'll never have to break anyone's heart to fulfill it."

"You'll never marry her, which is what a woman like that thinks she deserves. That alone will break her heart."

Would that break Selena's heart? He'd never considered marrying her. He didn't want to bring her into his world of cruel whispers and debauched souls. She was too good for all of that. And yet . . .

Canby thought about what life would be like with Selena beside him every day, sharing his frustrations and joys and privileges—and every night, sharing his bed.

"Well?" His mother pressed. "Do you see my point?"

"You know, Mother, you're right. I don't want to hurt her. So perhaps I *will* marry her."

Charity raised her eyebrows. "Don't be an ass. What will happen when she must stand in the same room with the likes of Lady Jersey and Lady Melbourne? Those two will devour her. And what will happen when the satirists make a mockery of you both? How will you feel?"

Canby felt the blood rush to his face. "I don't give a damn what Lady Jersey says, or the satirists, or all of England. If I choose to marry Selena Hewitt, I will."

"What about Selena?" Charity asked quietly. "How will *she* feel?"

Canby thought of the malicious stories he'd heard just yesterday at White's. Could Selena withstand such venomous attacks?

His mother laid her hand on his arm. It was the first time he'd felt her touch since he was a boy.

"People in our position have a responsibility. Not only to our kind, but to all of England."

He snorted.

"It's true. We are looked upon to set the standards—of

manners, of fashion, and most importantly, of morality. It's a responsibility I do not take lightly. And no matter how much you resent it, my boy, you cannot shirk it. If you were to marry Selena, you'd be ruined for the rest of your life, and so would she. You know our kind will forgive anything but scandal. Is that how you wish to live?"

He said nothing, because there was nothing to say. His mother was right. The ridiculous social mores he'd had to live by had always angered him. It was one of the reasons he'd decided to give this life up.

"Mother, you would be surprised how well I understand. But I cannot bend to all of that. I will live however I wish, with whomever I wish. And all I've ever wished for is Selena."

The cottage stood empty. No sign of Selena inside. But Canby was happy to see it had been restored to the tidy haven he remembered from his childhood. He could hardly blame Selena for wanting to escape Lockwell Hall to return here.

He followed the thick scent of leather to the workbench in the corner, and pulled a gauntlet onto his arm that Selena had almost finished sewing. In the fold just below the elbow, she'd burned three letters: JEM.

His initials.

He smiled. She was making the glove for him. Had she been hoping they'd spend more time together hawking, as he had?

He wished they could leave the world behind and take their birds away from everything his mother had described. Away from those who would judge his love for Selena.

Away from anyone who would look to *him* for moral guidance.

The only thing he knew for certain was that he wanted a life with Selena. But in some ways she was just like his mother, ever conscious of social boundaries, always talking about their places in life.

He was going to put her straight today. He would not leave her out here alone. She would come back to Lockwell Hall if he had to drag her by the feet.

He returned the glove to the workbench and headed for the mews.

Just outside the circle of the weatherings, a small cross fashioned from sticks protruded from a mound of freshly turned earth. At the sight of it, Canby broke into a run.

"Selena!"

She emerged from the mews, pale and wild-eyed.

"My God, what happened?"

"The falcon . . ." She dissolved into tears. In all the years he'd known her, Canby had never seen her cry like this.

"What happened to the falcon?"

"It's dead. It's my fault! I—" A sob tore from her lips.

Canby folded her gently into his embrace. "Shh. Be calm. Tell me what happened from the beginning."

Selena took a shaky breath and dried her eyes with her sleeve. "I left Lockwell Hall in the middle of the night. On the way back to the cottage, I thought I should come check on the birds, but I was just too tired. The next morning, I found the falcon dead." She rocked on her heels, her arms wrapped around her waist. "Why, Canby? Why?"

He stroked the braid that hung down her back. "'Tis the way of the world, love. Things die."

"It was killed."

"Selena—"

"It was!" She took his hand and pulled him into the building. In the aisle, several blankets lay spread out on the floor.

"Did you sleep here last night?"

"Yes, and I plan to sleep here again tonight. 'Tis the

only way to be sure they'll be safe." She retrieved something from a shelf beside the door and handed it to him. "I found this lodged in the falcon's chest."

He stared down at the small, pearl-handled knife in his palm. "But that's impossible. That would mean someone—"

"Killed my bird."

"I cannot believe it."

Selena made a sound of anguish. "Why? Why would someone do this?"

Canby slipped the knife into the pocket of his coat. A feeling of nausea settled in his stomach.

"I'm taking them away," Selena said. "I'm leaving tomorrow."

"You can't. Your name hasn't been cleared. You're still officially under Ethan's sponsorship."

"I don't care. I will not leave my birds in danger any longer."

He took her hands. They trembled violently in his. "Your arm is wounded. You aren't strong enough to carry all these birds. You'd do them more harm by taking them."

"I must get out of this place."

"If you leave, you could be arrested again," he said. He drew her to him. "Parliament is set to vote on the matter of my title tomorrow. After that, we'll figure out what to do."

She pulled her hands away, pacing the length of the mews. The birds stirred nervously, attuned to her agitation. "Fine. Then I will stay right here until I'm free to leave. I must protect them. Surely you understand that, Canby?"

"Of course. But you must take care of yourself, too. Come back to Lockwell Hall with me—"

"Never!"

His voice softened. "At least go back to the cottage. Get some rest. I will make sure the birds are safe."

"You will?" The anger had left her. Her shoulders slumped. He knew she must be weak with cold and lack of sleep.

"Go on." He turned her around and gave her a gentle push toward the door.

When she'd gone, Canby took the knife out of his pocket. He examined the mother-of-pearl handle closely. No initials, no markings of any kind.

He'd seen a knife like this before, but he couldn't place where.

CHAPTER 21

Though he'd searched it thoroughly, the area surrounding the mews gave up no clues as to who might have killed the falcon.

Canby left the weatherings and went to the cottage to check on Selena. She lay sound asleep, rolled up in a faded quilt in her bed.

He added a log to the fire and closed the door quietly behind him. Then he rode to the stables and sent two stable hands back to watch over the mews and Selena.

At Lockwell Hall, all was quiet. It was still an hour before tea time, and he knew his mother and Letitia would be napping. He had no idea where Randolph would be. The man was a mystery.

In his quarters, Canby went straight to his desk and unlocked the bottom drawer, removing his pistol from a polished wooden box. He tucked it into the waistband of his breeches and buttoned his riding cape over it. Then he wrote a note to Ethan and rang for Steeples.

In short measure, there was a knock at his door. He opened it, expecting Steeples but finding Randolph instead.

"I hoped I could speak with you about something." In his hand he held several large rolls of paper.

Canby stifled a groan. "I really must be going, Randolph."

"Please? Just for a moment."

"Come in." Canby held the door open as Randolph bounded inside with his papers, calling to mind an eager puppy.

Just as Canby was about to close the door, Steeples arrived. Canby handed him the note. "Please see that this gets to Mr. Gray in London as soon as possible."

"Yes, Your Grace."

Canby closed the door.

Randolph unrolled the papers on a table and smoothed them with his hands. He looked up expectantly.

"What are these?" Canby asked.

Randolph beamed. "These are plans for a coal mine. A highly profitable and efficient coal mine. Using a Watt's Engine, coal can be mined from depths never before dreamed of."

"A coal mine?"

"Yes." Randolph rearranged the papers, putting a different one, a topical map, atop the pile. "This is the estate. And this"—Randolph pointed—"would be the perfect spot for the mine. My surveys show a vein of coal running straight through the corner of the property."

Canby examined the map. "Isn't that where the mews are located?"

"Yes. But I thought we could build another home for Selena. A much nicer one, up here." Randolph pointed to a spot on the map. "And we would rebuild the mews as well, of course. Make them larger and better able to withstand the weather."

"Randolph, I cannot see destroying Selena's home for the sake of a coal mine."

Randolph's smile faded. "It would bring a great deal of employment, Canby. Not to mention the financial boon to the duchy."

Canby rubbed the back of his neck. All he wanted was to get to Selena. "If you leave the surveys and the map, I will take a look at them later."

"Very well," Randolph said. "Thank you for taking the time to listen to me. It's more than Lord Popper has ever done." He rolled the papers up and left them on the table.

"We will talk later. I promise."

Randolph nodded and scuffled out.

Canby felt a momentary pang of guilt before his thoughts turned back to Selena.

He wanted to be back at the mews before she awoke.

"What are you doing up here?"

Ambrose's presence in her private sitting room annoyed Charity to no end.

Her conversation with Canby had rattled her nerves, and she still hadn't fully regained her composure. Would he really consider *marrying* Selena Hewitt?

Charity's standing in society would never recover from such a scandal. The Hewitt woman had to go.

"Parliament resumed today. They are set to vote on the matter most close to our hearts tomorrow." Ambrose's usually pristine clothing was rumpled. He looked as if he'd been drinking, and she doubted he'd slept much lately.

"Will they restore his title?"

"I'm almost certain of it."

Charity felt the tightness in her shoulders ease. "They will, won't they?"

"I understand he was quite the attraction at White's, and at Lord and Lady Chadwick's. Smart of him to show his face about town."

"One could never call him stupid," Charity said. Even as a boy, Canby understood far more than he should have.

He'd always seen Kellam's rages coming on. Too bad he'd been too stubborn to get out of his father's way.

Charity supposed he took after her in that regard.

"The real question is, will he be smart enough to sell Two Moons back to me?" Ambrose said.

"I still don't understand why you want this all of a sudden. It's been nearly twenty years since Kellam won controlling interest of Two Moons from you. Why do you want it back now, after all this time?" Charity took a seat across from him.

Ambrose leaned forward, his eyes cold. "I want what is mine. Now, I asked you a question. Will Canby be smart enough to sell? Have you convinced him?"

With a confidence Charity didn't feel, she said, "He will sell. I'll make sure of it."

Ambrose settled back into the swan chair. It didn't take much effort to appease him. She'd found that Ambrose believed what he wanted to believe, most of the time.

"Come here," he said, his eyes darkening. Now that his mind had been put to ease, he was clearly in the mood for something other than conversation.

"You're not serious."

"Oh, but I am."

"Don't be ridiculous. We are not lovers. We haven't been for years."

Ambrose's gaze grew steely. "Let me make myself clear. If you expect me to give you the money you want, you'd do well to accommodate my needs."

Charity stood. "If you expect me to convince my son to return Two Moons to you, you'll do best to remember that you're not my husband."

Ambrose's arm snaked out from the chair and grabbed her by the skirts, dragging her to him. "No," he sneered. "I'm certainly not Kellam. He wouldn't take no for an answer. He would have you beneath him whenever he wanted."

Charity's heart pounded against her ribs.

Show no fear.

She extracted herself from Ambrose's grasp. "As soon as you have your company back, you will give me my due. After that, I never want to see you again."

Ambrose's laugh was devoid of amusement. "It will be my pleasure, my dear."

At dawn Selena awoke and realized she'd fallen asleep the afternoon before and slept through the night without stirring. She looked out of her bedroom window. A strange man slept on a chair outside her door.

She ran the short distance to the mews and pushed the door open, afraid of what she might find. But just as he'd promised, Canby lay asleep on the floor on the blankets she'd left from the night before.

In all the years she'd known him, Canby had never broken a promise. She kneeled beside him, touching his cheek.

His hand flew up and caught her wrist in a painful grip. She gasped, and the eagle shrieked.

"It's you," Canby said, releasing her. "I'm sorry."

She rubbed her wrist. "Your stay in prison has made you a light sleeper."

"What?" He rubbed his eyes.

"You were always a sound sleeper. Remember when I threw stones at your window in the middle of the night, trying to wake you to come look for owls? You slept through the noise every time."

He smiled. "I tried so hard to stay awake. There was nothing I would rather have done than gone owl-hunting with you in the dark."

Her braid hung over her shoulder, and he twirled the end of it around his finger. His gaze consumed her. An invisible thread drew them closer, until she felt his breath on her lips. She closed her eyes, and he kissed her so lightly she thought it might be her imagination.

And she didn't want it to be. She wanted—needed—something to be real. After the nightmare of the last few weeks, she wanted something real. Or perhaps she wanted a beautiful dream.

Their kiss deepened. Canby tugged her braid to pull her closer, and she moved from her knees onto one hip, stretching out on the blanket until her legs touched his.

She took his face in her hands and pressed her lips to his, pouring every moment of heartache and hope into the kiss. She tasted desire on his lips. He wanted her, maybe more today than he had when they were younger.

She had the power to refuse him again. To remain true to her conviction that she shouldn't be with a man who wanted her only for a mistress.

But what good was conviction if your heart was dead? She'd known that pain for half her life. She wanted to be happy now, convictions be damned.

"Make love to me," she whispered.

He kissed her hard, groaning against her mouth. "Are you certain?" he asked, his voice hoarse with longing.

She nodded.

"Selena, I—"

She pressed her fingers to his mouth to quiet him. "Please know that I expect nothing. Want nothing. Only you."

He pulled her to him, his chest solid against hers, his hands caressing her back, cupping her buttocks, stroking the back of her thighs.

Her skin came alive beneath his touch. She wanted to shed every thread of clothing, feel his skin against hers. Her fingers worked the buttons on his shirt, already half-undone and rumpled with sleep.

"No." He disentangled her fingers from his shirt. "Not here. Not like this."

He rose to his knees as he continued to kiss her, pulling her up with him. Then he gathered her in his arms and stood, pushing the door to the mews open with his foot.

The next time she opened her eyes, they were in the cottage.

Canby kissed her, and held her for the longest time as if she were as light as an armful of wildflowers. Then he carried her to the bed, laying her gently atop the quilt. He kneeled beside her, taking her hand, kissing her fingers, her wrist, the soft white skin on the inside of her arm.

Moving to the bottom of the bed, he unlaced her boots with trembling fingers, placing them neatly on the floor. His warm hands skimmed over her foot, circled her ankle, and moved over her calf, pushing her skirts up past her knees, exposing her to the chill air of the cottage. He bent over her, his lips grazing the inside of her thigh, igniting a fire in her middle. She struggled to sit up, but Canby quieted her with his hands.

"Lie still. Trust me."

She lay back on the bed. She would trust him, because being here with him made everything else disappear. All the horrible things that had happened to her since her father's death were merely dark clouds, receding.

His hands and mouth caressed her thighs, her hips, her belly, moving in an ever-tightening circle toward the wet heat of her center. When he finally took her with his mouth, she gasped, bunching the quilt in her fists.

His touch sent her soaring, like a breeze caught beneath an eagle's wings. She hovered at the edge of bliss, dipping and circling, anticipating something unknown. And then she dove, crying out his name. Before she had a chance to land, Canby came up and moved into her, fitting so neatly against her it was as if he were a piece of herself she'd been missing.

He moved slowly and with purpose, like a falcon's climb, teasing, urging, bringing her up to the sky again with him. Selena could hardly believe there was someone in this world who cared enough about her to want to make her feel like this.

A tear rolled down the side of her face and Canby

caught it with a kiss. When his lips moved to hers, she could taste the salt on them.

He tumbled onto his back, bringing her with him. Her braid slipped over her shoulders and he untied the leather thong that bound it together. Her hair unwound, cascading around them like a dark curtain. Canby combed the locks with his fingers and brought them to his nose.

"Your hair smells like rain," he murmured into the silken strands. "Like the time you rescued me from the ravine."

She kissed his neck. "I thought you'd been killed. I was so afraid to look."

"That's the night I fell in love with you. You rescued me, in more ways than one."

She turned her head away from him. "I'm not your savior, Canby. I never was."

He hooked her chin with his finger and gently turned her to face him. "You were. You are."

He rocked his hips, driving up into her gently, rhythmically. A moan escaped her. Butterflies stirred in her abdomen as he quickened his pace.

She couldn't catch her breath. She was liquid and fire, hot and cold, falling and floating.

He rolled her beneath him and buried his head against her shoulder, his body shuddering. She hooked her legs around his hips, pulling him tight against her as she exploded around him.

Gradually, her breath returned and the humming beneath her skin quieted.

Canby lay still, his beating heart the only sign he lived. Selena wrapped her arms around his head and kissed his hair, amazed at how much she loved him. Her heart ached with loving him. Her head swam with loving him.

For the first time, she didn't think about what would happen next, she just let things be. She and Canby were finally together.

Selena knew that when he was young, Canby wished he'd been born the falconer's son. However, he never knew she'd secretly wished she'd been born a lady.

But childhood fancies faded. One couldn't become someone else simply by wishing. Canby would never be a falconer, and she would never be a lady. But they could love each other in spite of that, couldn't they?

She kissed Canby's forehead. "Sleep well, my love," she whispered.

CHAPTER 22

Selena watched Canby sleep, his body wrapped in her mother's quilt. Was this how her mother had felt about her father?

She'd never had a woman to talk to about such frivolous matters as love. Her father was a pragmatic man who'd kept her close to him, giving her little opportunity to mingle with the opposite sex. The only boys her age she'd ever been around, aside from Canby, of course, were those who came hawking at Lockwood Hall.

The Duchess of Canby had arranged for Selena to meet her husband, a blacksmith who'd been hired to shoe the duchy's horses. The duchess had convinced Selena's father it was time to make a match for her. She was on the far side of marrying age.

Selena wanted Canby, but when he offered to make her his mistress, she knew he'd never marry her.

With his strong arms and big hands, Selena imagined she'd be safe with Garrick Hewitt, even if she didn't love him. She thought he'd protect her from the world just as her father had. She couldn't have been more wrong.

It wasn't too late to find happiness, though. She could stay with Canby now, rather than leaving. She could allow herself to be content as his mistress. As she'd learned from experience, marriage didn't necessarily guarantee happiness.

She trailed a hand from Canby's shoulder across his chest and down his arm, her fingers dancing over the hills and valleys of his muscles.

"Canby."

"Mmm." He rolled onto his side and opened his eyes. "Is it morning already?"

"Long past. We need to go back to the mews. The birds are alone."

"It's fine. I sent the man who was guarding your door to the mews."

"Oh, no! He saw us enter the cottage together? The way we were . . ."

Canby smiled. "Don't worry. Angus can be trusted not to speak of it."

"But—"

He groaned, pulling her into his embrace and tucking her against his side. "Put it from your mind, and kiss me."

She kissed the triangular patch of hair curling over his chest, and ran her palms across his belly.

They made love with reverence rather than passion, and by the time they'd finished, Selena knew there would be more days and nights to come. Many more. But she couldn't help feeling sad that this first was over.

She stretched her aching arm and tumbled out of bed.

"Don't move," Canby said.

"What?" She was suddenly aware that she had no clothes on.

"The sunlight on your skin . . . you're so beautiful."

Her face grew warm. She pulled a blanket from the bed and wrapped it around herself. "I'm not. I'm much too plain and tall."

"You're perfect."

"No, *you* are perfect. I am lucky."

He laughed. "Come over here and I'll show you how lucky you are."

They were interrupted by a knock at the door. Canby leaped out of bed and pulled a pair of breeches on. He rooted through the pile of clothes and withdrew a pistol.

"Canby!"

"Just in case," he said.

He went to the window and peered out. His shoulders relaxed. "It's Ethan. I'll be back in a few minutes."

"Your stablemaster told me you were at the mews," Ethan said, suppressing the grin Canby knew lay just beneath the surface.

He ignored the ribbing. "I'm glad you're here. I wanted to tell you what I found out."

"About the latest arms shipment?"

Canby nodded. "Most of the order was shipped legitimately to Africa. Care to guess which shipping company?"

"Which?"

"Two Moons."

Ethan expelled a loud breath.

"Quimby confirmed that some of the guns were recrated with other goods, as was done with prior shipments. They're being stored in a warehouse at the Dresden dock. He suspects, as you do, that they are bound for the colonies."

"Do you think Lord Popper is involved?"

"I can't say. But the way my mother has been pushing me to sell Two Moons back to Sir Ambrose, I'm almost certain *they* are. I plan to check Two Moons' records as soon as I get back to London."

"Who paid taxes on the gun shipment to Africa?"

"Couldn't find that out. The information had been ruined by spilled ink."

"Spilled ink?" Ethan shook his head. "Everywhere we

go there is spilled ink, water stains, lost records. Someone is concealing information."

"But why? Arms orders, arms shipments, and the like, they're all perfectly legal as long as all costs and taxes are paid," Canby said.

"Exactly. Which makes me believe that whoever is doing these things legally is also doing something *illegal,* and is trying to remove their name from all records."

"So you think whoever legally arranged for the Africa shipment is also the one siphoning weapons off to send illegally to the colonies?"

"No taxes paid, no record of export, no record of receipt in the colonies. The Crown would know nothing about those weapons, or where they were going."

Canby nodded. "I'll check the Two Moons records and see if I can come up with anything else."

"Very good," Ethan said. He leaned against a tree. The two were silent for a while, running the new information through their minds, looking for connections, possibilities.

"Oh, I nearly forgot." Ethan casually withdrew a packet from his waistcoat and handed it to Canby.

He unfolded it, and something heavy slid into his palm.

His ducal ring.

Ethan laughed. "They voted first thing this morning. Congratulations, Your Grace. You won by unanimous decision."

Canby slipped the ring back into the envelope. "I cannot wait to tell Selena."

His cousin grinned. "Go on. We'll talk later."

Canby ran into the cottage and up the stairs.

Selena had dressed and was braiding her hair.

He swept her up and kissed her hard on the mouth. "How does it feel to kiss a duke?" He waved the writ beneath her nose.

"Oh, Canby! That means—"

"They've restored my title. And if I'm officially the Duke of Canby, you officially could *not* have murdered me. You are a free woman."

"Oh, thank God."

"I know the perfect way to celebrate," he said, taking Selena's hand and leading her toward the bed.

She laughed, and wrestled her hand from his. "We have to take care of the birds."

"They can wait." He came to her and wrapped his arms around her, nuzzling her neck.

When his tongue brushed her earlobe, she said, "Well. Perhaps we can celebrate for just a little while."

It was nearly dark by the time Canby made it back to Lockwell Hall. Steeples met him at the door.

"Have they heard?" Canby asked.

"Yes, Your Grace. The whole household has heard. The duchess has arranged a celebratory supper."

Canby went to his apartment, where he stripped off his clothes and took a long, hot bath. Afterward, Steeples helped him dress in his most regal clothes. Then he donned the ring.

The band weighed heavily upon his finger.

In truth, aside from the fact that Selena's name had been cleared, Canby wasn't enraptured with the idea that he was officially returned to the status of peer.

Selena was free, but he himself was once again chained to a life he despised. And this time there would be no disappearing.

He would be John Markley, Seventeenth Duke of Canby, for the rest of his life.

After he completed the mission in Montainville, Jack Pearce would make an appearance only when there was a task that could be completed in a short time. The life of a duke was busy and quite visible, leaving little room to sneak away unnoticed. Certainly not for extended periods of time.

"Is there something I can do for you, Your Grace?" Steeples worked over the sleeves of Canby's coat with a stiff brush. "Is something amiss?"

Canby shook off his gloom. The important thing was that he and Selena were together. By resuming his life as the Duke of Canby, at least he would be able to remain with her always.

"On the contrary, Steeples. Everything is perfect."

Though the dining room was bedecked with the finest family china, the mood was far from festive.

His mother's air of tense expectance permeated the room like candle smoke. Letitia's mood hung one step below somber.

Only Randolph was smiling. "Congratulations, Canby. Well done."

Canby crossed to his brother and took the hand he proffered. "Thank you, Randolph. I hope we will have no animosity between us."

His brother seemed surprised. "Why would we?"

Letitia shook her head.

"Aren't you glad I planned the ball?" his mother said gaily. "It will be a most proper celebration."

Canby ignored her, and turned instead to Letitia. "It occurs to me that I failed to welcome you officially into this family." He kissed her on each cheek. "I would like to remedy my oversight. I'd like to offer you and Randolph Ansleigh Castle in Essex for your home. Though I've never been there, I understand the weather is mild and the countryside quite lovely."

"Yes," she said quietly. "Thank you."

"And Randolph, I trust you're still interested in building that new mine? Of course, you and Letitia are welcome to stay here at Lockwell Hall as long as necessary to complete the task."

"Thank you, Canby! Thank you." His brother's eyes glistened with tears.

"And what gift will you offer me?" his mother asked,

her voice a shade weary. "Have you decided upon the fate of Two Moons?"

"Randolph, Letitia. Will you excuse us for a moment?" Canby said.

Randolph took Letitia's arm and guided her from the room, like a shepherd guiding a lost sheep. Canby motioned his mother to her seat, and took his place at the head of the table.

"Exactly what interest have you in Two Moons?" he asked.

"Interest?"

"What do you stand to gain from it?"

Her expression was indecipherable. "I merely wish to help out an old friend."

"Of course," he said.

"Does this mean you plan to sell controlling interest back to him?"

Canby studied her. "I don't know yet. I plan to speak with Lord Popper on the issue as soon as I can get to London."

"Lord Popper? Whatever for?"

"I want to review the records. Make certain everything is in order."

She fidgeted with the sleeve of her gown. "May I ask you to hurry?"

"Why?"

She opened her mouth, then closed it. She shook her head. "Never mind. Take your time."

Canby chose his words carefully. "I assume completion of this transaction will be of some benefit to you?"

She was silent.

"No matter what happens, I hope you will sever your ties with Two Moons, and with Sir Ambrose. I don't like him, and I don't trust him."

"So noted. And while we're offering up advice, I'd like to give some to you. Forget the falconer's daughter, Canby. She isn't worth the trouble."

Canby held his anger in check. It didn't matter what his mother thought of Selena. Whatever happened with Two Moons, he'd make sure his mother was gone—out of his life for good, except on those rare occasions when they'd be forced to attend the same events.

"Selena has had enough trouble from you in her life, Mother. Though she's never said, I gather the man you convinced her to marry abused her readily. Then, when she returned to Lockwell Hall, you accused her of murder. And through it all, she's prevailed.

"I'm sure you don't know what she's worth," he said. "You never did."

"I know what she'll cost." There was a glint in her eye he didn't recognize. "You're a fool, Canby, just like your father was. When will you realize that lust will be your downfall?"

"It isn't lust, Mother. It's love. I love Selena. And I'm going to marry her. In fact, I'm going to ask her at your grand ball."

The declaration stunned Canby as much as it must have stunned his mother.

"You cannot be serious!"

He tested the words again in his mind. *He was going ask Selena to marry him.*

"I'm terribly serious. I'm going to marry her, and nothing, not even you, can stop me."

"At the ball! I won't allow it," Charity said. "I'd rather die."

"Wouldn't *that* create a proper scandal?"

She bowed her head. "She will ruin me. She will ruin us all."

"Spare the melodrama, Mother. Other families have survived improper marriages. Indeed, some have flourished in spite of them. I'm going to marry a falconer. It's not as if I'm committing a murder."

Charity's face went white. Her red-rouged lips formed a slash against the pale sweep of her face. She rose and, without a word, stalked from the room.

It was the last thing Canby had expected of her. She wasn't one to run from a fight. Especially not from a fight with him.

He stared at the empty doorway. The atmosphere at Lockwell Hall would most definitely be chilly for the next few days, until Randolph and Letitia and his mother had gone to London.

He would have to stay out of the house. Go hawking. Spend time with Selena.

At the thought of her, he smiled. He realized that he'd announced his intentions to marry her without even having asked her.

He wandered to the window and looked out over the countryside. His holdings stretched farther than the eye could see. What would Selena say when she discovered that she wouldn't merely live on this land, but that she would be mistress of it?

Would the prospect excite her? Would it frighten her? Or what if she refused him? She had once before.

Before he proposed, he would have to prove to Selena that she could hold her own beside any lady. And he'd have to prove to society that Selena was worthy of the title of duchess.

The ball would be the perfect place for it.

He would escort her. Let her know that he wasn't ashamed of her. He wanted the whole world to see how much he cared for her.

They'd put an end to gossip and speculation immediately by introducing her as someone he treasured, her station be damned.

"There you go, my love."

Selena returned the hawk, Diana, to her perch, having just checked her weight and replaced the bell on her talon.

She entered the eagle's mew just as Canby appeared.

"I want to take him out," she said. "His foot has finally healed."

"It looks as if you are healing, as well."

She smiled. "I am. I'm able to hold the hawks now without too much pain. The scar . . . well, you've seen it. But at least I have my arm."

"And I have you." Canby kissed her full on the lips, drawing an involuntary sigh from deep within her.

They collected what they needed and took the eagle from the mews into the mellow sunshine of the autumn afternoon.

They walked in comfortable silence. The calls of distant birds and the shuffling of brush creatures drew their attention until they reached a meadow.

Canby released the eagle. They watched as the bird climbed to the sky, spinning shadow-circles across the rippling meadow grass.

"Do you know where we are?" Selena asked. A smile played at the corners of her mouth.

"England, I hope."

She pointed. "Look over there."

His gaze swept the meadow, but no sign of recognition lit his eyes.

"Over there," she said. "Beyond the trees. It's the ravine you leapt into when we were children."

"You mean, when I was a child. I don't think you were ever a child, Selena. I remember you always as a strong, practical woman, even when you were a girl."

She stared off into the distance. "I know your life wasn't easy, Canby. But it was a different kind of life than mine. I had to work hard, even when I was young."

He took her hand. "I wish things wouldn't have been so difficult for you."

"Don't misunderstand me. I enjoyed my life with my father. But every now and then, I wished for something different."

Canby turned to face her, cupping her face in his hands,

stroking her cheekbone with the pad of his thumb. "Perhaps you'll have something different someday."

She looked into his eyes. "I have just what I want now. I wouldn't wish for anything more."

He kissed her then, his lips moving over hers with the perfect mix of strength and tenderness, passion and possession. She curled her fingers into his hair and tugged him closer.

His hands left her face to roam over the curves and hollows of her body. One of his hands strayed to her breasts, his palms circling, cupping her, teasing her nipples into furrowed peaks.

She leaned into him, pressing her hips against his. He fit perfectly against her. He reached around to cup her bottom, sliding his hand down the back of her thigh to her knee, raising her leg until it rested on his hip bone.

She went liquid, reaching between them to feel his hardness. Her belly tightened with anticipation.

The eagle's screech drew them apart. It had attacked. A fat hare lay motionless in the grass.

"We'll finish this later," Canby said, his words thick with desire. With promise.

They hunted with the eagle until dusk, gathering the bird's quarry in the falconer's bag. Canby promised to deliver it to the kitchens. "Then I have a few things I need to take care of," he said, "but I will come tonight to the cottage."

He left her on her doorstep, dizzy with thoughts of the days and nights that lay ahead of them.

CHAPTER 23

"Angus, why don't you come inside and get something to eat?" Selena called to the guard outside her door.

He reminded her of her father, with laugh lines around his eyes, and a deep, booming voice.

"I'm not supposed to."

"What? Eat?"

"Leave my post."

"For goodness' sake, Angus. No one is going to storm the keep. I think we both know that."

The guard shook his head, but stepped inside anyway.

"I've made a plate for you. It's on the table in the kitchen. I'm going to the mews."

"But you're not to go by yourself, Miss Selena."

"I will be fine. It's just a short walk, and Clive is there to meet me."

Truthfully, she was sick to death of being escorted everywhere she went.

Before he'd left for London two days before, Canby

assigned guards to walk her about and watch the house and the mews at all hours of the day and night. He assured her it was necessary if she refused to relocate to Lockwell Hall while he was gone.

While she welcomed the protection at the mews, she thought it completely unnecessary for herself. Frankly, it was difficult to find time alone with her thoughts.

Although, if she were to admit it, she'd thought of nothing else but Canby since he'd left. Everything reminded her of him.

"Set your mind straight, Selena," she chided herself. "You've got work to do."

With a new rake in hand, she hummed softly as she walked the short distance to the mews. Today she and the guard would give the quarters a thorough cleaning, and she'd make a list of the things needed to prepare them for the winter. Although she preferred to do the work herself, Canby insisted that, for this year at least, he would hire some men to do the work for her.

The screech of a hawk in a stand of oak trees startled her, and she dropped the rake. As she bent to pick it up, a telltale twang reverberated in her ear.

In the tree beside her, an arrow with bright red-and-yellow fletching trembled in the trunk.

Selena threw the rake aside and ran back toward the cottage, screaming for Angus. He met her on the path.

"What happened, missy?"

She clutched his sleeve, panting. "An arrow in the tree. Like the one His Grace and I saw before. Red-and-yellow fletching."

"Did you see who shot it?"

She shook her head. "It came at me from the woods."

"Here." Angus pushed his pistol into her hands. "Get home and close the door. If someone tries to get in, shoot them."

Angus disappeared down the path.

Selena bolted home and sat on the floor inside the door, the pistol resting on her knees. An eternity later, she heard a voice calling from outside.

"Miss Selena, it's Angus. Let me in."

She rose like a newborn colt on unsteady legs, her heartbeat loud in her ears. She opened the door to Angus, who held an arrow in his fist.

"Oh, Angus. If I hadn't dropped my rake . . ." The shaking started in her knees and moved upward until her teeth chattered. She had no control over it. She felt as if she'd shake apart.

"Lord," Angus swore. "His Grace will kill me when I tell him about this."

"No!" She grabbed his sleeve. "We cannot tell him about this. He has too many worries."

"Miss Selena, be reasonable. If someone is after you, His Grace needs to know."

"Then let me tell him. Please."

Angus shook his head, but said. "A'right. But you'll not be going anywhere alone again."

Canby's thoughts strayed to Selena, even as Lord Popper was explaining, in detail, all the intricate workings of Two Moons Shipping.

"I believe that's all I need to know at the moment, Lord Popper. Thank you. Now, if you'll excuse me, I would like to look through the records myself for a while."

"But of course, Your Grace." Lord Popper gave the books a final possessive glance before leaving Canby alone in his own, well-appointed office.

Canby flipped through the ledgers, searching for familiar names, going back as far as a year. Lord Shelbourne's name appeared quite often, as did Lord Chadwick's. They'd each paid the tariffs on several shipments of arms to Africa.

Sir Ambrose had, as partial owner, signed off on several

of their transactions, providing the link Canby needed between them.

But when he got to the entry about the recent shipment, the one Quimby had told him about, the information was gone. It seemed as if someone had spilled water on the pages, blurring the ink to indistinct brown splotches.

Canby strode to the door and flung it open. "Lord Popper!"

The man appeared at once, looking as if he were going to vomit. "You wished to see me, sir?"

"What do you make of this?" Canby pointed to the ledger.

Lord Popper walked as if on his way to the short end of a pirate's plank. "Of what, sir?"

Canby showed him the blurred ledger entry.

Lord Popper relaxed. "Why, it's a water spot, Your Grace."

"A water spot?"

"Yes. It would seem someone unwittingly spilled a bit of water on the ledger."

"Who?"

Lord Popper shrugged. "It could have been anyone, really. Many of our employees have call to reference these ledgers until an account has been settled."

"Is it possible someone might have done this on purpose?"

Lord Popper grew defensive. "Why would anyone want to do that?"

"Perhaps they didn't want anyone to reference this entry."

"But why?"

"Did *you* do this, Lord Popper?"

"Me? I would have no cause. These books are impeccable."

In fact, as far as Canby could tell, they were. Other than the problem with this single entry, Canby hadn't been able to find one fault with Lord Popper's business practices.

Canby gave Lord Popper a look of admonishment for

good measure, and sent him off again. With a sigh, he settled back down with the stack of ledgers.

Three hours later, he'd been unable to find one shred of evidence that Lord Popper or Sir Ambrose had committed any slight.

Canby rubbed his eyes. He hadn't counted on finding absolutely nothing. What a waste of time. Time he could have spent at home, with Selena.

He stacked the books in a neat pile at the corner of Lord Popper's desk and slogged to the door. Outside, Lord Popper's assistant Simpson had arrived, and now sat buried beneath a stack of papers. As Canby passed, Simpson made a small noise.

"Did you say something?"

Simpson looked nervously about. "I thought you should know, Your Grace," he whispered. "Sir Ambrose keeps his own set of books."

Canby's pulse surged. "Where?"

"There's been an interestin' development," Kincaid said, grinning across the table at the man who'd paid him to find the Falcon.

"What is it?" Smith leaned forward, wiping the ale from the corner of his mouth with his sleeve.

Kincaid stretched out a hand. The man laughed, and dropped a leather purse into his palm.

Kincaid scanned the room to see if anyone had noticed the transaction, but all seemed to be involved in other pursuits. He tucked the purse into his waistband.

"I've found the Falcon. And you'll never guess who he is."

"You are needed in France."

"Give me a few more days," Canby said.

Ethan gave a frustrated sigh. He leaned against the oak tree at their meeting place outside London. "I know you love Selena. But you can't protect her forever."

"I know." Canby looked down at his ring. "Have you heard from the Fox?"

"No, but I'm not surprised. The intelligence from the region of Versailles has slowed to a trickle. It's become too difficult to get messages through. We need to start using the pigeons for delivery."

Canby was silent, thinking about how hard it would be to leave Selena.

"Lord North is pressing for this," Ethan said. "You must go."

"Tell him I'll leave the day after the ball."

Ethan looked relieved. "Good. I shall arrange passage for you."

The two mounted their horses. As they rode, Canby filled Ethan in on his findings at Two Moons.

"So Sir Ambrose arranged everything?" Ethan said.

"He's siphoned weapons out of dozens of shipments that have gone on to other places. Chadwick and Shelbourne are most definitely involved. The only thing I haven't been able to find out is who the fourth person is."

"Don't worry. I'll work on that. Is everything set for the ball?"

"Yes. Lord Chadwick, Lord Shelbourne, and Sir Ambrose will all be there. Are you ready?"

Ethan smiled. "Of course. Are you?"

Canby fidgeted with his ring. Was he ready?

Selena stared bleakly out her bedroom window. Another day without Canby.

Through the persistent fog she could see Angus shuffling about at the end of the walk. She supposed she should be grateful for his protection, but at times she still felt as if she were at Newgate.

Suddenly, Angus came alert as a bright patch of blue emerged through the fog on the lane.

"Canby!" she shouted aloud.

She watched as he dismounted his horse and tied it to the post, removing his gold-handled cane from the saddle. He greeted Angus on his way up the walk.

Selena ran down the stairs and flung herself into his arms as he crossed the threshold. He laughed and gathered her up, spinning her around until she begged to be put down. It was something he'd done as a young man, when he'd grown tall enough to hold her.

"Stop!" She laughed. "You'll make me dizzy."

He took her hand and pulled her toward the sitting room, installing her in her favorite chair. "Did you miss me?"

"Terribly."

"Good. Wait here."

He returned a few moments later bearing a large box. "I have a gift for you."

He placed it on her lap and kneeled at her feet. The box was heavy, wrapped in thick paper and tied with twine. She looked at it for the longest time, unable to pose a guess as to what lay inside.

"Open it," he said, laughing.

She untied the twine and ripped into the paper to expose a beautiful green striped box. Carefully, she lifted the lid off.

"Oh!" Her fingers sifted through layers and layers of cool silk.

"Take it out."

Hands trembling, she withdrew the most stunning garment she'd ever seen.

Gray silk lay in gathers over thick cream-colored satin, like the feather patterns of a young merlin. The sleeves and bodice of the gown, seeded with tiny glass beads shaped like dewdrops, caught the firelight and shimmered enticingly.

"There are shoes to match. I hope I was able to guess your size."

She held the gown up to her body, mesmerized. "It's beautiful. But where would I wear such a thing?"

"That's the best part of the surprise." His fingers tangled around a bit of loose hair at her temple, and he twisted it into a curl. "There's to be a ball at Lockwell Hall, and you are going to accompany me."

"What?" Her voice was breathless, even to her own ears.

"You're going to accompany me to the ball to celebrate the reinstatement of my title. And your own exoneration, of course."

The breath stuck in her chest, thicker than the fog outside. She folded the gown and laid it neatly back into the box. "Thank you, Canby, but I can't."

He took her hands. "You *must* be there. I would have no reason to celebrate if it weren't for you."

She looked away, unable to meet his pleading gaze. "Canby, please understand. I am not ashamed to be your mistress. It was my choice. But I do not wish to be paraded about in fancy clothes for all the world to see."

"It isn't that way at all. It won't be . . ." He stood, still holding her hands. "What I mean to say is, you'll be treated with the utmost respect. Not as my mistress, but as my friend. As someone who paid a price on my behalf. As someone who's been an important part of my life, for my entire life."

Tears gathered in her eyes without warning, and spilled just as quickly. She swiped them away, angry that her feelings had escaped her control. "You know what everyone will assume," she said. "And for once, they'll be correct."

"No, they won't." He hooked her chin with his finger and tilted her head up to meet his gaze. "Selena, you aren't my mistress. You're my heart. I need you there."

She fought against the stinging in her eyes. Tears were such an impotent reflection of emotion. They accomplished nothing, and she refused to shed another.

"Oh, Canby. I—"

"Ssh." He kissed the tip of her nose and released her hands. "Please, give it some thought. I need you there."

* * *

Before Canby left, he removed the gown from the box and hung it on a peg beside the door so it wouldn't wrinkle too badly.

"In case you change your mind," he said.

Selena stared at it from across the room as if it were an apparition. Had it actually been a ghost, she couldn't have been more frightened of it.

The jewels on the bodice winked at her in the firelight, mocking her. Daring her to come and touch them. She was drawn to the dress, unable to resist the allure of such a decadent thing.

The silk was as soft as feathers beneath her fingertips. What would it be like to wear such a gown? Dare she try it on?

She stripped to her shift and stood shivering in the middle of the room. The gown moved slightly, whispering.

"Don't be silly," she told herself. "It's only a gown."

She removed it from the peg and slipped it on. As soon as the cool satin underskirt slid over her body, she was seduced.

The bead-encrusted sleeves weighed pleasantly on her arms, making tiny, musical sounds as she moved. She sashayed across the small room, the soft lace trim tickling the tops of her feet.

She twirled and swayed, admiring the way the skirt belled around her. She had only a small hand mirror, but she imagined she looked somewhat like the fairy-tale princesses in the stories her mother used to tell her before she died. From the neck down, at least.

Carefully, she removed the garment and hung it back on the peg, staring at it for another quarter of an hour. She had to admit, it would be her girlhood dream come true to dance at a ball in a beautiful gown, with the handsomest of men—just once.

But, Selena told herself, she'd given up fairy tales when her mother had died.

From the corner, the gown winked at her as if it knew better.

CHAPTER 24

The day of the ball dawned gray and misty.

Selena trudged to the mews with Angus, bleary-eyed from a sleepless night. She still hadn't made a decision. Would she attend?

Though she'd seen Canby each of the three days since he'd asked her, he remained true to his promise, never pressing her for an answer. But she noticed his eyes stray to the gown hanging on the peg each time he entered the cottage.

She should have put it back in the box, but she couldn't bring herself to do it. It was too fine a thing to look upon. A work of art, really.

"Here we are, Miss Selena," Angus said when they'd arrived at the mews. "Will ye be hunting today?"

"Not today."

"Then I'll leave you with Clive."

Selena hoped the birds would take her mind off her troubles. She took the hawks to the weatherings for some sun, talking to them as she tethered them to their perches.

"What do you think, Diana? Should I attend the ball? Perhaps you could accompany me. I would feel so much stronger with you on my arm."

Diana cocked her head and raised a wing, preening the feathers underneath.

Selena laughed. "Your beauty would most definitely outshine mine." She looked at Diana and Orion wistfully. The afternoon promised to be quite lovely. A perfect day for hunting.

She wished she and Canby could go. But she knew his days of sneaking away from balls were over. They weren't children anymore.

If she wanted him, this time she'd have to go to him.

"It is astonishing. Truly stunning." Canby picked up the ring and examined it carefully. Wings fashioned of delicate gold filigree held a round citrine, the exact color of a falcon's eye.

The piece had been made especially for Selena, modeled from elements of his ducal ring—the one she'd kept during his long absence. It would serve as her wedding ring, if she agreed to marry him. "I'm amazed you could finish it on such short notice," he said to the jeweler.

"For Your Grace, anything. I hope the lady appreciates it," the jeweler said, winking.

I hope she comes, Canby thought. "I'm sure she will. Thank you, Mr. Robards."

The little man rolled up the piece of velvet on which he'd displayed the ring and bowed out of the room.

Canby pushed the ring onto the tip of his finger and held it at arm's length, trying to imagine it on Selena's hand. She had such beautiful fingers, long and strong, and slightly reddened with work. So different from the porcelain-like twigs of aristocratic ladies, which Canby always felt he might accidentally snap should he hold them too tightly.

Selena was so different in every way. So substantial. He

couldn't imagine her ever having the vapors or lying abed for any other reason save making love to him.

He smiled at the thought.

He'd only left her late last night, but already he missed her. She was a passionate lover, adventurous and giving. Each time they were together, it was as if his dreams were coming true all over again.

He wanted her desperately as his wife. Perhaps even more desperately than he'd wanted her as a mistress. But if she refused to attend the ball, where would that leave them? If she were too afraid to face his peers tonight, would she ever face them?

A duchess held many responsibilities. Would Selena be able to handle them if she became his wife?

He had no doubt she could be taught all she'd need to know. When they were children, she'd learned all his lessons along with him, absorbing history and art and French as well as he had. But whether she'd want to learn the work of a duchess was another question altogether.

He rubbed his eyes.

In some ways, it would be better if things remained as they were. He and Selena were comfortable with each other at the cottage, away from this mad existence. She wouldn't want this kind of life any more than he did.

Unfortunately, he was stuck with it. Though it would be so much easier to bear with Selena at his side. And if they married, perhaps she could give him an heir—

He sucked in a breath. That thought hadn't occurred to him before. He tested it out for a few minutes, and decided he would be thrilled for Selena to be the mother of his children.

But he would not force the life of a duchess upon her. If she decided to come to the ball, he would ask her to marry him. If she chose not to attend, he would know she wasn't ready to be a duchess.

He stared down at the ring on his finger, wondering if he'd ever see it on hers.

* * *

Selena returned from the woods with an apron full of wild mushrooms, Angus trailing close behind, to find someone waiting at her door. From the girl's dress, Selena knew she was a maid from Lockwell Hall.

"His Grace sent me," the maid said, fidgeting with the basket on her hip. "In case you needed help."

"Help?"

"Getting ready for the ball, miss. Your hair and such."

The young woman looked at her with curiosity and expectation, no doubt wondering, as everyone would, why his falconer, the woman once accused of his murder, would be attending a ball.

As Selena stood on the doorstep, she realized she'd run out of time.

"Come in," she told the maid.

"Shall I kill him tonight?"

Kincaid waited impatiently for a reply. He would relish the opportunity to give Jack Pearce what he deserved, while at the same time bringing down the Falcon and collecting a hefty purse for it.

The fact that he'd also be ridding the world of an English duke was an unexpected bonus.

"No. I told you before, no killing."

"But why? It would be so easy. I could take him just about anywhere. In his home. At the woman's cottage. At the mews. He's having a ball—"

"No. A dead man can't provide me with the information I need." Smith slid a crudely drawn map across the table. "Take him here."

By the time the maid had finished, it was nearly dark.

"You look lovely, Mrs. Hewitt," the young woman

exclaimed. "Lovelier than many a fine lady I done."

"Thank you." Selena wished she had a proper mirror. She'd run the hand mirror about, looking at snippets of this and that, but hadn't got the full picture by far.

"Shall I walk with you to Lockwell Hall?" the maid asked.

"You go on ahead," said Selena. "I need a bit more time."

The maid patted her shoulder. "You'll do fine."

"Thank you." Selena returned her smile. "For everything."

The maid left her alone.

Selena took several deep breaths. Her heartbeat, which had grown steadily faster as she dressed, refused to return to its normal rhythm.

This was madness. She didn't have to go. She could spend the evening dancing alone in the cottage, then take the finery off, lie down on her mother's quilt, and go to sleep.

Or she could wear the gown to the mews and show off for the birds—hardly an appreciative audience, unless she brought them food. But at least she'd feel safe and welcome.

The problem was, Canby wasn't in her bed and he wasn't in the mews. He was waiting for her at Lockwell Hall.

Guests arrived in a steady stream until the ballroom was filled with familiar faces Canby hadn't seen since he was hardly more than a child.

He hadn't known many of them well. And of the ones he knew, most he didn't like. But he supposed if he were to live amongst them again, he would have to learn to tolerate them.

Besides, there were too many other things to worry about this evening.

Lord Shelbourne and Lord Chadwick had both arrived. Sir Ambrose would soon show up as well. The authorities had been notified of their misdeeds and lay in wait, to be summoned at the most opportune time.

Freddie arrived on the arm of Captain Blackwood, followed by Ethan escorting a long-faced young woman who looked remarkably like a young, female Lord Shelbourne.

"Lady Mildred, I presume?"

The lady in question tittered into her fan. "What a pleasure, Your Grace."

"Likewise." Canby turned to his cousin. "Ethan, I wondered if I might speak with you for a moment?"

"Of course. You don't mind, do you, darling?"

Lord Shelbourne's daughter pouted. "I suppose not. I shall be with Mummy near the refreshments."

Canby and Ethan watched her charge over the dance floor toward Lady Shelbourne.

"Poor girl. I feel sorry for her," Canby said. "She'll be ruined over this."

"Don't feel bad for her," Ethan said. "She was well on her way to ruination on her own. She's run up a fortune in gambling debts and has taken half a dozen lovers already. 'Twas merely a matter of time for her."

Canby laughed. "One would hardly think an offspring of Lord Shelbourne could be so adventurous."

"Indeed." Ethan scanned the crowd. "Is Selena here?"

"Not yet."

The truth was that Canby had no idea if she would come at all. The young maid he'd sent to assist her had reported back to him. Miss Hewitt had dressed, but had chosen not to accompany her back to Lockwell Hall.

"I've booked passage for you on a ship to France," Ethan said. "It leaves the day after tomorrow."

Canby committed the information Ethan gave him to memory. "I'll be on it."

"Lord North will be relieved," Ethan said. "Is everything set for tonight?"

"Yes. The constable and his men are waiting just a mile away. One of my footmen will fetch them when it's time.

Lord Popper will bring the charges against Chadwick, Shelbourne, and Sir Ambrose for tampering with a holding of the duchy. Lord North can handle the matter of the arms later. That way neither of our names will be involved."

"Excellent."

Canby searched the room for Selena for the hundredth time. His gaze locked with his mother's. He knew she, too, was waiting for Selena.

He turned away, refusing to allow her to see the uncertainty in his eyes. But moments later, she was by his side.

"Has she arrived?" the duchess asked. Tonight she dazzled in a turquoise gown shot through with silver filigree. Canby wondered how she'd paid for it.

"I think you know she hasn't."

His mother touched his arm. "I'm sorry."

"I'd like to believe that." He walked toward the doors to the terrace, suddenly in need of some fresh air. His mother followed.

"I wish you nothing but happiness, Canby. Why won't you believe that?"

"Because in all my life, you've never given a damn about my happiness. Why should I believe that has changed?"

Charity fidgeted with her fan. "I may not have been the most affectionate mother, but I made the decisions I thought were best for you. And now I need you to make a decision that's best for me."

"Ah." The light dawned. "Two Moons." The reason she was being so solicitous.

"Will you return it to Sir Ambrose?"

He took her arm and stepped out onto the terrace. His mother had never been known to make a scene, but he didn't wish to risk a first tonight.

"I have made a decision."

She looked at him expectantly.

"I'll ask you again, Mother. What involvement have you had with Two Moons?"

"Involvement? As I told you before, Sir Ambrose is my friend. I merely wish to help him."

"And as I told you, he is one friend you're best off without."

"Does this mean you won't sell Two Moons to him?" she asked quietly.

"I cannot."

"I beg you to reconsider."

He could not hide his surprise. "I've never known you to beg for anything."

"I need this, Canby."

"I'm sorry, Mother." Strangely, he felt no satisfaction denying her. Perhaps he could somehow keep her name out of the scandal that was sure to follow Ambrose's arrest. "Believe me, this is for your own good."

Anger flashed in her eyes. "You have no idea what you've done." She slapped her fan against the palm of her hand and stalked off the terrace without another word.

Canby sighed.

He suspected his mother was counting on the sale of Two Moons for some financial gain. After an exhaustive examination of the records, he didn't believe she had anything to do with the arms shipments. Her name was not mentioned anywhere in Ambrose's books or correspondence.

But her association with Ambrose would only hurt her. He'd warned her, and whatever consequences she'd face from this time forward would fall on her shoulders alone.

He had other, more pressing concerns.

He looked out over the lawn, eyes searching the shadows for Selena.

"Where are you?" he whispered.

After much protestation, Angus had left her alone at the edge of the lawn.

She stood there now, her heels in her own world, her toes in Canby's, amazed at how easily he crossed this line again and again. How comfortable he was in either place.

She, on the other hand, was acutely aware of the difference between marble fountains and rushing streams, between manicured hedges and ancient trees. In this world everything, including nature, was manipulated to whim. She needed the wild things.

No.

What she needed—what she *wanted*—was Canby.

She stepped onto the moonlit lawn and started up the gentle slope to Lockwell Hall. Music and candlelight and laughter trickled out into the quiet night.

Through the open terrace doors, she could see that the ball was already well under way. If she entered there instead of through the front door, she wouldn't be announced. Wouldn't have to face the stares and whispers when people heard her name. She hesitated, waiting for the opportune moment to slip inside unnoticed.

She should have known that would be impossible.

The moment she entered the doorway, there were stares and whispers aplenty. She pretended not to care, keeping her head up as she searched desperately for Canby.

She caught sight of a captivating woman in gray, her dark hair piled high atop her head, eyes shining. Startled, Selena realized she was looking at her own reflection in the glass of the open terrace door. The woman in gray was *her*.

"Selena, you look magnificent." Ethan approached her, an animated redhead trailing on his heels. "Do you remember my sister, Lady Frederica?"

"Of course. Although I doubt we've seen one another since we were children."

Lady Frederica flashed a dazzling smile. "Mrs. Hewitt, I always envied you. Able to run in the woods and play with the boys all day, while I was stuck in the conservatory at the pianoforte. So unfair!" Her mouth puckered into a pout, and Selena smiled. She remembered that pout well. If she wasn't mistaken, it had gotten Lady Frederica out of worlds of trouble.

"Freddie, you were only forbidden to play in the woods after you'd gotten lost there for six hours," Ethan said.

"I wasn't *lost*. I was having an *adventure*."

"Unfortunately, your little adventures always gave Father chest pains."

Lady Frederica waved him away. "Go on, find someone else to scold. Selena, your gown is absolutely gorgeous. Has Canby seen you yet? He'll be smitten."

Selena felt her face grow warm. "I . . ."

Ethan cleared his throat. "What Freddie meant to say is that our host, the Duke of Canby, should be made aware of the presence of all of his esteemed guests." He extended an elbow and Selena took it.

As they walked through the ballroom, Selena felt much like she had on the way to Tyburn. Lady Frederica trailed behind them, garnering her share of attention as well, which she seemed not to notice at all.

They found Canby on the dance floor, moving with surprising grace despite his limp, a beautiful woman encircled in his arms.

Selena's chest constricted.

He hadn't spotted her, and for that, Selena was grateful. She needed a few moments to collect herself.

"Is there somewhere I can go for a bit of privacy?" Selena whispered to Lady Frederica.

The young woman looked at her knowingly. "Come with me."

Lady Frederica led her to the perfect hiding spot—a window seat mostly obscured by velvet curtains. She held a panel back, and Selena slid onto the padded seat.

Selena tried to breathe, but the gown she'd admired so much just minutes ago now seemed a torture device bound to keep her from breathing. If she'd had any doubts about whether or not she belonged at this ball, they'd been confirmed when she saw Canby dancing.

It wasn't that she'd been jealous of Canby's dance

partner. Not really. It was just that the other woman had looked so *right* in Canby's arms.

These were the kind of people he belonged with. She should leave him to his world.

She squeezed her eyes shut. She didn't really believe that. Since she'd given in to her feelings for Canby, she'd never been happier.

This was only one night. Tomorrow she'd awaken in her cottage, and this all could have been a dream. Whether good or bad, she wouldn't know unless she braved it.

"Whenever we visited Lockwell Hall, this was my favorite spot when I needed to hide from Father," Lady Frederica said. "Needless to say, I spent a good deal of time here."

Selena laughed.

Lady Frederica sat beside her, letting the curtain fall back into place. They were completely obscured from view. "There are very few things in life worth fretting over," she said. "But love is one of them."

"Love?"

Lady Frederica gave her a knowing smile. "Yes, love. Like the love you have for Canby. And that he has for you."

"I—"

"Don't bother to deny it. I've known since we were children. I could tell by the way you both looked at each other."

"I did not know it was so obvious."

Lady Frederica laughed. "It wasn't, really. It's just that I was always looking for signs of love, so I'd know them when it happened to me. I was quite jealous of you and Canby, you know."

"You were?"

"Of course. I wanted so badly to be in love."

Selena smiled. "And now?"

Lady Frederica sighed. "We'll talk about me some other time. Now you need to go find my cousin. One look at you in that gown and he'll be the happiest gentleman alive."

Selena smiled. "Thank you. I think I will do just that."

She took a deep breath and followed Lady Frederica back to the ballroom, searching for Canby amongst the hundreds of people milling about.

When she saw him, her heart stopped. The look of joy on his face told her all she needed to know.

He loved her.

He loved her so simply and so completely, it made all the rest disappear. The ladies and gentlemen on the dance floor, the whispers and stares, the crystal chandeliers, and even her lovely gown—they meant nothing.

The only thing that mattered was him. Them.

Lady Frederica gave her hand a squeeze and slipped away.

Canby kept his eyes locked on hers as he came through the crowd. In a moment he stood before her. "You came."

She nodded, not trusting herself to speak.

"Will you dance with me?"

Without waiting for an answer, he led her onto the dance floor. His hand warmed hers, and she lost herself in his eyes. Canby's finesse soon put her at ease, and she learned the steps quite effortlessly. They moved as if tied to one another by silken strands.

His touch fed her hunger; his smile slaked her thirst. He would always be everything she needed. He had only to ask and she would be his mistress forever.

When that song ended, they danced to the next, and the next. Selena imagined that if there were a heaven, this was how it would be—dancing every night in a beautiful gown, with the handsomest of men. A man who looked at her as if there were no other woman in the room. Nay, in the world.

When the music stopped, Canby guided her from the dance floor to where Ethan and Lady Frederica stood.

"You two look marvelous together!" Lady Frederica exclaimed.

"We do, don't we?" Canby took Selena's hand and pressed it to his lips, drawing whispers from those about them.

All too soon, they stepped from the clouds, out of heaven and into purgatory. Canby escorted her through the room, introducing her to dozens of people, all of whom nodded politely and then proceeded to ignore her completely. But Selena refused to let anything ruin her evening.

Canby loved her, and that was all that mattered tonight.

He squired her about, holding her hand, touching the small of her back, making it clear to his guests that they were more than old friends. For just a moment Selena allowed herself to dream. To pretend that Canby was her husband as well as her lover.

It was a good dream.

After a while Canby steered her into the South Salon, where long tables bedecked in crimson linen held trays laden with food. Roasted meats and fowl. Pickled vegetables. Exotic fruits in every color.

He picked up a lovely porcelain plate and filled it with delectable treats. "I have some urgent business to attend to, so I'm afraid I must leave you for a few minutes. But I will try to find Lady Frederica to keep you company."

"Oh, don't trouble her. I think I saw her talking with Captain Blackwood."

"All right, then. Here." He handed her the plate. "I will be back soon."

Ambrose came up behind Charity, touching her arm in much too intimate a manner. "Have you been hiding from me?"

Charity nearly jumped out of her skin. Did she imagine the menace in his tone? "Ambrose. I did not realize you had arrived."

"Have you any news for me?"

She shrugged out from beneath his touch, and turned to face him. "I spoke with Canby, yes."

"And?"

Her expression must have told him what he wanted to know, for his eyes grew hard.

She opened her mouth to speak.

"Not here," he said. "Upstairs, in your apartment."

Charity lingered in the salon long after Ambrose had gone. She chewed her lip. What if she didn't bother to go? What could he do to her? The damage was already done. Canby had refused to sell Two Moons back to him.

But Ambrose would never leave it alone. Not until he knew every detail of her and Canby's discussion.

Not until he had punished her.

Gooseflesh broke out on her arms, despite the warmth generated by the crush of bodies in the salon.

She set off for her apartment, knowing that for each moment she kept him waiting, she would pay dearly.

Selena watched Canby disappear into the crowd. She tasted a slice of orange, closing her eyes to savor the unusual flavor. Heavenly.

When she opened her eyes, Lord Randolph's betrothed, Lady Letitia, stood before her.

"Well, Mrs. Hewitt, we finally meet face to face. This time I see you've dressed for the occasion." Lady Letitia unfurled a huge fan.

"I have," Selena said, meeting the lady's gaze and refusing to turn away. "Canby was most kind to give me this spectacular gown."

"It's lovely. But I think it might look better on someone else," Lady Letitia said casually.

"Someone else?"

"Look around you, Mrs. Hewitt. Any one of these women would be better suited to be a duchess."

"A . . ." She blinked. "A duchess?"

"Don't play coy, Mrs. Hewitt. It is well known that you aim to trap Canby. To trick him into marrying you. But I'm here to tell you, you are not fit to be anything more than his whore. You are not fit to wear that gown."

Selena's cheeks burned. "You are gravely mistaken. I

have no intention of marrying the duke. But if you covet this gown so much, I shall tell Canby to bring it to you later, after he's taken it off of me. I must warn you, though. It won't make you a duchess."

Lady Letitia gave her a chilly smile. "Enjoy your evening, Mrs. Hewitt. Have a taste of the lamb. It's delicious." She motioned to the table, where a servant shaved paperthin slices from a roasted shank.

Selena sucked in a breath.

The pearl handle on the knife he used matched perfectly the one she'd found in the falcon's chest.

CHAPTER 25

The room spun.

"You?" Selena whispered. Had Lady Letitia stabbed the falcon? It seemed so impossible, and yet Selena could see the truth in her eyes. She'd done it.

Selena stood on her toes, searching for Canby in the crowd, but he was nowhere to be seen. Nor was Ethan or Lady Frederica.

"Are you looking for your lover?" Lady Letitia smirked. "Go on, tell him what you think you know. Even if he believes you, what do you expect him to do? He would never openly accuse me of anything."

Selena knew Lady Letitia spoke the truth. Even if she told Canby her suspicions, what could he do about them? It would ruin him to take the word of a falconer against that of a lady.

"Go back to your little cottage," Lady Letitia said. "You don't belong here."

The room grew close. Selena needed air. She dropped her plate and staggered toward the terrace doors.

Outside, the cool air cleared her head. The stars seemed

close enough to touch. She immediately sought the constellation Aquila, the Eagle. It had been her touchstone after she'd married and moved away from Lockwell Hall, giving her a sense of companionship with her birds.

Tonight, though, it served only to make her feel insignificant. She realized now how powerless she was against these people.

She was only a falconer, a duke's mistress. And that was all she'd ever be.

Kincaid waited and watched behind a row of fan-shaped yew trees for another glimpse of his mark.

He cursed himself for not moving earlier. He'd had the Falcon in his sights, and then the constable had shown up with four of his men. Even Kincaid wasn't brazen enough, or stupid enough, to try and abduct a duke in the presence of the law.

Now he'd have to travel in daylight. Not an ideal situation, but he would have to make it work.

He waited until the terrace was empty, and squeezed through the line of yews. He crouched low, approaching the terrace from the left side. There he'd have a good view of the salon, but could remain hidden in the shadows.

Just as he was about to climb over the balustrade, *she* appeared on the terrace.

The falconer. And she was alone.

Lust coursed through him, sharpening his senses to an animalistic degree. He could smell her perfume on the breeze.

She looked up to the night sky, studying the stars even as Kincaid studied her. She was a vision in the gray-and-white gown, but he much preferred her in a more natural state, with her hair loose, and her body encased in nothing more than her simple frock.

Or perhaps, nothing at all.

A surge of desire pulsed through him, making his head pound.

To Kincaid's surprise, the falconer did not enter the salon again. Instead, she fled down the stone stairs and over the lawn, heading for the path Kincaid knew would take her back to the little cottage in the woods.

He smiled in the darkness.

He couldn't kill Pearce, but he could take something from him. Something he valued. Something he desired above all else.

His mistress.

And when the Falcon arrived to claim her, as he was bound to do, Kincaid would take him, as well.

"What are you looking at?"

"Nothing." Canby tucked the citrine ring back into his pocket. He didn't want to share his intentions with Ethan or anyone else just yet. Not until Selena agreed to become his wife.

"You and Selena are the talk of the ball."

"I'm not surprised. She looks beautiful."

Ethan smiled. "Yes, she does. But you know that isn't why—"

"Of course I do. But I'm going to pretend it is, just for tonight." He cleared his throat. "Has Sir Ambrose arrived yet?"

"He was announced, but I can't seem to locate him. I have to get Chadwick and Shelbourne together before I lose them, too. Will you find Ambrose?"

Canby fingered the ring in his pocket. He didn't want to propose to Selena until after the arrests were made. He wanted to be able to concentrate on her alone for the rest of the evening. "I'll find him."

Selena stripped off the gown and left it crumpled in a heap on the floor.

She pulled the pins and ribbons from her hair and plaited it quickly into a braid, then scrubbed the rouge from her cheeks. She wanted only to be herself again.

Once in her own clothing, she fled to the mews, resisting Angus's persistent efforts to escort her. She needed to be alone.

She ran past Clive into the quiet building, where she sank to the floor, pulling her knees to her chest, willing her heart to slow. Listening. Breathing.

The soft sounds of the mews failed, for the first time in her life, to soothe her. The tranquility she'd always had here had been destroyed.

She buried her face in her arms.

Until Canby had returned, all she'd wanted was solitude. Peace. A quiet life. Now that he was back, all she wanted was him.

But she had learned tonight that too much lay between them. No matter what she felt for Canby, or what he felt for her, they could never be.

She had to leave Lockwell Hall.

Canby searched the crowd, unable to find Ambrose anywhere. Nor, he realized, had he seen his mother. Were they together somewhere? In the gardens, maybe? Or her apartment?

His mother had always been so clear about the importance of avoiding compromising situations, and of the absolute amorality of taking a lover. But Canby had a nagging suspicion his mother didn't always practice what she preached.

If she and Ambrose were having an affair, it would certainly explain why she'd pushed so hard for him to sell Two Moons back to the man.

From the corner of his eye, Canby saw Lord Chadwick and Lord Shelbourne follow Ethan into the billiards room, and knew his cousin would keep them there until the constable arrived.

He headed for the stairs.

* * *

"What went wrong?" Ambrose's voice was calm, but Charity could see the anger churning behind his eyes.

She knew better than to answer him. She'd learned that lesson with Kellam. No answer she could give would be the right one. She sat completely still.

She would allow Ambrose to hurl his insults and profanities, and when he was gone, she would scream into a pillow, rouge her lips, and go back downstairs to rejoin her guests.

Ambrose moved closer. "You were unable to convince your son, your own flesh and blood, to do what was best for all of us."

Charity stared down at the fan in her hands.

Ambrose strode to the swan chair and jerked Charity's head up so her gaze met his.

"You failed."

Keeping the fear out of her eyes had always been the most difficult part. She donned an expression that was a careful mix of apology and defiance. "I tried, Ambrose. I did my best."

He slapped her cheek lightly. "I'm afraid, my dear, that just isn't good enough. Do you know what I stand to lose over this?"

"I will lose a lot of money as well, remember?"

Ambrose's laugh was harsh. "The pittance I promised you? You stupid cow, you have no idea. There is so much more than money at stake."

"I'll try again. I—"

He struck her, hard.

Charity's head snapped back, slamming her cheek into the swan's gilt wing. Ambrose grabbed the sleeve of her gown and hauled her to her feet.

He dragged her into the bedchamber and pushed her down on the bed. His hands worked beneath her skirts, clawing, scratching, tearing silk and flesh, searching for a way to inflict the most pain.

The humiliation of his touch jarred Charity into action. She drove her knee upward, making contact directly between his thighs. Ambrose screamed in agony.

She squirmed out from beneath him and scrambled from the bed. But Ambrose was quick. He grabbed the silver sash of her gown and yanked her back so hard she flew out of her shoes. Her head hit the floor with a sickening thud.

Ambrose was on top of her in a blink, straddling her hips. His hands encircled her neck, squeezing . . . squeezing . . .

"You bitch. For your lack of effort, I am a dead man. I promised someone something I cannot deliver. Something you swore to me you'd arrange. He'll kill me. But before he does, I'll kill you."

Through a cottony fog, she heard a voice. A pounding at the door to her apartment.

"Mother! Are you in there?" More knocking. "Mother?"

Canby!

Charity waved her arms wildly, tipping a crystal decanter from a small round table. The vessel tumbled noiselessly onto the thickly carpeted floor, spilling port across the fleur-de-lis pattern.

"Mother, are you in there? I need to speak with you."

A single breath wheezed from her throat.

The pounding ceased.

All but a few stragglers had gone, either home or upstairs to the guest quarters.

Ethan had left hours ago, bound for the quays, determined to find the hidden arms shipment before it set sail for the colonies. Although they had tried to keep it quiet, news of Chadwick's and Shelbourne's arrests circulated quickly through the ball. Sir Ambrose had disappeared, and Canby wondered if he'd somehow got wind of what was going to happen.

Canby had no doubt this ball would be the subject of conversation for the next several months, and not for the reason he'd hoped. If things had gone as he'd planned, his engagement to Selena would have been the biggest news.

As it was, Selena had disappeared as well.

He caught Freddie passing through the salon. "Have you seen Selena?"

"Not for quite a while. I saw her ducking out onto the terrace from the salon. She looked a bit peaked. I think she was quite overwhelmed by it all."

The two of them went to the doors and looked out over the countryside in silence. It was nearly morning.

Canby didn't know whether to be disappointed that Selena left without saying good-bye, or happy that she'd come in the first place.

Freddie gave him a sympathetic look. "Go find her."

"I have to finish things up here, and I must find my mother."

"You still haven't seen her?"

"Not since before midnight. I've looked everywhere."

"Why don't you let Randolph handle things here? He's much more competent than people imagine. And I'm sure Letitia would jump at the chance to be in charge of anything, even finding Aunt Charity."

Canby rubbed his eyes. He wanted very badly to escape all of this, to lose himself in Selena's arms.

He patted the ring in his pocket. "Tell Randolph I don't know when I'll be back."

The Dresden Shipping warehouse hunkered in one of the most squalid neighborhoods by the docks, looking as if it might decide to lie down one day and not get up.

It was an elderly affair, its bones groaning against the stiff November wind that rushed across the Thames. The cargo within was equally sad-looking. Some of it had collected so much dust that Ethan couldn't read the lists of contents affixed to the sides of the crates. Not that it mattered.

He was certain the cargo he sought would not be labeled STOLEN WEAPONS.

The lantern he held flickered as the wind entered the warehouse freely through gaping slats in the walls, stirring up dust and debris, sending discarded scraps of fabric whirling across the floor.

Taking a systematic route through the stacks and barrels, Ethan opened the ones that seemed least likely to contain what they said, either by virtue of size or shape. But halfway through, he still hadn't located the arms that had been siphoned from the African shipments.

If Chadwick and Shelbourne had given up the name of their fourth partner, he may have been able to check Dresden's records for the location of the export shipment in the warehouse.

Then again, he may not have. It was more likely that the records had already been tampered with and the man's name was already gone.

But Chadwick and Shelbourne had refused even to acknowledge that the man existed. They'd both looked terrified when the subject was brought up.

Ethan considered it a direct challenge.

He'd actually enjoyed this brief sojourn into the less civilized side of spy work. This was the way things used to be for him, before Lord North had elevated him to tactical head of the secret committee.

Ethan had to agree with Canby and Badger on one point—he'd grown soft since he'd retired from the field.

Dispatching others into dangerous situations while he attended social events, seduced women, and shared fine meals with dignitaries had seemed too good to be true at first. But after three years of it, he'd grown bored with it all and longed for some excitement once again.

He breathed the warehouse's musty air deep into his lungs. He longed for this type of action. This danger.

A gust of wind screamed around the building, and his lantern went out.

"Ballocks."

As he stood in the center of the warehouse trying to decide what to do next, Ethan felt something cold press against his temple. The click of a pistol cock sounded loudly in his ear.

He froze.

"Get out before you are killed." The threat wafted on the rich scent of tobacco.

The pistol disappeared from his temple. Nearly inaudible footsteps retreated into the recesses of the giant warehouse. Ethan stood in the dark, stunned.

The voice had most definitely been a woman's.

A stalwart November dawn drove the darkness back from the horizon as Selena left the mews. She'd spent the night there, thinking. Wishing things could be different. That *she* could be different.

She stepped over Clive, motionless on a pile of blankets just outside the door, and headed up the path toward the cottage.

As she passed the tree that had caught the arrows meant for her head, she wondered if it could have possibly been Letitia who'd shot them. It seemed as unlikely as her stabbing the falcon, but somehow, Selena knew it had been her.

She rounded the bend in the path, and her cottage came into view. Canby's horse stood at the end of the walk, but he was nowhere to be seen.

Her heart sank. She knew she'd have to face him soon, but she'd been hoping for a little more time.

Should she even bother telling Canby about Letitia? She had no hard evidence against the woman. Besides, what purpose would it serve?

Tears welled in Selena's eyes, and she slowed. She didn't want to arrive at the cottage looking this way. She wanted one more happy day with him, at least.

She swiped the tears from her cheeks with her sleeve.

When she looked up, the door to the cottage was open and Canby stood on the doorstep. What did he have on his head?

Behind him, a man in a black greatcoat stepped from the cottage.

He held a pistol against Canby's back.

Kincaid followed Selena noiselessly up the path, watching the sway of her hips, admiring the proud set of her shoulders. She'd put up a fight, he had no doubt. A fight he would relish.

He had almost closed the distance between them when Selena leaped off the path and into the woods. Beyond her, Kincaid saw two men exiting the cottage.

One of them was the Falcon, and the other—

The other was the man who'd hired Kincaid to capture him. Obviously Smith didn't trust him to finish the job.

Kincaid narrowed his eyes. He didn't like being cheated of a capture. Or of a lively hump.

His gaze switched to Selena. Crouching low, she moved quickly toward the men through the cover of the trees. She flinched as Smith raised his arm and cracked the butt of a pistol on the Falcon's head.

The Falcon dropped to the ground, unmoving, his hands tied behind his back.

CHAPTER 26

Selena's panicked gaze swept the surrounding area. Where was Angus?

Canby lay motionless on the ground in front of the cottage.

Keeping to the woods, she broke into a run, hoping she'd get close enough to help him somehow, before she was noticed.

The man in black disappeared behind the cottage, returning with a horse. He lifted Canby over the horse's shoulders and quickly mounted the saddle. Before Selena could reach them, they'd disappeared into the woods.

"Angus," Selena shouted as she ran toward the cottage. "Angus, where are you?"

The guard didn't answer. Canby must have sent him away when he'd arrived.

She screamed for Clive, but got no response from him, either. She had to face the fact that no one else had witnessed what she had, and there would be no help on the way.

With only a slight hesitation, she mounted Canby's horse.

The beast sidled, its sides rippling against her knees. She gripped the reins, her knuckles turning white. She knew she mustn't let the horse sense her fear, or she would lose control.

She fought the panic rushing through her limbs. She felt insubstantial on the back of such a huge beast. What if it reared? What if it ran? She would surely die . . .

Taking a deep breath, she loosened her grip on the reins and relaxed her legs, easing the pressure on the horse's flanks. The animal calmed, and soon Selena realized he was waiting for her commands.

Which way should she go?

She should ride back to the stables or Lockwell Hall and sound a warning. But that would take valuable time—and with each minute Canby would be farther away. He was in mortal danger, she was certain.

The man in black had taken him into the woods, and if she didn't follow them now, there was a chance they wouldn't be found.

Selena tugged the reins, guiding the great beast into the trees.

Again, he'd made a crucial mistake.

Kincaid had watched the Falcon and his mistress for days, and knew Selena Hewitt feared horses. But now she'd galloped away on the back of one before Kincaid had a chance to consider his next move.

He'd been debating if he should follow the Falcon and Smith to collect his due, or pursue Selena Hewitt. Now his choice had been made.

He would do both, for he had no doubt the woman followed her man—and he knew just where they were going.

First, though, he needed a horse.

He came around the back of the cottage, intending to make his way through the woods to the stables, when he nearly tripped over the body of the old guard, Angus. His throat had been slit from ear to ear.

Kincaid had underestimated Smith. Twice.

He wouldn't do it again.

Her own poor riding abilities and the abductor's speed conspired to keep Selena far enough behind that she never saw Canby and the man in black, but she never lost them, either. A man on horseback who didn't know he was being followed left many tracks.

They had stopped at least once, for she found the abductor's horse tethered in a copse of cedars where there must have been a fresh mount waiting.

Selena's own urge to dismount and ease the aching in her legs and bottom was great. But she knew if she got off the horse, she might not have to courage to get back on, and Canby needed her.

She rode on.

Canby lay over the horse, hands and feet tied, a quilt wrapped tight over his head. His ribs ached from the canter of the horse beneath him.

Finally, mercifully, they stopped.

He was dragged from the horse and set on his feet, every muscle in his body protesting his weight. Hands pushed him forward.

The earth beneath him, hard-packed and smooth, had a familiarity he couldn't quite place. He scuffled blindly forward until his knees hit something unyielding.

Canby went cold.

He knew exactly where he was. And the fact that he was there could mean only one thing.

Someone had figured out that he was the Falcon.

* * *

As she rode the perimeter of the meadow, Selena realized she'd been there before, by moonlight. Through the line of trees, Selena knew she would find the abandoned barn where Jack had kept her.

Had Jack abducted Canby?

She slid from Canby's horse. When she hit the ground, her legs gave way and she ended up on her very sore rear end on the grass. She struggled to her feet and led the horse closer to the tree line, wondering if she should try to hide it.

She decided not to waste the time.

Tethering the mount to a branch, she walked on shaking legs through the trees until the barn came into view. It was the first time she'd actually seen it, and it was a bit of a disappointment.

She'd built the place up in her mind to be a looming, frightening hulk of a place where all sorts of unspeakable things might have happened.

In reality, it was a rather small structure of weathered gray wood that leaned pitifully to one side. Jack had chosen his hideout well, for it appeared as if the place were abandoned.

The overgrown expanse of grass between the tree line and the barn stretched endlessly before her. How was she to cross it in broad daylight? She'd felt vulnerable enough by the light of the moon.

And what would she do once she'd gotten there?

She supposed she might find a weapon in the barn. There was bound to be something she could use against Jack.

She wondered briefly if he was alone with Canby. But then she realized that it didn't matter. Whether one man or ten, she would go in there for the same reason she'd ridden the horse. Because she had to.

Cold air shocked Canby's senses as the quilt was ripped from his head.

He'd been tied to a chair and sat in the center of the

room, in the circle of light cast by the lantern. He struggled against the ropes that bound him.

Shadows played in the corners of the room, obscuring the other occupant.

"Falcon."

Canby went still. "Fox."

"Did you suspect?"

"No."

Ned moved into the light. "You're losing your touch, Falcon."

Canby stared at his partner. "Why have you done this?"

Ned laughed, and squatted before him. "In case you haven't guessed it, my loyalties have changed."

"Why?" Canby said quietly.

Ned stood and paced before him. "There's money to be made on the other side, Jack. Or should I call you 'Your Grace'?" Ned chuckled. "You see, you've hidden things from me, as well."

"What of allegiance? What of duty?"

"Those were your reasons for spying, Jack. Not mine. For me, it was all for the adventure."

"I don't believe that for a moment."

"I don't give a damn what you believe." Ned hit him across the face with the back of his hand.

Canby reeled from the blow. When his ears stopped ringing, he said, "What are we doing here?"

Ned smiled. "Always to the point, aren't you, Jack? We are here because I need something from you. I tried to find it on my own, but I couldn't. I searched all of the other places, but you kept this one a secret, didn't you? If Kincaid hadn't met up with a certain loose-lipped coachman, I never would have known it existed. Why couldn't you trust me, Jack?"

Canby watched him pace.

"Do you know what I'm looking for?"

Canby was silent.

"It's the list, Jack." He entered the circle of light.

Canby's stomach tightened. "No."

"Yes, Jack. I want the list of contacts. Their codenames, real names, locations, everything. If you give it to me, I'll set you free. Well, perhaps not free, but I *will* let you live. You'll have to hope someone discovers you up here before you rot. By that time I'll have handed over the list, collected my fee, and I'll be far away from England."

"You might as well kill me."

Ned stopped pacing. "How about if I just make you wish you were dead?" He drew a dagger from a sheath at his side and pressed it to Canby's cheek.

Canby felt a sting, and then a warm trickle of blood running down the side of his face.

"What do you think? Should this ear be the first to go?"

The sound of footsteps above her gave Selena pause. She listened. There seemed to be only one set.

She kicked off her shoes and crept through the barn, checking each stall for something—anything—she could use as a weapon. The first stall housed a chestnut mare.

The second, a broken wagon wheel. A saddle. An old scythe.

She picked up the handle of the scythe. The blade disintegrated into a pile of rust. She set the handle aside with disgust.

Was there nothing she could use?

And then she saw it. In the corner beside the ladder sat a branding iron. She hefted it in her palm, testing the weight and balance. With the element of surprise, she could inflict some damage with it, she was certain.

But would she need to? She prayed not.

Perhaps she could reason with Jack. Make him see that only trouble lay ahead for him if he didn't release Canby immediately.

Taking a deep breath, she started up the ladder. It creaked mercilessly beneath her feet, though the footsteps on the floor above her never faltered. Soon she'd reached the top.

The loft was dim, lit only by a shaft of sunlight that shone down through a hole in the roof. She set the branding iron aside and crawled carefully onto the floor, her breathing shallow, her pulse quick.

She wiped sweat-damp palms on her skirt before picking up the branding iron again and tiptoeing to the door, hoping the door frame hadn't been repaired.

As she reached for the door, an arm snaked out from a dark corner and wrapped around her neck, taking her into a choke hold. A hand covered her face, muffling her screams and nearly suffocating her as well.

"The Falcon's mistress," the man behind her whispered. "We meet again." He turned her around and she looked into his face. It was the man who'd returned her to Newgate.

Kincaid.

"I've been waiting for this. For you." He pushed her back against the wall and cupped a breast in his hand, forcing a knee between her legs. "You and I are just alike," he said, his breathing labored.

He gripped the back of her neck, replacing the hand over her mouth with his mouth, pinching her nipple between his fingers. He pushed his tongue against her lips.

She gagged, and then bit it.

Kincaid jerked his head away. "Damn!"

"Jack!" she screamed. "Jack, help!"

She pushed Kincaid as hard as she could and lunged for the door. It flew open, and she stumbled into the room, Kincaid on her heels. She ran right into Jack's arms.

Or at least, she thought it was Jack.

He looked like Jack—the same height and weight, same broad-shouldered build. But on closer inspection, his nose was crooked and his eyes glittered in the light that seeped in through the open door. They held none of the warmth that Jack's had.

He gripped her arms painfully. Looking over her

shoulder, he said, "Kincaid." There was a note of surprise in his voice.

Kincaid wrenched her from the other man's grasp. "Did you mean to cheat me out of my due, Smith?"

"Of course not. You'll get your pay."

"I was supposed to take him." Kincaid jerked his head toward the center of the room, where Canby sat tied to one of the wooden chairs, his legs sprawled out, head lolling to one side. Blood oozed from a cut in his cheek. His eyes were closed, and Selena prayed he was still alive.

"I told you, you'll get your pay. But I began to wonder if I could trust you. I needed him alive." His gaze raked over Selena. "What is *she* doing here?"

"She followed you from the cottage. Weren't overly careful, were you, Smith?"

Selena twisted out of Kincaid's grasp. "Where is Jack?"

At the sound of her voice, Canby opened his eyes and looked up at her.

"I'm glad you're here, Mrs. Hewitt," the man said. "We can use you to convince our friend to talk."

"Let her go, Ned," Canby said, his words slurred.

Kincaid pushed Selena toward the man Canby had called Ned. Her feet tangled in the hem of her skirts and she fell face first onto the wood floor. The men laughed. Ned walked over and placed his foot on the small of her back, squeezing the air from her lungs.

Ned reached down and wrapped her braid around his hand, pulling her head off the floor.

"What do you think, Falcon? What if we relieved your mistress of a finger, or an eye? Would that help you to remember where you hid the list?"

"Please, don't." Canby's voice was tight with emotion.

"Then give me what I want. I know it's here."

Canby was silent.

Ned released her braid, but kept his foot on her back. "Kincaid, my knife is on the table. Get it."

Kincaid hesitated, then strode to the small table in the

corner. Selena's heart hammered against the floor. She struggled to take a breath, and looked up at Canby.

No fear there, just strength and determination. He spoke to her with his eyes.

She focused on him completely, shutting out Kincaid, the hideout, the foot on her back. Canby seemed to tell her there was a way out of this. He slid his foot toward her and a loose board beneath her belly moved.

Kincaid returned with the requested knife, and Ned removed his foot from her back. Selena questioned Canby with her eyes, and he nodded so slightly she thought she may have imagined it.

She pulled up on her hands and knees, and Canby brought his heel down on the loose board, hard. It sprung up, and something glinted in the hole beneath.

A pistol!

She grabbed it just as Ned rolled her onto her back.

He leaned toward her. "What have you got—"

Selena pulled the trigger.

CHAPTER 27

The flash of powder blinded her momentarily. The gun's retort rang in her ears.

"Shit," Kincaid said from behind her.

"Selena, get the knife!" Canby shouted.

She rolled Ned off herself, groping on the floor near his hand for the blade. Kincaid reached it first.

Still tied to the chair, Canby launched himself at Kincaid, knocking him to the floor. The dagger skittered across the floorboards, and Selena scrambled after it. Kincaid pushed Canby away and came after her with a roar.

Time froze.

Canby lay on his side in the chair, his eyes trained on her, willing her to move quickly. To survive.

Selena struggled to her feet.

Kincaid charged at her and she extended the dagger, gripping it with both hands. Too late, Kincaid realized his mistake.

He ran directly onto the blade, taking it deep in his chest. Blood burbled in the back of his throat.

Kincaid's gaze met hers and he stood there, suspended on the knife like a butterfly on a pin.

Selena took a step back.

Kincaid crumpled to the floor. She stared down at him, breathless, unable to comprehend what had just happened.

"Untie me," Canby said.

Selena looked down at her hand. The knife was slick with blood. She uncurled her fingers, and it fell to the floor with a dull thud.

"Selena, untie me. Hurry."

In a daze she went to him. Her fingers, slick with Kincaid's blood, worked the knots at his wrists.

"I can't do it."

"Get the knife."

"No!"

"Selena, get the knife."

She stepped over Kincaid and retrieved the bloody dagger, trying not to look at him. She cut the ropes and Canby crawled over to Ned, rolling him onto his back.

His face was gone.

Nothing remained but strings of bloody flesh.

"Oh, dear God." Selena bent, and vomited.

Canby rose and took her by the shoulders. "Come away."

He led her to the chair in the corner and left the room, returning a few minutes later with a bucket of water.

"Wash yourself as best you can."

Selena felt as if she were watching from a place far away. She followed Canby's instructions, moving as needed, like a marionette. But she wasn't there, really.

Something was dreadfully wrong. It was as if two parts of her life had twisted together, but she didn't quite know how. The events of the day were all a blur and she couldn't make them whole.

They were like pieces of a puzzle scattered across a tabletop. She knew they fit together, but couldn't quite figure out how.

Canby came to her and wrapped her in his arms. She buried her face against his chest, and wept.

Still reeling from the fight, Selena watched at the barn door as Canby emerged from the tree line with his horse.

She idly wondered how he'd known where she'd hidden it. The meadow wasn't visible from the barn.

Canby rode the horse into the barn and dismounted, leading it into one of the empty stalls beside the mare. He closed the stall door and walked toward her.

Without a trace of a limp.

The truth hit her with such force she had to clutch the barn door to stay on her feet. "Dear God, no."

"What is it?"

"You . . . you're . . ."

He reached out to her, but she stepped back, her heart beating furiously, painfully in her chest.

"You're not limping," she said.

He exhaled. "I . . ."

"You knew where the gun was hidden. And where the water is. And the meadow."

"Selena—"

Her voice climbed higher. "You looked up at me when I said 'Jack.'"

He moved toward her and she backed away again. "Come upstairs. Let me explain."

"It was you all along. The priest . . . Jack . . . Canby . . ."

"Selena, stop. Come upstairs, please. You don't understand—"

"I understand much more than you think. You tricked me. You tricked us all."

"That wasn't my aim. I . . ." He exhaled. "I needed to get away. It was the only way."

"Oh, my God." She bent over, drawing great breaths of air into her lungs. "I missed you so much. I wept for you for so many years."

She shook her head. "All that grief, and we might as well have been strangers for all we knew about each other."

"No, Selena. I know you. You know me. I've loved you nearly my whole life."

A tear slid down her cheek. "If only I could believe you."

"You can. Ah, Selena, I—"

"I'm leaving, Canby. Or do you prefer Jack?" She went to the stall and retrieved his horse. "I'm sure you won't mind if I take it."

"Selena, I want to explain everything. But we can't do it now, here. I have to take care of the bodies . . ."

At the mention of Kincaid and Ned, Selena's stomach turned.

"Take the pistol," Canby said. "Go back to Lockwell Hall. Tell Steeples to get Ethan and send him to you. And then tell Ethan what happened here."

She stared at him as if he'd grown antlers. Indeed, that might have been less strange than him ordering her about after what she'd just discovered.

"Please, Selena. I need your help. If you ever cared for me, you must do this."

She rode out of the barn without looking back.

Ethan had reached a dead end.

Neither Lord Chadwick nor Lord Shelbourne would reveal the name of the fourth man in the party, and Ethan had yet to track down Sir Ambrose Hollister.

At the moment he had but one lead.

He examined the letter he'd stolen from Lord Shelbourne's desk. It was the only piece of evidence he'd managed to gather that hadn't been destroyed or stolen before he could get his hands on it.

Could the woman who'd threatened him in the warehouse be the same person who stole the other letters from the desk at the soiree? He felt certain she was.

He held the letter up to the light.

He couldn't shake the feeling he was missing something. A code, perhaps?

Maybe Canby would be able to figure it out.

The return ride was a blur to Selena, as thoughts of Canby and Jack merged together in a grotesque stew.

Canby was Jack. Jack was Canby.

They—*he*—had put her life in danger on more than one occasion. She'd been jailed because of him, shot and nearly hung because of him. He'd frightened her, bullied her, threatened her.

She still couldn't believe it. The man she thought had never lied to her.

Could she have been more wrong?

She rode directly to the cottage where, as if conjured, Ethan Gray waited on the doorstep.

"Is Canby about? Randolph told me he hadn't returned since the ball, and I thought perhaps he came to see you . . ." His voice trailed off, leaving the last part of the sentence unspoken, she imagined for the sake of her modesty.

If she weren't so exhausted, so completely and utterly spent, she might laugh.

"We shouldn't speak out here," she said.

Once inside she told him everything, beginning with Canby's abduction the morning after the ball. Ethan didn't appear terribly shocked by anything she told him, except when she mentioned the name "Ned."

"Canby asked me to find you," she said dully. "I think he needs help."

Ethan reached across the table and squeezed her hand.

"I feel so betrayed," she said. "How could he have done such a thing? Why?"

"It isn't my place to explain," he said. "Canby must do that. But I know he had good reason. And if it means anything to you, he loves you, Selena. He's always loved you."

She laughed, but the sound was hollow. Devoid of emotion.

She walked him outside.

"I'll return Canby's horse to him," Ethan said.

"Thank you."

He gave her a sympathetic look. "I am sorry, Selena. Try not to worry."

He kissed her forehead. The tender gesture was more than she could bear. She ran back inside the cottage and straight up the stairs to her room.

Then she buried her head in her mother's quilt and wept until there were no more tears left to cry.

A stubborn sliver of moon hovered on the horizon, soon to be edged out by sunrise by the time Ethan arrived at the barn.

Canby had already moved the bodies into one of the stalls below, and scrubbed all trace of blood from the floors.

"How was Selena?" Canby asked.

"Distraught. Unhappy. Feeling betrayed."

"I should have told her long ago who I was. What I did. But I wanted to wait for the right time. I wanted to wait until I had asked her . . ."

"What?"

Canby shook his head. "It doesn't matter now. I'm sure she will never speak to me again."

Ethan was silent.

Canby pressed his palms against his eyes. "I suppose I cannot blame her. I never should have left."

"You did what you thought was right. The Crown desperately needed your services, and you needed to get away."

"I shirked my responsibilities. I played with people's lives."

"No, you didn't. You left your affairs in the hands of a man who had proven himself more than capable. Perhaps more capable than you. And even if Randolph had won the title, the duchy would have been in excellent hands. He's a good man, Canby. A bit absorbed in his projects, but he's a good man."

Canby sighed. "I know. He'd make a much better duke than I will ever be."

"But you are an excellent spy."

Canby looked at the now-damp spot where Ned's body had lain. "I thought Ned was, too. Dedicated. Loyal. I misjudged him. I don't understand why he turned."

"Greed," Ethan said. "It's a powerful temptation. But Ned's defection does create problems for us. For you."

Canby nodded.

"Your identity has been compromised for certain here in England, and most likely in France as well. You cannot go back to Montainville."

"But the delegation from the American colonies is due to arrive soon."

"We have other operatives near Versailles. We'll have to see if we can get them into the palace somehow. And of course, we have Franklin's secretary. If he accompanies the delegation to Versailles, we'll have all the information we need."

Canby rubbed the back of his neck. "I am sorry, Ethan. I never should have left my post."

"It doesn't matter. Ned contaminated the mission long before you left. Had you stayed, you only would have unknowingly passed him more information to sell. I am certain you would have been in danger, too. Besides, you had to come back for Selena."

"She was worth any cost." Canby swallowed back the ache in his throat.

Ethan squeezed his shoulder. "We have work to do now, cousin. Concentrate on that. Perhaps in time, Selena will feel differently."

"Perhaps." But Canby doubted it. The look of hurt in her eyes would haunt him for a very long time.

He only hoped she wouldn't allow his mistakes to poison the rest of her life. That she'd find happiness without him someday. He knew that he'd never find it without her, though.

He ran his fingers through his hair. "Now, what shall we do about Kincaid and Ned?"

CHAPTER 28

All of her belongings—the ones that mattered, at least—had been packed in two leather trunks.

Selena looked about the cottage, remembering all of the important events of her life that had unfolded there. Nights telling stories before the fire with her parents. Learning how to make her first falconry glove. Her mother's death. Her father's illness.

The first time she and Canby made love.

She pushed that memory to the far recesses of her mind. She didn't want to think of him.

She dragged the trunks to the door.

No matter how many memories this place might hold, she couldn't stay here; that much was clear. It was time for her to move on. This place would never hold the key to her happiness.

She left the cottage and set off for the mews, her steps slow and heavy. She walked the path as she'd done thousands of times, but this time she felt no anticipation. No joy.

Standing in the circle of the weatherings, Selena

thought of all the birds she'd trained and cared for and hunted with. Before she moved on, she left a flower on the grave of the falcon.

Entering the mews, she breathed the musky avian scent, tears stinging behind her eyelids. In turn, she visited each mew, saying a final good-bye to each of the birds.

She wouldn't take them. They belonged to the Duke of Canby's estate. Besides, she didn't even know where she would be going.

When she reached the hawks' quarters, the tears finally came.

"Diana. Orion. I will miss you both," she whispered as she held them on her arm, admiring their fine profiles for the last time. "Treat each other well."

When she had finished, she left her glove on a hook and closed the door.

"Mother." Randolph pounded on the door to Charity's apartment. "Mother, are you in there? I have something I must tell you."

He tried the door, but it was locked.

Randolph leaned his arm against the door and rested his forehead on it. No one had seen his mother since the ball, two days ago. It wasn't as if she'd never done that before, but he was beginning to worry just the same.

And then, with a small click the door swung slowly open.

"Come in."

Entering the room was like entering a cave—dark and cold. The curtains were drawn and the room was a mess. He stepped over a large wine stain in the middle of the carpet. Apparently she hadn't even let the servants in to clean or tend the fire.

Charity was wrapped in a coverlet, and her hair, so elaborately coiffed for the ball, looked like a tangle of weeds.

Randolph squinted at her. "My heavens, Mother. Are those bruises on your neck?"

She ignored his question. "What do you want?"

"I have news. Rather bad news, I'm afraid. I . . ."

"Out with it, boy. What bad news?"

Try as he might, he couldn't keep his voice from shaking. "You must come with me at once. Canby is dead."

Selena walked up the lane toward Lockwell Hall. She had no idea if Canby had yet returned. Thankfully, he hadn't darkened her door.

Though she didn't want to see him, she needed to collect her wages for the year, and request a coach and driver to take her to the docks in London.

She didn't know where she was going, but she knew it would be far away from England.

As she passed the stables, she stopped to peek through the doors, looking for Canby's horse. A black, windowless coach sat within.

A hearse.

Selena broke into a run, not slowing until she reached Lockwell Hall. She entered through the servants' door.

In the kitchen a small band of servants had gathered, and sat in chairs around the fireplace. A couple of them had testified against her at the trial.

One of the maids, the one who'd brought her supper when she stayed upstairs in the apartment, gave her a teary nod.

"I suppose you've heard, then."

"Heard what?" Selena held her breath.

"The duke. He's dead. Really dead this time."

Her heart clutched. It couldn't be. Had something gone wrong after she'd left? Had someone else shown up at the barn and killed him? She should never have taken the pistol and left him unarmed.

Selena wandered, dazed, through the kitchen and out into the dining room, toward the voices she heard in the Great Hall. Lord Randolph stood talking with a man dressed in black from head to toe.

The coroner.

She knew she shouldn't be there. What right had she? She'd been nothing to Canby, not really. He'd proved that in the last days of his life. But God help her, she had to know.

"Is it true?" she said.

The gentlemen turned to look at her. Randolph gave her a small, sympathetic smile. "I'm sorry, Selena. I know you and Canby were . . . Well, I know you were very good friends."

"How did it happen?"

"He was shot," said the coroner. "A traveler found his body on the pike about an hour's ride from here."

"And you're certain it was him?"

The coroner cleared his throat. "His face was . . ." He coughed into his hand. "We identified him by his clothing, and his ring, of course. The rest of him was rather difficult to distinguish."

"We can take comfort in knowing he fought back," Randolph said. "The highwayman who shot him was found stabbed to death right beside him."

"Must have been a hell of a fight," the coroner muttered.

Selena's legs gave way, and she collapsed on the marble floor. She sobbed uncontrollably.

"Oh, dear," said Lord Randolph. He and the coroner scooped her off the floor and draped her arms over their shoulders. They carried her to the closest room, the East Salon, and lowered her gently onto the settee.

Lord Randolph rang for a servant and requested a tray of tea.

"Please. Rest here for a while, Mrs. Hewitt. I need to finish things up, but I really would like to speak with you when I am finished."

Selena nodded.

The men left and she gasped huge breaths, laughing and crying all at once. Canby wasn't dead after all! Why she should find such joy in this, she didn't know.

Of course she knew. She loved him.

But he'd gone and done it again. Fleeing under the pretense of death, leaving destruction and heartache in his wake. And this time, she knew he wouldn't be back.

"Damn him," she said aloud.

"My thoughts exactly."

Selena gasped. The duchess peered around the back of a wing chair that sat facing a window. The whole side of her face was hidden behind a nasty purple-and-yellow bruise. She left the chair and came to take a seat beside Selena.

"He's really gone this time, isn't he?" the duchess asked.

"Yes." It emerged as a whisper.

Charity wept. Selena sat there looking at her, at a loss for what to do. Eventually, she reached out and put a hand on the older woman's arm.

The duchess cried even harder. "I am so sorry. Although it hardly matters now, does it?"

"Of course it matters," Selena said. "He was your son."

"Well." The duchess drew a handkerchief from her sleeve and dried her tears. "Perhaps I am softening with age."

Selena said nothing.

The duchess stared at her. "I would apologize to you, as well."

"To me? For what?"

The duchess smiled sadly. "I think you know."

Selena looked away.

"I'm sorry I convinced your father to marry you off to such an awful man. Canby told me of the abuse you faced with him."

"He did?"

The duchess nodded. "I had no idea he was so cruel. I just meant to get you away from my son."

"But why?"

The duchess looked up, her eyes hard. "I hated you, my dear. Canby always cared for you so much more than he cared for me. You made him strong. You taught him not to need anyone, least of all me." She gave a resigned sigh. "You held him in your power, don't you see? As long as you were around, he was never going to come back to me. He was never going to face his duties as duke."

"He didn't want to marry me, you know."

The duchess was silent.

Looking at the woman who had caused her so much grief and heartache, Selena surprisingly felt no anger. Only sorrow. A deep, deep sorrow. She had a feeling that she and the duchess led very similar lives, despite the social distance between them.

"I didn't take him from you, Your Grace," Selena said. "You pushed him away."

"I pushed him away from his father by sending him to yours. I thought he would come back when Kellam was gone, but he never did."

"That's because he fell in love."

"Yes, with you."

Selena shook her head. "With the falcons. I believe I was just the human embodiment of them."

The duchess sighed. "Men live for their passions, don't they? And God help us if we don't rank among them." She began to cry again.

Selena held the older woman's hand until Randolph returned. He was followed by Ethan, who seemed surprised to see the two women together.

"Aunt Charity, how are you holding up?" Ethan bent to kiss the duchess on the cheek.

"I'm tired. So tired."

"Let me escort you to your rooms, Mother." Randolph offered his hand and she took it. She leaned heavily on him as they crossed the salon. When they reached the doorway, the duchess turned.

She and Selena exchanged a silent look of understanding before Randolph led her from the room.

Ethan turned to her. "How are you, Selena?"

"As well as can be expected."

"I take it you've heard the news?"

"Yes. Canby's dead. Found with his face missing beside the highwayman who killed him."

Ethan studied her. "Shall I walk you back to your cottage?"

They said little on the way. Indeed, what could be said? Canby was gone. Again.

They went into the cottage.

"What are these?" Ethan pointed to the trunks beside the door.

"I am leaving, too."

"What about the birds?"

"That will be up to Lord Popper, I suppose. Or Lord Randolph, when he becomes duke. He will become duke, won't he? There is a body to prove his claim this time."

"Most likely he will. And I'm sure he'd want you to stay." Ethan followed her into the sitting room.

"There's nothing left for me here. Nothing but memories."

"It isn't for me to explain all of this, but Canby would want you to know. You should go and talk to him."

She shook her head. "No explanation is necessary, Ethan. He's left us again, and for no other reason than because he could. He's always looked for ways to escape."

"He had just cause, Selena. Then, and now."

"Why, because his father was a wicked man? Because his mother was spiteful?"

"Because England needed him." Ethan took her hands in his. "Go to him, Selena. Please."

CHAPTER 29

He was no longer Canby. Or Jack Pearce. Or the Falcon.

He was Trenton Meade, importer and trainer of exotic animals.

He was the Leopard.

The Leopard wandered restlessly about the cramped room of the inn, thinking about the mess he'd made of things with Selena. He should have trusted her from the beginning. Trusted her as completely as she'd trusted him.

He hoped she wouldn't hate him forever.

Sounds from the docks of Bristol—the clanging of chains, the shouts of lightermen—drifted up through the open window. He tried to pull it shut, but it stuck.

A knock at the door put him on alert. He checked himself in the mirror, satisfied that his transformation had rendered him unrecognizable.

"What is it?"

No answer.

He opened the door a crack. Outside his room stood the last person he ever expected to see.

"Selena."

She looked startled. "I . . . I'm sorry. Do I know you?"

He opened the door and pulled her inside. "Selena, 'tis me."

She looked deep into his eyes, and exhaled. "Canby? What did you do to yourself? Look at your hair."

"Black dye from walnut skins."

"Your jowls?"

He popped them out. "Wax."

She put a hand to her forehead. "I don't understand."

He guided her to the bed and sat her down on the edge. "I gather Ethan told you where to find me?"

She nodded.

"But he didn't warn you I might not look like myself?"

"No. Canby, what's going on?"

He sat beside her. "I should have told you this a long time ago. After I'd taken you from Newgate. No, I should have confided in you even before I left Lockwell Hall."

He took a deep breath, and told her how he'd taken small intelligence assignments as a young man because as a duke, he had access to many people others did not, and would draw little suspicion.

As his skills grew, so did his assignments. He soon adapted the persona of Jack Pearce, donned disguises, and used his talents with animals to infiltrate the private places where most gentlemen feel free to discuss their affairs without censure—stables, hunts, kennels. And eventually, the Royal Falconnerie at Montainville.

Selena was stunned. "And you came back to save me?"

"I had to. You see, I still loved you."

"But you were horrible to me when you first got me out of Newgate."

"I was angry. You married someone else. I didn't know why. And then when you told me how you felt, I couldn't believe it."

"But why did you tell me you were going to ransom me then?"

"We were getting too close. I couldn't take the chance that you'd figure out who I was."

She stared down at her hands. "You didn't trust me."

"I couldn't. I had no idea how you felt about me. And I couldn't take the chance that you'd tell someone who I was. You see what happened when my identity was discovered."

He could tell she hovered on the cusp of disbelief. "I know I lied to you, Selena. I hurt you and I put you in great danger. I'm so sorry. Will you ever forgive me?"

Her expression told him she was trying to absorb it all. It sounded so fantastic, he knew, like a story out of a novel.

"Why did Ethan send me here?" she said. "Why didn't you just leave again, with no one the wiser?"

He moved closer. "You know the answer." He kissed her lightly on the lips. "I love you, Selena Hewitt. I always have, and I always will. No matter how many miles or how many identities separate us. And no matter what happens, I trust you with this knowledge."

She slid her hands inside his open jacket. "How did you get your belly so big?"

"Only padding." He shed his jacket and waistcoat.

She pressed her palms to his chest, smoothing the linen of his shirt over his muscles. "Good. I was worried for a moment that you'd lost these."

Heat rose between them, almost visible, like the heat distortions over the sand of an Indian desert. He grabbed her wrists. "Don't."

He hurt too much from wanting her. He couldn't touch her until he knew . . .

He walked to the window and looked out over the water. "Do you love me, Selena?"

"I wouldn't be here if I didn't."

He closed the space between them in a heartbeat, sliding his hand into her hair and crushing her lips to his. She whimpered, the needful sound driving him insane with desire.

He held her tight against him and walked her backward

across the room. Her knees hit the foot of the bed, and they fell atop it, making it groan beneath their weight.

"I want to crawl inside of you and never come out," he murmured against her mouth.

They stripped all barriers between them and he plunged into her, reveling in the feel of her body beneath his. She wrapped her legs around his hips, and her arms around his neck, and when she whispered that she would always love him, he no longer felt like a duke. He felt like a king.

It didn't matter what his name was—he forgot it when he was with Selena, anyway. But no matter his identity, he would always be the man who loved her without reason.

They climaxed together, Selena trembling around him like the wing beat of a falcon.

When they glided back to earth, she was shivering.

He wrapped her in a blanket and held her close as they looked up at the azure sky outside the window.

"Ethan is sending me to the American colonies," he said. "The rebels have gathered many supporters. Someone must infiltrate."

She was quiet.

"You cannot be the Falcon's mistress any longer."

She closed her eyes. "I know."

He left the bed for a moment and returned to kneel beside it, a naked and desperate man. "You cannot be the Falcon's mistress, but I hope you will agree to be the Leopard's wife."

She sat up, eyes wide. He slipped the citrine ring on her finger.

"Oh, Canby—"

"Not Canby. Trenton. Trenton Meade."

She held the ring up to the light. "Oh, Trenton. It's beautiful."

The ballroom was packed with knights and ladies, animals and birds, angels and devils.

Lady Jersey's annual masque was a thing not to be missed. So why did Ethan wish he were somewhere—anywhere—else?

He adjusted his mask. Tonight he'd come as a tiger—the ultimate predator. Too bad he felt like prey. The harbormaster's wife, with whom he'd had a spirited and fruitful affair, but who had since lost both her usefulness and her novelty, stalked him through the ballroom.

Before she could pounce, Ethan spotted a pretty peacock beside the dance floor, looking for all the world as if she were standing in a pit of vipers.

He moved swiftly, taking her elbow and leading her toward the dance floor before she had time to protest.

"Lovely mask," he said. And it was. Colorful feathers framed green eyes and splayed across her cheeks, leaving only a pair of delectable pink lips exposed.

"Thank you. Yours is . . . interesting."

Her voice, low and husky, whipped his senses into a frenzy.

They plunged into the parade of couples entangled in a reel, falling easily into step. When she entered the circle of his embrace, his heart leapt.

His partner wore the most delightful scent.

The scent of tobacco.

EPILOGUE

February 19, 1777

Dear Mr. Gray,

Many thanks for your recent gift of a cast of hawks. They've been a welcome addition to our shop in Philadelphia, where the people have shown a great deal of interest in our unusual imports.

We've had the pleasure of serving many of this city's most prominent citizens, who have welcomed us into their homes and shared their most interesting opinions.

We shall be certain to write often, and keep you informed of the many events that occur here in the colonies.

Meanwhile, I am glad to know that my mother is doing well, and that my brother has decided to reconsider his pending nuptials. There is surely a more worthy bride for such a gentleman of distinguished kindness and intelligence.

We also were happy to hear that you've decided to pursue other, more stimulating interests as well, and hope you find all you are seeking.

Most sincerely,
Mr. & Mrs. Trenton Meade